RED PLANET, GREEN PLANET

An Empire in 42 Chapters

Glenn Preedy

Printed and bound in Great Britain by:
Book Printing UK Remus House, Coltsfoot Drive, Woodston,
Peterborough PE2 9BF

Dedication:
To my dear Grandson, Dylan Tanner

Special thanks to my friend Tony McTaminey for the cover design
and for his tireless support writing this book
Thanks also to Jozane Gray, my agent and supporter.

Table of Contents

Chapter 1

Helium was the name I successfully promoted for the capital city of the British Empire's province on the Red Planet. Governor Myrna Golden was happy to advocate it because it associated her with the popular favourite. She would have made a personal choice of something pretentious like 'Byzantium'. I was determined to persuade her of this choice because my market research had identified it as pleb-friendly. 'Helium' was used in the blockbuster, 'Under the Moons of Mars'. This melodrama was inspired by a nostalgic 'science fiction' book, written hundreds of years ago in the early 20th century. Any science in this fiction was there by accident. The 3D visual presented canals carrying water all over the planet, along with sword-wielding hero battling 15-foot-tall green monsters! This world-wide smash was what inspired the province's inhabitants in the naming of their newly completed capital, so Helium it would be. Hands up! I loved that kind of stuff myself, too. Snobby Myrna was so enamoured with me, she feigned admiration for it herself. Most of all, she was dazzled by my looks, my wit and my cleverness, as well as my glorious career in publicity. That is why she assisted in my sideways move into being her government's adviser and political propagandist.

With maximum media hype, I stood on a dais dramatically elevated far above the people and announced, 'Helium is the winning name – chosen by you!' Such a roar of popular approval came from every network and by-way!

Helium. I loved it. The punters loved it. It confirmed Myrna's faith in my skill as star bullshitter and supremo of the publicity machinery. All this was a novel experience for me; faking being sensible and competent. For at least a week, 'Simon Edge' was synonymous with probity. That went into reverse fairly quickly, as you might expect if you were acquainted with me. I even influenced the fashionable young Brits to wear 'Helium' clothing. Mind you, I did make this a personal little earner by registering 'Helium' as my trademark, despite it portraying Governor Myrna's face prominently in the midst of my design.

I studied the dull sky, a result of Mars being further from the sun than Earth. Multitudes of colourful airships drifted overhead. In that old science fiction tale, such inventions were how it was imagined advanced war machines of the future would look. They are regarded as low tech in today's civilisation, yet, as we know, they still play a major part in transport. They're favoured because of our low gravity and thin air, complemented by banks of circular anti-gravity devices laid in lines across the planet's surface. These lines of 'Grav Plates' resemble roads laid for land transport in past times. Along with airships being cheap and environmentally appropriate vehicles, they serve another vital purpose by creating warmth and increasing visibility using giant reflectors set along their sides. Their purpose is to maximize sunlight, as well as exploiting the low gravity and thin atmosphere of Mars. Ultimately, the simulated solar radiation provides us with fake day times, transforming selected areas of the sky from dusty pink and tan to blue. Over the centuries of human occupation, we have come up with a multitude of similar creations, making the air-filled domes more attractive as well as assisting the slow terraforming of the Martian deserts. One day we will sufficiently oxygenate our entire world to support grasslands, woodlands and animal life. Some science guys reckon that billions of years ago about 20 per cent of the Red Planet was ocean. A big question mark popped in my mind when I heard that one! Other 'experts' have estimated it could take a million years to terraform the entire world before we can get rid of the domes and send out gardeners to grow jungles!

I couldn't give a grub's arse whether the 'Zeppelins' – as old timers used to call them – were used as cheap taxis or giant haulage carriers. Many were mere tourist attractions anyway. As long as I could get low profile transport when I wanted it, that was fine by me. I didn't give a hoot whether it was a balloon, a personal jet pack, or even one of the costly war fliers. Today, I wouldn't be surprised if my brothel-creeping buddy, Manitoba Joe, decided to collect me in an extravagantly expensive strato-cruiser with en suite bars. He was too much of a snob to use balloons. Only flashy fliers would impress the kind of girls we wanted to pick up during our debauched sprees!

I convince Myrna to be lenient with me because, we only live once. Therefore high-powered stars like me need to let their hair down once in a while by zipping across the southern hemisphere in Joe's silvery littleship. Obviously, words like 'brothels' and 'tarts', or 'drugs and alcohol', were absent during our heart to heart. I'm not a saint, I admit that. But...hang on! That brings to mind a dead funny memory. There was one time I had begun to admit to Myrna, 'I might not be the perfect husband...' Before I could get out another word, she exploded in laughter that continued till tears ran from her watery blue eyes. God knows why. Eventually, I was able to explain how conscientious I had always been for her sake, how well I had served as her spy, not to mention my top-quality and inexhaustible sexual performance. I wanted her to believe in me.

I might well party freely with drugs, booze and whoring, along with a little illicit underworld dealing, *etcetera.* However, Myrna has received fabulous payback for acting like she's oblivious. No one needs to make themselves and others miserable with arguments. It must be clear to her, as to anyone else, I am so much more than a gigolo with a hunger for any woman in sight. Day or night I was there to serve as the most shrewd and effective spy and advisor she could ever have wished for. Our relationship has never been exploitative either. Sometimes my wife could be pretty okay. I won't say I would die for her, but I had knowingly risked my life many times, serving her with necessary assassinations and monitoring plotters I discovered on Mars or Terra. Our feedback sessions were frequent, honest and detailed. My political advice behind the scenes never failed to advance her ambitions and image.

I admit I don't give a toss about politics – except when it gives me access to wealth, sex, drugs and power. Today all avenues were open to me since I had made Myrna into Lady Big Shot. Thanks to my guidance, she was unassailable. During the last year she became odds-on for my bets to be the next President of the British Empire. She wasn't a bad shag either, though gravity has become detrimental to her upper deck. If I was less sensitive, I'd have said, 'saggy tits'. Her bonus was to have won a brilliant young sex god like me. In exchange, I'd pulled this mature lady who was rewarding me with power and status now I helped her become Governor of the Province.

All in all, it worked out like magic. Whenever I was asked to do anything dodgy, she made the request subtly and non-verbally because we understood each other so well. Our knowledge of each other sometimes assisted an ease of communication. Just to demonstrate how discreet we could be, I tell you a raised eyebrow or slight gesture was all I needed to alert her how to deal with any issue requiring my action. This seemed almost like the understanding reputedly shared only by lovers. It was another reason why she was prepared to be blind to my desperate urge to use that equipment Mother Nature gave me whenever I spied some tasty young lay. After all, Myrna – God bless her – was ten years older than me. Her bum cheeks were getting saggy as well as her tits, you know what I mean? I only fancied a nubile to pump away on for a quickie. Obviously, Myrna saw how good looking I am, and irresistible to all females. To my mind, Myrna's tolerance was totally deserved. You get my drift? Tonight was my date to meet up with my best mate and a group of the lads. That's when we young puppies go sniffing for bitches. Even if they're bug-eyed and green !

Chapter 2

Manitoba Joe was always late for meet ups. It was wise not to ask why. Most likely he had been commissioned, at the last minute, to perform an assassination or anything else sufficiently criminal for the husband of the Governor of the Province to be publicly unaware of.

I last had seen Joe was a week ago, Earth Time. We chatted about events that had affected the worlds while getting pissed. All us Fun Boys stagger into heavy discussions midway to being pissed, don't we? Manitoba and I let our brains totter into the history of Earth and Mars that day.

Over a century back, the eruption of Yellowstone National Park on Terra blew fragments of the most powerful nation ever into the heavens. The planet was in semi-permanent night for years after. Human history was re-directed in a fashion nobody could have anticipated on two worlds. I was not being melodramatic – though maybe pretty stoned – when I lectured Joe about how that cataclysm transformed more than borders on maps. It also altered humanity's sense of reality! Thousands of years of civilisation were terminated when the North American continent vanished below the ocean, leaving behind an expanded Sargasso Sea full of mud and debris.

Everything in life, is entirely a matter of chance. Every disaster offers opportunities for chancers though. I'm not just talking about me, the Super-Spy, Simon Edge! The first domino to fall after that BOOM was the European state. Their wobbly Empire tore apart without the USA's corporate investments to prop it up. Next, was the big event! Armageddon proved to be an unexpected gift for nations with piracy inclinations. Britain had been a nonentity for centuries. But long ago, it had been an Imperialist Empire and bandit of the land and seas. After Earth's planet-wide disaster, resulting from the USA blowing up and submerging, Britain burst out of nowhere, holding five aces. The fleets of opportunistic Somali buccaneers were overtaken with the speed of light. Pure luck it was when the British seized their chance. Me, being a history geek, I'd always liked England. My role model was called Sir Francis Drake.

11

I dug out my brain-linked history library. Then I bored the pants of everyone in our piss-ups when I rambled on about Cadiz and 'burning the King of Spain's beard' to show off.

Mind you, historians are nutters. Before the cataclysm, they all predicted Mars would see a three-way split between America, China and Russia for settlements. The instant the 'Yanks', as the sunken-nation's inhabitants were nicknamed, were eradicated, a fresh political geography was here. To universal disbelief, the British Empire emerged on Earth and Mars. Here was a new major power. The Brits were as bewildered as anyone. Pink shading on the computer graphics located its territories on Earth and Mars. Decades of secret technological and armament development had enabled the tiny Terran island to occupy swathes of the desert lands of Mars. That huge arsenal of technological and even radioactive weaponry, they accumulated from habit, protected the newcomers.

Their whole game was inadvertent and inspired. Historians predicted imminent conflicts, but they did not happen. Many attributed this to President Maddigan and his wife, Natasha. The openness of England to friends from Africa and India, the willingness of the British to acknowledge Chinese supremacy, and the threat of the Caliphate, accidentally created an umbilical association with Israel. That was what was so helpful. Historians never saw it coming, naturally! Maddigan, pompously Welsh, proclaimed, 'When the runes are cast, all nations shall realize Britain is a friend to everybody. And the Caliphate is an enemy to all civilization.' Blow me! It was all as chancy as throwing five double sixes in a row. I'm not some mystical head case! An accidental Empire just bobbed up. There you go!

As far as I could tell, Maddigan was a well-meaning eccentric. His British Empire was not interested in becoming a substitute USA. On Earth, the English were a mongrel nation of English, Irish, Scots and Welsh. More recently, they absorbed Africans, Indians, Germans et al. The mix was an advantage. What do Brits do if they find themselves in the A team on two planets? They went to work, terraforming their Red Planet Province and cleaning up their home world. Plus, they were polite to other nations.

They never threatened anyone regardless of all their stockpiled armaments.

Back here on Mars, most former Earth nations joined in land grabs: the Islamic Caliphate, India and mighty China came running across the 400,000 miles from Earth. Australia, surprisingly, seized but a small territory. Africa and Europe were diverted by internal strife and civil war. Russia was a total mystery. Initially, Russian holdings on the Red Planet were set to be considerable. Historians, political observers and other palm readers were bemused. They passively permitted their neighbours to move into their unused desert land. Remaining areas served only as airstrips and as markers for their presence. They made no attempt at terraforming or developments. There was a lot of speculation as to why. The most convincing was there was a plague, or toxicology experiment, that went belly up. I still don't know.

Three years after the worlds were blessed by my birth, President Maddigan rose to power. He was based in the southwest region of his tiny island. It's my guess that his passive calm was what convinced millions of people he possessed paranormal intuition. I found his success both fascinating and puzzling. Myrna was not going to disbelieve him. He had made her Governor of the English Province. That had confirmed a seat at the top table of nations for her. I hoped for an opportunity to meet this President. The old man was a maze of contradictions. Victory fell in his lap without him trying. Can't argue with that! Whilst the Brit's Empire enjoyed its lucky streak at the political roulette table, I made heaps of money from my real casinos on the new Martian territories. All that before I admitted to being 30.

Often, when I was bored, I used to distance-view Earth and Mars and the void between. The only place not worth bothering about was Earth's moon, a lump of debris formed from some space collision. There were no valuable minerals or brothels. 'Fergitaboutit!' as Joe would say. The bridge of 40 Rigs between Terra and Mars meant Terrans never needed it as a launch pad.

A surge of power jolted me out of daydreams. Joe liked to appear as unexpectedly as a genie from a magic lamp. His

Grav-sled slid neatly onto my apartment balcony even before I'd time to give him clearance. 'Security' was a concept that did not exist for him. He could outwit any of us and out-manoeuvred all systems. There he was, with his legs astride pose, imitating me. He was waiting for me to stumble to the platform where the transparent hood of his two-seater was rolled back for me. I exited my apartment's automatic doors and waved and whooped. To match his cool, I leaped up and landed in the seat beside him. Before I could blink, we were flying. That was easy – like my jump, I admit it – thanks to Martian low gravity. In seconds we were above Helium's imitation gold dome.

I loved Earth, though I had never visited in the flesh. I even almost felt nostalgic during my long-distance surveillance of the old planet. It was amusing to spy on England's windbag President. Myrna thought my voyeurism was part of my super-spy role. A multitude of surveillance teams worked under my control, dealing with all sectors of the Martian settlements, particularly the Caliphate. I ordered them to keep my eagle-eyes alert for the huge Chinese terra-forming and military movements on Mars. Two nations surprised me in their movements. Russia, once a major power, showed modest interest in terraforming on Mars, while following a silent isolationism on Earth. Secondly, it amazed me that Australia had idly missed out on expansion on Mars. Maddigan made friendly signs to them. They seemed to prefer to maintain their private fortress in the enormous Pacific Ocean. I guess they gave me the chance to quip: *How long till we have kangaroos on Mars?* The answer was: *That won't ever happen 'cos one leap will take the buggers to outer space.* Fair enough. At the time Joe and I were totally bladdered!

With Myrna so often irritating me, I needed a hobby. I picked history. I hired half a dozen students for free to excavate stuff I could use to support Helium Day festivities. They eagerly dug up a variety of oddball facts about London Bridges from Roman times to the mid-18th century. Hang about, there! There was a curious *relevancy* to my understanding of the interplanetary highway. You see, by the 1760s the Thames bridge became a major entertainment venue. Shops, bars

14

and whorehouses were packed into every vacant plot up above the Thames. Added to that, the research helped me get a pair of student chicks opening their legs for me.

Lights went on in my brain one day. London Bridge was equivalent to today's communications bridge between Earth and Mars. Instead of a brick-and-mortar bridge topped with slapper shag shops, we had placed 'Rigs' between two planets. They were an indispensable advance on using spaceships that took 400 days for the journey, even at the closest planetary alignment. Here is my associative genius at work. As a brat, old history inspired me as soon as I discovered Roman orgies. What a sticky mess in my teenage pants when I used my imagination! In sophisticated maturity, I announced: *Commercialized bridge across river equals broadcast Rigs between Terra and Mars.*

The Rigs – as they are known – carry visual broadcasts straight from the 1st to the 2nd to the 3rd platform and vice versa. Rig 1 was the first of the 40 platforms of the London Bridge in space that stretched from Mars to Earth. It was also closest to the Red Planet. Just like London Bridge, Rig 1 was filled with side-to-side whorehouses. Punters from Mars enjoyed a two hourly service to Rig 1 and the famous Anais Palace, the most extensive pleasure dome ever created by unique Anglo-Chino-Arabian-Afro-Indian co-operation. Of course, even London Bridge must have had a cover story for illicit enjoyment. Rig 1 was famous for domestic technology. That was something I found amusing. We never travelled beyond Rig 1. There was no point, especially when you're shagged out! I am told there was a decrease in depravity and fun if you visited the further Rigs. They only dealt armaments and drugs. Flight procedures were scheduled for upgrades, but at present, visitors still have to stop off at Phobos Moon Station midway to Rig 1.

Both Phobos and Deimos were dwarves, compared to many other moons of the Solar System. Deimos, the smaller, was unattractive and irregular shaped with a big bump on it. I thought it resembled a pock-marked pear. It was rarely used because it took 30 Earth hours to complete a circuit of Mars. Phobos, with three circuits a day, was more suited a destination for frequent flights from the planet. A Six Mile crater named Stickney, offered a launchpad from which we would transfer from our little flier to a full-sized vessel to take us to Rig 1, hanging in the void. Since Phobos is only 14 miles across and very fast-moving, pilots had to be careful not to miss its landing strip.

After a last glance at the orange bulk of Mars behind us, I turned to Joe and passed my time by educating him with one of my history lectures.

'Did you know, matey, the moons were discovered by an astronomer called Aliph Hall back in 1877? The crater where our launch pad is based was named after his old lady. How romantic! A pity her moniker was Stickney.'

'Boring,' Joe remarked, gulping old-time Earth beer straight from an old glass bottle.

I persisted. 'What interests me was a writer called Jonathan Swift; he wrote a book called *Gulliver's Travels*. Since you never read intellectual materials and it's not on video – not the bit I'm telling you about – you wouldn't know anything about this. Well, Swifty announced there were two moons orbiting Mars. How did he know that? He was of the 1700s. Astonishing! How could he possibly reach that conclusion?'

'Fuck knows. But I see you're going to tell me.'

'Well, you thick cunt, some people claim he was a Rosicrucian. I'm sure you've never heard about them, have you? There were other nutters who said Swift was an alien who came from the planet Latuna, the name of a world in one of his stories. But the general view was that it arose from maths. There were no moons for Mercury or Venus, one moon on Earth, three moons of Jupiter, so Mars, in between, had to have two. That was how he figured it.'

'Boring, Simon baby. Boring. Why you telling me this shit?'

'Take your mind off fanny on Rig 1, Simple Simon! You have a load of spy-time for plugging gash when you arrive at Anais's Palace. Yeah! For now, my duty is to brief you. Do you know why we're heading for Phobos?'

'Of course, I do, patronizing fucker! Shut your gob, Boss. Don't hassle when I'm getting wrecked.'

Pissed off with my dim mate, I shifted my brain power to our supposed mission of sifting some information held on Rig 1 about Maddigan. Myrna told us our sole purpose was to pinch this top-secret bollocks about him hidden on the Rig. The informant there was – here's the punch line – the Madam of the Rig's 'House of Ill-Repute'. I watched her face. President Myrna's sharp blue eyes pierced mine. My reaction gave no hint of guilt. Nothing could challenge the Master Mind of Mars!

Anyhow, her command was for us to bug any supposedly bug-proof monitoring devices and check for information leaks from England to the Rig 1 line. People who achieve great power inevitably drift into paranoia. Myrna had grown increasingly suspicious that Maddigan planned to remove her as Governor because he feared she planned a *coup*. To my mind, the President was too naive, too stupid to think such a thing.

That was why she had agreed so easily to our visit. She also said the superior scientific facilities concealed on Rig 1 guaranteed security of all visuals and audio. Using my duplicity, I could access the entirety for her.

Joe was obsessively shaping his forked beard and arched eyebrows. He was obviously aware of his inferiority to me in physical looks. I felt compassion for him and put him at ease with small talk. I asked him why he was called 'Manitoba.' He muttered about the name coming from a fish restaurant in a Canadian province: *Manitoba Joey's*. He chuckled, adding irrelevantly that Manitoba was the polar bear capital of Canada. I surmised he was probably named by a macho dad on Earth who wanted a kid as dangerous as a polar bear.

Before I could blink, we were descending to the Stickney Crater. Landing was smooth. Since we were regular punters, everyone knew of my personal tastes in working girls of the Rig area as well as my relationship with Governor Myrna Golden. Such common knowledge and sloppy lies established me with a most believable cover for espionage. None of the subservient ground staff

17

imagined I was any more than a frivolous, vain character, lucky to be the Governor's gigolo. Once I tugged my maroon *faux leather* military jacket into place, I alighted from our flier and led the way, Joe watching my back. With silk-smooth panache, I saluted every worker we passed. The salute was returned by all of them. Some, I noticed, did so with a poorly concealed snigger. Little did they recognize my status in major interplanetary politics. Joe wiped his nose on the back of his left hand, clumsily acting the common thug – a bloke no different from them. He was skilled in that sort of performance.

The military escort brought us to the First-Class Waiting Area. There we enjoyed some refreshments in the form of a couple of bottles of rather splendid sparkling wine and I took the opportunity to dress down somewhat. I did not want to draw attention to myself. I preferred extravagance. Pity I had to pretend to be Myrna's semi-rent boy. Wealth was a salve for my early life, and I deserved every reward I received these days. Not everyone is like spoiled brat rich girl, Myrna Golden!

On the brighter side – as far as far as Phobos was concerned – we located three bars on Stickney Crater. They would do for a few pick-me-ups before we had lift off aboard our passenger vessel. There wasn't much else to do on Phobos. Over the years, my missions to this shit hole meant everyone knew me as a merry piss head. Myrna would be happy for this episode to be leaked to her, when she checked up on me.

Balls to her! I was testosterone loaded and heading off to the brothels of Rig 1! I laughingly confessed as much to a salacious reporter with a nudge and wink.

Chapter 3

Our lift off from Phobos Station to Rig 1 was so smooth I scarcely noticed it. Eager for our mission and 'other', we went up, up and away into space. We acted according to our stereotype profiles. I lie! Instinct drew us to the nearby chamber where beer lived. The draw of alcohol is one constant of human evolution.

You can't beat the facilities you enjoy during space travel when you are one of the Government's elites. That thought always danced in my mind ever since Myrna promoted me to my illustrious status. Me and Joe slouched onto the couches in the private bar of the first-class area, an experienced drunkard's Nirvana. For at least 50 minutes (Universal Earth Time) we relaxed with old fashioned Earth-style beer, straight from glass bottles, having a good laugh and enjoying every service available to us. We even had salted peanuts, grown beneath the domes of the India province. All other requirements would be satisfied when we arrived at Rig 1, of course!

Even while I was at ease with my beers, I was prepared to slave for my boss/wife. I had to use all my available time during the day-long voyage to Rig 1. Joe leaned idly against the bar, but I isolated myself in the first-class area's observation booth. Invisible screens surrounded me to prevent interruption. I accessed my eidetic memory, so I could pick up the complex sequence of passwords enabling me to observe events 24 hours ago in England. That's round about how long it took for a transmission from Earth to reach me. A magic signal went 'Beep! Beep!' as the images leap-frogged through the void from one to another of the 40 Rigs between Earth and Mars. I was lucky to have my classy surveillance staff on Helium operating solely on monitoring President Maddigan. Any time at all I could watch his every expression, hear every word via my hidden super-drones that transmitted to Rig 40. Information came hopping over the transmission chain of an invisible bridge between two planets. All of it was illegal, according to International Dual Planetary Law, of course. But anyone with the top-ranking criminal contacts I built up could do the same. My entertainment enroute, therefore, lay in snooping on the President. I was not especially bothered about the time lag of the pictures reaching me.

Actually, I so relished my political voyeurism, I discovered that interpreting expressions and watching how people operated was better than entertainment drama. Dozy old Maddison was oblivious to it all. I had expected that. He was bound to be primarily concerned with preening himself and presenting himself as a charismatic leader of two planets. To give the old boy his credit, he was an excellent performer. Just a crap elected Head of the British Empire. I couldn't wait to present Myrna with his presidency like a bouquet.

Communication was 100 per cent ready now. I adjusted my 3D-goggles, and I was instantly dazzled by the unfamiliar brightness of Earth's sun. No wonder they named it the Green Planet. On Mars, the various nations had terraformed such areas as the South Pole, where China and India had located huge underground lakes that fed our world's single olive-green forest. Some maps even displayed pink shading to indicate they'd become protectorates of the reincarnated British Empire. However, on the real world of the 'Red Planet', everything was dull and subdued orange. The sky itself was barely lighter than the deserts awaiting terraforming. Our challenges were not only caused by our greater distance as the fourth planet from the sun. Human settlers had faced a dead desert world. Probably that was why ancient fantasists liked to portray vibrant civilizations on Mars that were destroyed millennia before our Earthly progenitors crawled out of the oceans. When I surveyed the fertility and brilliance of Terra through my 3D-goggles, I was confronted by the illusion that Terra was really paradise.

That fantasy was enhanced once I witnessed Maddigan's weird location. He had shaded his eyes to study a large hill with what looked like an ancient maze going round and around it. There appeared to be lines of trees or bushes planted on either side of a serpentine path leading to the summit. At the top of this curious mound stood a single ruined tower. Here was somewhere that genuinely disturbed me. Ridiculous as it sounds, I believed that I had seen it in my dreams. I knew they were dreams, not false memory of reality. I decided it was time to put hallucinations into the room marked, 'deja vu' or 'archetypes', then lock the door again!

I refocussed my spying. I saw a chubby man with receding ginger hair taking a big breath as he patted his gut. It was him! Most world leaders enjoy wearing combat gear to give an air of toughness and that. Not this old boy. Maddigan's choice was a blue t-shirt displaying a naked girl on the front. Over it, he wore a soft, velveteen jacket of light green with darker green trimmings round the dipped cuffs and deep pockets. His lower half was adorned with orange trousers with turn ups. Was he nuts? Or tasteless? Or was it a joke?

Experimental vid-trackers claim to be close to offering a sense of tactile and olfactory elements in the target areas of distance observation. I don't have the faintest idea how the scientist wallahs plan to do it! There again, I am merely a pretty face. Explanations aside, I gained a convincing impression of the freshness of the air and of a tactile breeze in the scene. It was further heightened by the illusion of sweet scents from flowers surrounding Maddigan, despite what appeared to be a soggy area of towering weeds and briars. There was no smell of decay though. Hearing was genuinely enhanced by my viewer. I heard the rustling of leaves in the aisles of small trees and bushes as if I stood next to them. The chirruping of scores of birds was a wonderful experience, one totally unknown on the Red Planet. I panned in on my subject. A sense of wonder was in his eyes when he leaned his neck back to survey a ring of standing stones crowning the summit. Both the megalithic circle and the tower disturbed me in a way I was unable to rationalize. Unexpectedly, I suddenly yearned for the security of the common-sense environment of Mars. Earth felt as alien and as odd as a dreamland.

A deep breath restored common sense. Maddigan had – allegedly – recently announced himself Head of the Druids. I was glad for Helium's atheism! Only perverts and psychopaths of Catholic Christianity or Arab Islamists carried the infection of organized religion. Such fanatics believed it was their religious duty to administer punishment and death to any other culture or those labelled 'Unbelievers'. The sodomite Christian priests went on buggering each other and their choir boys. They had become a lesser evil in that sense. The Caliphate committed genocide or *jihad* to punish 'Unbelievers'. My view, incidentally served me well in my public image of the Man of the People.

The Welshman was more complicated than my humble self. I had to re-focus to learn more on this day. With him was the First Lady, Natasha. He invariably revealed genuine affection for her by holding her hands and kissing her fingers even when they were alone. They stood together like romantic teenagers out together for the first time. I made a mental note to rehearse similar romantic gestures for Myrna.

I felt my lips squirm into a cynical smile as I watched the space age, elderly couple. During an earlier spying session, I noticed he left her at their residence, a town named Wells, when he visited this island. Also, I found several assassination attempts had been made on him and he had always tried to put her safety before his own. He and Natasha approached a shallow lake and area of swamp. He became more animated, and the volume went up, so his voice became clearer and I found it easier to make out his words. He referred to the 'Isle of Avalon'. Instant search function informed me the place had some sort of magical significance from the most ancient times of British folklore. The hill was an island 3000 years ago. Here, he had the air of someone hypnotized or subject to otherworldly visions. He hardly seemed a political man, ruler of an Empire that stretched between two planets.

As soon as they reached the expanse of water surrounding the hill, Maddigan peered across its margins to see a light-haired woman smiling at him from the opposite shore. She wore a green robe and a rugged cloak of animal skin. This was not the attire with which I was familiar in Helium, to put it mildly! My Info Check informed me the fur came from a real animal. A bear, it was called. I was shocked, although I did recall that Pagans favoured similar barbaric attire. As for the dramatically robed female, I detected deliberate artifice in her pose, there amidst the lush vegetation, where droplets of water fell from the large, pointed leaves beside her. Natasha's irritation was clear.

'Come over here!' the daunting woman shouted. 'We're waiting for you. You must walk the maze. You must do it alone,' she insisted. 'Your wife remains here.'

She seemed to be some sort of Druid Priestess. I found the entire situation baffling. I failed to comprehend how the figurehead of the British Empire was embroiled in this nonsense.

Maddigan gave his wife an awkward peck on her tight lips. He turned and giving her an awkward wave, plunged his feet into the waters dividing him from the Priestess. He was awfully inept and self-conscious. His bad balance and general clumsiness embarrassed me! Ankle deep mire beneath the water made it all look worse. The turn ups of his orange pants must be weighted down with muck. He kept going. Despite sweating profusely, he squelched to the other side.

A deafening chorus of shrieks and cawing of the birds exploded from the bushes. Their racket suggested avian laughter at this middle-aged clown in his ludicrous dress. Perhaps it occurred to him there might be concealed media surveillance from ionospheric drones. Unexpectedly, he laughed aloud in response to the birds as if he shared their twittering humour.

As he lurched onto drier land on the far side, he was watching the face of the woman waiting for him. She was suppressing her laughter at his awkwardness. When he came closer, she offered him her hand. He made an exhibition of not splattering her robe with mud. He definitely looked like he needed to chill out. Behind her were a pair of ancient iron gates. I wondered where they led. After a brief pause, she spoke casually, although her voice penetrated as sharply as a sliver of glass.

'One must put oneself in the right frame of mind. Pull yourself together.'

Appearing confused as to what frame of mind he was expected to have, the clownish President stammered, 'Are we really in the here and now? I've not been mesmerized, have I? Everything about this place is what one might describe as disorientating, look you.'

Checking the top left of my viewing googles, I found 'look you' was a 'Welsh Regional verbal mannerism'.

Maddigan was impressive in the PR releases that bombarded Mars. He was genuinely charismatic when he assumed his Presidential public address voice. His voice then was deep, vibrating in his chest with merely a lilt of Welsh accent. There must have been a considerable doctoring and enhancement in those transmissions. Even everyday English liked him. In my opinion, though, he ought to have dropped his 'boyo' and 'look you' bits that went well with working people. How could that be the same man as the idiot I saw now?

His robed Priestess waited impatiently in front of the bushes that made a corridor to the gates. Irritably, she fluttered her hands to hasten his tottering. I tried to shift the viewer's focus using a brain wave app. Being as crap as I am with new Helium technology, I found myself looking at the blue sky, instead of finding whatever mystery was concealed behind the big hedge and the portentous gates. I had to put my goggles on 'pause', then readjust my view with my fingers, instead of trying to use mental signals. My attractive artistic fingers have always been more reliable than my mechanical dexterity.

Opening the creaking iron gate, the green robed Priestess led him through the screen of bushes that hid a secret little area at the foot of the hill. There was momentary interference of transmission.

'C'mon, bastard!' I shouted, banging my vid-control.

Chapter 4

What was on the other side of the gate was a surprise. Instead of tangles of undergrowth and wilderness, I discovered my quarry had entered an ancient, cultivated garden. There was an unfamiliar tranquillity here. Nothing I could explain. After all, the Red Planet has a less than limited demand for gardens, so it was not part of my expertise. Descending on either side of Maddigan and his other woman, trickled two streams, one orange, one white. At the bottom of the garden, these waters joined to form a double mini waterfall. That, in turn, fed into an array of ornamental pottery goblets, with lips designed to carry the water to a pool at the lowest part of the garden. That was where the overflow vanished into the Earth, presumably feeding that shallow lake Tubby Taffy had waded through.

Wherever I scanned were swathes of long extinct blossoms of every colour. I touched my goggles to enable commentary and close ups. Despite myself, I was totally charmed by the flowers' beauty. The drone fed me detailed information. To the rear were lupins, delphiniums, convolvulus and also an enormous wisteria that sheltered and embraced them all with its delightful clusters of trumpets dangling from its arms. In the foreground grew many smaller, more lowly plants. I was fascinated; I adjusted my viewing angles. I had never seen anything like this in my entire life. When I looked downwards, I realized the flowerbeds formed a pattern of interlinked Druidic or Celtic swirls or mazes. I wondered what it meant. Maybe it stirred part of Maddigan's Welsh subconscious.

Three out of five senses were inaccessible during interplanetary surveillance: touch, scent and taste. Although I could see and hear from my millions of miles away, I could not experience Maddigan's shivers from being damp and chilly after paddling to his Priestess. Nor could I smell the fresh vegetation and flowers. From a different area in my brain came a recollection of sweet scents that hung in the breeze after rain and of a blend – not entirely unpleasantly – with rotting leaves and tubers. Perhaps all of us who have spent our lives on the Red Planet retained ancestral memory of the Earthly natural world. Nobody was likely to be dining beside at the well at the top end of the garden, so my taste faculty could not be tested. Curiously, I experienced another sense. It was memory. I knew this place was named Avalon. Without me downloading the history feed, I knew it also as 'Glastonbury'.

Madigan and his Priestess followed a narrow stone path to the top end of the garden where the source of the streams was hidden beneath overhanging olive-green boughs that I had glimpsed from the gates. A wrought iron arch announced, 'Chalice Well'. Passing beneath its frame, they halted as if they were entranced. Obviously, it held sacred significance. Beside the circle of the well that plunged deep into the Earth was a wooden throne. My viewer's info source informed me it was made from an ancient wood called 'oak'. The Welshman was anxious to sit here. The Priestess put her finger to her lips and shook her head, contemptuously, I thought. Like a disobedient dog, afraid of being disciplined, he followed at her heels as she led him through another barricade of vegetation. On the other side, they emerged from trees and bushes at the base of the circular hill called the Tor.

He was led upwards to a gigantic megalithic rock. It was likely to be a marker for a ritual that involved ritually threading the maze I had identified, running around the Tor. His destination would be the stone circle at the summit.

The woman in the bearskin cloak cried, 'I'll see you above in the stone circle!' Then she ran down towards the trees and disappeared. President Maddigan drew a sign in the air. His forefinger went upwards and down, then up again as if drawing a pentagram. He placed his palm against the monolith with the air of a man who believed this was a momentous moment. The tubby mystic looked all set to follow the maze as it wound up and down and back and forward on an irrational course to the summit. I wouldn't waste the next two hours watching him go round and round the turf labyrinth for some Pagan nonsense.

Some time ago, Joe had shown me a report from some of his intelligence mavericks about the religious revival in Europe, especially in Britain. Till now it never registered with guys like me from the Helium Province, how far England had diverged from the Christianity religion I found in the history accounts. Today, primitive Druidry and magic was in fashion. The real issue was the implication of the Head of the Empire becoming a tool of the occult revival. On the one hand, it might assist Myrna to remove him. On the other, we might end up with an equivalent of the homicidal lunacy of the Caliphate on Mars.

Before I switched off, I took a last peek at what awaited the old guy when – and if – he made it to the to the top. As Maddigan plodded along the ritual maze, I adjusted a space drone for overhead focus. What an appallingly tough trial the middle-aged Welshman had dedicated himself to!

That was my lot! I had got tired and bored with mystical bollocks. A stud like me bores easily, you know. Action was what I needed. I needed a few hours kip to be sure I would be at peak performance for banging Madame Anais's girls.

My viewer shut down. I was back in my tiny spy cell on our vessel. The warmth of the cubicle got to me. Believe it or not, I fell asleep where I was sat.

When I slept, I dreamed of the stone circle on the summit of the Tor. There was a ring of bearded men in long, white robes, chanting rubbish. One stuck in my mind, though. His hair and long beard were silvery white. He had an air of genuine authority. It was disturbing when he suddenly stared at me with eyes that were almost black. I imagined he saw my face. Then, it became a muddled nightmare. Miscegenated giants screamed for blood. Witches soared above the ritual. I had to struggle to wake up from it. Even then, I thought I had woken up and I was still dreaming, and I could not move. I wondered about having a brain scan, maybe minor brain surgery, which was currently fashionable for treating psychos on Helium.

Instead, I reached in my suit for a half hour trip tab. Far less radical. And it worked. I sank into a fantastic slumber in which me and Manitoba Joe reclined side by side in Anais's Rig 1 brothel, pumping endless gallons into and onto a line of obliging dolls of every colour and shape.

Chapter 5

The wake up came too soon. Joe was shaking me. I realized I was still in in the video spy chamber. He shouted in my ear that we were landing on Rig 1. I was not with it thanks to the pill I'd taken, so he dragged me on my feet, down the seating aisles and off our ship. When we stepped onto the surface of the satellite Rig, I was still befuddled. My hair was ruffled, and my buddy told me I looked like a mad scientist.

To rebuff him I instructed him that, 'Chronometric changes are unnecessary to Helium's advanced technology.' That was to prove how alert I was.

'What the fuck are you gibbering about?' Joe responded.

I flopped down on the exit ramp. He opened my mouth and poured down a gold liquid from a small bottle that appeared from nowhere. This was some sort of Earth alcohol 'spirit'. After gagging, choking and coughing, I revived.

Our reception was markedly low key. That was probably because security took me for a drunk or drugster. Joe used a timeless pacifier called bribery. I don't know what form of financial transfer was made, but they backed off. I began to complain this was not the red-carpet treatment I was used to.

'Keep your head down, wanker!' said Joe, dragging me away.

His political pull and bribery continued to make life easy for him. No one bothered us with intrusive searches. He reminded me to put my ego into hibernation and be invisible to hostile intelligence.

Manitoba was still in charge. He took us to the reception lounge, filled with artificially grown bright green bushes and trees. They were here to impress arrivals and feed the illusion they were on a planet, rather than a metal structure in space. I took an aristocratic pose, bending to sniff a dusty green shrub with tiny pink flowers, murmuring, 'Delightful!' I couldn't smell fuck all with my nostrils blocked thanks to snorting an array of drugs.

'The Honourable Simon Edge and Mr Manitoba Joe!' an unmistakeable female voice echoed through a speaker. Joe swore at our secrecy being blown. He was reassured when the speaker revealed herself.

Appearing miraculously in the lounge, we were greeted by our old friend, Anais, the legendary Madam of the Rig 1 Pleasure Palace. An alternative term was 'brothel'. But she did not like the term. Anais was as near as spit to being the queen of an independent planetoid. She was a tubby black woman of 'uncertain age'. Her lungs generated greater volume than a sonic cannon. The white-rimmed specs, an unnecessary affectation, were almost as big as her personality. These spectacles were intended to make one start, because of their contrast with her black face. Glasses had become highly fashionable. Any visual defect could be cured by simple operations. They were worn to establish her 'image', her copyrighted publicity symbol. They made everyone see her as a giant presence. I felt challenged by the quality of her PR. With immense skill, I countered her overwhelming presence with the slimiest depths of my charm. It was always a good move to feign awe of people with inflated egos. It appeared my act completely endeared me to her. Here was an invaluable opportunity for me to be in. Every grubby secret she secured about her punters, offered her infinite blackmail opportunities. By playing it cleverly, I might learn them.

Transport arrangements on Rig 1 were odd. We were carried across the space landing in a sedan chair, borne by two gigantic, white body builders. The Madam believed affectations of this kind enhanced the fantasy elements of her realm. A brief journey of 500 yards took us to the ground floor bar of her sex emporium.

I didn't bother my pretty head any more. A brace of totally delicious babes was hovering behind her. Each of them carried a silver tray. The first had a pair of champagne glasses sat waiting. On the other perched a lone glass. That was for Anais. My neuroses kicked in then. Were the two glasses for us doctored? I had those moments! She had no reason to poison her most influential sources of information. Especially me – her most handsome and attractive favourite.

When I raised my glass to clink it with Joe's I saw his eyes twinkling with amusement. He usually read what I was thinking. We synchronized when we both touched glasses with Anais. I gazed wistfully into her eyes. I became confident I could secure her in the palm of my hand. The dear old biddy still believed it was the other way around. As usual, she reassured me of my invisibility on Myrna's radar during sexual activities. She guaranteed whatever happened on her asteroid stew stayed confidential. Joe and I laughed simultaneously. I smooched her chubby black cheek.

In no time at all, we were special guests in her pseudo-gothic castle, housing that vast brothel that dominated the entire satellite. I didn't even pause to admire the intricacies of this 'House of Dreams' as our roly-poly bawd described it.

Diplomatically, I demonstrated my interest in her sons.

'You be meeting them rascals,' she laughed. 'I got one, he wants to be the hero of the space place and the other be wantin' to be like your buddy, tough boy, Joe. Just so long as they don't make a career living off older governor women, I approve.'

That was rather harsh, I thought. I chose to laugh with her. My mate diverted me.

'Try this, buddy,' Joe said, offering me a phial of blue liquid.

Since I felt recovered from my nightmares and in-flight excesses, I threw it back without even asking what it was.

He nudged Anais, a hint of a smile on his grim face. 'That won't give him the droops, Ma'am. You will make a fortune off him now!'

As if it had been choreographed, I discovered the balcony overhead had filled with a wiggling parade of at least a dozen 20-carat girlies. The potion had additional properties to the extent I couldn't distinguish fleshly girls from illusory ones! I identified the potion Joe had given me as 'Sceptre'. This is a hypnotic trip chemical providing the additional bonus of an instant, tireless erection! My fantasies went wild. I desired sex with a light green chlorophyl girl? Like a sexy plant. Bite her throat. Tasting bitter apple? Drink trippy Sceptre sap from her little tits? Or was that imagination? I salivated, not recognizing that this girl was my beautiful Alisha, who I remembered I once loved more than life itself for nearly six months.

In my drugged confusion, I waved her away before I recalled I was in love with her.

She registered my addled condition pretty easily. Her crimson lips pouted with her firm declaration, 'I'm still here and I'm staying put,' she teased. 'No other woman will be taking your wealth.'

I couldn't argue with that. She took charge and hurried me into a vacant sex room. Strip off. Onto silken sheets. And away I went!

Time slipped away. Alisha was of Indian nationality. Not a green alien girl! I had a vague memory of how she once she went spying for Joe. Most of the babes made extra income from their clients' indiscrete pillow talk. Her gorgeous pale brown skin and hooked nose were racial characteristics she and old Jewish Joe shared. I never trust people with small noses!

Alisha was slim, small, firm-breasted perfection – just like my hallucinatory chlorophyll girl. I sometimes suspected Alisha was telepathic because of her infallible ability of anticipating every decision of men. That included me. She was unlike any other prostitute in the Sex Palace. Sometimes I feared her intellectual dominance. That's because I was a control freak, I suppose. Anyway, I had bought her body, not her brain! She told me that.

The dose of Sceptre created slips in my sense of time. Abruptly, I was alone with her in a paradise of sky-blue silk sheets. Or was this what had I already experienced a while ago? Blank. Nothing existed outside Simon and Alisha. We were twisting and caressing, and I was kissing her hard brown nipples. Her eyes were blue despite her eastern ancestry. It was the first time I noticed it.

I rejected sentimentality. Words came thoughtlessly from my mouth: 'Double fee for your fleshy highway, my top harlot?'

Her reaction was violent anger that drove her close to a physical assault on me. A long, slim finger jabbed into my throat. My mind crumbled into psychological collapse. Why was I deliberately cruel and heartless saying shit like that? I was in love with her, despite her lucrative occupation. I hallucinated I was a therapist – a bearded, bespectacled elderly man – analysing another me who lay on a couch. When I concluded my findings about devious Simon who lay there, I concluded being despicable was a price he paid for his cunning genius. When I looked in Alisha's eyes, I saw a tremendous emotional debt I would be compelled to repay for years to come.

She determined my punishment. I think she realized I was incapable of returning love. To me she would remain the whore I had hired. She impaled herself on my chemically enhanced prong. I gave her tiny tits little slaps in order that that pretend sadism would help make me come like fuck. Trouble was I remained as stiff as a halberd. I banged away in desperation to come again. No more lava erupted from the old volcano. Just the same rivers of sweat ran down between my pecs.

'Let's leave it for now,' I told her.

She obeyed. Her lips curled in contempt, and she held out her palm for payment. Inappropriately as ever, I scribbled down my account code to pay. She crumpled it and chucked it. Seemingly, my generosity infuriated her even more for she spat, 'Perhaps you might grow up if you had a heart instead of a brain.'

Burying my face in her soft, little breasts, I sobbed as I explained how I suffered because of deep psychological issues from childhood. This made me always hide feelings from people. That line failed. She told me to fuck off. I wondered where the hell Joe had got to. He would get me off the hook. I did not need to call to him. A loud explosion rocked the building.

Within a minute, as I froze, heart pounding, there was a violent rapping on the portal of our re-enforced platinoid chamber door. He was bellowing, 'The Microdrone's on, you dozy fuck!'

Without doubt, Simon Edge was the number one target for assassination. Both the Caliphate and the Chinese colonies on Mars were hostile and suspicious, regarding the movements of a political genius who guided the Governor of Britain's colony. Worrying, despite being complimentary! Doubtless my unpredictable actions and range of personalities made it impossible for such dull, stupid people to decipher. My complexity would scare them. Pulling up my pants, I hoped the disturbance Joe had announced was just a media muck-raking ploy.

I clipped on my protective, moulded chest plate, as my impatient buddy kicked down the sex room portal even before it slid up to let him in.

'Transport outside. Balcony, Simon!'

Though I was on the tenth floor of the Pleasure Palace, I ran to the balcony and, without thinking, leaped off. Fortunately, this was an inspired impulse. A flier was perfectly placed for me to land onto the side section. Wearing a billowing scarlet cape – donned purely to upstage me – Manitoba Joe flew into space behind me. He landed on the roof of the vehicle beside me. Together, we tumbled through the entrance in the flier roof. His cape pissed me off. *What a fucking poser!* I thought. *I wonder where I can get a cloak with more swish than his.*

Once we flopped down inside the cabin, I had a moment of petulance. I took Myrna's mission because it was excuse for a monster shagging session. Instead, I'd been interrupted, and I wasted the high of the Sceptre trip! I thought this was as bad as it got. Mistake! My communicator indicated an incoming. I searched my pockets. Where the…? However, Joe had retrieved it for me. I tore the detector from his mitt, prepared for threats from an unsuccessful assassin. Alas, it was worse than any killer. The identifier showed it was Myrna!

I screamed, 'What the fuck? Why are you calling me now?'

Joe tried to calm me with, 'Only concerned for you, eh?'

'Myrna!' I shrieked, 'Cheers for your clumsy, shoddy surveillance before I got here. Are you going to tell me you never arranged a search of Rig 1 before we arrived? Or did you plan for me to be bumped off? Watch the news flash. See that bombing of my hotel room? Fuck!'

I realized she must know of the brothel provision that occupied 90 per cent of the platform. Obviously, we never discussed the prowling tom cat in my psychology. My sexual amusements didn't bother her. Or that's what I had believed. She was not so irrational as to murder me out of an unseemly jealousy after she sent me to recover secret information.

Oily charm is my finest attribute. This was the time to switch it on. After all, I am Lady Luck's favourite son. I had arrived instinctively in the right place at the right time. I would have got blown up without it my luck.

As our flier fled for the safe blackness of space, we witnessed, on the main screen, a second terrific rush of flames from the room I just fled. The shock wave was so intense that even our ascending craft was buffeted every which way. We went spinning down, towards the satellite's walkways. Gravity pinned Joe and me to the floor from the speed of our ascent into space. Suddenly we levelled out. I thanked my lfortunate planets that Joe's anonymous pilot was so capable! Seemingly, just feet from the ground, we slowed and reversed direction. We rose once more to hover above the palace.

Before the shock of it all could register, I began shaking, stammering and sweating from shock. I was ashamed of myself. To cover up my loss of dignity, I ran into the tiny cabin to thank our saviour flier. To my surprise, he wasn't Darren, my usual air-chauffeur, but his kid brother, Doran. The pair were Madam Anais's only kids. She adored the pair of them. A pity the names she allotted caused confusion whenever they were hired. My shrewd employment of them strengthened the bond between the Madam and myself. This lad, Doran, was nicknamed 'Light-finger' for reasons I did not ask about. Assuming a gruff, manly voice, I swaggered up to him to slap him on the back and express my appreciation of his skill.

He grinned boyishly and shrugged, 'Guess I was just born lucky.'

'Fuckin' hell, bud!' laughed Joe. 'Do you reckon Simon's bitch has gotten jealous? Have a beer.'

Our laddish performance was for the benefit of the teenager. I decided I needed to restore my popular image as the caring, laughing guy, loved by everybody across Helium and all the territories.

I instructed Doran to disable the spyware security so that I could be seen by everybody in audiences on two worlds who tuned in. They would witness the essential goodness of my natural personality. I prepared the appropriate caring voice pitch and tone, while forming my appropriate facial expression.

A thought suddenly hit me. Alisha! Had she been blown up? My concern was possibly genuine, I think.

I love that lovely Indian lady, my inner dialogue recited. Today I had reunited with Alisha after more than a year. She must have escaped to the safety of another sex room, when the assassins struck. I indulged my emotions like someone seeing a trash video-pulp romance. *Alisha! My blue-eyed, black-haired oriental beauty. I love you. Please be unharmed. I never revealed to you how I love you!*

Overcome by sugary sentiment, I was fuelled up with feelings when turned to the camera in order to exhibit my pain and concern for an innocent victim of such pointless terrorism by jihadists and all other political murderers. My loud soliloquy practically moved me to tears. A flashing red light at the top of the screen registered that my performance was being watched by millions.

Manitoba Joe was the coolest pal you could ever have. He knew what I wanted for my presentation. He focussed a viewer on the bombed brothel. With surprisingly professional skill, he brought close-up focus to my anguished face precisely the moment I begged for pity from of every Pagan, Scientology and Abrahamic divinity I could think of.

During my delivery, I was also calculating how astronomical the brothel's repair bills would be. Their big consolation was that insurance would pay for all maiming, surgery and loss of life. Fortunately, Madam Anais had fitted explosion-proof insulation between each and every girl's suite. She genuinely cared about the safety of 'my girls' as well as complying with security regulations. Along with Anais, I too prayed for the safety of all those delicious babes, packed into their silken business sheets like jewels.

I sat beside Doran who was hunched over manual controls. You cannot trust auto alone in an emergency situation like this one. Aware of the brotherly rivalry, I told him, 'I'm glad it was you flying support today, rather than Darren. He would've been more enthusiastic about taking out attackers than in rescuing passengers – or in casualties.'

He smirked. I had been successful in cultivating him! If I needed future favours, he would oblige me. Naturally, it would be undesirable for him to blab about my flattery to Darren, so I casually let slip some gossip about some situations his older brother had pulled me out of on several past missions. Some of this cloak and dagger – as they used to say – had even taken place under the mosque-filled skyline of the Caliphate's Martian territory.

Not wishing to be belittled, Doran said, 'Mam specially sent me to save youse from the attack. This is secret now. She needs you straight away for a top-secret meeting about...' He tapped his nose significantly, but wouldn't or, more likely, couldn't divulge any more. However, he did comment that Darren did not know about any of this.

'Hello, hello, hello,' said Manitoba Joe. 'What's that down at nine o'clock?' I spotted a lithe, green-skinned figure in the alley below. Female too. Something about the babe was familiar from my library of shagging memories. In a loud voice, I ordered Doran to approach ground level. Feeling inspired, I told him to drop a rope – a heroic technique from a thousand years ago. It originated from the time I saw an actor named Errol Flynn, in a 'movie' with no colour, perform the action. The ancient entertainment revealed a masterpiece of dramatic postures. I performed the daring action of swinging down a rope with style that Flynn might have approved of. The instant we hovered over the girl, I took the upper exit of our strato-craft and clambered back onto the roof. I stood there with legs apart and holding aloft a dowel rod I had grabbed from somewhere – believing it was an antique sword – jutting upwards. I was somewhat confused and thought my viewers would be awed. Recording this farce was Joe. That bastard was hooting with laughter at me.

I reassured the girl, 'You don't need to be afraid. It's me – Simon Edge of Helium!'

God, that sounded so impressive!

Miraculously, Tiny Tits' name came back to me at that moment. It must have been transmitted through chemicals in my bloodstream – or by the granite Sceptre in my pants! 'Melanie! You've been with me lotsa times at Anais's Palace. Me is Simon! You remember? You know, Manitoba Joe's mate.'

She stopped shivering. It pissed me off that mentioning Joe's name had prompted her memory of me. This was the time to remind her I was the Silverback Commander. My arm went around her slim waist as Joe pulled us up. He too got onto the flier's roof to assist us in getting aboard.

At long last I had returned to the cabin. I commanded Joe to fetch another phial of the hallucinogenic to offer relaxation for this beautiful girl. She tried to shake her head, but I popped a capsule into her mouth. Alisha was demoted from being love of my life. Her status was usurped by my slanty-eyed, light-green-skinned Melanie. In a haze of joy, I luxuriated in the perfume of her long, black hair intoxicating me. Amazing stuff was this batch of Sceptre! Our sex sesh was mutually enjoyable, I hoped. I'd even forgotten the dowel rod I had mistaken for my barbarian sword.

Before I shot my load, I pulled out of front entry and rolled her onto her side so that I could do her from behind while she wiggled her small, shapely bum cheeks. Throughout I was sensitive, slow and careful. I am lying! I banged away at her till she was ready to shoot into next week. She appeared content with my stamina. She was so quiet, so it was hard to tell. Too many women are neurotic, like Myrna. They want 'sensitivity' or 'consideration'. I was lucky to encounter Melanie. As a romantic thank you, I touched my pocket transmitter screen to pay almost double her usual fee, which went directly into her credit account. Mind you, an auto-deduction went to Anais as well. Drugs and sex drive wore off. While I washed my private parts at our bedside detox wash box, I needed to discover why Melanie was running down the alley when we saw her.

She was concise. 'I carry information. I hurry to get to Missy Anais. Report what I been told causes bad men to attack, but afraid more attack they come. You see? If more bomb. Even armed men. I run away, round block. Return to Palace when it all stop. Savvy?'

Her pidgin English was adorable. I did not want her to feel she was being interrogated. Just the same, I was a man burdened with duty and responsibility. I was advisor, secret agent and husband of the Governor of British Province on Mars. I was the exemplar of probity and duty.

Although she knew I was a sexual butterfly, flitting from flower to flower, Melanie acknowledged this. Without hesitation she became transparent to me, volunteering information before I asked for it. The 'interrogation' lasted over an Earth hour over drinks and a ten-minute sexual intermission. I suspected she and Alisha had been recruited by Anais for Myrna and briefed to watch out for any suspicious arrivals at the palace. Unbeknownst to me, Myrna might well have been using Madam Anais as her agent, set to operating independently from Joe and me. I felt decidedly paranoid. It was like we, the watchers, were being watched. This brothel was the base for Helium's technology. Being outside the radius of the Red Planet it was an ideal observation centre for interplanetary spying. Plus, it served as an early warning centre for threats of the Caliphate or China. I was awed by Myrna's genius. *Myrna, you scare me. You're so cunning! You must know everything about my sneakiness and adultery.* Some things are hard to admit. Particularly how Myrna Golden had so easily out-manoeuvred me.

Pilot Doran was banging on the fragile chamber door. That meant All Clear. Also, that Joe and I were required to return to Anais's secret den. My Madam was the last person I wished to offend. Immediately, we ascended to the atmospheric perimeter, to avoid possible ground assaults. Melanie sat at the front, behind Doran. Manitoba Joe and I both had protective arms around her.

I was fully down from Sceptre. The night sky over Rig 1 sparked a final glitter of hallucinogenic images. Zap! I slept and dreamed of my first encounter with Myrna and the appearance of Manitoba Joe.

Chapter 6

I often reflected on the meteoric rise of Maddigan in only three years. The British Empire was inflated with joyous arrogance, having been inexplicably transformed. By accident and luck, a tiny island emerged from nonentity status to re-emerge, almost overnight, as a major political influence on both Earth and Mars. The new power's first actions on Mars were grandiose. Firstly, this involved the construction of a gigantic geodome in the southern sector of the otherworld province. The real miracle was how the resources appeared to enable such a project. Seemingly endless quantities of diamonds and gold poured from Africa as the result of radical and mutually beneficial agreements between an unassuming Welshman and a distinguished Zulu warlord. Territory and shared sovereignty were at the centre of their odd agreements. English technology made it possible to reach the great mineral reserves that were previously inaccessible. The jewels and gold provided were wisely managed and invested by – it was said – the brilliant First Lady. Through her intelligence and Maddigan's openness and charm, Africa and Britain became as close as any two nations and races could be. The media term cliché "Win-Win" fits well.

Swathes of Britain's newly emerging islands were offered for African friends to occupy. Chief of them was Lyonesse, the massive land mass that rose from waters of the southern shores of England. The Afro-British partnership built towns and cities and engaged in joint military training and technology. Everything was shared without strings attached. 'Perfidious Albion' as it was historically known, kept her word and sought no advantage over the Africans. There were cumulative political effects. The positive outcomes emerging attracted India to become another potential partner in the alliance as well. They saw the Red Planet British Planet's resistance to the Caliphate. Then, they warily considered the threat of neighbouring Pakistan.

With boundless resources, material and political, the Brits began doing what they had done in their past history. They gave their all to the transformation of new territories they occupied. Helium and its surrounding country were the centre of human scientific innovation. After drilling to the core of Mars and bringing natural ice from the poles by canal paths, the engineers created a small lake under the four-mile geodome. Terrestrial shrubs, grass and flowers were cultivated. Such was the enthusiasm generated, there was no time for bickering amongst the coalition. Even birds and small rodents were introduced to settlements beneath the dome.

Catastrophe struck after more than three years of ceaseless labour. Extreme sandstorms once more blocked the main canals. Within three years, the water was reabsorbed by the desert. Trees, birds and animals died. The only word one could use was heart-breaking.

To be succinct – the blame game came.

However, this was when the unassuming President showed his mettle. Maddigan refused to assign criticism to anyone. Many politicians would have taken the easy path: 'It wasn't my fault. It was the Indians. It was the Africans.' Wisely, he took another course. This was the moment I suddenly considered that Myrna had undersold him through her own ambition to lead the Empire. He might be a decrepit idiot now; but once he had a spark within him.

No head of state can be as white as a spirit of purity. He 'fibbed' a little. But he did not blame his friends. His administration decided criticism could be distracted by cunningly disseminating elaborate conspiracy theories. The most popular one was that when Yellowstone erupted and the USA ceased to exist, a secret group of American survivors from the military sought revenge on the Brits for replacing them as a super-power. Their sabotage caused the disaster. I thought it was obvious to anyone why that was absurd. An alternative conspiracy involved the Caliphate. They had become a lesser power on Terra than they had become on the Red Planet. It had angered them so much they had planted explosives beneath the underground springs of Mars. Another theory was that the Russians sought to renew imperial expansion and planned to seize the geodomes as a starter to this end. The masses are idiots! At least none of them blamed the Australians' kangaroos for responsibility. Yet!

There were serious consequences back on Terra from Britain's squandering of wealth and resources. A period of prolonged anarchy struck the home island. That had magnified by an appalling natural catastrophe that shattered Scotland soon after Yellowstone. There's no point me rambling on about that stuff. A learned historian, literary and political giant of a sex god like me would be interested in such stuff, but not ordinary folk. What was pertinent to my future was what the Brits did next.

More by luck than anything else, that benevolent old chap who had come out of nowhere became a compassionate dictator. He was welcomed as the President of the British Empire of Earth and Mars! Maddigan's charisma was based upon his benevolent manner, his reassurance and his lilting oratory that reassured confused and nervous nations who had coalesced to form an imperial and interplanetary union. People knew he was reluctant to accept the position offered to him. They believed in him because he calmed uncertainty and convinced them he could bring them safety. Most of all, he was incorruptible. My suspicion was that his wife, Natasha, was the PR genius who swayed the greater number of thorough-bred English. Though it goes without saying, despite the fact she was far from being my equal, she was sufficiently adequate to win over all her husband's peoples. That paid off in every way. Impressive military support was willingly offered by his African and Indian friends. It added to the reassurance of all the races within the Empire. I must admit, 'honesty is the best policy' was what served him so well. His next step had to be to appoint a tough, ruthless Governor of the Martian Province.

The turning point for my position within the Empire seems unbelievable to me. In the final year of the Brit's attempts to maintain the water supply of the lake-cum-pool beneath the flexi-dome, everything seemed ready to collapse into anarchy. I might be regarded as part of the scum that rose to the surface. At that time, I was a different me. I had no real interest in the workings of government. I was on a criminal errand.

Waiting for people is boring! I had to chill till my main man arrived. I fell into conversation with a tall older woman who stood near my lakeside bench. Not bad for her age. I'd seen her face before. She mentioned she wanted to be nominated for some government job. I studied my reflection in the water, pretending to be deep in thought. I remarked that if the post she was after related to terraforming, she should start running in the opposite direction. When she started in surprise, I saw I had made an accurate guess. She asked me why I said that. I explained politicos always wanted a patsy to blame for any a disaster. She had reached the same conclusion, it seems, although she arrived there via facts and secret information. My conclusion came from intuition or hunches. Without realizing it, we were sowing the seed of a fruitful future partnership.

We surveyed the waning reservoir. Two gorgeous white swans descended on the calm surface. I don't know how they were important. As they glided serenely past us, Myrna and I looked at each other. Both of us felt a sentimental gush. They would not last long here. However, that was a crucial moment of us sharing feelings. Once upon a time, she told me, she dreamed of terraforming the entirety of the British Empire's province, despite a dozen catastrophes. Being four or five years older than me, she would have to struggle against the competition of my innumerable nymphets. I could use her for more than sex, though. Something alerted me to her potential importance. There was a lot of intelligence in her pale blue eyes that captured my interest. Win her heart, use her brain, give her a fuck. I could see I had brought out a maternal protectiveness in her because she found my immaturity sweet and charming. I failed to spot how hard she was. Using her would go in the opposite direction if I was not alert. This occasion was the day of mush. None of it mattered as we enjoyed one of the most rewarding conversations I have experienced in that brief hour.

After she was gone, I checked all around the lake. I decided my drug man had let me down. I followed a muddy little track that led to a hut belonging to an ancient gardener who had given up a losing battle. Then, a stubble-faced man emerged as unexpectedly as a djinn from a magic lamp in a puff of smoke. He was scruffy; faded denim jeans and jacket in the style of the distant 20th century were his preferred attire. During our last few meetups, I called him 'Manitoba Joe' because he was shedding a previous identity as 'Spikesy', the drug-dealer cum hitman. When I came to know him, he revealed that the grubby narcotics trader served as his front for his true occupation as an agent for the Kidon. They were the elite of Mossad, the Israeli assassin group. I did not realize it, but I had long been 'talent spotted' by Israel when they were looking for a foothold in Helium. Sophisticated psychological profiling by his masters indicated my potential as a rung on the political ladder he was mounting. Even today's meeting with Myrna had very likely been engineered by his handlers' predictive psychologists, as I was to discover.

Two hundred years ago, the Kidon branch of Mossad was known as the Caesarea. Later research told me, 'Little was known about this mysterious unit, details of which were some of the most closely guarded secrets in the Israeli intelligence community.' They had recruited former soldiers from IDF Special Forces, right up to the emergence of England as a major power. Spikesy – or 'Joe' – became the most senior Mossad agent. Largely through his espionage and planning, Israel was able to grow into a significant bi-planetary operator. Mossad subterfuge on Terra was so successful that Egypt, Jordan, Syria and Iraq deteriorated into being lowly fiefdoms of Israel. Their decline was not entirely the result of Mossad. The creation of the Caliphate on Mars seriously weakened the resources of Arabian states on the home planet. Initially, Arabia had celebrated their Red Planet Province as 'the Miracle of the Prophet.' Such blind faith inspired credulous believers to achieve dominance over a third of Mars. And the Earth became of small importance. Manitoba Joe was more important to two worlds than his drunken dealer in faded denim might have suggested! I missed the coincidence of my first romantic encounter with Myrna happening so closely to meeting Joe on that first day.

In future months we became a highly effective team, backing Myrna's campaigns and machinations to secure the governorship on Mars. Joe masterminded the selection process with bribery. I used the media in making her appear the strong administrator President

Maddigan sought. Being her lover, I accepted credit for planning her victory. Obviously, I asserted to relevant cabals, I was in charge of Mossad's top man. That did not offend Joe. He found it amusing to act as my 'minder' and hitman. I pranced in the public eye as the governor's wheeler-dealer and strategic advisor. I ran the head of Mossad. In political perception, I was never Israel's servant. My personal gratification came from acting as the irresistible young male for a powerful, and still attractive, cougar wife who headed the Empire's territory on Mars. As far as I was concerned, Joe and I were genuine sex, booze and drugs buddies. Joe, to me, was the only guy I met lacking ego and personal ambition. Naturally, he adored me. He loved to serve me.

Joe was assigned to be Myrna Golden's opposite. She projected moral rectitude, upper class values and 'responsibility'. Joe, however, sold himself as a dodgy, untrustworthy tramp. While he gobbed and said, 'Fookin', she pronounced, 'Fecking'. Whether I wrapped an arm around her shoulders in her favourite woolly jumper or relished swearing and shoving Joe during ear-splitting play-fights, I loved them both. Between themselves I witnessed one of those love-hate relationships. She hated him for leading me into bad ways like drugs, drinking and whoring. Without doubt, I was sure he loathed her for being a snooty bitch who tried to boss him around. At the same time, Myrna knew how useful he was, especially in his willingness to protect me with his life.

Chapter 7

Once we approached Anais's Palace, Joe attempted to contact the Empress of Whoredom. I hadn't bothered about it. My interest involved kissing slender Melanie while playing with her lovely little nipples.

All of us jumped when Doran exclaimed from the cockpit, 'Shit! Gotta land. Police are hailing.'

As always, the bastards were impatient. They were public servants who did not know their place. A magnetic field hit us with a bang! You can't argue with that. Little Melanie thought we had been shot down and huddled against my manly chest. The bastards had frozen our gravity elements. We oscillated ground-wards like an ungainly goose, till we were stationary beneath two police fliers.

I was first out, making an insouciant stroll across the landing strip toward the police vessel. Despite all the weaponry aiming at us, the law enforcers didn't demand the antique 'hands in the air' stuff. Manitoba Joe shared my contempt for all servants of law and order. With a bit too much melodrama, he staggered out with a bottle in one hand, while his other was reaching out towards Melanie. He wanted to protect her, no doubt, hoping for a free ride on her when I was done. Doran was the last out. Understandably, given some of his mother's activities, he was trembling.

These were Rig cops, not international agents. Police here were supposedly independent of Martian nations. Their main duty involved drug issues – overdoses and violence and murders around that enclave of off-planet recreation. Around the grey eyes of the man who addressed me were tired lines and good humour. His intentions in stopping us seemed to be unthreatening.

'I know your face from somewhere,' was his laid-back lead in. 'We shall discover where and why as we have a chat.'

'We were escorting the young woman here back to work,' I replied casually. 'Providing you think it's safe.'

'You didn't return to check if your handiwork had been successful?'

I was irritated I was not recognized by the fellow. After a skinful, Manitoba acted like he was in the mood to fight anybody, with or without a reason. He snarled, 'Look, you fuckin…'

I told him to shut up. We did not want a big scene because of our mission. I preferred to keep everything as low key as possible. Only if it looked hairy, would I disclose my diplomatic immunity.

A female voice said, 'I know who they are. Permit me to assist.'

The speaker, who came out of the second flier, was a tiny, gorgeous Chinese chick. Although information files informed me that she was in her forties, I found her stunningly attractive. Irresistible, in fact. Her hair was long and black with a cute fringe, and she wore extremely high heels. I identified antique shoes that had been fashionable 300 years ago. If she intended them to give her height it was pointless. She already had an aura of authority and perception, when she spoke in a calm, deep voice.

'These individuals, Officer Perkins, they are very important persons from your own birth nation. They are notable as Governor Golden's 'wild cards'. By that, I mean they engage in espionage and assassination when it is required to maintain international peace.'

Was she presenting how she regarded Simon Edge – secret agent and lover of Governor Myrna and a thousand beauties? Or was she mocking me?

Expressionless, she added, 'I also spotted Mossad Academy's most elusive killer. Currently, this man, holding the beer bottle, has the appellation "Manitoba Joe."' She bowed her head to him after her observation. 'Truly, it is a privilege to meet you at last, face to face. I admire what I have seen of your work, sir.'

For the first time in his life, Joe was nonplussed. I, meantime, drew back the drug and booze curtains in my brain to decide the most debonaire bullshit I could come up with.

Wrapping my tongue in sweetness, I answered, 'The honour is ours, Janine Suee, Head of the Chinese Peoples' Empire Defence Service. Forgive my hesitation. I am overwhelmed by your loveliness.'

'This is indeed the name and title by which I am known. I compliment you upon such excellent recall,' she replied.

That meant she was surprised I had her online records at my fingertips. She turned to the police officers, who were seemingly still wary of me and my Mossad pal.

'Gentlemen? Please to be so kind as to permit me speak privately with Commander Edge.'

I puffed up with pleasure at her use of my honorary rank. Myrna had awarded it last birthday. The change in her police escort's attitude was immediate. Joe had expected to be invited into the 'private conversation'. Knowing Janine would not agree to it, I wafted him away. He frowned at being slighted, no matter how sensitively I had done it. With a shrug, he slouched back to chat with young Doran. His arm crept back around my skinny Melanie. Talk about making a point!

'By heaven, Janine!' I exclaimed as soon as we stood away. Gazing at the brilliant pinpricks of stars above the clear space of Rig 1, I repeated, 'You are the loveliest and most observant lady I have ever known.'

'You're most gracious, Simon Edge,' she responded. 'To business, shall we? We monitored your espionage with regard to the British Empire's President on Terra. And we were conscious of your supposed purpose on behalf of the Governor of the Helium Province. You made a specious journey to the sexual pleasure house of Madame Anais which, we have been long aware, is the main British security station.'

'Specious?' I answered. 'Do we have the right word? Salacious maybe? Whatever. I only came for sex with a few young females. I think my pal might be doing some for my partner. But I don't know anything about that stuff.'

Janine was as direct as Alisha. 'I have no time to waste with games. The bombing. Who? Why?'

I gave a winsome smile saying, 'I sincerely admire your directness. In return, I must confess we have no idea at all. One potential enemy threatens us though. To be certain, I want to ask you something without any intention of offending. Where does the

47

Martian Empire of China stand regarding the present military situation?'

She said, 'The balance of power is very different on Mars and on Earth. On Earth, English friendliness with Israel was a threat to the financial status of China. Once the Arab States poured their military resources into Islamic domination of Mars, they weakened their home base. Israel moved into its former birthlands and smashed Arabian power across the Middle East. Then, they commandeered all sources of Arab wealth and became even more welcome as a partner by Britain. Without Jewish support, England would have crumbled long ago. Different story on the Red Planet, though. There, the Caliphate was China's greatest foe. I would say to you, our mutual enemy. Yes?'

'There's nothing you've expressed I could disagree with, lady. But where are you going with this? Alliances? Information sharing? Suspicion?'

Janine continued to fulfil that stereotype of Chinese inscrutability. Or, I should say more accurately, I was unable to read her. After a long pause she said, 'Mars? Allies against Caliphate. Earth? China hesitates about President Maddigan. Who might be your next President? Myrna Golden has ambitions. Culturally, we share a literary metaphor for the birds. President Golden is the hawk; Maddigan is a dove. Or perhaps that is incorrect. Yes? If I allied my humble self with a man who would assist by convincing your British President to work alongside China, we could eradicate the Caliphate's nests of cuckoos. Should China offer her friendship to Britain on Earth, the Caliphate falls there as well. These are just my personal reflections for consideration by the perceptive husband of the British Empire's Governor on Mars.'

Her meaning had was expressed with oriental precision! Anais and I shared a secret, that I did not intend Janine should know with any certainty. More on that later.

Her implication that the brothel bombers came from the Caliphate had been her small gesture of goodwill. The Chinese ran the finest intelligence service on two worlds. I was still concerned how China's intentions might alter once they realized the full extent of British innovative technology being concealed by Anais within Rig 1.

Janine, smiling serenely, weighed up my reaction and trustworthiness. Chinese public statements proclaimed their commitment to religious toleration for Druidism, Islam and New Catholicism. Those platitudes were not credible to anyone, particularly the Prophet's believers. Nor to anyone who knew China.

On Earth, Saudi Arabia barely managed to defend their black meteorite at Mecca. All their military strength was tied up in their theocracy on Mars. They intended to intimidate and crush every British, Indian and Chinese settlement on the Red Planet. Foolishly, most of our nations had fallen behind the Arabs during their preoccupation with terraforming their territories. Janine's friendlier tone towards Britain arose from a common fear. On my advice, Myrna had leaked hints about her new technological weapon. That offered us a particular advantage. No one, not even Maddigan, knew with certainty the nature of her 'secret device'. China was desperate to discover what it could be. Chinese ambassadors bluffed they were party to what was happening whilst they made unusually friendly overtures to the British provinces. Disingenuously, Janine had referred to England's 'magic bullet' during discussions with other nations. I had uncovered a cryptic reference she made to 'alternative means of movement.'

Today, she had tried to overwhelm me with her charm and friendliness. Her parting words were, 'I honestly welcome any proposal you can offer to build any alliance we might both consider with favour.' Then, she smiled sweetly. Without waiting for a reply, she started to totter back to the police flier.

I called, 'Janine! I appreciate your frankness. I mean that.'

'A pleasure, Simon,' Janine smiled, gazing back at me. 'We might meet next in a place you do not expect. It would be a particular pleasure for the two of us to talk as friends.'

The police strato took off with China's Head of Intelligence aboard. I re-joined my party, waving them into our own vehicle. When Joe growled in my ear, 'Whodunnit? Chinks?'

I replied, 'Caliphate.'

Up, once again went our flier. Within moments, we were descending onto Anais's private roof top landing. Seconds later, we stood beneath the dome that covered Anais's Pleasure Palace. I paused to stare at the stars and endless blackness through which they shot silver beams across the blackness of space. When I turned my eyes around on the city that filled Rig 1, I felt emotional, beholding the ornateness and magnitude of such architecture in the void of space.

Impulsively, I flung my arms around Manitoba Joe and Melanie, holding them as close to me as a kangaroo with her joey. I declared, 'reality is so scary!'

'The Pleasure Palace ahoy,' cried Joe, ignoring my trippy shit, while young Doran was admiring the perfection of his landing on the roof.

Three heavily armed security guys appeared. They escorted Melanie away from the normal top-level entrance to the building. Manitoba Joe and I, however, followed our jaunty young pilot through a concealed panel in one of the four towers.

We had entered an anti-gravity tower. We all took the jump and slowly descended to the 40th floor, avoiding the extensive security of the top two levels. After floating down seven floors we came to a halt at an ancient stairway. It was dark and deliberately off-putting. Having circled two flights of stairs, I sensed we were on ground level. I looked around, a bit puzzled, until the smell of perfume, dope and sex escaped from reinforced security doors. We were outside Anais's Operations Room in the core of the satellite.

Doran keyed in his entry codes. The panels slid up to admit us to the inner sanctum. Being only human, I thought of Melanie within the palace sex chambers. Although I still throbbed to fuck tiny tits Melanie every which way, our meeting with her Madam was top priority.

I knew Doran would already have messaged Mother. She was sure to be waiting impatiently to quiz us as soon as we entered. Beside her was Darren, her eldest son, who towered over her. This stocky woman could fill any man with a greater terror than her other companion, a black mastiff, snarling and slavering beside her. The bitch – I refer to her pet – was trying to suss out Anais's reaction to us. Her moods directed her pet's actions. Fortunately, Anais was relaxed and charming. She practically purred as she embraced and welcomed us. The thought occurred to me how like her pet she was: always prepared to change mood, give a sudden leap – and rip your throat out. The animal relaxed again and renewed gnawing a bone that seemed, suspiciously, as big as a human thigh bone.

Our discussion was informal. Whisky, supposedly pirated from an Earth ship attempting the year-long Mars journey, assisted the mood. Darren, the more macho brother, informed us he was part of the daring whisky looters. Joe and I looked impressed. We enjoyed this feel-good mood, relishing the comfort of this most luxurious suite in the whole brothel. Our feet sank into a deep-piled carpet of green and maroon; it was patterned with flame-breathing dragons, pagodas and exotic trees. The walls were bare of ornamentation, mirrors or pictures. This was reassurance, I supposed, there had been a recent detailed security sweep, probably with Anais herself supervising, preceding this meeting. A soothing perfume of rose incense hung in the air adding a further calming ambience.

At last, we were ready for some top-level discussion regarding the teleporter hidden within Rig 1. Myrna's creation was to occupy our next four hours.

Chapter 8

Joe and I were livid to be summoned back to Helium immediately. Myra is such a bitch! I had a quick one with a Russian babe. Ruski girls were a scarcity. There was no time for that three-day debauch we had planned.

The return from Rig 1 had an air of tension, absent from the journey out. Myrna commanded Joe to video report back to her the moment we left Anais's hidden chamber. She had not asked for me, her husband, for fuck's sake! When I attempted to hack Joe's secure line, it was blocked. I rounded savagely on him. What the fuck was going on? At first, he could not defend himself. All I could get out of him was that Myrna was up to some scheme which would endanger my life if I were associated with it. He denied any knowledge of what that could be. In my Book of Rules, mates come before your women. Obviously, not in his.

I admit I went bang out of order then. I shrieked he was plotting to pull Myrna and so the pair could seize control of Mars before they overthrew Maddigan. When his denials became more heated, I punched him in the face. Considering his reputation, that was dangerous. He reluctantly defended himself and refused to belt me in return.

In the end, he gave his most solemn word that he would never do anything that would harm me. He said that Myrna had involved herself in something with Israel. As a senior Mossad officer, he had been in a situation where he could be assassinated if he divulged anything whatsoever. I knew that was true. Mossad never messed about. Even more, I believed his word of honour. Odd, isn't it, with an arsehole like me? Anyhow, I had no choice. Regrettably, I was not quite the omnipotent Mr Big I pretended to be.

We did not speak in our sedan chair to the landing strip. Myrna had commanded us to make a single non-stop voyage back to Helium. For this purpose, she had arranged for a full-sized cruiser direct to Helium. There was no Phobos transfer to a flier. Within moments of boarding, we strapped in and shot into the emptiness of space.

Despite my rationality, I found myself on the brink of crying. Perceiving my distress, Manitoba Joe spoke with tears in his eyes, for certainly the first time in his life. I sensed it was related to something else he had concealed from me and that he was unhappy about.

'I'll tell you something I'm not s'posed to, but I owe you, mate. Remember when I was Spikesy, the dealer? I'm other people too. I've a good half dozen different whatdoyacallits, y'know.'

I supplied him with the word, 'Identities.'

I dreaded what he might be about to confess, some betrayal behind my back. I grew horrified to think my dearest friend was a fake. 'Manitoba Joe' was all an act. He didn't exist. I looked into his beady, black eyes, feeling bereaved.

He read me and begged, 'Please, Simon. Don't get upset. Our friendship is true. It's genuine. Solid as a rock. If anyone monitoring me picked up the full reality of me, I'd be a dead man.'

In an uncharacteristically generous gesture he offered, 'Buy you a drink? On me. That's if they charge in the VIP lounge!'

'No sweat. They don't, dodgy fucker! Beer?'

He nodded. After setting up sound blockers round us, then an anti-lip reader distorter, he began an out-pouring. It was not about drinks. His distress appeared genuine. I wondered how I could be sure.

'You've always known I was an Israeli Mossad agent doing a favour for your Brit Empire. I was open on that one to stop suspicions. I'm more than I first told you,' he chuckled nervously.

'Like fuck you are!' I exploded, for I was conscious that I was still emotionally unstable. That contemptuous tone in his voice, when he said 'Brit Empire' like it was a joke, had suddenly antagonized me. His edgy chuckle really pissed me off. There was a choke in my throat when I replied, 'I opened my heart up to you. You've treated me like a fool all this time, cosying up as my best mate!'

He yelled back, 'Get fuckin' real, Edge. Takes two. When we first met, you spotted me as a dog's body to use for black ops you took credit for. And I was an alibi to hide your whoring from Myrna. We became genuine buddies along the way. Absolute truth. I swear it! To begin with, I obeyed Mossad's order to monitor the British Empire and report on everything they were up to. After Britain became an ally to Israel, my spy-work paid a double benefit. Britain and Mossad both rewarded me for sharing the same fuckin' information.'

Although I believed him, I trembled. Something else was coming. His account continued, 'I must confess to only one deception I regret. You are truly my one and only friend. I owe you my honesty. Okay. Israel sent me to meet India's secret sleeper agent. Imaginatively, their agent had been planted on Rig 1 for over three years. Like China's Janine, the Indian top espionage operative was female. Her name was Alisha.' He paused. Then, weakly, 'I guess she never told you.' I started involuntarily. I had been played as a fool. Worse was that I'd had an emotional thing about her.

Joe noted it, but, gritting his teeth, continued, shame-faced. 'There was liaison between our controllers, matey. After the atrocities in London and Delhi, they saw why alliances had to happen. Behind the scenes, naturally. The Israeli government had to admit Mossad ran the nation. Not the other way round. Same sort of confusion involved with India's prime agent. Alisha was told to work with Israel with the British Governor on Mars. Myrna was line manager, sort of, co-ordinating both allies. I'd guess Maddigan must have demanded that as part of the deal for mutual support. What the Indians and Israel received was direct access to most of Britain's inner workings. Naturally, that was only partly true. In Helium, the people were happy to believe Myrna Golden would reverse the sloppy blancmange liberalism that slithered through from a President. He was an idealistic wanker. The British Empire increased its power by the day. It had access to wealth and influence that bought the respect of Israel and India. There was still popular scepticism about what was happening in England, the centre of the Empire. The President based there was a stark contrast to draconian

Governor Golden. Maddigan believed he could set up liberal governance as the model for all races and all faiths. That could be acceptable to India and Israel. Trouble was a turd, named the Caliphate, continued festering on Mars. Even Alisha felt Maddigan was not up to stopping them. She declared he was a clown who had, "opened the gates to Trojan horses called mosques."'

Manitoba continued. 'Maddigan realized there was a further split which many on Earth were blind to. The Roman Catholic Papacy, who won all their power and wealth through murder and torture, preferred the Arabs to the Jews. Catholics were as evil as Islam, but their control over Christianity undermined concerted resistance. As far as I could deduce, Maddigan attempted to counter it in the most bizarre way imaginable. He affiliated himself with the rise of new Paganism. I don't know if it was for real, or he was pretending. But he was seen as a believer in Druidism that would counter both evils of Mecca and the Vatican.

'What do I know, Simon, mate? I'm a dumb Jewish terrorist and strong-arm man! I got orders from the Israeli PM's Summer Residence HQ, to work with an Indian spy chick. I'm Israel's top *katsa* on Helium, so Mossad chose me to join her and direct the show. There used to be 30-40 of us on Terra but now we have only a dozen on Mars. It's stupid. The Caliphate is the biggest nation on Mars. Mossad's 300-year-old model of three *"jumper" katsa* territories per region is outdated today when you have agents jumping between two planets! Tht had to be a spy alliance of me and Alisha.'

That was the longest, most eloquent speech I ever heard from my taciturn bodyguard. He had revealed how much of his intelligence he had always hidden. He named each of the *katsa* bases of three on Helium, China and the Caliphate. Such openness from Manitoba was unlikely to be repeated, so I stayed silent. He again checked our audio and visual blanketing was fully impenetrable before producing his mini-screen device.

'Eyes on screen, mate. For starters, let's watch the Helium Mosque. Boom! Boom!'

On screen I watched a pair of agitated, ragged junkies, shuffling in the shadows of the mosque. The Catholic Church would have taken them off the street, imprisoning them inside what they called a 'soup kitchen'. They received no food until they did confession, of course. This was their attempted PR for Christian compassion. The victims from the gutters would become financially useful. A kindly Father gave them Bibles and trained them to be free labour for Our Lady, the Pope, and God.

Islam was more openly cruel. No pretence of compassion there. The whip was their solution to mendicants. Their most ideal victims for Islamic sadism were drug addicts. Imams instructed their abstemious congregations these losers were the most despicable of all sinners. They polluted body and mind. Maybe, they were envious because opium offered a more convincing paradise than the Prophet's wet dream promises of renewable virgins in the afterlife.

On Joe's screen I saw a tall male beggar with a forked beard and his companion, a dusky, hawk-nosed maiden. I identified them easily and raised an eyebrow to Mossad Joe.

'My diversion, shit-head,' he explained to me.

Myrna had been instructed by the President's First Lady to organize a deniable attack on the Helium Mosque of Ayesha. Britain's Indo-Israeli allies provided superb prior surveillance. Mossad already knew of experimental transporter labs in the mosque complex. Caliphate exploratory tests of new weaponry would be set back by at least six months after such carefully targeted damage. The Imam's security people saw the brawling and drunken shouting around the mosque as entertainment. Armed guards charged the supplicants and vagrants giving a deserved dose of brutality! Many of the Faithful ran, laughing, to the front of the building to join in the sport of throwing stones at this gathering of stinking, ragged Unbelievers. With relish, they began kicking many random unfortunates into unconsciousness. Injuries sustained by Joe's and Alisha's disguised team were unavoidable. Lots of other junkies had been lured here by social media boards and rumours of free drugs and knives. Those top-secret labs inside branches of the mosque were protected far less conscientiously by the Arabs.

'Fight Moslem oppression!' Joe incited the demonstrators who came from other minority religions and free speech believers. He manipulated them ruthlessly to hot up the violence. The climax came when he and Alisha simultaneously lobbed Molotov cocktails at the Blessed Steps. All was recorded by security cameras. No evidence could be proven of British political motives, especially of any involvement by Governor Myrna Golden in the rioting. President Golden had pre-recorded her official condemnation of this situation in advance to be broadcast down the Rig network and across the planets before the Caliphate had time to get on air. I saw Manitoba's grim sneer when the maddened mob grabbed material to use as missiles he had seen was laying around.

Acid-filled containers smashed against the intricate religious facades. Above the double entry doors, ornate arches were defaced or merely broken away from the facade. He fulfilled his order to ensure a blitz of noise, panic and flames. Slowly realizing what was happening, the mosque's security force raced back to the front to defend it against the maniacs getting inside. Just at the same time, deafening explosions erupted from the concealed experimental labs. The defenders were too late. Waves of 'rent a mob' flooded through the entrance and into the immaculate forecourt of the mosque. Senseless violence always entertained me. I especially enjoyed a slightly grainy recording of some bearded vagrant handing out home-made bombs to every junkie, party goer, wrecked revolutionary, or authentic parasite in the looting and vandalism. Isn't there something infectious about explosions, chaos, wrecking and violence? Gripped to Joe's screen I was loving every moment. Who in the world can resist an opportunity to fling bombs, ignite fires and most of all yell abuse at holy fraudsters, and let yourself go, punching all the forces of piety and lies?

Joe touched pause to explain. 'Me and Alisha needed to vanish asap. If Mossad or Britain's agents were identified, our pre-emptive terrorism would be exposed. Myrna had withheld her conspiracy from security and the Police so their reaction would be genuine. That would make it more credible to dual world audiences that this was sabotage by some mystery enemy. Nothing could be traced to her.

My super-spy buddy narrated, 'Our fuckin' time was running out. As far as we could tell, it was "mission accomplished". I delivered a goodbye rocket through the mosque entrance doors. Alisha launched a mini drone inside dropping drugs all over the show. Her idea was to give planetary media a juicy "shock and horror" scandal exposing how hard drugs had been stored in the mosque. Beautiful!'

I saw my earlier anger about romance between Joe and Alisha was unfounded! It was just a mission for them. My antipathy towards my mate was dissipating now.

I squinted at Joe's screen. He and Alisha were taking off in a flier that looked more like scrap than transport. It had been stashed in a pile of rubbish a short distance from the mosque. Even their pilot viewing window was cracked. They flew off as low profile as could be. As they were rising higher, something hit them. The recorded picture spun around. They had crashed. They looked badly shaken, before screen went black. Joe must have adjusted his portable viewer. Presumably, he had secured it inside his jacket pocket with a hole in it, making it possible to show events around him. Anyway, the visuals came back. Fury swept across his face. Forgetting to check that Alisha was unhurt, he swung out of his vehicle to confront whoever smashed into them. Joe, angry, was lethal.

The guilty driver was a vicious looking fuck with tats on his shaved head. He came, feet first, out of his flier because his doors were also too battered to open. Obviously, it was stolen. When he stood up, he was a foot taller than Manitoba. His ugly mug must thrust inches from Joe's face. Certainly, he filled the screen of the recording. Talk about gripping media!

'You're Caliphate fuckers, aint yer?' he spat.

He swaggered forward, wagging a fat stump of a forefinger towards Joe growling, 'Don't fuck us about you Arab fuckers. We're going to carve you up and your scabby-cunt Muzza whore, yer bastard. Yer off to plant a fookin' bomb in revenge for us patriots.'

The problem arose from skin colour. Baldy and his mate were sickly white. Alisha was Indian and Joe was a Jew. The latter could think as quick as lightning.

'You thick twat? You calling us fucking muzza cunts? You know who I am?' Joe screamed, tearing his shirt open. On the front of his black t-shirt was the seven branched candelabra of Mossad. Walking up to the hairless lout Joe shoved him into his mates. In case they didn't understand the symbol, he cried, 'we're fuckin' Israel's Mossad. We're the fuckin' heroes as blown up the fuckin' mosque. We bled them wogs on the Arabian deserts. We kill kids like you for breakfast. Fuck off or we killin' you now.'

They ran. They had kept their lives. Joe and Alisha wasted no precious time. They had to escape the chaos in the streets of Helium. Detonations were going off over all parts of the city. The only really deafening sound coming from the device were explosions from the mosque. Then, the sirens of dozens of police fliers made the screen vibrate.

Joe moved to lower the audio, but I gently stopped him. I needed to know how his 'mission' with Alisha ended. He watched while I continued studying. Some visual blurring indicated they were lifting off again. As far as I could guess from their porthole shots, the battered flier was sputtering barely 30 feet above the chaos and wreckage surrounding the mosque. The police below appeared to be knocking the shit out of the mob. That was show for the Imam's benefit. Politically speaking, Myrna needed to prove Britain had no part in the 'terrorist attack'. I guessed that mobs of thugs and junkies Joe had imported to bring chaos to the capitols shadowy streets were 'disposables'.

As always, things started going wrong. Visuals flickered on and off. It was clear their flier had lost altitude too. Finally, it died and dropped into a gloomy alley. Very slowly, luck returned. The Martian night descended, restoring their cover from the cops. After another three-minute blackout, they reappeared for us, on foot, crossing on a playing field. Since it was Helium's only one, I knew where they were heading. On the far side of the fake grass recreational area was my ground floor flat. I used it to bring pick-ups for shagging sessions, telling Myrna I was meeting an informant. Most importantly, it was here I used to bring Alisha. I had a sinking feeling.

However, it was a safe house for Joe and Alisha to hide. To deter local kids coming too near to my lair, I had installed convincing recordings of bestial roars all around the bushes; even inside the flat itself. That had proved an incredibly effective shocker. Only those few in the know, such as Alisha or Joe, were aware my flat was more an intelligence centre than a knocking shop.

When they arrived, Alisha's palm recognition gave access through an imitation wooden door. She led the way across the hall, at the side of which was a mirror that slid back to reveal the concealed entry to my ground floor hideout. No alarms either visual or audio were activated.

I had believed only I knew how to dampen the sirens for my own entry. I was wrong about that. This was further evidence that Alisha and Mossad Joe were more familiar with my secrets than I was. I was an information cuckold! I'd been deluded into the belief this was a place I could smuggle in chicks behind Myrna's back and nobody on two planets would ever uncover the little scandals. It would have rubbed more grit into my ego to ask Joe what further information he might have stored in here. I had no option but to appear to fix my entire attention on what was revealed on screen.

Dim lighting came on as Alisha flopped onto the bed, the sole substantial item of furniture in the single room 'apartment'. In precise English tones, she declared, 'I am frightfully stressed, Joseph.' For the first time Alisha was no more Anais's whore who provided any men with her endearing Indian pussy. I had been so engrossed with staring at her face, I had not noticed a board on Joe's knees upon which he was chopping lines of a brown powder for them to snort and chill out on my bed. I wished I had a visor to cover my eyes. Anticipating what might happen next, when Joe sat beside her on the bed, I said I had seen enough to get it. Before I could debate whether I was experiencing a broken heart or deflated ego, Joe intervened with an openness I was not accustomed to.

Apart from occasional interventions from Alisha, he began emphatically tos set the record straight. He explained my kindness had been used in the way everyone in the spy business should expect. I had been the courier of information exchanged between Myrna and Anais via Alisha. Simplicity itself! Alisha had pinched my mini communicator from the secret hiding place in my jacket lining nearly every time I hired her. It was easy for such a beautiful woman to remove a slim piece of perspex from the attire of a lust-blinded male. I'd always known Alisha made frequent journeys between Rig 1 and Heliopolis. I assumed she was moving between 'pleasure houses' so clients were offered variety on the prostitute menu for many premises on the Rig and Mars. Anais had few rivals on Rig 1. On Mars there were a wide range of men from Helium, and, most of all, the Caliphate. So much info came from them!

I was a prize idiot. I was the blind mule for espionage – not the VIP punter I had believed I was! Our return to Helium began to fill me with dread and embarrassment. All my lies, deception, sexual acts, had provided amusement for Anais, Alisha and, probably, Myrna. I was completely exposed. Such emotional muddle was impossible to process. I believed I was the master of wheels and deals but really, I was a prime sucker. Manitoba wasn't my dumb sidekick. He was Mossad's super-spy and light years brighter than I was! Myrna, Anais and Alisha had all used me as an oblivious delivery boy to carry all their information. That included the plots I was involved in. Things they were bot supposed o know about. Once upon a time, I fantasized about being a heroic leader who led a dangerous mission in which I would die in an act of glorious bravery. Tears would pour from Myrna's pale blue eyes when she gazed on the memorial statue they would raise in my honour. That was swiftly being erased. I could only defend my ego with deliberate self-deception.

Alisha had silently disappeared from the bar. She saw Joe and I needed a bit of space to talk to each other.

Wrapped in the body armour of my cool persona, I enquired, 'I am so relieved our chick and you made it safe out of the bombing, bud.'

He caught on. 'Yeah, fella. We all did a good job for the Brits and Mossad. Israel owes us.'

'We acted out as the perfect team,' I said casually. 'Celebration!'

I signalled the monitor for a brace of 7.5% ABV "Olde England Ales." They arrived instantly, bottle seals off. Joe still avoided my eyes. I stared till he met my gaze.

'We right again, mate?' he asked.

I had nowhere else to turn. I embraced and hugged him. We needed get back to normal relations once more with assistance of multiple nutty and orange tasting beers. Time flew. We grew familiar and normal.

After a number of hours, we focussed blurry eyes on the central screen. Our vessel was orbiting Mars, prior to entering the thin atmosphere. 'Dream Gas' began circulating as in standard procedure for re-entry. It calmed potential panic amongst passengers as the result of the vibration, speed and imaginings of crash landings. Another pleasantly drowsy stupor created by 'Dream Gas' lasted about five minutes. It helped me de-stress in my anticipation of the reunion with beloved Myrna. Vague plotting continued during my sedated mind. Nothing was my fault. Myrna had used Alisha as an *agent provocateur* or an old term – a 'honey trap'. Bees didn't exist on Mars, though. Scientists had tried to introduce them as part of terraforming. I wished we had bees to fertilize blossoms like the ones around Maddigan in the Chalice Well garden, so far away on Earth. I was still confused, I guess. I floated out of the fuzzy blue mist that had sedated my mind.

Ah! We were landing! Welcome! Helium spaceport greeted our homecoming. I looked for Alisha. She was gone. How and when added to her mystique. On the other side I forgave Joe – yet I would never trust Alisha again. I was better alone. Romance is a sick delusion. Never again!

Chapter 9

As elite passengers, Joe and I were first to disembark. I shaded my eyes while I adapted to the muted sunlight of Mars. That gave me the opportunity to prepare myself. Being the epitome of efficiency, as always, Myrna had arranged for a conveyance to be waiting beside the landing strip to whisk us away immediately. *Security or affection for her Simon?* I wondered. Once we alighted, the side panels of our little flier slid down for us to board.

This was an improvement on Anais's sedan chairs. We were on a two-seater private passenger vehicle. Being by portholes on opposite sides of the cabin, we each enjoyed clear views. We simultaneously pressed the overhead buttons for refreshments. In seconds, we were 2000 feet above the planet and a *Ding! Ding!* sound alerted us to the arrival of our beer cartons that dropped from the ceiling. I glanced down on the dazzling metal roof of the spaceport as we started for the Governor's Palace. We circled in an uncharacteristically bright, light blue sky, which briefly brought to my memory the summer times I had spied upon on enviously, on old Terra. However, the bleak orange sand and rocks of the Red Planet's rock-strewn deserts were unaltered since our last flight over this area. And all other trips here!

But it did seem to me that there were twice as many of the silver wind turbines criss-crossing the landscape around Helium since the last time I had flown over the southern region. They were a significant, major investment the Empire had contributed to Mars. England was historically an innovator of wind farms. On the Red Planet, however, they were essential in both ecological and financial ways, for they would harness the energy of the sandstorms that had been one of greatest challenges on that New World. Curiously, the avenues of turbines followed the lines of the legendary 'Canals of Mars', popularized by a popular astronomer named Camille Flammarion more than three centuries ago. He never considered his 'canals' might have originated as run-off water from the poles millennia before.

I recalled a student article I did about the wind farms of England, which was a topic of my youthful research. The island to the southwest of a region called Devon and Cornwall, was once connected to the mainland. Today it was called Lyonesse. There had been violent territorial dispute here between North African migrants and the Pagan forces just across the narrow stretch of sea. The latter had named themselves 'Druids'. They were based on the northern side of Devon in a fortified area where they established their mysterious Druidic School of Tintagel. In less than 30 years they became a major religion. With that came substantial political influence.

Tintagel had been enhanced and expanded through generous support by President Maddigan as part of his plan to attempt to extend his power. As a result of his donations this seminary was able to create more fortifications than a medieval castle. He also supported a major development on the Isle of Anglesey, off the west coast of Wales. In my opinion, all this tremendous cost was folly. The President had no hope of securing political support from the Druids. Their intention was to have him dancing to their tune rather than the other way round!

To give the man credit, his truly significant achievement for England was embedding that cheap wind and tidal energy throughout his realm. While I was a student – and gigolo in training – I was awed by drone views of hundreds of wind turbines that encircled Welsh and English shores and extended south, far across a shallow sea. Wherever I looked were lines of spinning windmills decorating the glittering waves. Such grand innovation made an enormous contribution to the Empire's development of Mars. Although the President was condemned for his wasteful extravagance in all his enterprises, he had uncanny luck in generating more and more wealth for the Empire. Those silver turbines, glittering on the sea, remained a treasured image for me. I always hoped to set foot on Earth one day. Joe nudged me out of my contemplation saying, 'We're here!'

We were circling the Government HQ, while the dual airlocks of the protective dome were gradually opening for our entry.

While we hovered, I thought how impressive the turreted walls around the building were, seen from the air. Day and night Myrna needed to be defended against any surprise incursions by Caliphate saboteurs. We landed between the walls and the central building close to an area of lush greenery. I regarded the scene with fresh eyes. Scores of trees were being cultivated between the rock defences and Governor's Palace. For a moment, I imagined I was on a green planet instead of a red one. Our little flier was met by armed soldiers. We emerged onto the stone forecourt in the most dignified manner two sweaty, beer reeking men can manage.

Though I would have liked a blare of trumpets to herald my arrival, it was still a great feeling to be welcomed by such smart, well-organized soldiers. Joe and I bounced about with a happy feeling of, 'The heroes of Rig 1 are back!' It was a little undignified! We synchronized the removal of our space jackets and our stylish way of slinging them over our left shoulders. The escort appeared to be unimpressed by the governor's husband and number one advisor. I deserved the deflation.

I looked up at the main building. The Governor's Palace was considerably more tasteful than the Pleasure Palace on Rig 1. It was attractively designed. Impressive in every detail. There were sculpted cornices and miniature human statues in alcoves, elegantly decorating sixty-foot rock walls and the adjacent features were aesthetically placed. It was made more aesthetically pleasing by the fact that all the work was reminiscent of Terran ancient Greece and Rome. The common mass of people would find the ornamentation excessive. I had the impression the architect had checked every part of the entablatures, door columns entryways and windows for opportunities to embellish and impress. Probably, this was inevitable on an alien planet without history, art or civilization. All of it was fresh, new and significant.

In a similar manner, the greening agenda of our province also combined the practical and attractive. As was the Presidential policy, terraforming was a prime objective in all our endeavours. This was not done in a mechanical chessboard of water-bearing canals. He wanted beauty to be as important as functionality, most especially in terms of flowery gardens and oxygen-rich trees, that filled the Great Dome. The government building boasted a beautiful ring of woodland and shrubbery. Dreamy old Maddigan insisted we import and breed colourful singing birds for all the fragile oases of his Empire's settlement. For an instant, I had an image of the lovely garden at the base of the Tor where I watched the President. On Mars, nature demanded the commitment of heart and soul to persist in creating a whole new civilization. Although the avian displays and melodies filled even me with happiness, they had been far from successful. Most wildlife under the domes of our world was hybrid, modified to survive in an environment that was 400 million miles from their place of origin. Many species died despite endless research. Yet Maddigan had tremendous faith it could be done.

The officer in charge of the escort disliked me intensely – and obviously. To her, I was a sickening toy boy using the governor; a corrupt, brothel haunting, sneaky spy and a liar. That just began her list. Manitoba Joe was, as far as she was concerned, a druggie Jew boy thug. I had my patience tested to prevent Joe decking this butch bitch. And that captain's face showed all her contempt. I doubt if even seeing the size of my dick would have won her over.

We were marched in silence down the corridors of multiple security devices to the reception hall, where Governor Golden greeted diplomats. At the high golden doors to the hall, Captain Sewn-Up Cunt snapped, 'Halt!' Without as much as a grunt, she turned and marched her people away. We were kept waiting till our usher emerged.

When the embossed doors opened, we found we were facing Alisha. Her eyes were averted. This was no, 'How wonderful to see you, Simon. How are you? I've missed you so much.' Quite the contrary.

Everybody liked to embellish their rooms with hologram technology. Tropical islands with palm trees set amidst oceans, used to be favourites in Helium. Nostalgia from Earth always pressed the buttons. Simple folk like illusory palaces with intricate golden embellishments and heavy drapes. It was a favourite with Anais in her brothels, understandably enough. However, a Head of State like

Myrna Golden avoids off-putting distractions. Psychologists point out that gaudy illusions indicate deviousness. A plain, clean reception, with lots of light implies sober reliability. I had sat beside her on many state occasions and summits with a variety of dignitaries in delicate, aesthetically designed settings. Not today! Joe, Alisha and I stood in a rough cavern. On a first glance the walls appeared to be in their natural state after they had been drilled out of the virgin rock.

A cough came from the blackness at the top end of the room. Someone sat on a high-backed chair in the shadows of at the far end. I just about made out the familiar posture of Myrna. After a minute, dim light enabled me to distinguish two columns upholding the roof on either side of her. I thought she might be imitating a mystical figure of some sort. If so, Myrna was being a ham actor. Either she wanted to intimidate or disorientate us. I refused to react.

With an irritating chuckle, I strode confidently towards her. It was obvious she was giving us the works. I could match her any day. Lumpy mounds were scattered around to provide a mood of primitive barbarity. They might have been some new fashion in bullshit art. I was unable to interpret her intentions behind dropping us into this setting. I was bemused as to why she had ordered her designers to painstakingly produce carvings of gigantic monsters from Earth's prehistoric times. Of course, she loved to 'double double' me. In common parlance, send me on a quest to interpret some meaningless puzzle in order to divert me. Before I completed the thought, the sides of the cavern were reshaped again. Now there were arched cloisters cut in the rock, leading to who knew where. The uneven floor had no carpeting. Instead it appeared to be composed of painted serpents. Finally, she conjured up for us groups of phantom people. Rough wooden tables appeared to be around us, all crammed with ghostly students, devouring massive half French rolls packed with slabs of cheese. This was a unique trick - and unexpected. I was lost for words.

Joe wasn't. Even if her trickery was aimed at him.

'Fuck me!' he exclaimed. 'I remember here.'

A hooded, solitary figure at the top of the hall appeared, sounding pleased: 'How sweet, my lad! All those years ago too. Look over there.' Definitely this was Myrna the ham actress.

She gestured to the table that was conjured up before us. A couple chatting there were easily recognizable as the young Myrna and Manitoba Joe in their student days. I was seeing a dramatized memory. Ghostly Myrna offered a few words of conversation to Junior Joe. The young guy with the hooked nose said, 'I'm Joe Amit. They call me Manitoba Joe. Tell you the story later if you want to stick around. I know you. You're Myrna Golden – college star. Plus, you're the Chair of our Jewish Society. Do I say, "Shalom"? Or is there a secret signal?'

I was less insouciant, In fact, I was stunned. Another ball rolled at me and knocked over my mental skittles. There was too much to absorb and interpret. In the era of potential Anglo/Israeli alliances everyone had been sneaky. Mossad selected and assigned a former university boyfriend to ingratiate himself with the potential future Anglo-Jewish Governor of Mars and, later, with me, calculated to be a likely partner. Such calculation was incredible!

My dear wifey beckoned me with the little finger of her left hand, crooning, 'No need to feel insecure, my handsome, darling toy boy. Think of how much I must love you despite knowing about all sorts of naughty behaviour. I still pledged myself to you.'

'Know all!' I started to stammer something. But I failed to connect words into a sentence to convey my emotional chaos. How I wanted to make her feel guilty for wrong-footing me!

She delivered a superior performance, kissing me lightly, stroking my hair and seeming like the adult of the cave. She placed her long, artistic fingers on my lips, she shushed me, explaining, 'I am not a jealous child. Silly boys fuck about. As you endlessly tell me, it was just sex. Please don't be upset.' She pointedly gave Alisha a fluttery wave. Illusions vanished as I realized how cunning she really was.

We sat in the reception hall with its true appearance at last restored. Myrna took the solid wooden high-backed chair at the head of her conference table. She patted a chair next to hers where I was to sit. Joe and Alisha faced me. With a faint smile, my wife reached underneath her seat to produce four bottles, two of real ale for me and my mate, two of fruit flavoured cider for Alisha and herself. It worked. I relaxed. Nothing else to do! Winning matters. Not being right.

'The full story can come later,' she smiled. 'If I might borrow another phrase of yours, Joseph, "let's cut to the chase".'

My buddy guffawed. He felt as outplayed as I did. So, he fired off a surprise revelation of, 'Fuck it! Melissa rescued the key codes when she escaped just before the bomb went off…'

It upset me instead of diverting Myrna.

'So, Melanie. Melanie as well? She's a…?' I cried.

'Yeah, yeah, yeah. Leave it. No time to piss about with that. Just a minor task. Most of Anais's girls are agents. Gives 'em extra income. All the girls are brilliant with using diversions to fool or confuse their bastard Caliphate clients while we spy on them. Mossad runs most of them.'

Eagle-eyed, he noted my querulous expression. He continued, 'I tell you this, mate, there ain't no one comes near you and me at espionage. We're the ultimate spy-guys. That's why we're setting up the biggest interplanetary scam there's ever been. You'll be in the history records, Simon, buddy. You know how you always told me how you wanted to go to Earth in the flesh?'

My brainbox was spinning so fast I thought it would fall off, and Joe, Myrna and Alisha could kick it to and fro beneath the table.

'In less than two years Earth Time we will be living in England. We'll teleport there from Rig 1,' he explained. 'Some preparation is still necessary. No sweat. We will reach Terra in two or three minutes. None of the old 400-day space voyages.'

Yet again, I was speechless.

He ignored it, continuing, 'Point two is a shocker for a guy as vain as you, mate. We won't have the faces we have today. When we infiltrate Maddigan's's Imperial Guard, we'll receive more than new names. We're getting new faces and bodies. Don't interrupt. I promise you'll still be as good looking as you think you are today. Put you back as you are now when we done what we do. Swear to you, baboon arse! It's me has to arrive first. If my molecules are teleported to the far reaches of the universe, you'll have advanced warning. On Earth, Alisha and I will be slaving away to prepare for your arrival. You see, the psychology profilers calculated you were the one and only guy with the right amount of empathy to get close to Maddigan. You'll be a legend, mate. You'll be the man who altered the history of two worlds.'

Chapter 10

Psychologically, it was complicated. Especially the way they ignored my feelings. Surgeons performed operations on my brain alongside hypnotic recalibration. There was no, 'Goodbye! Good luck!' All I am aware of was black eternity. I never felt more alone in my life as when my eyes opened, and I discovered I had been teleported from the hidden labs of Rig 1 to England.

I had materialized into an isolated location to give me time to adjust to my internal 'terraforming'. That was the extent of consideration I received. It wasn't just brain landscaping either. My body and my face were physically transformed. An unfamiliar looked back from my mirror.

For many months I was to be secreted in an old stone cottage halfway up a hill in a region of Wales. My time was entirely occupied by distance observations of President Maddigan and his court. I was empowered with access to the ring of spy drones at the edge of Earth's atmosphere. This was to assist me to study every action of my target and his retinue. My only human contacts were Joe, apparently in an even more challenging situation, and Myrna, back in Helium. I watched, updated and gradually adjusted to Terra and England. Endlessly.

No doubt it was hellishly difficult for Janine Suee as well, when she arrived on Earth. How could China's super-spy identify two Helium agents also teleported to Earth in alien bodies? That was an amusing reflection for me. Safe in my secluded adjustment centre, I relished her difficult situation. Her condescending, mocking attitude towards me had always got under my skin. Now the tables were turned. Using British drones, which were far superior to China's, I located her very quickly. No way would she recognize us, with our new names, new faces and modified personalities.

Two things about her appearance at the President's HQ amazed and worried me. I wondered how she had arrived in Wells at the same time as Manitoba Joe and me. Our finest intelligence – by which I mean Mossad – assured us the Chinese lacked access to teleportation. Wells was established as the English capitol. That was a dramatic evolution. Aftershocks had obliterated vast landmasses all over Earth following the Yellowstone cataclysm. Eruptions, ten-mile-wide sinkholes, flooding, earthquakes and conflict across every continent had spared 'the smallest city in England'. Historically, London was England's capital. Today, the government was based in the 13th century Bishop's Palace of Wells. It was located close to Glastonbury Tor, where I once saw Maddigan prancing around like a Druidic baby elephant.

I often scrutinized the troops guarding the President in his converted ecclesiastical palace. Their one duty was to check visitors' credentials before they were admitted. Their performance did not match their pompous strutting. Security was shambolic. Maddigan was the face of British Empire and its territories across India, much of North Africa, as well as anarchic Northern Europe, in addition to being President of the Imperial Province on the Red Planet. Yet I could easily have walked in the palace and blasted him. He only survived, I thought, because most of Earth's nations were overawed by an illusion that Britain had the best equipped military forces on two planets. In addition, some form of super technology was whispered about. Even the Chinese were convinced they were nowhere near to Britain's technological advances. That was all PR, not reality.

My continuous task was to provide Myrna with appraisals and assessments of the British Empire's capabilities. Certainly, there were scientific advances and innovations that generated the wealth to fund tremendous military power. However, the true core of the power lay in key human personalities. The helmsman of the warship was of the major importance, not in the armaments. Two charismatic individuals directed Britain's dominance on land, sea and air. In material terms, First Lady Natasha and her loyal champion, 'Rastaman General' Alassam, drove England's emergence from the shadows. Despite their achievements, one individual was the representation of the Empire and its values. Everything radiated from Maddigan. He was the polar opposite of plebeian expectations for a master of worlds. The majority of his people might have expected a brutal warlord to sit at the head of an Empire. Popular history knew Emperors to be tough, brutal individuals, surrounded by bristling bodyguards who crushed every threat before them. Although Maddigan was likeable, he appeared a clown, a bumbling, absent-minded old fellow. Nobody was certain this was a pretence. How he had survived this long was a mystery I was curious to discover. There was more than met my eye.

Before I awoke in my lonely, Welsh cottage, I was convinced the Druids were his puppeteers. I had watched the ginger Welshman at Chalice Well acting like a humble supplicant. There wasn't an iota of assertiveness in him. Even the marital confrontation I peeped at confirmed his lack of common sense. Improbable as it seemed, the man had the unbelievable stupidity to appoint the Head of the Chinese Secret Service as one of his secretaries. He compounded his indiscretion by appointing the utter stranger, who said his name was McNulty, as joint commander of his army. What kind of fool would do such a thing? Perhaps insanity was a prerequisite for world ruler?

Another mystery unravelled in Maddigan's weird fantasy world. I often observed how the beady black eyes of Janine, his 'secretary', watched every moment of McNulty. I could not believe he was blind to the swamp of subterfuge all round him. I enriched my isolation by spying on everyone in the palace all day long from my hideaway. I particularly watched Janine. That included her in the shower. Well, we all have little peccadillos! One professional lesson I learned was how good an agent Joe could be. His Mossad training helped him pick-pocket Janine's visual device. The cunning bastard posed as a delivery guy for the palace. When she reached out for her goods, his fingers dipped in and out of the side sheath where she held her recording card. Within three minutes of his departure, he had duplicated all the cards store of confidential records. She had no time to block his recording her hard drive of all information before she realized it had been stolen.

What an eyeful her visuals turned out to be! I couldn't believe her cleverness when I hunched over my own screen to discover the contents! After collating information about troop movements, Janine even caught an intimate moment between the inept President and his wife. I found it shocking that this pretty Chinese woman, lacking any security clearance, had freely monitored him and caught every private event. It was simplicity itself for her to assassinate him. Yet, her failure to do so proved that China's proposals for an alliance were genuine.

Later I re-watched an episode downloaded to my 12-foot screen size and settled down for the entertainment.

Maddigan and his wife were in a secluded grove in the Abbott's Palace gardens. His habitual pacing up and down, his gesticulations, suggested he was guilty and defensive also. Natasha, being a tall lady, with jet black hair and unblemished complexion, was in superior physical condition. Though both were in their mid-forties, she looked at least a decade younger than her husband. His shirt's gauze fastener had come unstuck at the bottom, allowing his fat white belly to peep out, supported by the top of his pants. His faded ginger hair was tousled and failed to conceal his encroaching baldness. In most visuals, put out for public consumption, he wore a toupee. Actually, it worked even better when he wore a wig for major state occasions. Sweat streamed down his cheeks and he was trying to convince Natasha of his love for her. His accent added a poetic sincerity to his words.

'Isn't it sufficient to have been in love? It can't continue all through our lives with the same intensity. Emotions must constantly be renewed. At some point in the future that intensity will flame once more.'

'So, you're fucking Sheila again. Is that it? You want to pester me with us having her with us in a threesome again? Last time we discussed our 22nd century liberation that was meant to be a one-off.'

He seemed hurt by her lack of understanding. As he explained, the Welsh lilt resumed the defensive tone.

'Darling, sweet Pork Chop!' he began.

Even I was embarrassed by it.

'How dare you? Your conversion to Paganism was not some shrewd political act as you claimed. It was a plan for sex magic, involving Sheila. Am I expected to be mommy, holding your hand and approving of you fucking your Eco Minister?'

Maddigan threw his body down onto the low, ornamental stone wall around the trout-filled pond. His head was buried in his arms. Natasha would not let him off the hook.

'Come along, man. How stupid do you think I am? Why did you appoint Sheila as Eco Minister? Your long self-justification to me makes clear why your detractors call you The Welsh Windbag! Come along. Man up! You lied about her possessing essential knowledge. You're an old man who wants to fuck blonde corpses.'

Bitchy! Bitchy! I thought. Janine must have jumped so high with delight her head hit the ceiling when she forwarded this episode to China! A brilliant fabricator like me, Simon Edge, would have made up half a dozen believable lies. No way did the President equal me in deception.

Instead, obese, ginger and mystical Maddigan went off on one as emotional therapy. 'Please pity me and forgive me', whining, referencing his 'suffering emotional centre' and the 'scrutiny of the intellect' and then to his 'mechanical centre's compensation element'. The latter was performed by him pretending to unconsciously light a ready-rolled tobacco/grass cigarette.

What a pat on the back I deserved! Two days after teleportation I had hacked it, already busting the vid files of China's Intelligence Chief. I turned down my spy-screen and opened a beer. Joe had not failed me in that way. The cottage had a concealed cellar, containing 6,000 assorted bottles. Given I was to be a hermit for almost a year, it was essential!

While I relaxed, I speculated how Janine managed to record the soap-opera episode of domestic conflict in the palace garden. I couldn't help but grin when I deduced Janine must have been hiding amid the shrubs. It was ludicrous! Besides, her subterfuge was elementary compared with how I used to spy on them from 400 million miles away!

My real challenge would be how and when I could leave my isolated den, get to meet the President and make contact with

Manitoba Joe, and be anonymous and unnoticed. I didn't have a clue how to accomplish it.

Chapter 11

People are addicted to gossip and scurrilous rumour. At the same time, there is no better means of gauging the public mood. Frequently, a brain-dead celebrity reveals truths sober commentators miss. The news infos said Maddigan's new Head of Security, was a Scottish heavy called McNulty. Already the public liked him. Therefore, he was built up in reports. He was hard-line, pushing the President to take a tough approach to impose his own control over players like General Alassam and his African mercenaries from Lyonesse. That was the kind of tale that would sell transmission subscriptions. How the masses love tough talk!

The next juicy story was a sensational dramatization of governmental in-fighting. Alassam had upset one particular seller of sensationalised "news". He had refused to discuss rumours of a military build-up in Southwest Britain. The media worm sought revenge and used the rejection became a tasty story 'leaked by an insider' that McNulty, the newly appointed Scottish General, actually swore at African Alassam for being so 'uppity'. Then he shouted so loudly that Presidential aides rushed into the private quarters to ensure he was not being killed! A follow-up whispered that Natasha Maddigan was set against any idea originating from General McNulty. The Scottish general had hijacked resources allocated to the Rasta general. He used it to upgrade the technology of his own regiments and not his colleague's. Illicit bugging by the scandalmongers got hold of an old summons to Alassam to join a conference HQ in Wells. The emphasis was on a summons. Not a request!

Natasha was sceptical about the random event that was to inspire her husband's appointment of McNulty to an absurdly senior position. The motivation for his whim came from a single dramatic event that took place four months after my own arrival in my Snowdonian lair.

The drama took place the day the President made a physical appearance at a major public rally. This spectacle would be watched all over the planet. Everybody wanted to see him in the flesh. Within a day or two, people on the colony on Mars would also celebrate it.

Attendees on the actual day were local, arriving from Wells, Bath and waterlogged Glastonbury. Because it was a special event, he requested attendance by his Druidic subjects. He planned on them following the Dragon Line from Stonehenge and Avebury to add a mystical quality to his celebration. Instead, an insultingly small representation wandered from Haggard's Tintagel School. Regardless of the reality, technicians were told to fake images of half a million people of Britain celebrating Maddigan's achievements. The phrase 'you couldn't believe your eyes' acquired a literal truth!

Everybody, not only his red-jacketed, gold braid 'security', had warned Maddigan of the potential danger from flocks of unidentified outsiders, gate-crashing that day. An eagle-eyed Scot at the front of the crowd had braced for action well in advance. He overheard Natasha confiding to the President she dreamed she was the wife of an ancient dictator from ancient Rome named Julius Caesar. The Scot, a man by the name of McNulty, did not understand the reference, but he passed this titbit to his contact in Snowdonia, an isolated bit of North Wales. His recipient, a man called Masque, was an ancient history buff. He said Natasha's allusion came from the famous English dramatist named William Shakespeare who lived more than 1,000 years back. Natasha, an equally educated woman, had experienced a dream that preceded Caesar's murder in the play. Ergo, she grew extremely upset and warned her husband. He laughed and hushed her with a clumsy kiss. Nonsense, he reassured her! She was supposed to be the rational partner in their marriage. More than that she should realize everyone loved him. Publicity caught the kiss and put it on screen. British subjects on two planets around cheered, out of sentiment and on affection for a clumsy, but likeable, clown.

McNulty was perfectly placed for the drama about to ensue, having shoved in front of other spectators. He looked back, noting the contingent of Anglo-Indians and Africans, most likely refugees from Lyonesse. He seemed amused by the security guys in scarlet and gold braid, trying very hard to appear eagle-eyed, showed minimal interest in white English or even the Chinese or Orientals. Being professionally trained, McNulty was more thorough. Playback of recordings were evidence, when viewed later, how eager he was to watch out for his President.

As I viewed the show in my cottage, I checked out people around him as well. I saw some bearded bloke in dark shades, sporting a ponytail and silver earrings, clutching a fishing rod wrapped in brown paper. By him was there was an elderly lady booing and blowing a whistle. My eyes next stopped at an oldish black fella in a tweed coat, waving and smiling; his eyes paused at an Afro babe with those huge bazookas. Not surprising! Close by her was a bespectacled young guy with spikey red hair. I moved to a woman who looked like she was with the Speccy Fella. She was of medium height with long, highlighted hair. She looked Arab or Indian. She frenetically waved a white flag with a red cross on it. All of them were odd. Suspicious too! England – land of eccentrics and oddities.

A subtle sign by Maddigan's left hand signalled the musical crescendo was due. Now it rolled forth, all perfectly choreographed. This was the moment for him to raise his arms over his head as the lead into a patriotic speech. An escort from his Gold Regiment loaded gunpowder into antique rifles. The touch of nostalgia. Dramatically, standing on either side of him in two lines of five men they fired. Antique weaponry, with the loud bang and the smell of gunpowder, provided a marvellous novelty.

As some master of criminality had intended, those guards letting off shots was the signal for a brown-skinned woman with white highlights to jump from nowhere. Screaming insanely, she broke through the spectator line, letting off shots from a revolver as ancient as their rifles. The President held up his hands in an optimistic attempt to stop her 300-year-old bullets. His armed escort fell back in terror. Incredibly, this mad-woman, shrieking throughout, missed her target half a dozen times. At this point, a heavily armed, stubble-faced man performed the legendary Celtic 'Salmon Leap' over the heads of the shocked spectators. Fearlessly, he tackled the woman, who had modified her old handgun to store a score or more cartridges. She proved an accomplished fighter when she and the man,

79

McNulty, hit the ground, because she was brandishing a dagger before he could restrain her. She slashed wildly, her blade glinting in the bright sunlight, before she raised the blade above her head to stab him. Fortunately for McNulty, he wore heavy body armour. At long last, several useless bodyguards around the President joined in the scuffle and secured her. They were too cautious though and failed to hold on. She rolled free and ran for it. When the bearded Scot attempted to grab her ankle, he misjudged and brought down a pair of some clumsy would-be helpers instead. They came crashing down on him, so the assassin made good her escape.

Regaining his feet, McNulty instantly apologized to Maddigan for his botch-up in stopping the woman. The Welshman instinctively recovered his outstanding gift for identifying PR opportunities. This was even after he had nearly been killed! He looked around for his oriental Secretarial Assistant. When he spotted her, he indicated she must be sure interplanetary cameras were recording everything. People on two worlds were to watch with admiration, as their unshaken President took immediate control of the situation. He stepped up to his rescuer to offer his hand. When they shook, he offered thanks in his loud voice, demanding his saviour's name and identity.

McNulty supplied this information awkwardly and muttered that he had been fighting alongside Britain's Israeli allies against attempted Persian incursions. That's why he had, fortunately, still been wearing body protection. Shyly he made reference to how he once led one of the country's top-notch regiments. When pushed, he mentioned various military campaigns in which he had been engaged. Maddigan was aware he could revoke anything said at a later date when public recollection faded. Without more ado, he placed his arm around the hero's shoulder and proclaimed that henceforth this man would be in charge of England's military planning. If the Scot proved effective, he could be awarded a more sonorous title. The crowd applauded with delight. They love to watch spontaneous acts of chivalry. Among that audience was Janine, the oriental secretary, still revealing nothing of her private thoughts. From my own distant screen, I noted the First Lady pursing her lips in distaste at the glibness of her spouse's performance.

Subsequently – and it was many, many months later – even Natasha grudgingly recognized McNulty's genius in all matters strategic and military. He would serve as the iron fist within his master's cute fluffy glove; most importantly, he appeared content to remain a shadowy background figure, with neither personal ambition nor the slightest desire for media glory. Day and night she observed his tireless dedication to the task of creating blueprints for efficients defences for the realm including the wider Empire. He was delighted to submit everything to her for approval. Sadly, the Governmental Palace stayed as chaotic as ever, due to the President's fantasy he would never come to harm because his people loved him.

The First Lady never tried to act beyond her strictly defined areas of accountability. Helium, for example, was her special responsibility. This initial aversion to McNulty was similar to her continued dislike of Myrna Golden. That woman's ambition to usurp the presidency of two planets was blatant. Frequently, Natasha's reaction to her verged on paranoia. Love for her open, caring husband lived in the core of her heart. She worried about his blind optimism. Was Myrna plotting an invasion and a bloody usurpation? Or maybe, Helium's fruitful alliance with the Martian Chinese had spread to Earth? None of this concerned Maddigan as it ought to have done. His attempts to divert her worries with ludicrous Pagan regeneration blather about Earth energies and so forth, baffled her. She hoped it was his act, not a genuine belief in supernatural bullshit that endangered material concerns.

Like I said humans love gossip and salacious fantasy. The story of McNulty and the failed assassination was a gift for them to hear, see and discuss. For an observer like me, there is no better means of gauging the public's mood than by popular fictions. The news scavengers were excited by the very appearance of Maddigan's new Head of Security. A Scottish heavy like McNulty was a singular novelty. Already the public adored him. He was built up in reports as being a heroic barbarian. Even my John Carter of Helium was eclipsed by him. What everybody wanted to see was a man who was unafraid of being hard-line. Here was the tough guy who pushed the President to take a firm, uncompromising approach. By making himself the personification of Britain, he convinced antique English nationalists the President would always to impose his authority over newer settlers like General Alassam and his African mercenaries from Lyonesse. I guessed his performance owed a lot to the shrewdness of First Lady Natasha. She perceived that Our Fighting President, Soul of Albion was the kind of melodrama that would sell transmission subscriptions as well as win hearts and minds. How the masses love the man of steel!

Using charm and bribery, McNulty established his credentials to the President and his people as a loyal military strategist. Following a sentimental reconciliation with Alassam, the pair dined with the Maddigans. A heart-warming account was composed by me, for him to divulge to media sources.

While they dined, he casually described to the group a strikingly brilliant person he once worked with. This individual, he said, was an expert in security matters. A totally brilliant guy. Like himself, they fell foul of Governor Golden. The crime was expressing to Myrna opinions she considered too favourable to the President and proposing tighter links between Helium and Wells. The only way to stay alive was to flee, before the bitch ordered a murder.

'Bit of a wimp,' McNulty remarked. 'Be useful if we found out where they went. A genius with organizing. Stuff that bores me shitless. Someone lacking ambition in him. Efficiency and organization! Who gets their rocks off on that? I bet you, Ma'am, Golden's regretting making someone with those gifts do a runner. She'd have contrived an accident or poisoning, I bet, if I hadn't sent a warning, you know.'

Natasha frowned, but said with her icy politeness, 'That is a curious tale. I'd never appreciated that woman's murderous tendencies before. Have you no inkling where your remarkable individual went?'

Maddigan seemed reluctant to divulge. He began, 'Tell you the truth, I'd guess on North Wales. Myrna Golden's claws reach anywhere. She'd think of Arabs, not somewhere as dead as there. I have suspicions about who sent the loony bitch to swing a blade at you, Sir.'

His implication was clear.

During sex was when Natasha's beloved went indiscreet. When she asked about this refugee from Helium, the name 'Masque' popped out of his mouth. As soon as Maddigan started to snore, she initiated many scores of search programmes. I sent Joe a big thank you!

Chapter 12

While matters unfolded, McNulty was in constant communication with Jon Masque, Man of Mystery. The pair of us had been given the most sensational espionage mission in modern history! For nine months, Charismatic Jon had been isolated in Snowdonia. McNulty had been his only friendly contact as he hid and waited in the cottage in the mountains of north Wales. McNulty's messages adopted blunt humour that concealed information so blatant that sophisticated technology would miss it. The latest one said, '*two faced devious liar required to assist Head of State. Location, Bishop's Palace, Wells. Travel expenses and accommodation covered.*' Messages were never aural or visual. Masque's replies were as concise as, '*What the fuck?*' I can't help my repartee, whether I am Simon or Masque! I imagined Janine had set Chinese techies on days of seeking hidden reverse framing and stepping video and audio links. The simpler and more transparent the communication, the more sophisticated analysis would tie itself up in the pit of nonsense!

Frequently, McNulty posted me comic strips with stick figures and speech bubbles that he drew himself. A cartoon of Natasha Maddigan had a halo and label saying, '1st Lady'. She was chatting to a kilted ape with the name 'McN' on his chest. The speech bubble was unnecessary. The next cartoon showed McNulty pointing to a sign reading, 'Well. Well.' A third panel portrayed who I was to go and see. The identity of the stick man with a paunch and a crown on his head was pretty obvious. The fat stick man said, 'Er what washes ter dishes wants uz to invite me mate, what I sez to 'er iz an organizational genius'. To further obfuscate the meaning, McNulty added an odd ancient phrase: 'Me bees' knees! Did a saver for the Taff an' all.' Many Chinese scientists would be head-scratching!

I enjoyed the way McNulty contrived a fake rescue of Maddigan from assassination. Even better, McNulty anticipated being rewarded with a job for a really important mate of his, he could locate for the President. The final comic frame showed the fat stick man bawling, 'I can use him. Get him here! Now!'

At last, here was the action I had itched for during my agonizing isolation on the slopes of Dinas Emrys, up above the Glaslyn River valley. When I was first concealed here, I needed a relaxing break. During this time, I could work on political and structural planning while recuperating from what they had done to me in the Rig 1 lab. But enough was enough. I missed my life as the celebrity socialite and womanizer. All I could do to pass the months in my hermitage was cruise endless cyberspace in loneliness.

That now deceased flier had awaited, in clever concealment, me when I arrived from Mars. How McNulty arranged this, or who he used, I'd no idea. The thing lay between a pair of jagged rocks, surrounding a pool in the middle of some ruins, that gave Dinas Emrys its name. Security demands had meant that once I wrecked his vehicle, I had to painstakingly shift and conceal its debris in the nearby cave. I didn't want to reflect on that. The tale I told my friend of how it got written off bore no resemblance to the truth!

However, the flier disposal helped me develop the character of Jon Masque, which had been merely latent within Simon Edge. That was a positive to my period of solitary concealment that would prove useful in the future.. Although folklore rubbish never appealed to me in the past, the isolation got me into new interests. I studied things like a legend about that pool at the centre of three ramparts. They were what remained of a prehistoric fortress below his cottage. Some Briton King, Vortigern, was told by Myrdinn the sorcerer that red and white dragons lived in the pool, waging a symbolic war, like the one between Celts and Britons. Although it was rubbish, I liked a prediction that its mysteries would be uncovered by a golden haired, blue-eyed young man. I thought *This sounds so like me in my new body!*

I polished my fashionable spectacles and squinted at my screen, feeling enormous relief that those yawning months of surfing the entirety of history, space and political mayhem across two planets was ended. Within an hour of McNulty's summons, I was bumping down the steep track on the west side of the hillock on my motorbike relic.

This was a 350-year-old Norton, converted to normal energy in place of a primitive oil derivative they called 'oil'. However, I managed to keep it operating on petrol in case of emergencies. I 'acquired' the petrol from a storage area of a building in the tiny settlement I ransacked every now and then. I enjoyed the fun of looting all sorts of food in tins and novelties of every sort. During the months of boredom, I became quite the master of my machine. Being, at the same time lazy and mechanically inept, I ran on petrol until I botched up a radio-power modification. My riding skills were honed to a perfection during my frequent descent of the magic track lined by my slender trees and wildflowers, It was a refreshing change from sitting inside my cottage up the hill.

I made great progress toward those roads built between Welsh towns long ago. The present geography bore little resemblance to the spider's web of land communication that apparently covered Britain prior to the Yellowstone's decimation of half the planet.

Distance motorcycling was fun for the first hour or so. Then my arse felt sore, and I suffered cramp in my right thigh. Here was my time to rest and pull the day's treat from my pack. I was surprised how difficult it was to open the 21st century beer bottles with the metal caps I had looted from the village store. After much swearing, I got it open. Inevitably, the bastard exploded in a beery flood. I clamped my mouth over the top. As soon as it had vanished down my eager gullet, I contacted McNulty with my warm greeting: 'Hello, mate. You fine and fit? Eh, now? I still ain't got used to what a thug you look these days.'

His new ugly mug growled, 'Fuck off, pretty boy. Go and do what you're good at. Wave your bum for your new boss and slime up to him. I've got it all in hand for you to meet General Alassam as well. Do you remember who he is? You know fuck all about Lyonesse, where he was based, do you?'

'I know fucking everything since Atlantis, you ignorant twat! What's this Mrs Maddigan like, Babe-hog? Bit of a goer?'

'Sort of lady who'll send her Chief of Security to blow the head off any fucker that makes a pass at her. Comprendo?'

McNulty switched off and an encrypted file arrived. I scanned it briefly before starting up my Norton again.

In less than a day I reached the north side of the Bristol Channel. The sight was fantastical for a man familiar only with desert and dry channels criss-crossing Mars. To my left was the Atlantic Ocean. Today new islands emerged, created from Yellowstone's debris and the underwater volcanoes that erupted while the cataclysm destroyed the American homeland. I studied the wide, deep channel feeding into the Somerset Levels, which were become an expanse of lakes and rivers. I shut my eyes to visualize how the British Isles might once have appeared.

Night fell, and I found shelter beside a white hawthorn hedge. In olden times peoples called this a 'Shepherd's Bush'. Another useless fact learned in my eternity of boredom. I stabbed open my millennia-old tins of spaghetti and sausages to heat over a low fire. This was like being in the Stone Age! Still, the odd grub met my needs. The expedition from Snowdonia on an old motorbike across muddy tracks had already made me, in my own mind, a heroic wanderer!

While I rested, I checked news on the Red Planet and, more thoroughly, what was happening in England. Reports of bandits and tribes from the European Alliance received maximum hits because of a panic about rumours of incursions by Islamists. It was nonsense. Arabia was the womb of the Caliphate, but today it was utterly insignificant. Allah was a Giant on Mars but declined to lesser proportions on Earth. Laughing at my own colourful mental metaphor, I forced the top from another beer.

I confirmed my location on my mini vid-screen. My plan was to ascend the low hill between Pen Hill and Arthur's Point and, from the top, be able to view Wells, before making my dramatic appearance at the court of President Maddigan.

I awoke for the final day of my journey. Chance was kind once more. I messaged Myrna I was Lady Luck's favourite. That would help me stay in the good books if she thought I had her constantly in mind. Not a chance! She replied I was nuts.

As I completed my bumpy my to the top of the hill I found I was in sight of me in sight of an old stone cottage that must be less than 10 miles away from Wells. The place was sheltered by a sheltering outcrop of rock and bushes. It was well-maintained and fossil fuel smoke billowed from a 'chimney'. Fate had given me an opportunity to study the lay of the land and try to talk to some ordinary person to sound out what they thought of President Maddigan.

Chapter 13

I revved up to the stone cottage's low door. I got off the bike and walked up to the door with my hands by my side, as an assurance I was not carrying weapons. Like a traveller in the olden days, I knocked upon the door with my bare knuckles. That was weird! Whoosh! The wooden door opened and I faced a small, stocky, black bloke, dressed in an outfit like shepherds wore in antique oil paintings. He even had on a floppy hat. This was an elderly bloke with a strong regional accent. The variety of different accents in Britain was peculiar. Heliumites all speak the same way, sharp, crisp, easy to understand.

'I'll come outside if that don't offend thee,' the elderly man said, with a flash of brilliant white teeth. 'These be times of disturbance. I's sure ye unnerstand. I seen thy spectacles glitterin' in yon sun. That tells me ye bin not likely an invadin' foreigner. So, bein' as 'ospitality ain't ever wasted in our fair land...' he paused, dipping into spacious pockets of a tweed 'overcoat' as they used to call it. Each pocket held two bottles of beer. He offered me one, then put the other to his mouth after he removed the fixed metal lid with his teeth! 'Wow!' was all I could say.

His friendly, old, dark face wrinkled up in laughter. 'It's what most folk say when I does that,' he said. I collected the biggest stash of ancient bottle beers from this side o' the Channel.'

I grinned, 'I expect you want to know where I come from, or what my business is?'

'Don't worry me, son. Folk reckon me a good judge of people. I judge you to be the joker on the gamblin' reel. Dead dodgy. But you gonna tell truth to me 'cos you not seen no one in a long time. An' I am all I seem and no danger to you. Tell whatsoever ye wish. I'm not a man to pry.'

Here was an effective approach and one worth my using in future. Bearing it in mind, Masque explained, 'I've been living up on Dinas Emrys. Planning, scheming, getting me brains together. Then I got a message from my mate, who's cosying up to Maddigan big time. He's found me a job with the Big Man. I figured I needed to check out what normal guys like you think of President M. And what is really happening here.'

Another bottle was dentally removed before the shepherd lowered himself onto a huge log. He gestured to his visitor to sit down on a log opposite.

He began, 'Since you was honest, you'll get the same back. That tubby prick has more failings than as I could count. But his great virtue is that he don't bully. He bain't what folk might call tyrant. Everyone is free to say what they think. I'll not be in fear of my life, if I be honest with ye. What does I think of him? Good with his gob and little else, I'd say. His missus is the one with brains. You know about Governor Golden? I see you does, son. I think both of us, and everybody else as thinks, agrees when she thinks she would make a better President. There's them thinks she be happy to cut loose and rule her own country on Mars. Does yer know as much about General Alassam – him as was drove outta Lyonesse, now?'

Shaking his head slowly, I admitted, 'Nothing. That's why I'd really be interested in everything you tell me about what's happening nowadays. It will help if I get this job the President wants someone for.'

The African shepherd told me I was a 'good boyo', which was too Welsh to be real. He gave his name as Glendower! Suspicious by nature, I wondered if Glendower was acting undercover. My fear grew as the old man became even more blunt.

He said many in Britain suspected that Maddigan might be removed. Nobody trusted his cosying up to 'them Druid weirdies'. Also, they feared he was not up to stopping an Arab invasion, directed by the Caliphate. In old Glendower's opinion, it was only England's alliance with Israel and Mossad that protected ordinary folk. He also feared the 'Yellow Peril'. At present, China acted friendly. That was now. Maybe the Chinese planned to attack the British Province on Mars.

Glendower had one positive angle. General Alassam was wonderful. Even there, the old guy was cautious. The general was a brilliant commander. But he was from North Africa. So were most of his troops. Added to that, divided loyalties for the Anglo-Indians too. Without either of those racial groups putting England first in their hearts, the Empire could collapse. How would they feel about protecting the British Empire? Uncertain times. I gave a rehearsed half-smile with raised eyebrow. Glendower was an oddball, Welsh negro shepherd. He wasn't dim despite his years and instantly saw my unspoken thought.

However, my fears were laid to rest the further we conversed. After all, we both had been isolated for long periods. A lively discussion developed over a subsequent two hours. Only the clink of bottle tops, unplugged by big white teeth, punctuated the exchange of questions and answers.

I laughed loudly. Our last topic was the Druids. Glendower's vehemence took me by surprise. Druidism, he declared, was the greatest dread for all the Terran English folk. He used to think of them as a few nutters. Now there were few ordinary people who were not afraid of them. The Tintagel School was a place of terror and evil without doubt. He hoped that Maddigan was trying to use them. He was not a man to be so stupid as to allow them to influence him.

Fortified with more beer, the two of us moved closer together as I asked the old man, 'How come a Somerset shepherd like you knows all this? Are you Alassam's mate? Retired soldier or something?'

Glendower stared at his knees before answering, 'I show you mine if you show me yours. Get me massa?'

The dig of 'massa' pissed me off. Show yours, eh? I would. Sometimes you unbalance people with an unexpected shock of truth. Acting sloppy, I grinned, 'Do you want to know where I come from and why I'm here?'

The old Welshman told his visitor, 'reason is, boy – I mean as I see strange depth in 'ee. Might be me eyes needing restoration. When I watch your face it's like I see a king of genius in midst of a shit heap of stoopidity. No offence intended. Ye got a mind like a spaceship between Mars and Earth. Apologize to 'ee. Elders get confused and gabble rubbish.'

I confessed close to all: 'You know that that outsider from nowhere Maddigan put in charge his troops? He's my best buddy, name he used here's McNulty. We were blacklisted on Helium by the bitch of a Governor. Fuckin' contract out on us 'cos we were high up in the services. We did a runner. McNulty was high up in her army. He got out. Saved me too. A few months back I heard he got a promotion and said to me to shift my ass down to Wells asap.'

That was a major gamble particularly if the old fella turned out to be an informant. It was done on a drunk whim. Ludicrous! Yet I liked the black Welsh shepherd. I have made a rule of doing business only with people I like.

I ended with more of my secret. 'I've been on Dinas Emrys nearly a year. I was planning, scheming, getting me brains together. Then I got a message from my McNulty now he's cosy with Maddigan big time. He found me a job with the Big Man. Being an intelligence agent from your Mars province I got sent to check out what normal guys like you think.'

No secret police came for me. Then. Or ever. I made a wise choice.

We parted with back slaps and hugs. After topping up with the last of the petrol I sped away towards Wells. It was bound to be an eye-opener to see McNulty after all this time. Most of all, I really wanted to meet President Maddigan in the flesh. I was confident I would do a successful selling job on the tubby figurehead of England.

The final lap of my journey began well. I left the muddy track leading from Glendower's cottage and came onto a cracked, tarmacked road. Fliers and balloons had made roads redundant in most ways. Martian cities, like Helium or New Pekin, had a network of grave-plate highways that were interconnected and immaculately maintained, land traffic practically ceased though For all its other technological advances, the neglect of England's land routes had reduced too much terrain to wasteland. Nature had got out of hand.

Then, my Norton conked out. No warning, such as a stuttering engine or slowing down. The bastard just went dead on me.

Dusk was descending. When I looked southwards, I realized I had come to the top of a precipice, within sight of Glastonbury Tor.

Mists were swirling over the waters surrounding the island. I experienced a moment of fairy-tale magic. I laughed at myself. Bidding goodbye to the ancient motorcycle, I left it at the side of the road. Boyishly promising Miss Norton we would be reunited one day, I slung a pack on my back and descended, aiming towards Wells.

I discovered I was in a flooded area. Twelve-foot reeds grew thickly wherever I stumbled. After a life spent on rock-strewn desert, this place felt like a peculiar dream. A red sun sank into a purple horizon. Behind in the east was a stark contrast. There the skies were vivid turquoise but ripped apart by blood red clouds trailing the setting sun. Clouds. Shadows swept across the swampy ground, to become lost in sombre twilight, making progress harder. With darkness came silence. Even the twittering birds, which had fascinated me when I first arrived on Earth, were hushed. What a totally alien world!

I retrieved my common sense. From my left pocket I extracted an infrared scanner to detect obstacles. To my surprise, it revealed a score of soldiers guarding the entrance gates to Wells at the bottom of the steep road. I considered how to play it.

It might be advantageous to make a bold appearance. Being bluff and hearty might help me to avoid being screened by dozy security monkeys because dusk had descended. However there could be some easier way to gain access to the small city. I left the track and squelched over the meadows and fields to my left. Though it was heavy going, I blundered through grassy tussocks and mud until I reached a fence. It creaked and swayed when I clambered over it, into a cornfield. As the darkness deepened, I stumbled over more clumps of turf, making my way towards sporadic lines of trees I had discerned on the skyline. By now I could hardly see anything at all. I was desperate not to fall over and get further plastered in mud or cow shit. That would not make for an impressive appearance!

Unexpectedly, dazzling lights came on, catching me by surprise. The beams were directed from a great medieval building, presumably the government's HQ. What was this about? I would have expected armed sentries, but there were none. The array of lights here were an entirely inadequate deterrent. Their function was not security. In fact, their purpose gave an impression of being more to illuminate the impressive gothic buildings, where the President of our British Empire dwelt, than to ensure his safety. In addition, the canopy of clouds parted so the brilliance of a full moon burst through. I might as well have adorned my head with flashing lights the way things were going. I cursed myself for selecting this ludicrous route to the Abbot's Palace. All I could do was plod on until I reached those woods. From there, I had to follow the line of trees.

At the worst possible time, the clouds scudded back over the moon's face. In the blackness I plunged into a pond. 'Fuck medieval England!' I roared, regardless of caution. Fortunately, there were no ducks to start a quacking symphony because the water was shallow. I pulled off my water-filled boots and slowly dragged my feet from the pool, then bumped into a stone wall. Luck changed at long last. Right beside me was a flimsy gate composed of rotten wood. When I pushed, it opened. A miracle! I was standing on a closely cut lawn. Remembering my preparatory evaluation of the area I identified 'The Bishop's Pond'. That meant I was about 100 yards from the entrance to the palace! There was still not a single guard in sight. Nor did alarms go off. Perhaps security was some kind of joke to the President of the British Empire?

Once I drew nearer, I was overwhelmed by a terrific din from the Presidential residence. After strolling through the open entrance doors, unchallenged, I finally came across a security guard. The laser-armed fighting man looked up and down. I had prepared a fantastic lie about being lost and seeking directions. It was unnecessary. The man chuckled, 'Yer in fer the party, ain't yer? ID, have you?'

'McNulty,' I said, being my polite Masque self.

No further explanation was required. He told me to go right in. If I needed to freshen up, he said, the men's room was second on the right. His sentry duty done, he returned to the ornamental shelf where he had chopped a line of white powder. He snorted noisily. I knew that as soon as I went, I would disappear from his thoughts.

Shocked by the security, I joined the festivities. Helium's Governor always maintained impenetrable rituals of security. Anybody who attended her governmental receptions would have been incredulous faced with the scenes here. The first face I identified when I entered the party was Maddigan, in the flesh, barely 20 feet away. The President was relishing his freedom from responsibility with the maximum volume of inhibition.

Rising grandly from an elaborately carved Bishop's Throne, the Great Man held aloft a pewter tankard – a priceless relic like much else in this historic place – and casually splashed beer from it. The ecclesiastical ghosts must have shuddered at such goings-on! Music blared, coloured lights glittered and the merry crowd, packed together, were dancing and chattering. However, the party was stage-managed to present the man on the carved throne as the master of everything around him. To the delight of millions of interplanetary audiences, Maddigan assumed a picturesque pose, assisted by seven gorgeous girls who leaned on the sides of his throne and lounged at his feet.

Chapter 14

An anachronistic collection of paintings from the previous four hundred years decorated the mediaeval walls. My knowledge of static visual art is minimal, but I identified the majority of works as being from the 'School of Kitsch'. A tasteless clutter of painted pottery figures sat on a display shelf. The fake golden rabbit and silver dog made zero impression on me. I liked a few of the framed prints, however. These dated from the 1960s. In particular, I recognized work by two popular artists who were a joke to the artistic establishment of their own time. Three were reproductions of Vladimir Tretchikov's work: *Chinese Girl, Balinese Girl* and there was one with a girl with greenish skin, called *Lady from the Orient.* One era's garbage is a later era's art. A couple of other paintings, attributed to J. H. Lynch, caught my eye when I got through the crowd. One was *Autumn Leaves,* the other was *Tina.* Blending both European and Eastern traits, her face had been described as 'erotic' and 'mysterious'. It was handy to have the universal library on my vid! Now I was ready to meet the president of the British Empire!

Maddigan seemed well into his cups. His sonorous Welsh baritone came through an auto amplifier, assisting his voice to roar above the voices of his joyful guests. An imitation of the ghost projector I saw at Myra's reception creating armies of illusory hybrids on the walls, on the ceiling and across the floor, where fantasy forms mingled with flesh and blood humans. A blonde mermaid floated up to me as I reached the President. Then she dissolved. No one could have prevented an assassination, had that been my intention. I noted four indecisive armed soldiers had their hands on laser holsters. I ignored them and shouted to the President, 'Sir! I was summoned here. And I have arrived.'

The response was casual. Maddigan was not pompous. He simply raised a bushy ginger eyebrow, as he sipped from his tankard and looked at me.

'I'm Masque. Friends call me Jon,' was what I had rehearsed.

Somebody placed a high stool behind me so I could chat with the 'Boss'. The stool-bearer leaned forward as he sat and whispered, 'Not going to say hello, speccy wally?'

The voice was familiar, yet I failed to recall the speaker's low-browed, stubbly features. Eyes are what give people away. These were dark brown, beady and challenging. This was Maddigan's new silverback gorilla, appointed as an advisor and strategist of the Empire. I weighed up General McNulty with fresh eyes. This was Manitoba Joe, dressed up in his new body. I should have recognized his face from all our vid chats.

I hoped my old friend had been able to secure his position alongside the popular General in-situ, Alassam. What struck me more was that McNulty addressed the President with an offhand, almost bullying, demeanour. I was confused and watched for cues. Miraculously, McNulty had found an opening for him at the top table of England's administration. How was he meant to act towards him? How should I behave for Maddigan? Briefing errors! Still, the crowd's din muffled McNulty's words to his commander.

Aware his orgiastic guests required reassurance, Maddigan's theatrical instinct kicked in. Raising his arms above his head, then sweeping them downwards, he commanded silence. The hubbub ceased immediately.

He shouted, 'Quiet, everyone! Tonight, it is my privilege to introduce you all to two brilliant men who will assist me in creating yet greater military strength and prosperity for all peoples.'

A conditioned burst of applause demonstrated the extent of their President's popularity. Awkwardly, I waved, smiled and adjusted my glasses. McNulty glowered at them. That worked well! Maddigan posed with a hand on a shoulder of each of his new officers. This picture transmitted straight away to audiences on two worlds. There was further clapping and cheering.

'I shall see you all later. Jolly General McNulty will remain with you. I'll have a long chat with Minister Masque and welcome him to our land. Soon, I shall reveal to you exciting developments that will emerge from our talks,' promised the President. He touched the wall to reactivate the special effects for his guests' celebrations.

Again, music blasted out from walls and ceilings; out poured a bestiary of men with unicorn heads, sexless but shapely angels, and sinuous, naked snake girls of all races and hues who swam through the dancers' bodies, while glittering multi-coloured stars filled the air. From the top and bottom corners of the hall multi-coloured mists appeared. Each new dancer was accompanied by their individual perfume. I relaxed amidst the scent of lilies blowing towards me, followed by rose perfume from a pink mist. I was delighted to see Maddigan's superlative stagecraft.

I realized the Welshman was beckoning me. I obeyed and followed him into a small adjacent chamber. Nobody appeared worried about the President's safety. When we entered, the first thing I noticed was a mediaeval font in the centre of the stone walled retreat. Maddigan casually slouched against an ancient metal studded oak door. But he did bolt it for privacy. The racket of his supporters was muffled. For the first time, I could study the man thoroughly. For the monarch of the British Empire, he was unprepossessing. He was average height, a couple of inches shorter than me, in poor physical shape, being overweight, and he had dark bags under his eyes. His ginger hair was thinning and tangled. An unsuccessful attempt at a comb-over was merely embarrassing. *Modern treatments would have rectified it simply enough*, I reflected. Or maybe should wear his wig more often. Why not? Perhaps he was in some fad of being 'natural', or of "letting his hair down so to speak!

Finally, I noticed how he dressed. He favoured black, velveteen robes. They were tasteful, impressive even. They concealed his saggy belly! I was taken by surprise when he dramatically pulled open his garment and cast it aside. Beneath the robe was simple a white cotton surplice. It was somewhat different from his chable well attire!

Suddenly, Maddigan lurched up to the font and cupped his hands for its water. Slowly, he trickled it in a circle around them and declaimed:

'Eternal Goddess and Horned Cernunnos,

All power be yours!

Protect your servant within this silver circle,
Which surrounds us as the seas,
Encircle fruitful land of Earth,
From the red fires of Mars.
And direct the Druid's Chosen One.
Eko, Eko Azarak,
Eko, Eko Aradia.'

Bollocks! I thought. *The bloke must be the Druids' deranged puppet after all.*

That appraisal was immediately corrected. Maddigan, the mystical Druid, disappeared, replaced by a more obvious act. He became the simple beer-swilling old man, a down to Earth fellow from the Valleys. At last, a pair of strong, deep blue eyes rose from behind the eyebags like the sun emerging from behind mountains. Maddigan grinned. He had deliberately revealed his real self to me briefly. I was worried I had been so easily fooled.

Sounding more Welsh by the moment, the President proposed, 'Let us commence afresh, young man. I am Maddigan. You're welcome here. Introduce yourself properly. Your go, boyo. You're fake too!'

'Me? I'm Masque. John Masque.'

'A start,' said Maddigan.

We shook hands. This was an odd interview. I removed my glasses and began polishing them with Forever Cleaner. This helped me reassemble my perception. My host indicated we should sit together on some old oak stools, beside a stained-glass window on the far side of the font. The glass portrayed an elfin figure in a pointed green hat, playing a flute as he danced through the bordering green leaves. *Funny stuff to put in old Christian churches!*

In response, I demonstrated my Pagan knowledge. I asked, 'Is this figure the Green Man? Or Pan? Or is it our antlered Cernunnos?'

Having said this, he watched my eyes keenly. I must have passed the test because the President grinned and remarked in a mildly mocking tone, 'You're an anti-Druid sceptic. Fine. Rather obvious, you know!'

The amusement in his gruff voice was not hostile. Being proficient in subterfuge myself, I saw it was wise to be more open. Returning his smile, I admitted, 'No, Sir. You are right. I am here because I want the senior post in your government for my personal interest in you. However, none of it will be detrimental to your vision. McNulty invited me here. I know you are aware of that. I promise to serve you faithfully.'

'What can you tell me of McNulty's military credentials?'

Once more, Maddigan revealed he was a shrewder operator than anyone realized. He was casually testing me and checking on Joe at the same time. Our preparation had been immaculate. McNulty and I knew each other's cover story perfectly well. I memorized every minute detail of his, of a spurious career history on Helium. McNulty's biography, or bogus story, was fed into the interplanetary media long ago. Thanks to highest grade techno allies of Mossad, everything could be substantiated. With disingenuous awkwardness, I admitted, 'You ought to realize my view is biased. I'd be dead if my friend's contacts hadn't rescued me from that murdering bitch.'

'Hmmn!' Maddigan considered that. Finally, he responded. 'Natasha is my wife, old style, boyo. Ours isn't a Druidic seven-year renewable. It's a lifetime marriage. She loathes bullish me. McNulty irritates her. Look you! See, she is a clever, clever woman. A bit too superior, you know? Always it is my heart that leads me. But Natasha? She lives in her head, if that makes sense. You might have knocked me down with a deciduous leaf when she advised me, that the "obnoxious man" (your friend, I mean) was someone who was indispensable. Turnabout, eh? Mind you, Jon – alright to call you that, is it? Dear me! What was I saying? Oh, yes! Sometimes she tells me I am a proper fool too.'

As if to demonstrate this, he bumped his bald spot on the stone ledge before the stained-glass window, when he bent down for a flagon of Somerset apple wine, concealed under the table. I studied this puzzling individual, while he gulped chilled, sweet wine that had appeared in his hand. Before I could play gullible myself, so I could dig up more information, there was a loud knocking on the oak door.

'Piss off! I'm talkin',' shouted the President.

The offender sounded female. Swearing all the way to the studded door, Maddigan unlocked the bolts. He held it open a bare inch or two but spoke gently to the visitor. 'I'm in the middle of something of importance, honey. I swear I'll join you the minute I've received counsel from my new friend here.'

My reshaped nose came with a heightened sense of smell. I, Masque, detected a perfume from an ancient era. Such a luxury must be worth a king's ransom! Maddigan was beaming as soon as he had restored the iron bolts to prevent more disturbance. We sank two more chalices of apple wine. Maddigan told me he needed to sit. I became the young man listening to the wisdom of a sage.

He unburdened his ideas on me. It was as if I had passed the test and now that I wore his coat of arms, I must be clear where he stood in order that I would serve his wishes with the maximum accuracy.

His beliefs were utterly the reverse of Myrna Golden's. Like her, he recognized the Caliphate threatened all civilisations on two planets. However, the Pagan fanatics had a stronger hold on Earth than on Mars. Arabia's Islamic maniacs had been crushed between a pincer movement by China and Russia in the East and by Israel in the West – with some degree of assistance from England and from African citizens with memories of Muslim slavery. The British Empire on Earth enjoyed respect, thanks to historic alliances with India, distant Australia, and a variety of African mercenaries. The more immediate danger for Britain came from the Papacy and Druids. Although the Catholics were weakened by Islamic conflicts, English Paganism had grown in the heart of the Empire. The previous President had mounted a major attack on the Druidic centres. Before his troops engaged, a recent, random event – Act of God, the Christians called it – obliterated much of Northern Britain and a large proportion of his forces.

Disaster came in the form of a meteor that destroyed most of Scotland. Worse, the earlier President was assassinated by an unknown knife-man. The tale given out was his death was heroic, leading the army to deal with the Pagans. Fighting, looting and barbarous tribalism endangered the seat of the Empire. Despite the odds, the Empire survived, although England was seriously diminished by comparison with Helium Province.

By luck – some said a miracle – an unknown politico from Wales emerged from Powys. He was able to impose law and order across the entire South of England. By maintaining an illusion of the great British Empire, he used patriotism, jingoism and alliances with countries and races across the globe to restore peace. He was also blessed with an invasion by an external enemy that united England. A heterogeneous force of bandits from North Africa and Somalia joining barbaric looters from Germany, France and Spain under the leadership of Pagan Scandinavians. Despite their racial mixture, Britons, naturally, called them, 'the Vikings'.

While Mars directed all its technology and army to combat the powerful Caliphate, there was no opportunity to 'assist' Britain. England remained heart of the Empire and successfully escaped external attack while foreign forces engaged in fighting each other. This information stunned me. So much had been concealed from our Martian settlers!

I tried to readjust everything I knew about Alassam's rescuing soldiers, the Druids and how Maddigan had restored wealth and power to the British Empire. It was to take me weeks to uncover suchcoded secrets from the interplanetary web. And to accept, yet again, a new reality.

Maddigan abruptly hit me with a fresh piece of information. At this moment, England was endangered by another invasion, this time, of the Isle of Wight on the south coast! Adopting a tone of disarming honesty, Maddigan declared, 'My domestic organization is an utter mess. So much of our military and scientific strength depended on our friends in Scotland. The disaster there had terrible consequences, you understand? Many of my finest commanders were Scots. I suppose, me boyo, that inclined me towards the miraculous appearance of a Heliumite of Scottish origin and led to my spontaneous decision about him.'

The trust the President gave me was both a shock and flattering. Also, I had never before realized how tenuous was the position of England. Little wonder the man turned to chance and miracles when he had to make decisions. If I was manipulated, I accepted it willingly. I wanted to assist him. As if a floodgate had opened, Maddigan continued to pour out his dilemma in the here and now.

'Do I send my shambolic armies across the water to Shanklin? I know I am not a trained soldier. Not a fighting Emperor who will lead my forces into battle. Nor am a strategist. Destiny presented me with McNulty and then you. I believe it. I appreciate you think me insane.'

The opposite was true. I was convinced this seemingly bumbling fool was inspired. All his actions in the material world really were accidents. His decisions were random. The President was not finished.

'I'll tell you something few might credit. I went, must be nearly two years ago, to Glastonbury. I climbed the Tor and entered the Henge that crowns the summit. Tintagel's Druids were assembled there, eager to be seen when they accepted me as their disciple. They thought it'd be telecast across the solar system. Greedy fuckin' morons. For all that, I swear to you, Jon, I received a blast from the energies flowing through Earth's arteries. Natural, they was. Not magic gods.'

A miracle brought the answer to my heart. The Druids were fraudulent. Alassam it was as saved us. Good man. Go check your history stuff. There were ten attempts by Haggard to murder me. A record, I do believe! Astonishingly, number 11 try was prevented by a stranger, a Martian exile of fine military reputation. The rescuer's name – well, you know it was McNulty. Soon as the boyo popped out of nowhere, I'd had a Mossad check on him – they're the Israeli Secret Service lot. Totally positive they assured me! Four weeks later, there comes a mad woman with a dagger. Immediately, on the spot where he saved my life, him as one of my top officers in the land. Alassam, a man of absolute integrity, completely agreed when he saw my secret intelligence. You know your history of him. A little bit later, Grumpy McNulty draws my attention to another Helium refugee. If McNulty hadn't delivered, he'd have gone.'

Although I knew all the details, I enquired sweetly, 'What has my referee, McNulty delivered?'

'Everything and more, boyo. Most recently was only a week ago. Unexpected trouble came out of nowhere. Vikings, thugs, maniacs were moving south from Salisbury. Alassam still tied with Lyoness refugees. Who appears and saves the day? Here's McNulty with 200 lads he'd been training on the plain, faced off them rabble. Came out of nowhere! They were spectacular. I allowed McNulty only ten armed fliers. Caution, look? Some say we of Welsh origin are tight fisted. McNulty had to use a 1000-year-old cannon as the unexpected weaponry. See, I wanted to test him to the bone. The clever fellow had concealed them north of Stonehenge. Troublemakers were decimated. That's why I appointed him, General McNulty, Co- Commander of all English forces.'

'Sir? Here's my hand. And with it my heart,' I responded.

Though Maddigan took my hand, he went on full flow: 'With him proven as true, I've taken to you, lad. From this moment, you have access to all my files and technology. All is as open to you.' He flopped down on the tabletop, acting elderly and dumb again. As a casual afterthought, he sighed, 'Friendship is the outcome for us, I hope. No matter. McNulty awaits you outside. He'll take you to your suite. If you're not too weary, he'll explain anything you want to know. Happy to have met you.'

Somewhat startled by Maddigan's unpredictability, I left the chamber and found Manitoba Joe, a.k.a. General McNulty, awaiting me.

Chapter 15

McNulty upped the volume of his implanted growling voice: 'Haggis and bacon!' he exclaimed. 'It feels years since I pulled you out of the shit from yer bitch of Mars!'

Before I could answer, I was crushed in a bear hug. The Scot ape whispered in my ear, 'Stick to being our fake selves, nob head. Every part of the place is bugged.'

When he let go of me, he whispered, without moving his lips, 'Tell you what, Simon, even I didn't recognize you at first when you gate-crashed here. Those specs suit you, by the way. You look like a fuckin' assistant wimp in the records department.'

His physical alterations were less dramatic than mine. I had become a skinny, speccy lad, and an academic upgrade, as a well-intentioned bonus. Joe had merely been modified to resemble a gorilla. The bones of his brow were lower, harder. That must be an enhanced head-butting design. As Simon Edge and Manitoba Joe, we both used to have brownish hair. However, his rugged McNulty beard and locks were brutal black now, in contrast to my blonde innocence as Jon Masque.

Pushing and jostling like boys in scrapping displays of playground affection, we acted up for the benefit of any vid snoopers. It was a way to let off steam for me. My mission, even my loyalties were in chaos. Our original duty was to uncover information that would defend both Earth and Mars against the nightmare of an interplanetary Islamic Empire. Implicit in our errand was to check if the President was sufficiently competent to sit at the Head of the Empire. We were placed, with amazing ease, in the centre of power. The extent of our support of Maddigan was left to our discretion. Also in our remit was to decide whether or not it benefited the people to assist replacing the President. There was no doubt who planned to replace him!

Helium was entirely ignorant of the complexity of the dangers England faced. Collateral injury to Helium was brushed aside. Technological superiority, especially teleportation, was the be-all and end-all for Myrna. Slowly it dawned on me, her pragmatism was insignificant beside what Terra possessed. If England fell, Helium and the Terran Empire would also be lost. Thanks to Maddigan's alliances with Africa and India in England, these alliances would carry across to Mars. Even China would work with Helium to some extent, as they had grown to respect the President. For all its amorality, Mossad was not, as Myrna assumed, a pawn she could use. More likely, the Israelis, as the result of Joe's counsel, had grown more inclined to partner Maddigan. Much of the Empire's wealth was reliant on partnerships and intellectual contributions to England, widely regarded as a seat of learning. Such views were held in high esteem by Israel. Without a similar cultural perspective, Myrna had little in common with her fellow Jewish allies in overthrowing the Islamic *jihadist* heritage. Personal ambition blinded Myrna to English peoples' perceptions of Maddigan's virtues. He himself to be proved himself to be a benevolent Head of State. And they believed he was totally responsible for rescuing them from anarchy after a century of multiple natural disasters. Despite affectionate jokes his people made about him, they fet his every endeavour – and blunder – culminated in final success. More than anyone I've known he possessed that indefinable quality called 'charisma'. Myrna was the reverse. Even in Helium, she was regarded by the populace as cold, distant and she was feared. In some quarters, I fear, she was even hated. When I considered her today, I saw the potential of a tyrant.

Deep below the ocean depths of my psyche, I sensed the stirrings of dark currents about to turn. They were different in nature from what had come from those operations on my brain tissue.

Militarily, Myrna alone was in charge. She demanded her generals deliver results. Maddigan was relaxed, knowing he could rely upon the loyalty of Alassam's African soldiers. Myrna lacked any true allies to share her burden. Helium was oblivious to the challenges Terra dealt with – particularly, the serious threat the Druids posed to all England. The most Mars achieved with Israel, India and China was a diplomatic balancing act. All of it was a complete contrast to the shared interests and established trust that the

Empire had built with other nations on the home planet. The repercussions for Myrna's isolationism were not considered.

Joe and I could only discuss such issues well away from Wells, preferably somewhere deep in the heart of nature, and unwatched by drone eyes in space! We walked together, talking about the weather!

There had been extensive modifications to the Abbot's Palace. Our accommodation was on the second floor of the central tower. When my buddy led me into my rooms, their size and opulence left me lost for words. I had been given an enormous briefing room with screens and some elderly surveillance equipment. Joe led me to the dining area. It was ridiculous! Someone had the idea to fill it with works of art worth a fortune. The same was true of my sleeping chambers. Luxury, luxury everywhere!

'Spyware?' I asked Joe.

'No way, mate. The President knows me, and he knows I am one million percent loyal. I am the same with you. If you were an enemy, I'd execute you myself.'

That was an appropriate reply for anyone spying! We had to remain 'in character' as per our training. I was entirely Jon Masque, the geek, Manitoba Joe was McNulty, the Scottish macho man.

'Are you winding me up, pretending to know about spying and cameras?' I shouted. 'Happy days when you were brawn and me brains. Tell you what, mate. Us two are going to crack bitch Golden's security. I can make Maddigan proud. I want to impress the boss.'

We suspected there were people analysing every word we spoke. I studied the equipment supplied for me. It was a joke. This was children's technology by comparison with what everybody had on Rig 1. If I used this for interplanetary snooping on Mars it would take a day to transmit. That was like stuff I used two years ago. Nowadays, Helium would perform such tasks in less than an hour. This was the same time it used to take for transmission between Dinas Emrys and Wells!

Time was getting on. I'd had a busy day. I felt dog tired. Joe, I suggested, could crash in my guest bedroom. That way we could resume our discussions first thing in the morning. His military duties did not resume till mid-day tomorrow. So, he nodded. I showered, put on silk nightwear, provided by the British Empire, and wished him a good night. My head hit the herbal-scented pillow and I slept. I was rejuvenated by a dreamless nine hours in the astral world.

Chapter 16

Golden sunlight shone through my closed eyelids. I was waving a happy goodbye at the gates of a wonderful other-world. Such warmth! I had never felt so happy and rested as I was that moment.

Reluctantly, I opened my eyes. Natural sleep on Terra was always tranquil by comparison with the induced rest I was familiar with on Mars. I padded into the shower room, still dreamy. Was it imagination? No. A delicious aroma wafted from the dining area. It was a smell of breakfast. Earth technology might be bollocks, but accommodation and food were superior to anything I'd ever tasted with Governor Golden. McNulty's face met me, bringing me back to reality like a kick in the nuts. He was in the middle of ravenously scoffing a pyramid of full English Breakfast such as I had only encountered in ancient fiction. I'd expected him to be an organic food fanatic. No. Bacon, eggs, sausages, beans. Unbelievable. Delicious. Even more impressive was real, proper coffee that was carried to us from the kitchen by drone.

We play-acted a political discussion for the benefit of observers. I needed to ask about McNulty's counterpart, General Alassam. What, I asked, were his plans for dealing with the imminent invasion of the Isle of Wight? Was he okay to team with McNulty? Joe insisted, very loudly – and genuinely, I felt – that he and the 'Rastaman Commander' enjoyed mutual respect and liking. Already they had shared had the task shaping up an army of eager, incompetent trainees. Maybe my position required discussion?

We had an unanticipated interruption. When the alert went, I checked the monitor. On screen, I saw a red-haired goddess, stylish glasses cutely perched on her nose. I fear I leered. She demanded a full screen body augmentation! Talk about worthwhile! Her long straight hair ran down her back to what seemed a delightfully firm bum. Added to this, she was dressed in a retro leather mini skirt, fishnet stockings and high leather boots. I gaped. I am sure Joe was doing the same.

With a flash of perfect white teeth, she introduced herself, 'Hello! I'm Teena. I saw you last night, handsome. Jon, isn't it?' A nod was all I managed.

This young female was like a rose-scented breeze, completely self-possessed and confident any man she encountered would be swept away by her loveliness. Even Manitoba Joe was tongue tied, captivated by her within seconds. My fortune would be made if I could market her essence, I thought. She appeared to be deciding which of us to overwhelm first. Lowering her big spectacles to the tip of her nose, she looked into my eyes, and enquired, 'Was it you who abandoned a vintage Norton on the brow of the hill above us?'

I looked at Joe to reply on my behalf. Like all professionals he knew the maxim, 'Answer a question with a question if you want to unravel a mystery.'

'How come you know about that?'

'Old Butch told me,' she tittered.

'Butch?' I asked

Joe interpreted, 'Maddigan, she means.'

I was too flustered to invite her into the lounge. I let her take my arm and lead me instead. She sat on the top of a chair-back. Her long legs crossed when she leaned back, and her toes made circles. Aware my mate might feel ignored, she re-directed her radiant beam to him and giggled. 'A girl gets thirsty biking around the hills in the early morning.'

Joe's grin was the first of such breadth I ever saw on his grim visage, whether he wore the Manitoba face or the McNulty one.

Teena tapped her glasses frame on her lower lip and declared, 'A legend is lost!'

'What do you mean?' I asked.

With another sweet smile, she explained, 'Legend is the translation of *Oustoure*. You know, the swish motorcycles? That's what I was riding around on when I spotted your poor, abandoned Norton. Legend's the appearance, more than performance. Usually, I'm an AER electric rider. Dear old Butch gave me both of them. They must have cost him a king's ransom, as they used to say.'

Any suspicion that Maddigan had deviously sent her to spy on us was dismissed from my mind as soon as I looked into her huge blue eyes. Teena acted completely openly to us. She explained her visit very simply.

'My Welsh admirer has gone to receive counsel and instructions from Natasha. That's his wife. You won't have seen her yet. Afterwards he'll probably see his mistress. That's Sheila. Officially, she is England's Eco Minister. But she is also one of the priestesses of the Tor. I figured it was a good time to vanish and try to meet you two mysterious men. Plus. The Norton!'

McNulty still had suspicions about the girl.

'Och! Speccy's motorcycle? I might be daft as a spud, you know. There again, I might not. Ye was sent visiting by Maddigan, weren't yez?' he growled in a rough voice he assumed as required. He maintained that blunt McNulty persona, Scottish accent and so on. Both attitude and tone would have intimidated the majority of people. Not Teena! Completely unphased, she giggled as if he'd been teasing her, and she had the gall to ruffle his short curly hair. 'You big hunk! My poor dear couldn't *make* me to do anything. Just the same, I'll tell him I came to see you. I don't lie to my darl'. Our ages aside, we've a close relationship, you know. He's a treasure. Get real. You've hardly poured all sorts of your secrets into my shell-like ears, to report to anyone, have you?'

She was impossible to not like. Even Joe almost smiled. He relaxed, allowing her to chatter about things I might need to know about Wells and Britain. She was a mine of information too.

Without any prompting, she asked if I wanted to take a look at Alassam. As she focussed her hand-held scanner, she added that General McNulty could put her right about wherever she'd got things wrong.

She commenced her documentary by connecting us to drone cameras over the southern tip of England. She wanted to show us one or two of the islands that emerged from the sea during the geological upheavals. She showed us an aerial perspective of Lyonesse, once Alassam's land. The land that had emerged from the sea was long and narrow and larger than I had realized. It was around

111

seventy miles in length and thirty miles in breadth. The northern tip had absorbed one or two of some islands once known as the Scillys. Teena's commentary became gabble in her enthusiasm to present us with a sight of Alassam's previous kingdom.

Her viewer swung abruptly from overhead views to pan in on an impressive figure well over six feet tall, broad and with gold-skinned arms that bulged with muscles. His hair was dreadlocked and his beard artificially curled. The ornate armour and shining hand-weapons made him yet more daunting; so too did the proliferation of Ju-Ju and other heathen pouches, lockets and chains. As far as I could see, every part of the light brown skin was adorned with occult tattoos. Above and about him on the screen were the vast force of Afro soldiers. Here was a man to be reckoned with by either Druids, Vikings, Arabs or any other enemies.

Teena had no hesitation about disclosing any information she thought might be of assistance to us. She handed her scanner to McNulty, offering him whatever military or psychological material that he might require. He took the device without even a 'thank you' and sat in a far corner of the room to browse. He wanted a break from her enthusiastic chatter.

With her disarming directness – and a flash of her bare thighs above her olden-style fishnet stockings to assist her – she shot at me: 'Did you signal him out of earshot?'

This was a rare occasion of my being wrongly suspected of deviousness. She thought we planned to do a good cop/bad cop on her. Innocence was so unfamiliar to me she believed my denial. I explained what was really on my mind was Maddigan's relationship with her. Awkwardly, I muttered he was old enough to be her grandfather. I thought I had annoyed her. But it was the opposite. Far from being offended, she squealed in delight at her opportunity to gossip. I was still uncertain whether she was open and indiscreet, or a cunning *femme fatale*.

The silken blouse tightened about her young breasts when she leaned forward to explain. 'Old Butch is as complicated as. Half the day he's the blundering fool you were meant to think he was. My life, Jon! You said it was alright to call you that? He really needs a clever smoothy like you to sort out the pickle his administration's got in. No one's sure if they're coming or going. Our armed forces are even worse. There were so many of them and only one commander. That's why he grabbed McNulty. I can tell you Butch's less warm towards your buddy than he is towards you. I'm the same. I always think our new general has more secrets than a beggar has fleas. It was different when you gate-crashed. I knew Butch'd take to you just like that.' She snapped her long fingers with their scarlet nail polish.

We laughed. I trusted her. She went on to give her view of President Maddigan's psychology. 'You're dead obvious about what you want to get out of me. He's self-conscious and the most hidden man I ever met. The opposite of his cuddly Butch character. as well. I love him for being, like, so real. He knows he's a wrinkly, ugly old man. It doesn't matter to me. I'm for how he is as a person. He's spiritually deep when he removes his mask. That wasn't meant to be a joke, honey! Mask, you know? I like that he enjoys my brain as well as … You don't want to hear that though. You're a younger, so much better-looking version of him. Both of you's ladies' men too. Tell you the truth, I was really pissed off with our randy old goat banging that cow he made Eco Minister. Fuckin' Granny Sheila. She's older than his wife, you know. Natasha is a woman I admire more than any woman I ever met. I don't know how he was so stupid. She's really nice to me. I am an airhead bimbo. She knows I'm just what you blokes call, "eye candy". I play clumsy eyelash fluttering for her sense of fun. All that confirms for Natasha I am no threat and we both know what bad news that Sheila Shit-Heart is...'

I was more baffled by women than I had ever been. None could ever approach Teena. Although my lovely redhead was approachable enough to offer all the information that could assist me, I had fallen for her. Just like that. Interestingly, she had clarified my reasons for my growing empathy and respect for President Maddigan and Natasha. Lastly, back to my Simon Edge side – my odds of bedding her within the next week were 100 per cent better than Manitoba Joe's!

Chapter 17

Two months later, chaos began to spread across the islands of southern Britain. The problem for me, and all the team I'd been given, was the sheer volume of information we had to process. Visual surveillance posted us minute-by-minute updates. Further information was arriving constantly from our many allies. Most of it was contradictory. Moreover, each member of the government had a different take on the situation. India and Africa shared information about every Terran nation, including the European wastelands. China permitted us limited perspectives, although its own reliability was questionable. McNulty filtered updates from Mars, always from Mossad contacts. Closer to home, Natasha and Alassam sought proof and justification for their antipathy towards Tintagel's Druidic School, something about which President Maddigan appeared deaf. His First Lady attempted to remind him of their danger. Even Alassam had lost his kingdom of Lyonesse to the military strategies of the Druids. Added to that, Natasha forcefully impressed on him Alassam's warnings of an imminent invasion of the Isle of Wight, and of the endless rumours about plundering hordes progressing toward Stonehenge. Her husband still insisted it was not yet the time to act. Some, or all, such information could be false or misleading. Possibly, she had concluded she would be no worse off employing unknown factors like Joe and me to influence him. She argued we were at least professionals in our work. Hence, our banishment by a jealous Myrna Golden!

It was a funny thing. After my elevation to Chief Advisor to the British Empire (Yes, I really had that title!) I grew increasingly fond of Maddigan. I felt honoured by his innocent trust in me. True, from one perspective, I could see the deluded idiot that both the Caliphate and Governor Golden believed him to be. In reality, I realised he was a fascinating mix of a uniquely honest politician, a simple duffer, then that charming old reprobate I first met. His motivation for dissembling so effectively came from was a part of him that actually was a deluded idiot. However, I had to give him full credit for his skill in creating illusions too. Despite being fat and balding, he could make himself irresistible to women, especially young and beautiful ones like Teena. I made the obvious assumption it was because he was President of the British Empire. When I observed him more closely, I detected no trace of a lecherous deceiver, but a genuine, benevolent person, goodness emanating from him.

I sensibly supplied Myrna with accurate political updates of events in England. I no longer confided all my thoughts to Joe as I once had. His ultimate controller was Mossad. I am sure he was aware of the ambiguities the situation, but he always kept of his own council too. I was confident that he was proving a wise appointment as general. The President treated him with great respect towards his effective military organization and strategy

One firm indication Maddigan liked me for personal, not just professional reasons, was that within a month of my appointment he almost always invited me to_join him for breakfast. This was a leisurely, enjoyable beginning to our day, I knew he listened carefully to my views as well as noting my information. He seemed to find breakfast more useful to him than holding regular formal meetings.

One spring morning, I arrived for our early morning breakfast. It was held in the flower filled dining area of the Abbot's Palace where he was chatting to a curious selection of his retinue. I sat quietly, slicing off the top of my boiled egg, observing them all. The President sat at the head of the table, an embroidered napkin over his belly. Natasha was reminding him Emperors undermined their dignity if they attended public events with tomato ketchup down their attire! He sat close to his wife. She wore an elaborate gown. I could tell she was not prone to spilling ketchup! I still had not had an opportunity to get to know her. It was a loss. She was the power behind the throne in many ways. Although she sat beside him, I was curious to see that Teena was next to her, and opposite was Sheila, Eco Minister. I recognized that she was the Priestess I had spied on at Chalice Well, not simply his mistress. The company was relaxed, laughing at the morning's live news on three of the room's vid-walls. Some teenaged musician was being interviewed. I had no idea who he was; my own interest was classic rock of pre-Yellowstone cataclysm days.

They all gave me a cheery welcome when I sat at the lower end of the table, facing the President. The finest tea, fresh from India, was poured by a serving boy. Then three boiled eggs appeared on my plate. My love for eggs at breakfast was now well known. Back home on the Red Planet, animals and birds were scarce. Most food was created artificially and given varieties of artificial tastes and textures. True, hens had started to be bred under a few Martian geodomes, but it could be another century before we achieved sufficient geo-forming to provide suitable environments to wildlife. Eggs were a rare luxury. Earth inhabitants were unaware of their good fortune in having forests and still so many species that survived climate change and man-made catastrophes on Earth. I used to agree with Joe, mankind left there just in time before the planet nearly died. Recently, I changed my view. I felt it was in the power of a leader like Maddigan to restore Terra to its previous fertility and learn from the consequences of 'wreck and run'. My conversations with the President had played a significant part in my ecological conversion. That would never have happened if miserable Sheila, sat further up the table, had attempted to preach some self-righteous dogmatism. Sulky, miserable cow!

Natasha Maddigan was such a contrast to Sheila! She did not indulge in the cosmetics, which Sheila had adopted in excess, to attract the elderly Welsh Casanova. Natasha preferred her natural exterior. Her hair was immaculately arranged, and she chose not to conceal her silver streaks which, curiously, added to her mature beauty. Even, I thought, to a fit and handsome younger man like me, she was interesting and attractive. For all her commanding manner, particularly with regard to her husband, there was nothing bullying or devious about her. Her intelligence impressed me most of all. I was surprised how pleasantly she responded to radiant young Teena, who was pouring out her naive ideas without a pause for breath. It was blatantly as obvious to her, as to all of us, the nature of the girl's relationship with her husband. I was amused to note Maddigan seated himself between Teena and Sheila. From one side of him came happy laughter, while from the other, sulky silence.

The President had confiscated the channel changers for the trio of surveillance screens. He preferred to do the tuning via his brain implants. He asked us what we wanted to see. We must all be bored, he observed, with this young musician exuding his visual accompaniments. Perhaps current African news would be interesting? Or time-delayed views of Helium?

'Let us see what serious spiritual affairs are dealt with at Tintagel,' Sheila scowled. 'If serious issues of a Druidic Priestess any longer have a distant interest?'

Maddigan obeyed. He directed his drone cameras onto the triple 3D presence of an ancient man with a waist length white beard preaching atop wind-swept rocks. Crowning his sweeping hair were ivy and oak leaves. He wore a long white robe. At last I saw the legendary High Druid Haggard in his rousing performance! His voice was so powerful that the President had to reduce screen volume. I was uncertain how much was genuine live performance and how much had been enhanced by the Tintagel technology. Those ragged storm clouds, racing across the heavens behind him, were especially dubious. Real clouds did not move like this! They supplied a dramatic backdrop. I observed Haggard's voice, tone and gestures were more compelling than his verbal logic. Subliminal technology was certainly at work here; no doubt about that.

'Faithful brothers and sisters of the Earth! Threats strike us from evil Christian offshoots of Arabia! The Saracens are returned, my people. We sought your salvation. We offered Druidic elevation to our President in name. My heart breaks as I realize, he is unworthy of the Goddess. Still, he tolerates atheist territories upon Mars. He appointed an unworthy materialist as Governor of your Martian Province. This Jew woman, Golden, rejects the Goddess, who sought to spread fertility to Helium's sands. Small wonder war spreads and a plague is coming to destroy two worlds!'

Teena giggled, 'The old creep never even took a breath, I swear. If you ask me, Butch, he's taking the piss out of you.'

Natasha put a finger to her lips in a gentle, semi-parental reprimand. Haggard began moving into an unexpected area. He told his audience they could be saved by his 'super soldiers' and redeemed by the Goddess-given 'eugenics'. What the fuck did he want to let loose on humanity?

Maddigan looked as shaken as all of us were. The body language of his hands gripped between his knees, indicated inner conflict. Abruptly, he declared we all should relax to at 'brckkie' time. The screen blanked. To calm matters further, he restored the channel, that present us with the face of General Alassam. The latter was performing some kind of troop inspection. Terran technology was so 'iffy', compared to Helium's, his location was unclear. I knew, by contrast, the superior surveillance of Myrna's team on Rig 1 enabled her to monitor everything Maddigan watched and most of what he did. No time delays, either.

Like the majority of the Terran population, Natasha appeared unaware of the extent and speed of the technological advances made recently by Helium. She commented, 'One wonders, my dear, how far one should rely on the Afro-Brits. Might their allegiance shift if the Druids were to extend their military resources? McNulty still needs to prove himself as exceptional a tactician as Alassam.'

When the President stayed silent, she concluded, 'Geographically, it'd be easy for his Afro-Brit loyalists to turn, then regain Lyonesse or attack Tintagel and ignore your enemies' invasion of the Isle of Wight.'

Maddigan started to devour his toast and imported marmalade. He answered questions in a vacant manner, still munching. 'Talk to my friend, Jon, here. He was appointed to calculate the odds for stuff like that. Me? I heed my heart, Madam. My heart says Alassam's an honourable man.'

I shuffled uncomfortably. But nothing more was said or asked of me. Maddigan surfed the drones around the English regions in a cursory fashion. Many of the images were disturbing. Salisbury was suffering strafing by unidentified fliers. For no obvious reason, he panned slightly further north toward Stonehenge. He made no comment about it. Silence usually indicates some private knowledge.

The Welshman was far from being the simple clown he pretended to be. No one spoke, although all of us glanced guardedly at his bland enjoyment of a post-breakfast fruit wine.

I wanted to postpone Natasha's questions. Acting as if I was the person who was a bit slow, I asked if I could have a beer. Like magic, it appeared before me. I lifted the bottle with a hearty toast of, 'To your victory in Salisbury, Sir!'

Maddigan surprised everybody, suddenly revealing, 'McNulty's strato-fleet is approaching Stonehenge. I'm glad your buddy keeps his own counsel, young Heliumite. I'd assumed he'd told you about it.'

I've always been quick with appropriate responses: 'Discretion works both ways, Sir. McNulty isn't yet aware of all my organizational plans for domestic infrastructure as well as means to support his tactical moves.'

At my request, Maddigan ran back through three days of my recent recordings of operational retructuring in practice. About 100 yards from the palace, were training phalanxes stretching as far we could see. I explained I had adopted some degree of my fakery and enhancement I created for propaganda purposes. Mind you, those armaments were genuine. I'd set workers doing overtime day and night to upgrade weapons the generals could use in southern England. My re- organization had quadrupled stocks of protective shields. To be honest, I had nicked the entire catalogue I'd used from Helium, thanks to Darren's pirate pals and his mother's Rig 1 teleporters. I gave the impression it was all my own work. Obviously, I ensured the site was secure enough to deceive observers about the real details. Teena leaped up and scurried down the table to place a kiss on my forehead squealing, 'And you are so clever and sexy, Mr Masque. Don't we all love him, Natasha?'

The First Lady managed to smile and nod.

This was a brilliant coup for me. Distrust of me was melting away.

'Pwyll of Dyfed!' cried Maddigan, unintelligibly. 'My heart opens to you, Jon, my boy. Here's the reason for Natasha's fears!'

Transmission shifted to the English drones broadcasting from above the Channel. We saw an armada of sailing boats, no less – a water navy, it might be called. The variety of protective armour worn by the invaders was odd. But whoever they were, the crucial issue was that they were drawing closer to the Isle of Wight off the south coast.

Here was a dilemma for me. I did not know what the two generals had planned or how I could provide back up to them. I was desperate to discuss it with McNulty. Were Helium or Israel involved in the assault? Were the opposing invaders Chinese, Arabs, European bandits or Scandinavians? A selfish thought half-entered my mind. If the worst happened, Myrna would teleport her loving husband from Terra.

I felt sad. I enjoyed the company of Maddigan and his other breakfast companions. I had grown closer to them than I ever was to the ambitious politicians on Helium.

Chapter 18

Like a divinity descending to the mortal world, Maddigan appeared on the summit of Badon Hill, arms akimbo. Every special effect my technos had created, heightened the tableau for audiences across Earth and Mars. A sky of delicate gold and pink had been created as the backdrop for our President. His black tunic displayed three moons representing Luna, Deimos and Phobos. A reminder of his dual world Empire! I was proud of my work !

His ministers, advisors and generals were arranged in a pyramidal hierarchy, standing on camouflaged platforms. A cynic like me enjoyed such blatant theatricality. Beside Maddigan stood his statuesque Natasha, with subliminal feeds to suggest she was an incarnation of the goddess, guiding Britain's destiny. I thought it might work on a few Pagan suckers.

The placement of the military was significant. Generals, not politicians, were on the first level of hierarchy. They stood beneath Natasha and Butch. One placement really caught my eye. Eco Minister, Sheila was the epitome of sulky and scowled at me because my own unprepossessing figure was stationed parallel to the military leaders and above her. I was relieved that I was not too top league beside McNulty and Alassam. Joe looked as smug as fuck on screen. My muttered, 'Tosser!' was satirical, not spiteful. Alassam's face was worn by care, with no trace of arrogance or pride.

It was almost a week later that I discovered a confidential file Myrna had transmitted to Joe. Her encryption had not copied me in. That pissed me off! The devious bitch had anonymously tried to sow seeds of doubt in Maddigan's mind about Alassam .

She inflated the significance of the General's relationship with High Druid Haggard. Initially, the Druids had demanded Alassam and his people on Lyonesse would support an assault on the Isle of Wight. Haggard planned to use their support for a pincer movement that would meet up with the Scandinavians and the other opportunists and malcontents. The latter were preparing to move furtively over the North Sea in boats and strato-cruisers.

Myrna's version was that Alassam had committed to an alliance with the pagans. He only came over to Maddigan to save himself after he was doubled-crossed by Tintagel.

The reality, I had long since uncovered, was very different. Loyal Alassam had told the white-haired old Druid to stuff it. Haggard exploded when his arrogance was so unexpectedly deflated. To add to his fury, was the fact he had already financed armament for the Afro soldiers, being confident of their supportive action. Thus, without warning, the High Druid changed target and went for Lyonesse. His announced intention was genocide. Surprisingly, given Alassam's reputation, he suffered a shattering defeat. Haggard struck with assistance from berserkers and mercenaries. Their unexpected assault kicked the shit out of the Anglo-Africans. Alassam had never anticipated such violent reprisal. The Rastaman's response was equally as unexpected and shocking. He wanted to save the lives of his outnumbered people. Lyonesse was abandoned. A few remaining civilians surrendered to Haggard. They were slaughtered.

Alassam, personally leading his army, fought back. He sailed over the Channel and crossed the peninsula in order to attack Tintagel. This attempted retribution failed. His forces were annihilated by undreamed of weaponry, developed within Tintagel's top-secret labs. Their technology was many times superior to anything Lyonesse, or even Wells, possessed. This event was blurred in Myrna's secret propaganda. Personally, I was just a bit unsure whether Alassam's judgement was askew or if he had already made a ruthless decision to align with Maddigan for revenge, instead of trying to recover Lyonesse. Maybe he decided to cut his losses, rather than engage in a battle he could well lose.

The end result was that a massive Afro-English army magically appeared on the outskirts of the Abbot's Palace. Everything went to high alert. With a sense of drama to match Maddigan's own, Alassam strode from his troops, alone and unarmed. He hailed the President as his Commander in Chief. Whether his action came from the heart or the head, he was greeted with incredulous adulation. He received a warm welcome as the champion of the Empire. Some described him as the Sir Launcelot to Maddigan's King Arthur. It was a useful legend to counter Druidry. The Afro-Lyonessians were citizens and provided with accommodation in military barracks and private homes where necessary. Alassam was appointed the military commander of all British forces. Why then had Myrna still tried to muddy the waters and send scurrilous information to McNulty?

Anyway, here we were with the British government posing on Badon Hill in a worshipful assembly around Maddigan. I studied the two generals for indications of rivalry or resentment. I reached an unfamiliar conclusion, being accustomed to the stab-in-the-back world of Helium's politics. These men were genuinely open and relaxed with one another. What I did notice were the injuries Alassam had suffered in the latest in a series of raiding parties from Tintagel. Brown make-up concealed bruising to his face, and he was leaning on a carved ritual staff for support. His shades were not a fashion statement either! The lengths to which he had gone for Maddigan's sake still amazed me. McNulty deserved credit too. In the old days he had honed his deception skills, by posing as my humble bodyguard, Manitoba Joe. I observed he was careful never to publicly contradict the black giant. He deferred to Alassam as the senior general. I would swear on my life this sensitivity was genuine. Eventually, I accepted the popular sentiment that they were twins of different colour, like you would find in a cat's mixed litter as Alassam once joked, such was their good-natured friendship. The only participants on Badon with snouts slightly out of joint were a few minor ministers who resented standing on the tier below the generals.

Maddigan delivered a slick morale-boosting speech to assure his people on two worlds of their safety and of the inevitability of their triumph over the host of pitiful enemies. All the rebels of Stonehenge and Wight would be punished. Any misunderstandings between Lyonesse and the Druids could be resolved, he lied to the cameras. Technology made their uniforms look like gold and each had a halo of light above his head. This was my creation, of course. Some might be embarrassed by my enhancements, feeling I went too far over the top. However, the popular audiences loved my melodramatic touches. Alassam and McNulty were cued to scowl like tough guys. The final extravagance of my production were views of a sky, seeming filled with fliers and British land troops at the foot of Badon. Special effects showed them spreading to the horizon, as if they numbered millions.

Straight after my fantastic presentation there was no rest. Key personnel comprising Alassam, McNulty, five cabinet ministers plus Natasha, myself and the cabinet, assembled in 'bug-swept' briefing room. I was there to present new super-security measures I had devised. Accomplishments like this were my pride and joy. Beside me was Teena, appointed as my administration assistant. That was Maddigan's idea.

I was proud of the high-grade technology that ensured our safety. None of it had existed before my appointment. I had 'borrowed' Helium's scientific blueprints. *Why not accept the praise for it?* I thought. Slightly tongue in cheek, my ministerial room replicated the interior of the Borgia's secret planning room as it was in Rome, back in the 15th century. This was from the idle research during my isolation at Dinas Emrys. My intention was to create a sense of dignity, sophistication and cunning to replace the previous lackadaisical design applied equally to layouts and administration.

I had been assigned as chairman by the First Lady after she gave me a one-to-one briefing. That was unexpected. Her intention was to assess my abilities and to emphasize my position for the ministers. After thoughtfully surveying the wooden ceiling, I stood up. I did not say a word, just stared at the gathering until I achieved respectful silence. An old trick. There would be no time wasted in democratic debate. I prefaced my presentation with a smile as dazzling as the sun rising on a clear summer's morning on Earth. The introduction was short. They liked that. I saw only one frown. That appeared on Sheila's brow. It was clear to her and the rest of the group that it would be advisable for anyone with reservations to keep it to themselves. I stressed that I spoke according to instructions from the President.

I was concise. This was to attune the Cabinet to the streamlined, efficient organization I had been instructed to set up. Wells would be under Natasha's regency. A quarter of the new model army McNulty had trained would transfer to Alassam's command. They would protect the capital and the First Lady. Such a responsibility visibly delighted Alassam. It gave him time to recover from his wounds too. Also such actions sent a message to Arch Druid. But he was was subtle. Haggard still paid lip service to Maddigan. The unrest and rebellion were theoretically nothing to do with him.

A concealed threat was uncovered by both my own agents and Joe's Mossad. They identified evidence of fliers, laser tanks, explosives, hallucinogen bombs, nerve gas and so forth stockpiled off the west coast of a secret Druid centre on Anglesey. No hostile alliances could be proven. There was no evidence that Haggard had links with the bands of brigands and malcontents converging around Stonehenge. There was similar uncertainty about the sea and air threats assembling in the North Sea. McNulty could stamp on the seemingly chaotic Salisbury Plain offensive, but there was the still a horde from Europe heading for the Isle of Wight. This was a dilemma.

The council's first proposal had been for the President to stay safely in Wells while Alassam went to repel the raiders on Salisbury Plain and McNulty would be the Isle of Wight's protector. I announced that Maddigan had made a spontaneous decision that he must be seen by his peoples as their heroic leader of the Empire. Perhaps the myth of his predecessor's last stand was at the back of his mind. I denied the Cabinet any debate or discussion. This was by Presidential order. Some members were disgruntled. However, Alassam's happy obedience to the Supreme Commander's wishes cooled them down. I would welcome an opportunity to talk to him and get to know him. Unfortunately, I was unable to do so right now.

When the meeting ended, several attendees gave me hard looks. Neither I nor McNulty were fully trusted by the higher echelons of the government.

Chapter 19

I resumed my role of Master of Disinformation. Myrna's communications were light years ahead of England's. I embedded delay features into newscasts our enemies might hack. Recordings of Maddigan ran more than six hours in retrospect. He could massacre his foes before they knew he was there.

During his seemingly live performance on Mount Badon, his army were making a strike 100 miles away. Disbelievers mocked his promise to rescue England's southern seaboard before dusk. They had been convinced the limitless military forces – made by special effects – were marching to the Isle of Wight. He convinced them this was his greatest concern. With my assistance, he led the world to believe that fiction. In reality, his troops were preparing for an imminent strike against the threatening hordes around Stonehenge. Viewers saw him and General McNulty shaking hands, crying 'Away for Victory!'

For undisclosed reasons he insisted that Teena and I physically witness the action. More puzzling was his insistence we should travel alone to Salisbury Plain. Why did he wish Teena to accompany me? Perhaps he wanted her trained in fieldwork espionage? I had an intuition she was privy to instructions I was unaware of. He was too devious by half!

Teena and I took off in a nondescript mini flier. Technos shuffled the British guidance satellites into fresh orbits, so our high-altitude fliers vanished into cloaked positions from which they could direct laser fire from space. Only Helium, and maybe Peking, had the ability to expose my surveillance and time lag trickery. McNulty's reputation would depend on how effective he would be in eradicating the ragged rabble on Salisbury Plain.

I had expected my beautiful colleague and I would go east to the battle. Instead, Natasha messaged we were to turn north into Wales. I shrugged. That might confuse or avoid hostile trackers. Another change of plan came five minutes later, ordering us to land in a small grove of trees.

'Fabulous fresh transport!' exclaimed Teena as we bumped down. She treated everything like a kid's adventure. She led me to a great clump of branches and bushes. Concealed beneath it all was a cloaked mini transporter. Access was given via her iris recognition. Inside was a treat! There were two glorious motorbikes. They were my *Norton* and her *Oustoure*. As we admired them, our transporter took off under automatic operation. As soon as we set off, Maddigan was on screen, ordering us to circle round and back to Dinas Emrys, my former home in Snowdonia. I obeyed. The President's subterfuge became clear. A fighter fleet cut across the flight route we would have taken. They came from the west. That was where the huge complex on Anglesey was located. I began to enjoy the unpredictable fun! The trickery of changes of identifiable vessels and direction. Maddigan appeared on screen, nodded to me, then instructed Teena, 'Sweet child? I want you and our young man to visit that concealed site. Eighty miles north-west of Salisbury Plain. Use the bikes now.' Although it made little sense to me, she understood.

'Lovely man!' exclaimed, shaking her long red locks. 'Fun begins. Away!'

Maddigan's goodbye words were, 'Jon, boyo? You will take care of her?' He should have known I would!

Teena kick-started her legendary *Oustoure*. I mounted my magnificent *Norton*. An inspired specialist had restored them to tip top shape. These formerly ludicrous petroleum fed machines were souped up beyond all recognition by the top grade of radio chargers. We celebrated by circling, doing wheelies and so on. Then we rode another ten miles and sat down for Cornish pasties and beer, olde worlde style. Having rested, we went off again.

It was not enemy soldiers who caught us by surprise. The attack came from an unexpected source. We paused at the crest of a wooded hill. From the corner of my eye, I glimpsed wild hounds, racing from the trees. They sensed we had spotted them and gave vent to savage baying. Inappropriately, Teena exclaimed, 'Doggies!' These 'cuties' were clever bastards.

Before we could accelerate from our steady 25 miles an hour along the track-cum-derelict road, they were on us. Half a dozen of them tried to hit our cycles from the sides. The main body slowed our progress by racing to and fro before us. Maybe they were once domestic pets from various species. Today they were similar, with fawn, short hair and physically slighter than the packs of wolves that infested Europe, but infinitely quicker. Their fangs were more terrifying; they were sharp as scythes and so long, they grew over their lower jaws like those of sabre-toothed tigers. All canines, though, need a leader to direct operations. In this pack he was a red eyed horror with a scar running along his left flank. Somehow, he decided Teena was the softest target. Or maybe he'd recognized the laser pistol I tugged from my holster while I kept my machine on the track.

Teena accelerated. He sprang up, snapping at her fingers that gripped the handlebars. I managed to draw my weapon. I fired a beam which went yards off its intended target. It is impossible to fire diagonally behind yourself while you try to control a *Norton* going at 60 mph. Of course, I lost control. The energy tank burned inside my thighs, and I went careening off the former road. I knew Teena's 'doggies' were about to dislodge her. She held her nerve. Meanwhile, I fell off my machine, and it tumbled into the thorny undergrowth, wheels in the air still spinning. The pack raced in for the kill. I heard a high-pitched scream. Full throttle Teena had accelerated into the slavering beasts surrounding me. She knifed through them. I could not decipher what she was shouting until she braked, waving with her gun. The hounds scattered. Finally, I rallied. Smashing aside those eager fangs, I swung up behind her while she still lasered them. We roared away. Going at top speed, she cut through a roadside screen of wild shrubbery and ferns. After 50 yards, she spun round, back in control, and had us back on the track.

My arms gripped tightly about her slim, firm waist. Even the unexpected sexual stirring did not console me for the loss of my lovely Norton. Her 'legend' cycle bellowed at full power, carrying us away from the pack. Before long, I signalled that I had seen a pot-holed road that would take us to our destination. When we came to a scattering of standing stones, maybe just glacier-carried rocks, we halted, so we could calm down and recover. The respite was brief.

We relaxed on sweet, green grass, our backs to a ten-foot monolith. I thanked this beautiful girl for saving my life. For the first time, brushing aside her veil of red hair, I kissed her. She responded gently. Suddenly, she announced, 'Look where we're sat! It's a ring of mushrooms.' She was right. They looked like magic mushrooms, the sort that don't grow on Mars. Any chance to research psilocybins was rudely interrupted.

'Hey, Ginger! Wanta real man's beef bayonette up yers?'

Four lumbering lads surrounded us. The leader was a long-haired kid in his twenties. Beside him towered a teenaged apprentice thug. Honest! He was seven foot tall! The others were ginger twins with watery blue eyes that reminded me of Myrna. The last was a tattooed black monster. I despaired of the body I received on Rig 1. Despite being skinny, speccy and frail, I stood up impersonating a confident guy. I answered their opening line as if it was a friendly quip. That was not easy!

'How do, mate!' If I'd acted too self-assured and said, 'son', I would have antagonized him. 'We got a beer left. Fancy one?'

'We fancy your bit of gash more, fucker.'

The teen giant suggested, 'We tie him up so's he can watch? Blow the cobwebs off his nob, eh?'

'Why the fuck you want to do that with an old bloke and his bit of candy?' I said, relaxing my body and smiling at them.

The leader whipped a 12 inch blade from his belt. He smirked, conscious his buddies were enjoying his bullying techniques. I would not last two minutes against one of them. A gamble was all I had for our defence.

Looking at his big blade, I asked, 'Making up for a little dick, are you?'

Aware my life was in my hands, I looked into his eyes and said, with a lazy chuckle: 'Here you are, mate. Have a drink.' I offered him a large bottle of eight per cent stout. His pals started laughing at him. He hesitated. I knew I had won. He had chosen to join in the joke to keep face. He must act as if he thought what I'd said was dead quick and funny.

'Get our friends some more of them other bottles,' I ordered Teena. To assure them we weren't planning to escape to the bike, I began skinning up a joint. I lit up, inhaled, and passed it round. They responded, clearly impressed by my balls. Unbelievable! The knife vanished. So did all our bottles and the block of solid I had placed on the grass. I maintained my grin. Thankfully, they did too. Happy, they swaggered away, appeased.

About a hundred feet down the primrose meadows cloaking the hill beneath us, there was a flash. Four laser hits killed them instantly. The funny thing was that I felt sorry for them. Simulated charm can mutate into genuineness it seems. Shit! Minds work weirdly!

Out from the sparse grove of trees behind us, strolled two hooded assassins. Their gait was female. Only when they were within a few yards of us did our rescuers reveal their identities. One was Chinese. It was my acquaintance Janine, Head of Chinese Espionage. She was the one who had dispatched the four muggers with those rapid blasts. She'd changed her of undercover identity, from being a Presidential secretary!

Her companion was the greater surprise. I did not even know who she was her at first. She had silver white hair, shaped into spikes like icicles that stood out from her head. The effect was more startling because of her coffee-coloured skin.

'Alisha!' I exclaimed. 'I'm over the moons to see you. How did you get here? No one would recognize you as that femme fatale who pretended to try to stab the President, so Joe got his job!'

'Idiot!' she replied with a hint of her Indian inflection. 'Not being identified was my obvious intention.'

How was I so thick as to have believed she was one of Madame Anais's working girls? I suddenly remembered her hostility at our last meeting in Madame Anais's Rig 1 'Palace'. She was hiding it. But it was still there.

I retrieved my confident veneer by greeting her companion: 'Janine! I am so happy we meet again! Tell you what, if one of you ladies would be good enough to recover the bottles and blow from the deceased's pockets, we'll toast you by way of thanks.' I admired my own charismatic cool. Certain admirable traits cannot be denied!

Janine inclined her head by way of greeting. I wondered why the most senior head of China's Secret Service was here, literally in the field? And why on Earth was Alisha beside her? I waited politely. It could be my request for this Chinese lady to collect bottle was a faux pas. Her reply made me think she was telepathic. Not forgiving. More like I was simple for her to read.

'You should have paid greater attention, Simon, to security on Mars. After all, for years I've followed all your nightly private conversations with Governor Golden.'

I was shocked. 'I knew that,' I lied. 'More to the point, how did you identify me in my new face and body?'

'As easily as I hacked into that travel technology centre and your secret place on Rig 1.'

I said nothing. We all sat on the grass. I had been shut up. The beer never tasted better, though! I noticed Teena's restraint. She stayed uncharacteristically silent, I guessed because she held more information about these women than I was aware if.

Alisha also remained silent. Much to my surprise Janine opened up about the political position of her secretive Empire. She laughed (I'd rarely seen that before) and said I had missed China's overtures to India. Since India was Britain's dearest friend on the Red Planet and on Earth, she was astonished how blind Joe and I had been to that development.

I suspected teleporters brought the Sino-Indian allies to Earth. That would explain her confidence and preparedness for entente cordial. She gave no hints how much she knew about the Empire's teleportation.

Actually, my own transformation affected me at present more than political games. I suddenly asked Alisha how I looked best – as Simon or Jon? Teena spontaneously answered for her, 'As you are now, Jon! Sensitive and clever.'

Alisha pursed her lips and went for a smoke behind the monolith.

Teena murmured "I will be expecting your explabation of who your ex-whores are."

Chapter 20

General McNulty's Mossad-woven web was impossible to unravel. My suspicion was that his Mossad Israel spy network had worked with Maddigan and Natasha to organize the Salisbury action. In addition, Israel could well have facilitated Janine's dialogue with India and even other nations on Terra as well as their provinces on the Red Planet.

I would discover some explanations imminently. As I was thinking over our position, a huge military strato-cruiser descended in the meadows next to our fairy ring and monoliths. We marched to meet the vessel, me in the lead with Teena wheeling her priceless *Oustoure* and Janine and Alisha behind. A party of smartly attired soldiers emerged from the ship to assist and escort us. They brought us and the bike aboard.

McNulty was waiting for us and we boarded the craft immediately. His hug was strong and affectionate, though abrupt. He barely nodded to my babe trio, Alisha, Teena and Janine. I wanted to check if he would to be particularly cautious about the latter. After all, Janine Suee was the supremo of China's Secret Service. There was no time to discuss anything because he was in a frantic hurry to launch the offensive. As a precaution, he told some guys to fit us up with breathing apparatus as protection against hallucinogenic gasses, that might be launched in armour-piercing mini missiles. Later, we found this sophistication was beyond the abilities of the Salisbury Plain thugs, looters, barbarians and mercenaries.

When we were equipped, our flier shot off, vertically, at breathless speed to the edge of the ionosphere. Joe's full attention was on the screen. Without hesitation, he barked an order. Instantly, I mean that literally, his forces stormed into an overwhelming offensive from land and sky.

He made no attempt to prevent Janine from studying our military strategies or weaponry. She leaned towards me, inscrutable as ever, with an aura of sweet perfume emanating from her long, shiny black hair. She explained, 'You will be unaware that Governor Golden and President Maddigan just confirmed a formal alliance between the People's Republic of China, India and the British Empire. It's applicable on Terra and Mars. Myrna Golden would have been unable to inform her husband. Your graduated security link must have prevented it.'

She was taunting me. She was amused by my anger at being excluded from the loop! Myrna, perhaps like the Maddigans, was using me for some unknown reason. Janine gave me the impression that she had credited me with greater subtlety. She must enjoy my humiliation.

I watched in fascination as 'Mossad McNulty' implemented the Maddigan and Natasha strategy. Just as cabinet calculated, this horde descending from Stonehenge was unprepared for being attacked itself. These bemused adversaries had been easily fooled into believing we had a doddering fool for President who would go charging from Wells to the Isle of Wight in panic to stop an invasion there. The 'Stoners' – as Teena named them – thought they were only a stand-by ready to hit the British from the rear, while they were being beaten trying to stop an overseas invasion of the Isle of Wight. The reverse was true. McNulty's impeccably uniformed troops were professionally trained and knew exactly what he expected of them. The Stoners lacked even uniforms or compatible arms. On screen, we witnessed white-robed Druids, Scandinavian giants in jeans and T-shirts, a sewer load of Arabs, and a mix of Caucasian garbage in tabards displaying coats of arms from half a dozen European countries. I was amused to see a significant number of fighters displaying stars and stripes of the long extinct USA. Presumably, these were cut-price, second-hand or surplus army stock!

When we rose to the edge of Earth's atmosphere, McNulty drew my attention to our opponents' hilariously inept use of drones and lasers. Joining in with Joe's laughter, I drew Teena to the screen to take a peek. To my concern, her face was as pale as what was called snow. She was struggling to put on a breathing mask but did not secure it. Stupidly, I forgot she had never been in space before. Alisha watched me contemptuously. Probably jealous!

Very quickly, I wrapped my arms about Teena and held her close to reassure her. I made soothing noises, although I kept my eyes on the screens. The majority of 'Stoner' satellites, including military ones, were built from organic materials. What madness! There was sufficient wood for a forest in orbit. Which lunatic created this? To replace steel with tree trunks offered disadvantages that would be obvious to a drooling idiot. Their sparse electronic shields provided a feeble defence.

Our crew hooted at the cluster of enemy sputniks, performing a light show for us. They apparently fired randomly to assist their comrades around Stonehenge. Prior to our shooting down every one of them, something disturbing caught my attention. Much of the other side's fly-ware displayed a star within a crescent moon and, oddly, a human head with antlers. Though more curious than the surplus uniforms, it made no more sense. Before I could set my mind to it, McNulty's strato-cruiser wiped out the last enemy satellite within our orbit. It had taken a matter of minutes. By comparison with Maddigan's technology, and the refinements I had stolen from Helium, the organic spaceships had been as sophisticated as clubs resisting lasers!

McNulty swooped down to participate in engaging the Salisbury marauders. 'Massacre' would be a more accurate description than 'engage'. The rebels, mercenaries, or whatever, were being wiped out with minimal effort. They had never anticipated such an attack. They believed they were only back up for an Isle of Wight invasion. Being so unprepared, three quarters of the soldiers and the entire flier fleet were out of action, mainly thanks to Joe's ruthless laser fire and clouds of hallucinogens that created a madhouse of men and women screaming, violent with fear and unable to distinguish phantoms of nightmare from reality. His own regiments were highly disciplined, wore filters and masks and outnumbered them. His Mossad maxim was, 'efficiency not mercy.'

Troops streamed from Maddigan's cruisers. Teena and I were monitoring events. However, a surprise participant appeared; a screen scan revealed Maddigan was beside the battlefield. Although he was being kept away from the slaughter for his safety, no one could accuse him of cowardice. He proudly personified the British Empire. When his flier deposited him dangerously close to the hand-to-hand skirmishes around the Stonehenge monolith, he apparently had no trepidation. Unsurprisingly, the paunchy old man in military fatigues was not an identified target for the retreating rabble. When a rock narrowly missed Maddigan's bonce while I was recording him, the viewers could see he was unperturbed and looked alert.

A powerful explosion came from the direction of the Stonehenge stone circle. A rock of several tonnes hurtled through the air. An ogre must have got loose and wanted a go at chucking boulders! What the hell was going on? Before I could find out, bodyguards swept me away. They said I was needed to direct the live broadcast. I had no time to argue. My holster vibrated. A message coming through. I pulled out my device and scowled at the screen. I saw Myrna's immobile face. Mockingly, she asked if 'hubby' had avoided having his head blown off.

'Head still intact, Ma'am,' I snapped. 'If you check transmission, you'll see I'm entering the stone circle. McNulty's guys will lead me across the field. My assistants are here to present the victory speeches.'

Myrna asked what else I would show on screen. Auto-censorship was applied, as she knew well. The President authorized what would be reshaped for general consumption. To annoy her, I said I was too busy to talk. I had to provide instant access for the First Lady, Natasha, to view in Wells. Myrna snapped, 'That Chinese woman must stay well clear of screen. Make sure to do it.' She had hacked to my secret feed. Unless the myth of female intuition was operating. That ridiculous suspicion about Janine had stirred her fury. She cut me off.

By coincidence, Natasha's dignified features instantly replaced Myrna's on screen. Her calm, deep tone made a pleasant contrast to the previous shrill venom. She asked me to ensure McNulty would be at the centre of mopping up operations. His peak of acclaim was scheduled for after the Isle of Wight battle. That victory was far from certain. Realistically, if he perished, I was still tasked with creating PR for billions to celebrate him as a tragic dead hero.

Nataha's toughness shocked me. I managed a warm smile, explaining to her I was needed right now to stage-manage the riot taking place at Stonehenge. To show my consideration, I zoomed into close ups of Maddigan on the field. He looked good: the garish battle kit, a smear of blood over his forehead and he carried a 4-foot portable laser in the design of an antique gun. The familiar Welsh voice was full of confidence: 'Friends and allies of our proudly united Empire! Today's outcome will affect human history for the next thousand years. In less than thirty minutes, we have eradicated these rebel scum at Stonehenge. Here, in Britain's heart, Fate guides our war against the forces of evil. Behind it all are vile religions. The Caliphate are a malevolent power that, like disease, infected all of our dominions on Mars and now look to England itself. The British Empire welcomes the friendship of all nations and all races. Thus, all you free people have chosen to join us. Our clarion call was answered by the entire human race. Thank you, dearest India, standing shoulder to shoulder with Britain. Thank you persecuted Israel for recognizing our integrity and, like us, pushing back tyranny whether from Arabia or nearer home. Most of all, I thank Africa for giving us General Alassam and his soldiers who guard our capital. And what praise can I find words for when I behold General McNulty, who has driven vermin from sacred Stonehenge?'

Naturally, everything was pre-recorded. But it was true and accurate as to what had occurred in reality. For closure, I directed a golden panoramic swing around the battlefield of our triumph and dubbed inspirational music to the views of our mighty fleet coming down from the heavens.

The President wrapped up with inspirational words, 'Beware, all, of evil intent! We march. NOW!'

Blank screen.

Chapter 21

Teena and I had felt completely unnecessary during the Stoney campaign. The sole explanation for it was that she had been assigned to observe me and assess my commitment to England.

Again, I remembered her trips behind the bushes for a pee when we were biking across the country. On one occasion, I had definitely spotted the lined Taffy face on her screen, when I checked she was safe. She told me nothing about it. I could only assume she was receiving secret instructions. The length of time she was behind the hawthorn suggested she had a seriously full bladder – or it was an order for her.

After one of these 'comfort breaks', she let slip that our next mission was one involving a flier, rather than our beloved motorbikes. I said nothing at the time. I nearly forgot that until McNulty passed on details of the President's next mission. While he finished his 'mopping up' on Salisbury Plain, Teena and I were to make our way, alone, to the Solent, facing the Isle of Wight. We travelled in disguise and by a disappointingly shabby, wreck of a flier. I speculated we might serve as a decoy for enemy bugging before their air and sea fleets arrived for the invasion of the island. Even a meaningless action creates immense confusion in hostile minds searching for plots and espionage. Maybe my own reputation might set them thinking it was I who would initiate our actions. If so, they would squander resources and intelligence on us. I do not mean to be egoistical, though.

Conversely, travelling by this rusty can could be intended to enhance our disguises as semi-tramps. That might mean an enemy would not spot us. I dug deeper and decided that they were likely to hack into our transmission but dismiss our rust heap as the source.

My devious abilities were working brilliantly. Nevertheless, I was worried, at the back of my mind, about after effects from the surgery on my brain. Occasionally, I acted bizarrely out of character, especially in a peculiar suggestion I made to Teena. I said I'd a fantastic idea to decorate the vessel with magical symbols. Being Teena, she expressed no surprise. Almost instantly she hauled out half a dozen colour containers conveniently stashed in the litter at the side of the flier. I recognized that she was painting what is called an I-Ching Hexagram, comprising a straight line between two broken ones, topped by a broken one beneath two straight ones. My red-haired sorceress informed me this was Hexagram 59, named 'Dispersion (Dissolution)'. I couldn't understand a word of what she read to me from her tablet. Something about an army sounded appropriate. Like all predictions, it was gibberish.

That rig 1 trepanning must have enhanced my artistic skills. Simon Edge never had time for arty shit. As Jon Masque, I did. On the opposite side of the flier, I did an amazing, brilliant picture of a youth in a blue tunic and a sack on his back, followed by his pet dog or cat. He was looking up at a blue sky and walking off a cliff. I was immensely proud of it. Teena whispered, 'Tarot', but I did not understand what she was talking about. It was a bit creepy the way it appeared in my head. Sometime, I must have seen a picture like his, my Simon reassured me. As Jon I relaxed again.

Being in a peaceful, dreamy state, I let Teena take my hand and lead me back inside the ship's cabin. We made love. Then we slept, arms around one another. This girl loved the qualities of Masque, not Simon. Just the same, Simon's rationality dealt with the oceanic turmoil in my brain. He programmed my synapses to return my consciousness to what we call 'normal' when I woke next morning.

We slept late. We kissed, held one another, and made love again and again. Our relationship was deepening. But we had a part to play in protecting millions of people. We must continue the slow journey in the direction of Southampton and Portsmouth.

A transmission came through that explained the art of my function. It was the President himself. He was ruddy faced and jolly.

'Well, well, my master of subterfuge. Look you at you, the cat has drunk the cream! You have anticipated the plan. No matter, Hayling Island. Misdirection is essential as well you know.'

He over-estimated my deductive gifts. Also, I knew nothing whatsoever about Hayling Island. With his habitual sonorous voice and poetic fancy – some said 'verbose' – he led me through my task.

There must be confusion as to his whereabouts. I was to direct a fake appearance of him on Hayling. His visit would be accompanied by a visit to a sacred yew tree. This, he explained, was thirty feet in girth, claiming to have been there over 3,000 years. Special effects were required; a golden aura would shine around him there, and as he went to the nearby Iron Age shrine. Was this proof of his return to Druidic friends? It aimed to give Haggard pause. The Vikings, mercenaries and foreign marauders would suspect this was a sham. Too overdone to be for real. To compound their fear, I must simulate him ending the tour by arriving at a pile of grey rocks that were the ruins of Sinah Heavy Aircraft Battery. The main espionage advisors of the invaders would interpret this as absolute proof that the armies and fliers of his people were about to assemble on Hayling Island in order to strike at the attack on the Isle of Wight.

I was very impressed, though I lied that I had anticipated this diversionary scheme. He beamed and said he was 'chuffed' – another dialect word, though not of Welsh derivation. Like a conjuror, he revealed a further piece of skulduggery.

'I hope you won't be upset if I show you how I used Myrna Golden for further confusion. Your lads in tech-espionage have been magnificently trained by you. Cast your gaze on what they achieved for me.'

He passed me his large screen device; Myrna's face was on screen! Here was a transmission that did not actually take place.

My team had delivered a miracle. It was a cut-up of recordings from the enormous library of the Governor of Helium. Even I was unable to detect the joins – as you might say – for face, lip-synching and dialogue. How on Earth had they achieved this?

'Dahling!' she seemed to gush, shifting to 3D mode to be more imposing. 'You must be aware of the new threat to me. It's essential you continue your sterling support of Madigan. This McNulty man achieved an overwhelming victory at Stonehenge. Unexpected and impressive. However, I believe the Caliphate here on Mars manipulated him as a diversion from their own plan to lead *jihad* across Mars and overwhelm us. If we fall, so too will the British Empire on Earth. Moreover, impeccable sources inform me that the Caliphate has gained access to a technological wonder. They are able to teleport ships and soldiers to England in a flash.'

I heard a mock-up of my own voice mumbling about how we would fight our enemies wherever they were. None of my wit, I observed.

Myrna's laughter was created to come across full volume. She revealed the purpose of the *jihad*. After the rabble of invaders had done the hard work, hundreds of vessels would teleport to Europe and Arabia, eliminating Israel, Druids and the Papacy. And creating an Islamic theocracy throughout the entirety of two planets.

My judgement was, 'Wow!'

'Tell you what, my boyo,' chuckled Maddigan. 'That masterpiece equals any of yours, eh?'

He was a hard act to follow. We had to try when the time came.

Once more, our rattling transport managed to fight gravity and continue the journey to the south.

The plan was for us to reach either site of Southampton or of Portsmouth in another hour and a quarter. I decided a very slow zig-zag course was required. The indeterminacy resulted from an unexpected blackout of all transmissions north of the Isle of Wight. It included satellite surveillance. Here was the most sophisticated technology we had encountered from the enemy. Who was responsible? Haggard's lot had topped my suspect list for the overthrow of the President. That felt wrong. No way would the Pagan fraternity use this level of scientific sophistication.

In the cloudless blue sky, the sun reached its zenith, its brightness dazzling us. Unfamiliar brightness was reflected back at us from the water as we reached the Channel. I became aware we were losing altitude. No time to act! Mercifully, we dropped to the ground with a padded bump! The cause embarrassed me. In a wonder age of science, where we can fly between planets, all machines require power. Ludicrously, we had forgotten to recharge our flier. Being such an antique, this blasted thing was dependent on electricity.

I swore. Teena laughed. Nothing could ever dampen her optimism. For her everything was a delightful surprise, a new adventure. She told me to calm down because it was such a lovely fresh day. Attempting to recover dignity, I pulled out a little treasure from my pocket. I spread an old paper printed map on the short grass on which we had landed. That was my act of pretending to be competent in map-reading.

With a tone of authority, I explained, 'Over here – that pink area is Lymington and northeast of it is Brockenhurst. I've decided to swing off east toward Portsmouth, rather than Southampton. That will take us above a town named Waterlooville. This hill goes from there down towards the sea. It was where Portsmouth city was, a big, big naval base. That was in an age of battleships on the oceans. Amazing, isn't it?'

Teena's greatest attraction was in her ability to appear fascinated, impressed, by my learning. My truncated history lesson was a winner. From the height where we had come down, we had a perfect view of the sea and sky beyond the harbour.

The invasion fleet appeared on the horizon. They approached very rapidly. Sea warfare was completely alien to me. McNulty warned me earlier these boats were bigger than old time ones. Each of them carried hundreds of fighters, intending to land with overwhelming firepower that would ensure immediate occupation of the island. Soon, fliers would come from the blue horizon with the hardware to support the slaughter of remaining defenders. Physical occupation by foot soldiers was an essential preliminary to full control. Forget lasers and drones, soldiers with hand arms are needed to terrorize and subdue a population.

Geometric applications on my vid triangulated the point where the invaders and sea power would meet. This was a time to check in with McNulty. I activated the amusing transmission protocol.

My screen lit up and I spoke to 'Granny'. The face and voice concealed the identity of McNulty. Natasha had helped me set up this little fiction. With the assistance of a dreary background and uneven volume, the special effects were very convincing. One glance, and most hackers would start to yawn with boredom.

'Good afternoon, Granny!' I greeted Joe. 'My girlfriend and I ran out of fuel before we got to the camp site. Can't complain, mind you. Lovely view of the fishing boats. I never knew how popular it was, here by the stream. I swear to you there must be 20 parties of anglers. They do trips down the river too.'

The imitation old lady's voice sounded concerned: 'Oh, Grandson! I so worry for you in these country parts. I heard there was another outbreak of those flying ants close to where you are. They were all over my geraniums last month.'

'Yes, Gran. We've seen lots of them already. I need to begin spraying repellent within the next half hour, so we're not bitten. An elderly man I spoke to said we'd have been better going to the seaside. And going walking on the beach.'

I had warned Joe a strato attack was imminent. My implication was he should act immediately. It was easy enough to work out that Ryde, guarding the eastern side of the Solent, was the prime strategic site. The air attackers would inevitably sweep south to rendezvous with the sea fleet heading for Sandown Bay.

Granny excused herself to alter the setting of her din-din up from 5 to 8. Teena was muffling her giggles until transmission ended. For her this was immense fun, all a hilarious game. I hugged her, nuzzling into her glorious red hair, blowing in the breeze.

War broke loose. From the sky and sea lasers were targeting the Isle of Wight. So sudden, so intense, was their fire that the sunny day was dimmed by smoke clouds blowing from burning buildings all around the shores. The sun was eclipsed as it thickened. My message to 'granny' was barely in time.

The invaders prepared for their second wave of attacks. In the nick of time the coalition appeared as if by a miracle to block them. The black clouds formed by fire and destruction tore apart to let through daylight. The immense strato-fleet of Britain and its allies emerged from the blinding brilliance of the sun in overwhelming numbers. The raiders had insufficient momentum to press on with their advance. McNulty's armada rent the heavens once more with laser lightning. Additional firepower and even more awesome support from the drones and satellites orbiting the planet. Silver beams struck the invaders from the invisible margins of the sky. The seas swallowed dozens of their cruisers within minutes.

Our flier may have been a scrap heap, but my recording equipment was the best I have ever used. I focussed into the heavens to record the most dramatic record of battle the world ever saw. A group of vessels belonging to one of our allies – I'm fairly certainly China – created what was later known as a 'fire wall'. A score or more of the enemy fighters were enveloped by huge clouds of flames that came pouring through the air. All that remained was twisted, blackened wreckage dropping into the waves. Despite my shock, I was able to continue to record some survivors who managed to eject seconds before their ships were absorbed by fire. They were thrown higher into the heavens by the force of the explosions and then they fell, somersaulting towards the water. Survivors would be the quicker thinking professionals from the leading cruisers. They must have remembered their training and activated levitation wrist bands to give them more chance of survival when they hit the sea.

The Solent and the Channel were filled with multitudes of swimmers and dead bodies. Luckier individuals directed their levitation kits to land along the eastern beaches of the Isle of Wight. The marauders in sea ships were the most fortunate because many made it to safety to land on the shore they had intended to invade.

While I was oblivious to anything except what I was filming, Teena coaxed our humble two-seater, barely six feet above the ground, up Portsdown Hill. Finally, using manual control, she brought us down on the other side to a swamp, once a town known as Cosham. I was really glad I had spent so many hours confirming the geographical minutiae. It paid off. A short time later, the little flier collapsed upon the sandy shore of the Solent.

Even before we could alight, Maddigan was on screen. He was the consummate diplomat, making everyone feel special.

'My dear Jon, you and Teena! Hello, poppet,' he waved to her coyly. 'I have not the words adequately to thank you.'

He could be as sweet as honey.

Chapter 22

Barely a quarter of an hour later, the multi-national fliers began landing across the beach and a swathe of flat land that would once have been a common. The Strategy Team had determined the troops needed a period of relaxation before the next nexus of action would be dealt with. Viewers all over Terra and Mars would be impressed by the scene of thousands of fighters from many nations flowing onto that wide, sandy expanse of Southsea's coast to stretch their legs and breathe in fresh sea air. My PR crew were exemplary in their dramatic presentation. The hearts of our viewers would be uplifted by the wonder of the British Empire and its friends.

Apart from his care for the soldiers and the publicity angle, the President also had a practical consideration. Wisely, I thought, he decided he did not want armies storming across the Solent, so soon after the battle that had already terrified the population of the Isle of Wight. He wanted feelings of reassurance to be brought to them.

From behind me, a voice growled, 'How you doing, my mate?'

'Fuck's sake! McNulty!' I shouted, almost forgetting myself and calling him 'Joe'.

He looked good. I'd have chosen scarlet and gold, like a space opera hero. His choice was low profile khaki fatigues. I did observe a brace of medals recently pinned to his chest for his services. I wondered what message it would send to key individuals in Mossad and in Helium. His beard had been pruned to a macho heavy stubble and his hair had grown longer. The masses would love that touch!

I gave Teena a kiss before Joe and I strolled toward the sea edge, for a private chat, well away from human or machine spies. We kept our hands moving across our faces to frustrate lip-readers.

Now was a time for us to appraise ourselves and our place in this multiple espionage. Bonds between Israel and Myrna were strong and had been maintained with Maddigan at the same time. Although we were aware of Alisha's negotiations with Janine, I remained cautious of the latter. China was likely to go along with an alliance with Britain on Mars because the Caliphate was an infinitely greater threat there than Arabia was here on Terra. I might still be a casualty of Alisha's deviousness which had involved secret schemes involving Janine. As for McNulty? After her affair with him, my closeness with the guy might be gone forever. It upset me.

I planned to lead into it by means of a man-gossip about Alisha's spikey silver hair. But when I turned to check the beach behind us, I spotted the lady herself. The President was beside her and she was leading a black horse for him. I needed to have a word before he fell off and killed himself.

Once again, I was interrupted. I felt the vibration of a live message come through. I pulled out my viewer. Myrna was on screen.

'I'll leave the lovebirds with privacy,' McNulty snorted. 'Still think that babe's hair is right bleedin' crap.'

'Hang on matey boy! We're doing a dual greeting,' I told him, shifting focus so Myrna saw us both.

Something about her shagged out appearance was really sexy to the lurking Simon in me. I wanted to beat her; give her a slap at least. 'I have followed Mister Madman's faster than light triumph,' Myrna commented bitchily. 'Congratulations to you, General Joe. You are in line for a Mossad Agent of the Year award, no doubt. No injuries, I trust? Simon's not been too rough?'

Nicely done, bud, I thought. Then I went business-like as Myrna liked me to act, by enquiring, 'My sources indicate you've a reason to speak to both of us together. You see how well I know you, honey?'

Perversely, her ravaged face and body made me eager to have sex with her. I longed to beat her, give her a black eye. Simon wanted to punch and kick her. After, she could punish Jon. For a moment I wondered if I might be a bit unbalanced.

There was a sneer on those thin lips as if she guessed what I was thinking. She asked Joe, 'Are you still hiding things from your stupid friend? Like troll corpses?'

I saw she ambushed him successfully, because he threw his arm round my shoulder to hug me, stuttering, 'I'd no time to update him. You want to stir trouble.'

This time the interruption was ludicrous. Maddigan had tried to dismount his black steed and got a foot caught in the stirrups! McNulty broke away from our discussion and raced to assist him. When the Welshman attempted to control the beast by tugging at its reins, it tried to savage him with gnashing teeth.

Alisha saved the day. She had a way with animals. While she soothed the stallion, McNulty helped Maddigan down from the saddle. The expression on the Welshman's face assured me he might reconsider attempting this kind of stunt again. How wrong I could be.

Chapter 23

There was little time to rest on our laurels. Within 24 hours Maddigan, in his competent avatar, required McNulty and his 'shock troops' to begin cleaning up the mess on the island. Every detail came to me – snap, snap, snap. There would be total clearance of the invaders who were trying to fight against us in a hopeless cause. The President wanted them either dead or imprisoned. My propaganda responsibilities were of equal importance as the battle strategies. The whole allies must be portrayed as glorious heroes in the liberation. The population of the Isle of Wight should be rapturous. It would culminate in the Triumph procession by our commander in chief.

Where deception is required, I can be tireless. In less time than it took Teena and I to get from Stonehenge to Portsmouth, my multitude of technicians, scientists, tacticians and adepts of IT sorcery had been established in units beneath protective camouflage with detailed instructions regarding the special effects I wanted them to create. Using sky drones and a few brave souls on the ground around Ryde, they were to broadcast McNulty's cleansing the land of the forces of evil. The phrase was added subliminally to transmissions.

By sunrise I implemented my schemes as the General swooped down on the enemy. My own attention flickered between two screens. One showed the true situation of his retribution, the other my enhancement of our number of troops, fliers and sea fleets for the benefit of audiences across both Earth and Mars. The latter was also impressive thanks to world-wide allies. I observed that the numbers of friends, particularly from China, had rapidly increased once the action went so decisively in Maddigan's favour. Even Australia and Russia publicized their token presence. There was absolutely no doubt now that victory lay ahead for Britain and her friends. However, I wondered whether alliances would be as firm if open war with the Caliphate broke out on the Red Planet.

This thought impelled me to check my own back. I recognized my former butler, bodyguard and buddy, Manitoba Joe, outranked me in his military importance. Just the same, my role appeared to free me from accountability in most actions. I did not have to justify my private contact with General Alassam, protecting the President's wife back in Wells. Previously, I speculated that the African would grow envious of McNulty's glory. In his place, I would deeply resent it. I felt an urge to check him out. Although I was not fully certain of my own motives, I did fear he might be uncertain about my own loyalties. He had seen much evidence McNulty and I were once close. He knew my reputation for being devious too. I hoped a friendly, 'How you doing?' contact could be taken at face value.

On screen I greeted the immobile dusky face. The dreadlocks, plaited beard and ancient studded leather armour he wore added to his striking presence. What made him even more impressive was the aura of physical power. His massive and powerful body, along with the two-foot-long machete he clutched in his left hand, would daunt anyone. Let alone me in my wimpish Masque form. What can you say as openers to a fella like that?

'Hello, General. I'm Jon. Jon Masque. Not sure if you'll remember me?'

Humility was my least used trait. Today it worked like a dream. His white teeth flashed. With a 'Hey, Man! I remember you', he set me at ease. I presented myself, jokingly, as 'a town planner on a national scale.' But I coyly confessed I was a town planner who found he had been dropped on a battlefield. He loved it! I declared I wanted a chat with him while McNulty, the man who had recommended me for my post, was in battle and so forth. I wanted to be sure Alassam wouldn't think I wanted to step on his toes. If he was having any difficulties, I would be more than happy to serve him in any way I could. For my own part, I wanted him as a friend. No bullshit, I told him. I wanted him to judge me by how I kept my word.

Already he was warming to me. My choice of words was careful. Actually, it was genuine too. He replied, 'I see you a man with honour. Respect for that. You don' need to be shy, man. You got same rank as me and McNulty. Civilian. That's all, ya know? You're a brave guy, you know that. Youse the one that went to spy on them bastards what attack us. You no coward. I say again, respect.'

Perhaps to put my mind at rest, he revealed he had contacted McNulty to offer military reserves if they were needed. There was no threat to Wells. He hesitated. Then he said, the Eco Minister had tried to encourage him to strike Tintagel to recover Lyonesse.

'That Sheila, old babe's a bitch. Don't trust her none. Let's get real, Jon, we're guys. Biology sends us shagging anything coming on to us. Even a Sheila. Buy. I be a'telling. The body, the face – not too bad at all, savvy? Only sometin' 'bout her sends spiders up my spine. Be wrong I feel. Most of all, I don' trust her. Danger there. Poor dumb Maddigan doesn't realize, I guess. Envy you, my friend. That kid with the ginger hair to her ass, she is ultimate. You wake up with empty pocket one morning. But worth it.'

He was a great guy. He thought Natasha was impressive in her running of the southwest area. He had a genuine liking for her as well as her husband. We agreed ordinary people, Anglo-Indians as well as Anglo-Africans, believed in the President. They were all resistant to the religious doctine and sorcery peddled by Druid and Roman Catholic enemies.

'But it is not religion we need,' he said, holding up an amulet on a cord around his bullish neck. 'We need the magic of the good heart. That's what President Maddigan got. Druids? Evil, man. Evil.'

We ended our communication on a friendly tone. What stayed in my mind were his closing words: 'What bugs me is own people of Africa, got no presence on your place. I mean, like, on Mars.' That was an issue where I might assist him to negotiate with Myrna?

Moments later, I received a peculiar order to go to the beach and look to the sky. Things were 'hotting up'! I explained to Alassam, who assured me he would be watching out for whatever bulletin came from me. We exchanged friendly goodbyes.

I did as I was told. What met my eyes was extraordinarily impressive. This was a sight unfamiliar to the little island where the world-wide assault had been directed. I had prepared to impress my audiences and fake the extent of our strength. McNulty had gone one better.

Like hornets – a species never seen on my home planet, but I like the sound of the words – swarms of fliers buzzed in circles overhead. In awesome formations they then dipped towards the island. A flash of light blinded me. Our lasers were converting the hostiles into bloody joints of meat. A series of explosions and dark clouds of smoke over the east side of the Isle of Wight demonstrated the zeal and overkill of our forces. The invaders' position was hopeless. It was vital i to confirm the identities of our enemy; more importantly, we had to uncover who had inspired their disastrous invasion.,

Viewers panning to the fighting showed a predominance of white skins, although there were also a number of Arabs as we had anticipated, given the rumoured *jihad* against Earth by the Caliphate. Druids were simple to identify with their occult regalia, especially the robes, which appeared to impede their effectiveness in battle. As Myrna and I had always believed, the President's Glastonbury performance which I had spied on nearly a year ago (Earth calendar) from my Martian home world, had proved an abysmal failure for the English. How, I wondered, did Sheila, Eco Minister-cum-Priestess, who had such a prominent role at Chalice Well, fit into this? It was very unlikely that malcontent Druids could mastermind such a scale of world war.

The failed invasion forces my voice-overs described as 'riff-raff' or and 'scum' because street language invariably makes listeners feel tough.. The enemy were largely tall,blonde or ginger Scandinavians who had bathed in the pool of ancestral memory to go 'a-viking'. Contrary to romantic legend, the originals were not noble, fearless adventurers but thieves, killers and rapists. These were no different. I knew their kind from my youthful escapades in the criminal underworld. There was no possibility the anarchy had been brought about by such bone heads! Who had inspired them on this chaotic looting? I was obliged to leave my speculation because I was summoned for a key 'photo-op', as they called it.

I caught a glimpse of McNulty. He was still in the midst of the fighting to mop up the foe on the shores of Ryde.. He had engaged in the primitive brutality of hand-to-hand combat while his fighters attempted to round up prisoners for interrogation. This was heart stirring stuff! Around the millions on two planets, I ordered his live action to be beamed to interplanetary 'fans'! There was a degree of a gamble in his participation in battle. What a disaster if he were killed! However, heroic death would not be a presentation problem – except to friends like me. Martyrs break their friends' hearts.

Something else caught my attention in the midst of my propaganda team's dramatization of our general's bravery. I zoomed back to a pair of fit, trained men with intelligent, European features. It was not just their faces that interested me. I shouted urgently to Alisha. The platinum haired Indian sex bomb paused in her spying and came to me immediately.

I stammered, 'The insignia! On these guys. Again! See it?'

'Spirits above!' she exclaimed. 'I recognize that! It's that eagle with spread wings above stars and stripes. How? We've got to get them in. Mercenary survivors, or what?'

It seemed increasingly possible the war was led by an internal rebel, using mercenaries to overthrow Maddigan! Or might it be someone even less principled like gangsters, the Europeans or the Papacy?

When my message to seize those two reached Joe on the far side of the shore, he was the middle of another brawl. A group of prisoners had tried to make a break. Joe, being Joe, went to handle them single handed. Guys he had nicknamed 'the Specials', his physically enhanced 'super soldiers', had to pull him out. The publicity people caught it. Real warrior stuff! Within three minutes viewers saw a full screen focus on his face, immobile, determined, as he headed to join me. Such drama could not be bettered. Hands covering his mouth, he spoke to me in muffled communication.

Quite obviously, the worlds-wide audiences neither heard nor saw what transpired. He started by telling me, 'Bollocks! It's like the tip your girlfriend, Janine, gave Myrna.'

I was furious. Myrna had been a sneaky cow, telling Joe and giving me no idea about any of it. I should have known that by now. Throughout our whole relationship she had deceived me into believing she detested him for being my drug-dealing mate who led me to whore houses and participated in druggy and piss up sessions while assisting me with my many deceptions. Again, my anger transferred to him. After all, I still felt bitter about the way he had been fucking Alisha at the same time as conspiring with her, as well as Myrna. This must have been directed by Mossad. Was there no one I could trust? I knew where I stood with Janine. That sensuous woman never pretended to be other than the head of a spy system traditionally hostile to the British Empire.

Before I had time to submerge in self-pity, I had a message. Mr Macho McNulty, the reconstituted fugitive from Mars, was making a casual enquiry about my PR. His words were clipped, 'Hiya, buddy! I hope you made me look good for our patriots. I'll get the Yanks to you within an hour. That's after me and the boss man have had a chat with them. They're old-style cunts. The guys holding them say they only gave us name, rank, number. One says he's Admiral Barker. Other gave us a name of Lieutenant Kirk. Hold onto your nuts. Over and out.' And he was gone.

I needed to hang onto the old gonads like he suggested, by keeping all my balls in the air, to continue the metaphor! Top of my list was misinformation that would confuse spies of all types...

That familiar Welsh voice made me jump with the remark, 'Hayling Island was very 'andy, young man. Confused 'em to fuck!'

'Hello, Sir. You took me by surprise. I didn't realize you were creeping upon me. Have you abandoned horse riding?'

Madigan was ruddy faced and sweating from his exertions; but he always enjoyed my friendly sarcasm, so he chuckled easily, saying, 'I got meself a right sore arse from that stroppy brute, you know. Got to make my posterior fit to mount again when I do me triumph through Ryde.'

His eyes were warm and friendly. He was waiting to hear my opinion. I felt it was sensible to wait until I had time to talk to McNulty and Alisha as well as find what came from the interrogation of this 'Barker' and 'Kirk'. Besides, the President had more immediate concerns he seemed to need me to deal with. Maddigan had a sonorous voice. He was also close to the ancient stereotype of the Welshman in as much as he liked to use it in ways that some might describe as 'verbose' – others as 'poetic'. Fanciful metaphors and images were scattered throughout his speech like the many-coloured, perfumed flowers in the green meadows that I found so breath-taking on Earth.

When he finally got to the point, it involved Myrna. He softened me by reporting that he had spoken to her, and she had said my fictitious visuals of the President's Pagan piety on the Hayling Island sites were brilliant. However, her response dealt with a fresh issue. That was why he needed me to use charm and reconciliation on her. She spoke of a more serious development facing Helium. McNulty's defeat of the invasion of England was unexpected and impressive. She doubted it was prompted by a discontent on Earth. She claimed to be faced with the possibility that it could have been entirely organized as a diversionary method by the Caliphate.

I had a distinct impression that Maddigan's strong position and increased threats from the Caliphate on Mars had led to a modification of the Governor's aspirations. Rather than wishing to topple President Maddigan, she needed his assistance.

Chapter 24

After a mere 24 hours, we had regained full control of the island. Even though I say it myself, I knew I did a fantastic job of heightening the drama of our thrilling 'Liberation of the Isle of Wight'. I was determined to advertise my own high profile by riding alongside Maddigan during the planned Triumph. This day was history in the making!

I had a feeling of unreality after 12 hours sleep. Instead of the familiar crimson sands, intersected by eon-old canals and a gloomy red sky, I was about to ride out beneath Earth's dazzling light azure sky through fresh greenery that smelled fresh and sharp from the light shower that had fallen earlier in the morning. My boyish fantasies had become a reality. I was the fearless champion from another planet preparing for the acclaim of the free people of Ryde.

I flew back to Ryde with a strato-fleet still based on Southsea beach. Even as we travelled, I delivered a breathless live broadcast, watched by billions of viewers on the Rigs, Terra and Mars. They were awed when they witnessed the national insignia of the fliers circling Ryde to celebrate the friendships and alliances between England, Israel, India, Australia, numerous African republics and even China. The armada hovered spectacularly above the glorious golden sands of the beaches running along the northeast coast. This brightness and colour enhanced a world-wide good feeling for the Isle of Wight.

I went a bit over the top when I ordered my team to superimpose a huge ghostly image of Maddigan's face across the heavens. I figured this would create further mystique about the saviour of the land. My guys tinkered slightly with the image in the sky to give the impression of him as a deeply reflective person; everything the people wanted in the Empire's President. Moreover, he spoke of international harmony on two planets. I aimed to show Helium that he would be their bastion against the Caliphate threat.

McNulty was occupied with more practical concerns. He was calculating how many invaders had made it through our lasers and landed successfully, still hoping to do some sacking and looting. He assisted my broadcast by providing me with images of smoke rising from ancient homes and shops along the hill leading to Ryde's centre. I wanted to create more shock. I spotted several dead bodies. I ordered close ups of their corpses and then artificially added more red blood to incite the anguish and anger of our audience who might have lost friends and neighbours.

I felt satisfied with the effectiveness of the Operations Centre, where I had sat directing with bottles of beer from Maddigan's secret hoard. Everything had been re-assembled with miraculous speed back on the mainland, I added in my own link sections.

The stars of the supporting cast included McNulty, Alisha and Teena, who were about to join the Presidential Triumph. I was certain how highly I'd scored when I was asked to join him and his top brass outside Ryde to give final approval to the plans. I relished riding beside Maddigan during his Triumph through the High Street of the town.

My escort was familiar. I couldn't place the black guy with the Welsh lilt. When he took me to shower, change and heighten my handsome features, it clicked. A cottage. Near the Welsh border. Admired my Norton on the way to Wells. What was it? Click!

'How are you now, Mr Glendower?' I enquired. A grin twisted his white stubble. It is always good psychology to remember somebody's name. The old man chattered ten to the dozen now he felt he had been noticed. He congratulated me, 'What a long way you been coming, young fellow, since the last time I been seein' you!'

'You're not wrong, Sir. I trust you won't consider me rude if I ask where you fit in the scheme of events.'

''Tis not a mystery. Our Butch and me, we grew up together. Both of us born in the valleys. Then, it did happen his parents went up north toward the mountains. Aye! As a lad I missed my friend a long while. Some of 20 years it was till he got the hand of destiny upon his shoulder, and it was by that very same shape of fate that we did meet again.' I feared an interminable life story was about to burst the dams of nostalgia. Furtively, I reached inside my upper garment and pressed the button programmed for such occurrences. A loud siren went off. I pulled out the viewer like my life depended on it.

'Come on! Quick, mate! He wants us. Now!'

He stumbled after me as I went trotting towards the President's location signal. I rushed through security. My badge with a red dragon on green background and with the gothic letter 'M' over it was all I needed as ID. Our heroic leader was sitting in the centre of a circle of fliers on the grassy area that was once, I learned, Ryde Golf Club. I couldn't be bothered to discover he nature of 'golf', though it was obviously some ancient outdoor sport. The business of the afternoon was to select sequences of commemorative images showing Masque and his bosom pals in a victory march – or Triumph as he preferred – up Ryde's decrepit High Street. What he wanted was scenes that would be indelibly imprinted onto billions of optic nerves across Earth, then – via the forty Rigs – across Mars. With eccentric reasoning, he believed such indelibility could only be produced by a procession on horseback down the High Street of a tiny town on a little English island. Would he wear a laurel wreath, I wondered, like those Romans in distant millennia? Being an exhibitionist, I could quite enjoy it, but I imagined McNulty would go going purple with the idiocy!

Once he spotted us, Maddigan beckoned Glendower and me to join him. He was midway between laddish affability and shrewd showmanship. After he had endured hugs and verbal gush from his schoolmate, the elderly Welshman was sent to mingle in the crowds, alert to any threats. I had to ride behind him with General McNulty guarding his right, alongside Alisha, At the last minute, he asked Teena to ride on his left. I thought, *Dozy sod! Natasha won't be delighted with this one! I imagine you've over-used the mid-life crisis excuse too many times by now.* Probably he required me within hearing distance to direct a record of favourable poses and angles. Also, while McNulty's eyes were alert to dangers lurking amongst the crowds, I had to keep in touch with lasers in space which were programmed to take down any suspicious individuals a hundred miles beneath them.

Once this had been battered into my aching head, the biggest challenge came. This was in the form of that very big black stallion upon whom Maddigan had already demonstrated his ineptitude.. The true obstacle was that an overweight, middle-aged Welshman was not made for riding, and even had to be placed in the saddle! To tell the truth, I was too embarrassed to watch. I had hope he had learned his lesson about horse riding. It went down well. While the 'inner circle' saw how Maddigan was crane-lifted and lowered onto the embossed leather saddle, the crowds along Ryde's thoroughfare were diverted by silver fliers beneath the clouds, pouring golden foil stars on them. Music played and there were puffs of Happy Dust pumped along the lines of excited people. McNulty glanced back to exchange a mocking smile with me. Still acting too buddy-buddy, I thought.

I was aware of a shadow or a movement, I am not sure which. Without warning, a hail of missiles hit the procession. Teena, in front of me, screamed. Something struck her. I feared it was a laser or even an old-style bullet. I moved to catch her backward fall, and McNulty threw his body over Maddigan. That must have been instinctive, for it revealed his true feelings for the Welsh Emperor. No spy who lives till retirement is ever truly a totally obedient robot. Old Glendower was stood in the crowd where the shots came from. He was more professional than I'd given him credit for. He threw his antique body into a pack of adolescents. I clocked some 15 or 20 evil-faced brats in their early teens. Their heads were shaved, same as the thugs who had tried to mug Joe and Alisha in that recording after Helium's mosque was bombed. That recollection might have rung the same warning bells for General McNulty because he spurred his horse directly into them.

A pair of teenage thugs were trampled. A ferret-faced 12-year-old holding a catapult tried to run for it. He was grabbed by the incensed crowd, who were eager to rip him apart. They backed off at a roar from the general, who slung him over his saddle, so he could be interrogated. McNulty stopped dramatically. It was impossible. Squinting, he stared, unable to believe his eyes. He identified a tall, elderly man with a white beard, lurking in the shadows of the porch of a ruined Art Deco building down the High Street. The towering place was once the Royal York Hotel, probably preserved as an historical curiosity. The man with long white hair and beard was no other than the High Druid, Haggard. No way would that old devil be here to celebrate the apostate President's Triumph. The young rodent hung over Jo's horse's back was an irrelevance now. Before he jettisoned him, McNulty forced a couple of hallucinogenic pills down the brat's throat. That would be salutary when he tripped in nightmares for the next eight hours or so.

The General did not dismount when Haggard disappeared into the hotel. Rather than be delayed by doors, he acted like the Joe beloved by me and Mossad. He lobbed a light explosive towards the entrance to clear obstructions. There was a blinding flash, then a bang and dark smoke. His quarry ran inside the entrance. Without hesitation, McNulty charged into the building, desperate to arrest the High Druid.

Alisha vented fury on the processional soldiers. They had been frozen by their commander's speed. On the other hand, I applauded how quickly Alisha had reacted. *I am a blind fool,* I admitted to myself. *For two years she was a working girl in Anais's Rig 1 brothel. At last, I realize she's a top officer in India's Intelligence Service.*

My self-flagellation was interrupted when the roof of the Royal York exploded as it was blown off by a volcanic eruption. The source was astonishing. What must have been the most powerful flier ever created smashed through the roof. With tremendous velocity it shot vertically upwards. There was no levelling off. The High Druid was accelerating through the atmosphere and into outer space. I never saw such force from so a small a vessel. McNulty's horse needed to sprout wings to follow that!

Maddigan realized the importance of calming the mood of confusion and apprehension before it totally sabotaged the Triumph. He turned up the volume control of the micro device under his collar in order to project his voice across the whole of Ryde. Being blessed with an unexpected innate skill of a dramatic director, he set about pulling rabbits from his hat. Come to think of it, he possessed many aspects of the conjurer at a children's party, including the voice and mannerisms of a loveable old uncle. All of this was assisted by a major leak of more 'happy gas', a tranquillity enhancer. The audience understood that this kindly old man, with his Welsh lilt as he talked, had liberated them from those evil marauders who had slaughtered their friends and burned their homes. Their President was no arrogant conqueror. He was a good person who was friends with people from so many nations. And they had come willingly to assist his benevolent mission. They were moved and horrified by the thought he would shed tears for the Druids of Tintagel who had so cruelly betrayed him. I understood why he was the Head of the Empire. I had never seen anyone so adroit at manipulating mood and feelings. Facts were an irrelevance. Emotion was everything. When they looked about, his citizens could see people and insignia of India, Israel, Africa and even – as an anonymous Janine appeared from nowhere – China. Adding to their empathy, they saw he was surrounded by other brave, good advisors – the general and I with noble poses and the beauty of Alisha and Teena.

The latter, giggling as always, improvised a special effect of her own. She noted the preponderance of males round her. She raised a big jar of cider and let it drench her flimsy t-shirt. Never subtle, she responded to the roars of approval and threw the wet top to me! Never have I seen such beautiful breasts! Clearly the majority of the crowd, female as well as male, felt the same. It became a party mood. Still being Uncle, the President passed her the leather jacket from the back of his saddle to cover her 'modesty'.

Here was a party, a celebration. Everything was harmless fun. A Big Bad Wolf was banished from the Isle of Wight. True magic!

Chapter 25

The Triumph was a resounding success. This was despite the surreal appearance of Haggard, described in my broadcast as 'an unknown terrorist'. The anonymity of the High Druid was a political necessity at this stage.

I wanted an opportunity to have an encrypted discussion with Helium. Maddigan had requested a sweetener for Myrna. I needed some quiet and privacy. Poor Maddigan was obliged to accept Ryde's finest accommodation because he suffered the obligation to maintain the appropriate status of President of the British Empire. I was luckier. I demanded to be away from it all. Bluntly, I reminded him, 'You owe me.' Politely, I requested that McNulty and I should have the sole usage of a small 'bungalow', as it was called, away from the town, with a sea view, as well. The boss smiled and consented.

I braced myself for the conversation with my wife. She was essential if Maddigan could maintain his position and authority on Mars. Transmission time lapses made conversations stilted and difficult. Speech and visuals took ten minutes to Mars and another ten minutes back to Earth. This was a tremendous improvement on the old days when my surveillance of Terra suffered almost day-long lapses. However, it was still frustrating.

On the positive side, I found myself in a relaxing place with two soft, fluffy sofas. The decoration was what I would describe as 'tasteful' and 'nostalgic'. I needed this environment right at the moment!

I prepared an opener such as, 'my love, here we are once more. I cannot wait till we are back together.' No. Not any good!

During the pauses I knew my eyes would have a plenty to study. The low walls were occupied by beautiful oil paintings, largely concerned with Scottish subjects. The most impressive of these was an old painting from long ago. I guessed it would be worth a fortune for so scarce a work to have been preserved, then maintained over the years. I used the magnifier on my viewer to read a title on a small brass plate. 'Rivers of Fire from Torness', it said.

Throughout my updating from Myrna, I studied its history on my device. The title, I found to be a quotation from a 20th century 'prophet' called Jean Darnell. She described a green fog descending on Britain with pinpoints of light. The light proved to be fire. These flames would pour down across Britain, from Scotland to Land's End, and even across the Channel. This was bizarre. The origin was itself pinpointed by the woman. It was named as Torness. In my own age, Torness was the location of the explosion at a nuclear reactor, which had obliterated two major cities of the country. A further search gave the name of one of these as Edinburgh, which had once been the Scottish capital.

Next to this painting was another prophetic revelation. There was an explosion of a red and yellow whirlpool. The name was a simple, 'The Meteor Hit'. That, I knew, was what caused the appalling devastation of northern Britain. Some small rock out of space was not spotted by the doom watchers. When it hit it re-animated the volcano, dormant it was believed for millions of years, a couple of miles from Edinburgh. Much British, never mind Terran, history was unknown to me. Events like this and the real cataclysm of Yellowstone, were familiar throughout our planets. Never this chilling prediction and fulfilment. In addition, the Rig 1's implants in my brain accidentally activated a cultural feed which invigorated my interests in historical matters. Even without using the viewer access to the library, I could get info about the tartan display garments displayed in the cottage alcove by focussing my grey matter. Even the hessian curtains were automatically identified.

My fascination with these matters distracted me from my purpose. I had not contacted Myrna. Instead, it was she who took the initiative.

The screen lit up and that familiar haughty, posh voice greeted me with, 'Welcome, mastermind and hero of the British Empire!'

With reciprocal sarcasm and with a much rehearsed raising of my right eyebrow, I said, 'The praise belongs to Manitoba Joe, your Mossad informer. You recall the fellow you employed to spy on me? He deserves your congratulations.'

162

'False modesty ill suits you, dahling. Tut, tut! You are not all huffy and jealous, are you, my pet?'

Possibly my altered face and voice would give me an advantage. People are uneasy if the face of the 'beloved' is no longer familiar. Here was my opportunity to use my psychological modifications to be less subservient to my governor spouse.

'My, dear,' I announced, calmly, 'I am in a position to assist you in your defence of Helium. This is not a time to rake up personal bitterness. There was no argument when you wished to alter my face, tamper with my brain and accept the danger of teleportation. I acted from my heart. Because I love you, I would do anything to help you. I was deeply hurt at how you pushed aside your emotions when you risked my life? I forgive you. Despite it all, I still care for you.'

Her reaction was unexpected. Even with the slightly imperfect visual from the 400,000-mile transmission I saw tears trickling from those pale blue eyes. Myrna put her fingers to her lips to conceal a sob. She shook her head, unable to speak for a moment. After a pause she averred, 'I ought to express my feelings for you, my Simon. I am sorry for all of it. I try too hard to bear responsibility of my position. Don't doubt there's always feelings you.' Love was a word she unable to say.

'We need to spend time with each other and no other people or politics in our way. I accept this isn't the time,' I explained. 'May I present my experiences with Team Maddigan? It will help you.'

She was relieved by these words. She listened very carefully to my descriptions of the President and his people. Her greatest concern was the President's alliances with India, Africa and Israel. China was the same big question mark on Earth as on Mars. My revelation that two Americans had been amongst the invaders shocked her. Surprisingly, her questions revealed she saw the Druids as more dangerous than I did. I immediately knew that both bits of news related to events on the Red Planet. When she spoke, I sensed she was thinking aloud, rather than saying what she had planned to tell me.

She reflected, 'You're exuberant about all your friends and allies assisting England. I realize warmth and friendliness are

163

qualities you value – even more than that teenaged girl with spectacles and long red hair.' She couldn't stop that popping from her thin lips. I was shocked that obviously, her surveillance from space had been as much directed on me, as it had on the battles, strategic meetings and activities of the Maddigan administration! I chose to accept it as a compliment and as evidence of concern for me. I smiled and listened to her soliloquy.

'Remember that although it's lovely to find friends from all over the world helping you drive Maddigan's enemies away from his neglected country, it's risky. What will he do if his friends of convenience decide they'll settle in England?'

Those history implants kicked in again. I agreed, adding, 'two or three thousand years ago Scandinavian pirates known as Vikings did that, my love. There was a Saxon warlord named Alfred, wrongly called 'the Great' for bringing peace and stability to England. However, he only achieved it by giving away half his country to the Vikings. The north was all under 'Danelaw'. Alfred's kingdom was essentially just the southwest. Maddigan the Great? I wonder.'

Myrna Golden's laughter was like her surname. I refrained from poetically shaping it into a clumsy compliment. That laugh made me happy none the less. Then, her heart closed once more, and she was back with the voice of Governor of British Mars.

'Your academic analogy is apposite my dahling. However, historical evolution is going beyond Wells or the southwest. I believe that the deciding outcome will be on Mars. Moreover, that will not be a deal like that Danelaw you told me about. Your destruction will come from the Druids and the Caliphate. There was something monstrous appeared at Stonehenge. You aware?'

Her words set off something in my mind. I began, 'What was...?'

'Something that I dread is coming from Tintagel to the Caliphate on Mars.'

There are always interruptions at crucial moments in our lives.

There was an explosion and the sound of splintering wood. McNulty fell through the ruined front door and landed half in and half out of the entrance to the cosy little lounge. His head was bleeding profusely.

Chapter 26

Despite being the hero with a brow of solid bone, General McNulty whined like a Caliphate slave girl while he was dripping blood over the priceless antique sofa. When I questioned him about his door- wrecking entry, he only gestured with his device. I needed to see what happened in the interrogation immediately. Myrna still watched from her palace in Helium. She offered me helpful instructions on how to bandage his low forehead. Maybe she did not want me to switch off nor ignore her. A flannel of hot water – ancient doctoring – was followed with a healer pad. I secured it with the protective bandage and gave him a blast from a heroin inhaler. That knocked him out. When the moans ceased, I linked online to her transmission. My decision was to put aside secrecy so we could share Joe's recording of the Yanks' grilling. Myrna's input could help to interpret what had happened during their questioning that led to his dramatic arrival at the cottage with such injuries. She entered my own viewer's reception of his recording.

His picture flickered, then lit up with clarity. His cross examination began in a small room, requisitioned for the purpose. I noticed the President was not present. Both Yanks were scanned for implants that might serve murderous or espionage purposes. The pair were supercilious throughout.

My own scans located their personal histories were still ongoing. I had hoped to dig up something to help Joe. This exercise was, to say the least, challenging. The prisoners' entire country had been blown into the skies and its detritus sunk beneath the ocean. For a century Americans were believed to be rarer than unicorns. My intuition awakened and went to high alert when no solid facts came. An auto-search started up so I could check if either man was registered as having undergone physical or mental reprogramming like me. Nothing. No medicals. No personal info of any sort. They did not exist. I thought about their belongings. All that was found, it seems, was a crucifix on a chain, worn by the Admiral, and a St Christopher amulet, belonging to the Lieutenant. I was alert for a clue that might suggest they could be emissaries for the Papacy, that evil Christian equivalent on Earth to the Caliphate on Mars. The Roman Catholics once infiltrated many terrified nations after the cataclysm.

Myrna and I watched and listened from our separate worlds. These men were professionals. They kept their cool. Admiral Barker was in his early forties. His hair was short, impeccably neat and dark, with barely a trace of white. A downward-curled moustache gave him an air of determination. Despite emerging from combat, his uniform was smart, uncreased and clean. Kirk was about a decade younger. I judged him to be about mid-thirties. He had longish blonde hair. His teeth were slightly protuberant, though sparkling white. He had an irritating habit of frowning, or nodding in agreement, with whatever his senior officer said.

Both of them recognized they faced an expert interrogator. Mossad training had made Joe a master of every technique for extracting information. Neither of the pair doubted that his arsenal included torture, were that necessary. That possibility would excite Myrna! McNulty's lead in was to share an admission that they, like him, were professional fighters, yet also men of the world with sufficient realism to discuss their situation in an honest, open fashion.

'I'd bet you laddies would appreciate a good hot drink?' he enquired in a respectful manner.

Barker studied his own immaculate fingernail nails and paused before drawling in a laid-back voice, 'You got bourbon, General?'

Mirroring him, Joe looked carefully to his own grubby digits, 'I'm partial to the aqua vitae too. Prefer proper Scottish, whether it be malt, blended and so forth, ye ken? But we shall oblige once we have shared some pertinent information?'

'We're goddam lucky to be in the hands of a proper military guy,' the admiral remarked to his partner, who nodded. Casually leaning back on his wooden chair, he asked, 'Ever hear the name Edgar Cayce, Sir?'

'Tell me more,' replied McNulty in a neutral tone.

I smiled at Myrna on my screen. I remarked, 'What a master of evasion Barker is!'

'Let us see, dahling, if Joe has met his match in this American.'

Barker talked calmly: 'Cayce was an old guy in the mid-20th century with the rep of being the best psychic on the planet. Psychic spying was nearly as big a deal in that era as it is again today. I won't insult you by asking if you have heard of Atlantis. For a whole lot of years Cayce read what he called 'Akashic Records' of past lives on Atlantis. I ain't no spiritualist. Damned if I remember the name of who he was on Atlantis. Then – this is the real doozie – he shocked the faithful by announcing that Atlantis didn't go under the oceans in the days of ancient Greece. Nope. It was all going to happen in the future. Lots of people now tell as he was seeing Yellowstone blow up. Yep! Atlantis was the future United States. Even when Cayce was alive, many weirdo guys made the same kinda connections. Particularly when they read about the super science, moral laxity and whatever that old fella went on about.'

As Barker intended, McNulty was briefly lost for words! Kirk smirked, becoming silent. A signal from Mars interrupted my concentration. I paused, irritated I snapped, 'Fuckin' what, Myrna?'

'An old saying was used once on Terra, to say you were being led astray. It was, "to be led up the garden path" Simon, dear.'

'What're you on about?'

'The Americans believe you Maddigan Boys are as mystical and superstitious as the old man pretends to be. Your history upgrade can inform you that the ancient world was eradicated in the eruption of Krakatoa in 535 A.D, leading to a period named The Dark Ages. That pattern was repeated by the eradication of America when Yellowstone exploded like a million, million nuclear bombs. Ignore Atlantis. Think about why he wants to divert you from rational explanations for the USA's destruction. Pay proper attention.'

I returned to watch. It looked like McNulty was letting Barker ramble on for as long as it took about sunken Atlantis. When he ran dry, it would be the time to resume.

Joe went to a slide drawer in his cabinet and pulled forth a litre of whisky. He sipped slowly. Then he poured himself a second. Barker tugged his moustache.

'You wouldn't like to join me?' asked McNulty.

Making his body relax, the American answered, 'That, Sir, is entirely up to you.'

Now the Yank's thirst had been worked up, McNulty grinned in a man-to-man way, and filled up a soft cup with what could be 35 cc of Scotch. Barker ignored his companion and automatically knocked back half of what he was given. Finally, Joe filed a cup for Kirk, touched a 'Cheers' with him, before turning to the senior officer again.

There was a potted palm beside Barker's seat. Not artificial like the ones in the Governor's chambers in Helium. Alert as ever, Joe moved it a few feet to the side, to prevent the captive furtively tipping away his drink. McNulty encouraged the prisoners by example and tossed back his own generous whisky in one gulp. Yank males hate to be unmanly. They both did likewise. The strategy was heading in the intended direction!

'I have two questions for you,' smiled McNulty, leaning back in his chair. 'Number one: are you mercenaries hired by the dickheads we polished off? Number two: how many of your people survived from when the USA homeland was destroyed? Take your time.'

Barker became animated. 'You Brits are duplicitous, brownnosers. Get that, Mister? America was the defender of the free world. Today we got no homeland. We got to work for any goddam guy who'll fuckin' feed us. If you Brits had helped us evacuate...You saw your chance. Fuckin' British Empire...What a joke!'

McNulty did not react. Of course, he was not British anyhow. He recognized Yanks were little different to Mossad, Britain or any other power. Everyone worked what served their interests. He sneered, hoping to get a rise from Barker. He topped their glasses. He prevented a refusal by asking a question and winding them up more.

'Scots like ma' self, we faced the same disaster as the USA. We didn't sob like brats to be rescued. We never begged of the Sassenachs. Sense of honour. And we are proper soldiers today. See how's we popped you from yon sky? Did it wi' our eyes shut.'

The term 'Sassenachs' made Barker hesitate. However, the insult about their fighting skills made Kirk's face redden. He spoke in a southern drawl.

'It's never been the way of an American fighting man to sit in comfort, directing other men, armchair general. Admiral Barker and me, we was in the middle of it. Someone got lucky. Probably one of your Chinky buddies, cos it weren't no satellite laser. I was pilot. Ain't easy when you start to go into a spin. You wouldn't know, would ya? Tracers were flashing. I was a proper man. We all were. Burst of cold air made us all gasp. Goddam. Friggin' hole on the flier under-carriage. One slip, one error of judgement, I knew we was done, mister. The admiral here had to stop any panic from his forty soldiers on board. You was a proper man, Sir, if I might give praise where it's sincerely due.' He paused for a few moments, with a deferential nod to his superior officer. Before their interrogator could demand answers to his questions, Kirk went on with further defence of his masculinity.

'We ain't pen-pusher limeys. Jagged hole was next to my feet. The land under us was all blurred. We could buckle up. But my duty comes first. Our Terran turbos, I tell you man, they was howling like demons. Looked like we'd be blown out the sky if we don't explode first. Admiral had our men in a double line, with anti-grav kit if they had to jump. Me? I held on to manual control to give them more time. See, mister, I am a man and a soldier. Admiral had to drag me away. Checked my stuff was sound. Then he pushed me out the hatch, like old style. You know what I'm saying? I knew the Admiral was behind me. Last man to leave.'

I sensed that Kirk was about to lose it in his building anger. Barker had knocked back his whisky and took the bottle from the table without being invited. He was signalling his lieutenant to do likewise. He was eagerly obeyed. This was their small a way of challenging McNulty. Feeling he was psychologically taking command of the situation, Barker filled both glasses for himself and his lieutenant. He offered nothing to his interrogator. With a friendly smile, McNulty produced two more bottles of spirits. He topped his own glass from one, and sipped it slowly, calmly surveying them.

Barker laughed. 'I saw my brave Kirk wobbling on his jet pack underneath me. As I descended, I got my first panoramic view of your Isle of Shite. Pretty place. Excepting there was hundreds of your multi-nation armies waiting to do whatever beneath me. One day somebody will invent jetpacks with sufficient power to help a guy shoot fifty miles away. We were lucky to land with what we had. Shame so many attempts ended with disasters.'

'I heard you had lotsa deaths from explosions and overheating your crap equipment,' McNulty agreed. 'Plus, there's them poor suckers in the wrong body position, went and burned off their feet with the flames. Badly trained by their officers I should imagine.'

In the top corner of my screen, Myrna was studying it all from her governmental chamber. She was anticipating a McNulty inquisitorial ambush on the wily the Yanks. The alcohol was working well, too. Instead, something unexpected socked McNulty. This was Barker's plan all along. The north side of the interrogation building blew up. A fog of dust rose from the rubble of the two demolished walls. Yelling soldiers in gas masks, armed to the teeth, charged through the debris. They had come for our American prisoners. There were around a dozen marines. Automatically, both Barker and McNulty seized a bottle of Scotch and held it protectively against their chests. I freeze-framed it. Even in life and death situations there can be comedy.

What happened next was sobering for me. I heard a shot and saw Joe fall. He could never have anticipated anything like this. He had no security guards on hand to assist him. The picture fuzzed up and went offline.

'Shit!' I cried. 'We've lost it!'

Myrna could never resist a put down. 'Dear hubby! How can a boy so devious and cunning be so stupid? How accomplished you were in serial unfaithfulness, but you always fail to consider the obvious. Surely, you could expect a competent President's Senior officer like Joe to make back-up recordings in an interrogation room. Do you need me to tell you how to access them?'

'I love you too, Governor Golden. Just piss off! It's obvious to anyone it will be channelled toSecurity,' I sneered.

In fact, it did not reach Security. Possibly the other area had also been damaged in the explosion. I avoided humiliation when I hacked into the signals from Joe's stratosphere drones. Ingeniously, I retrieved back-ups transmitted from the three angle cameras on the walls up to a space drone. I had a frustrating 20 minutes collating the post-explosion information. Bouncing the shared information between Terra and Earth delayed me a bit. Myrna observed silently.

Finally, I got us back in. We heard coughing of those in the fog of dust in the interrogation room. My mate was down, almost buried in debris. Barker's SWAT team were true pros. One aimed his hand laser and blew apart one of our spy-cams. I saw they wanted McNulty as well as their comrades. Miraculously, he emerged from the bricks and planks burying him. I can't even guess how he did it, but he was up, swinging a club of broken wood and prepared to fight. His physical reconstruction must have doubled the solidity of the bone in his low forehead!

He managed to stagger towards the rescuers, smashing a path through the wreckage. Unfortunately, he was still weak. His broken chair tripped him up and he went skittering over the debris. When he tried to get up, the leader of Barker's SEALs ran at him, kicking him down again.

I never knew how tough he was. Mossad training was better than the best of the best. He head-butted one guy in the goolies and got his fingers round the man's neck. When he doubled up, Joe twisted his head and banged it onto the desk. There was a choked yell. Whoever he was, the soldier was big and tough. He managed to pull free, arms flailing. McNulty grabbed his laser pistol and whacked it into the guy's head. There was a helluva lot of force behind it because blood spurted all over the place. Another soldier hit Joe with something hard in his fist. McNulty was out of it all. An Afro-English voice was shouting, 'Get the boss!' Help could have come quicker, but they arrived at the last moment. Our lads came charging in to rescue their general.

The SEALs abandoned McNulty. Their priorities were Barker and Kirk who they dragged out of the building with desperate speed. All the dust and smoke from the flames and broken walls gave cover. I had to admit they were superbly trained. They were from a different *milieu* than any foes we had previously encountered. Double powered jet packs enabled two pairs of soldiers to carry our former prisoners some 200 feet into the air. The most expensive flier I ever set eyes on was hovering to accept them. They and the American officers vanished into its hull. For an instant the ship hung above Ryde; next, in a literal flash, it streaked out of the Earth's atmosphere. Our own exterior cameras recorded it, accelerating into space till we lost it.

Governor Golden read my concern about where this level of technology originated. She declared, 'China? Caliphate? How? You need to use your skills, my dear. If it is either of those, you can say farewell to your cushy life with President Maddigan.'

She turned off. At least I had established dialogue with her.

Chapter 27

I could not resist from my career speculations. My buddy on the sofa could be out of action for a quite a while. I was the President's key advisor. A pity I had been oblivious to this recent threat. I needed to associate myself with the military glory of the rescue of the Isle of Wight, to enhance evidence of my capability. Of course, I would care for Joe. The most luxurious recovery facilities and best doctors in the little town were at our disposal. I would be decent and have a clear conscience! That's human nature for you!

Joe moaned and slipped, in slow motion, from the settee. He lay prone on the deep pile carpets, again bleeding profusely. The atmosphere was not tranquil. The sky was alive with sirens. Through my tiny diamond windowpanes, I saw laser lights flashing. Suddenly, I heard a landing outside. I pulled out my laser shooter, before looking out of the door. Unexpectedly, it was the President. He possessed a genuine sensitive human touch. Thus, the man ruling the British Empire arrived in person for this loyal general. My publicity teams were briefed to promote this golden opportunity! I looked at the concern on Maddigan's face. I could not be so cheap, I decided.

A chilly sea breeze had disordered Maddigan's combed-over tresses as he strolled up with his hand outstretched to me. Still unused to Earth's damp winds, I shivered, but managed to clasp palms with him. I was affected by the Welshman's authentic concern for General McNulty. Even at this unhappy moment, however, he could summon up fun. He chuckled with his familiar 'look you, boyo' throatiness and indicated behind him with his thumb,

'You been training our new nurse, 'ave you now, see?'

Teena had rushed over, wearing the nurse's costume she obtained for the Halloween party held as a part of the victory celebration. She loved to give a performance as much as Maddigan did. Perching on the old man's knee, she exhibited her 'Naughty Nurse' kit, so the tiny skirt rose up her long legs to reveal fishnet stockings and scarlet suspenders. The President was in paradise, sat there with a glass in his hand and a bonny lass perched on his crotch!

174

Brushing back my own fresh blonde locks, which I had implanted individually to enhance my appearance on the networks, I responded, 'I need a fucking proper briefing, Butch. Not hazy pleasantry. If there's something I need to know, tell me. No pissing about.'

I'd had more than a few drinks to talk to him like that. Unperturbed, he answered with a smile. It was reassuring there was nobody recording our discussions. As always, the old bugger read my mind, because he smirked as if he was amused by my furtively darting eyes. His open honesty embarrassed me.

'Now let me see, boyo. I 'ave a few notes on me sleeve here, you know. They're prepared for when I have to impress folk.' He studied his grubby shirt cuff. It really was covered with smudged reminders.

Was this his pose to disarm foreign diplomats or spies? Or was he still, underneath it all, a naive mystic who became leader on two planets by a ludicrous accident? Maybe he was simply nuts? Or pissed up. I lurched, took the flask from my pocket for a swig, and passed it to him. Whatever caused it, he could be wonderful company. I admitted to myself he was a loveable bloke too.

Turning to fantasy nurse, Teena, he dipped into his jacket and produced several tiny bottles.

'Dearest, cute young lady! These cosmetic items evolved from being dumped as trash centuries ago to become exotic rarity in this age. No wonder you are awed by my maturity. Feel free to enjoy a full appraisal of them for, say, 20 minutes in yonder bathroom. Commander? Is that the title I gave you, Masque? We are about to mull the pasture or some such bovine metaphor. When Teena returns, she will dazzle us with her perfumed radiance.'

Teena, understanding he wanted a private chat with me, tossed back her waist-length red hair and giggled, holding one finger between her front teeth. She leaned forward and kissed his saggy cheek, 'Dear Uncle Butch,' she whispered. 'Such a sweet request. You only need to call for me whenever you're ready.'

I had a moment of fear he might have set me up with her and was slapping me down again, to remind me she was really his. There was a click as the shower room door locked. Maddigan and I faced each other in silence. He smiled. His benevolent manner confused me. I recalled his pretences and devious actions, of hesitations, speaking of irrelevancies, he used while he plotted ways to confuse potential opponents. I had learned how to deal with such techniques. I grinned and stayed dumb. He stood up and surveyed the comfortable, lavender-scented lounge with approval. He looked casually around checking where our booze was concealed. Immediately, his eyes were caught by those paintings of the destruction of Scotland. He was wide mouthed in admiration at the skill of the oil painting. I tried to deduce his thoughts. I failed.

'Whisky?' he asked. 'Or has McNulty sequestered all the store for his reward for interrogating American renegades?'

He wandered towards an antique wooden dresser on the far side of the lounge. It was a fine piece of ancient craftsmanship. Mysterious human shapes were carved upon the cabinet doors, and they were framed by leafy vines that derived from Celtic culture. He stooped and opened the bottom compartment. Again, I knew important ideas were in his mind.

'It is to be hoped, young man, no children have access to this unlocked hoard?' he commented, producing an unopened bottle of 'Johnny Walker Black Label'. His smile stretched from ear to ear! 'Oomph! The old bones are aching, young fellow. Might I beg your assistance by bringing us a couple of yonder tumblers?'

I fetched them as he demanded. He half-filled each, then plonked himself heavily onto the sofa beside me. 'Aah!' he sighed. 'Scotland's *aqua vitae*! What magic in it! Even to a Welshman such as myself.'

He raised his glass to the portrayal of the Highland apocalypse on the wall facing him. With a dainty sip and a heavily exhalation of breath, he announced abruptly, 'Do your job, Mr Masque! Provide me with information about five important matters.'

'Number 1. Those Americans. A hundred years ago Scotland blew up. Some say it was volcanic activity and quakes following the meteor strike that set off Yellowstone. Myself, I doubt it to be true. Northern Britain has no connection to the Pacific Ring.'

'I completely agree,' seemed a wise response to him.

Rather pointedly, he asked, 'You're my Head of Intelligence, aren't you? I have some ginormous questions for you to find answers for. How did these Yanks emerged from nowhere? Where have the fuckers been for the last century? You observed their rescue party had the look of SEALs, I trust? More how and why to be answered there, wouldn't you say, boyo?' His tone hardened. 'What do they want? Who sent them? Anything of this nature is absent from your reports.'

That loveable bumbling Taff was gone. His tone felt threatening. He shouted his own answer, 'The Caliphate! Why conceal it if you have?'

There is a time to stay silent. He prepared another response.

'I shall tell it to you in your to-the-point Martian manner. I see *jihadist* devils close to dominating the Red Planet. On Earth they are not worth shit, my clever lad! People from my province on Mars, believe England is in their past. It is said their governor wants me dead. Especially those near to Myrna Golden. Is that true? Am I right? Don't act dumb.'

He had ambushed me when I was wide open. I felt afraid and became entirely Jon Masque. I was unable to call on Simon Edge of Helium. His implication was that I was making a devious alliance with the Caliphate.

'You're likely right about the Mars situation, mate. To be blunt, if you think I'm disloyal to you, you can fuck off. Get on to the next question you wanted answers to. I'll do my best.'

His reaction surprised me, 'Is Myrna Golden getting in bed with our enemies? Tell me what you really know.'

I answered as quick as lightning, 'That bitch tried to kill me. She's capable of treachery. But you told me to play her sweet. I did. What you asking me? Surveillance of her? Or is it assassination you have in mind?'

'You're admirably quick at the game, Jon!' he exclaimed. He squeezed my shoulder and topped up my tumbler with whisky before I could object. I attempted a diversion of lewd humour, 'Golden's on the skinny side. But if you want me fuckin' her for the Empire, I'll fill her fanny with fun.'

I was confident that had absolved me from suspicion. The Welshman let loose a burst of uproarious mirth. Instead of the shoulder squeeze, I received a slap between my shoulder blades as hard as a punch. He joked that when he had the popular Quiz Night at the Bishop's Palace, he would select me as his team captain. I didn't know what on Earth he meant by it. Everything made me nervous.

He went back to the Caliphate. I paid close attention. Confusingly, he offered a reverse conclusion to his previous one. He proposed the Caliphate was only interested in threatening Myrna and other nations on Mars. On Terra, Islam beaten, as successfully as the Papacy. Soon they would huddle around their black rock in Mecca while Mossad blew it up!

I shuffled on my chair. Perhaps I was in the clear. Again, I tried to relax. The President returned to his amiable, rambling persona until he slowly came from yet another angle.

He confessed, 'Haggard's the one who causes my deepest concern, Jon. I didn't convince them when I joined their Pagan rituals at Glastonbury. You know that? I've an unsubstantiated fear – and this is confidential – that the invasions and England's unrest are of the High Druid's making. I need you in the Abbot's Palace. From there you can do reconnaissance on the Druids. Report to me everything you can learn about Tintagel and Anglesey. Talk 'off the record' first with General Alassam. Observe him too. My other fear I'll also tell you. It's the American soldiers. I require details of where their high level of military training took place. Those who got them away from us were marines and their weaponry equalled ours. Examine all recorded files of McNulty and Alassam – or any Martian sources you can access. I have to know all you can get.'

His harsh insight and tough commands took me aback. I worried why he thought I had access to Myrna's intelligence too.

The bumbling old Butch personality reappeared. Exuding goodwill, he embraced me, remarking, 'My beloved advisor, you have a monumental task. I get an easy job of requesting Alisha's

Indian soldiers to assist McNulty's fighters while he recuperates. You are my Sherlock Holmes of interplanetary espionage. You, Commander Jon Masque, are the cypher to the future of two worlds.'

Before these responsibilities had time to germinate, Maddigan escorted me from the cottage, explaining, 'Your personal pilot and flier await you. More pleasing to you, I'm sure,' he added with an elbow nudge. 'Teena is already waiting to travel with you. Our fair young lady is ecstatic at the idea, young buck!'

On cue, she emerged from the doorway. 'Am I okay to come in?' she asked, adding, 'That eyeliner, you gave me, really knocks me out!'

She was so beautiful! An aura of sweetness hung about her, enhanced by the scent of that rare perfume which was still evident when we made our way outside into the fresh air. I wondered if she had blended it with a sense-heightening hallucinogen. Chemical innovation was one area wherein Terran scientists were more advanced than those of Mars. They must owe it to Pagan traditions of magic potions.

Teena had but one question. 'Are Jon and I off on that holiday you promised me, Butch?'

'Naturally, you are,' Maddigan lied, a beatific expression on his chubby face. He held a hand to his ear and told us, 'I hear the hum of your flier descending.'

What awaited us was entirely the reverse of a romantic holiday.

Chapter 28

I hugged Teena while we watched our silver strato-craft land. I was intrigued to discover the identity of the pilot when the hatch opened.

'Doran!' I greeted Anais's lad. 'How's yer belly off for spots?'

'Fine boss. Ma sends her love. So do dozens of girlies! She's hired lots of new gobblers, queueing to work in the Palace. Know what I mean, mate?' He raised the rim of his cap and gave me a sleazy wink.

Security contacted Maddigan. He shook Doran's hand, embraced me and Teena, then hurried away to the edge of the little flower garden where the Presidential super-grade cruiser was landing to carry him away.

As soon as he was gone, I asked Doran to explain his appearance in Maddigan's service as an Imperial pilot. He was the last person I dreamed of meeting in England. His explanation appeared straightforward. All his life he had longed for an opportunity to get one over on Damian, his older brother. After repeated begging, his mam organized his teleportation from Rig 1. This was over six months ago. Yet again McNulty was involved. I might have guessed that. He and Anais had created fake credentials of his history as a bodyguard who piloted fliers for dubious private clients on Helium. There was a background story, suggesting these individuals were disaffected from Governor Golden.

Most mobsters on our home planet resembled the robber barons in a period of English history called the Middle Ages. Myrna was suspected to be implicated with them. Such gossip was attractive to the Maddigan devotees who doubted her loyalty. The conclusion was simple enough. Doran, as a known associate of the whisky-looting pirates, said Anais learned he was in hot water. With her assistance, he fled. The time frame seemed dubious to me. However, criminal stories usually are. He ended up on Terra, with forged references and miscellaneous documents he claimed he had to deliver to McNulty. That provided his pathway for introduction to the President. He handed everything over, got the job, did it well. Voila! He was appointed to fly confidential missions.

Experience taught me folk who give intricate explanations are generally lying. What worried me was if Mossad was involved in it? Whose benefit might McNulty be using Doran for? The possible suspects were English plotters, Helium Province or Israeli intelligence? I could not see how Mossad or Israel could gain significant benefit. Everything was so duplicitous I could not be sure I hadn't missed anything.

Today Doran had orders to fly us northwards and approach Wells from that direction. He was told he must not take the direct course from the east. The reason was 'above his grade' to ask, he said. He was so cocky nowadays he addressed me by the incorrect name.

'Tell you what, Simon,' he said. 'I hear rumours. They're saying your hag – whoops! Gob slip, I meant Governor Golden, warned the President about danger above Mona – that's Anglesey. Top Secret shit I got my ear to.' There was another significant wink.

That was probably correct. In the current position, Myrna would see little reason in being other than obliging to Maddigan. I left it to ferment in my mind.

I felt an urge to peer down on my former hermitage on Dinas Emrys, now only 25 miles away. Very firmly, Doran refused. He recited his order to stay as far as possible from Anglesey. Being irritated by the boy, I accessed the computer bank for an explanation. It came up blank for Anglesey. Mona was the same. When I persisted, a red 'Warning!' flashed on and a universal security alert lit up. I shut down instantly. I couldn't afford to draw attention to us.

I did not speak again. A few minutes later, the brat brought us down beside ancient Wells. Ignoring diplomatic convention, I emerged from the ship with my arm round my lovely redhead. I recognized I was inappropriately scruffy for a senior Presidential advisor. Aware of my gravitas, a senior Minister of the Empire nevertheless, I remained where I was, awaiting my escort. It would be undignified to shout, 'Hello, everybody!'

Cloaking had been in operation over Wells. When it was lifted, the visual spectacle was overwhelming.

General Alassam stood at the head of a force of over a thousand troops. They synchronized their salute and vocal greeting. They were all trained to perfection and clothed impeccably in scarlet jackets with gold braid and black pants. Simultaneously, every soldier raised a shiny new laser pistol, then re-holstered it in a leather holster. By a curious quirk, many bore swords, with ornate hilts in sheaths on their backs. I wondered if it was some nutty sword and sorcery fantasy of Maddigan's. This was the sort of pretence both he and I enjoyed. It wasn't what an Afro General would come up with. All the same, as Stonehenge had demonstrated, even in hi-tech culture, ancient weaponry could be useful.

The giant, who commanded the Empire's domestic defence, strode toward our flier. A Westerly wind was blowing about his mane of dreadlocks and his curly beard, adding a natural dramatic effect to his presence. In the brilliant sky squadrons of fighters from India, England and Africa buzzed in a perfect arrow formation. They provided awesome visuals for my news and propaganda crew to transmit. I enjoy stardom. Today I achieved a small dose of ego gratification. Audiences would be awed by their Commander Masque, a brave and unaffected man, wearing torn pants and other practical attire of a genuine combat veteran. My red-haired companion, in her leather mini skirt and high-heeled boots, faltered awkwardly. However, I demonstrated myself to be the perfect gentleman, as well as a fearless warrior. I held hands with her while we walked slowly to meet Alassam. That added a touch of romance that would stir the hearts of our audience. I prepared to salute the general. He rejected formality and simply smiled from ear to ear to welcome us. Bless him!

'How ya do, Commander?' he shouted and held up his hand for a high five. I knew this guy was as sound as they come! He would never stab his President in the back! A lifetime in Myrna's cynical world had led me to attribute devious motivations to all movers and shakers of the political milieu. Without such inherent suspicion, I would have perished many times over. Previously, en route to here,

I actually considered the possibility of Alassam leading a coup against his absent leader. Alternatively, I had wondered if he aimed to usurp power from Natasha Maddigan, by calling his African troops her 'protectors' in imprisonment. My last scenario had the Druids unexpectedly attacking, repeating their defeat of him on Lyonesse. Or arranging a furtive poisoning of him. Instead, I was facing a beacon of nobility and compassionate intelligence. Our eyes met and he realized the warmth I felt towards him. Once more, his large white teeth flashed. Putting his arm round my bony shoulders, he escorted us through our parade of honour. The troops split from their previous arrow formation to provide a corridor of immaculate military training.

The Afro General's achievements equalled McNulty's. At this moment the latter was accepting accolades for his victories at the Stonehenge and Isle of Wight campaigns. In short, the two generals were equally impressive. A complete integration of Anglo-Saxon and African British patriots had been successful. Other ethnic groups of Britain's soldiers were also forming unbreakable bonds. United nations are undefeatable if they are built by friendship and trust. The idea was fresh to me. On an abstract level, the common history of India and England returned and evolved as they became united to resist the Caliphate's fanatics.

During this period of embarrassing sentimentality, I imagined Maddigan being the redeemer of a dual planetary Empire. Naturally, all of it would be set up by his wise guide, Jon Masque, political planner and visionary. The legendary name, Merlin, entered my brain. Just before I drowned in my heart-manufactured syrup, I was rescued by Simon Edge's cynical intelligence. What about McNulty?

Once he was my closest intimate, my spiritual brother. But my buddy had become a mystery. As a result, I feared him. Militarily, Joe was a master of pre-emptive strategy. However, he was primarily the servant of Mossad; he shared more secrets with my wife, Myrna, than I did. I found it sinister.

I experienced another of my recent mood shifts. I was pleased to march side by side with Alassam, toward the palace for a reception. At first, I wondered if I were impressing the crowds. I need not have bothered. All eyes, especially of the male soldiers, focussed on Teena's bum as she tottered beside me in her provocative, tiny leather skirt.

The general's gold-flecked, hazel eyes were watching. With a chuckle he said, 'Me Deh Ya, Rude Boy.'

I saw he had spotted my earlier moments of mental disorientation and he was teasing me out of it with a bit of Jamaican patois.

In a flash, I accessed my implant library and came back with, 'Wah Gwaan' which made him splutter with delight. I explained, 'I found a bit more of it. I hadn't spotted your Jamaican ancestry. I figured you as fourth generation English with Somali roots. Or are you being a fraud and winding me up?'

'Nuh romp wi mi,' he answered. 'Ma ancestor dey deep under da sea. Some ting you Martians don't savvy. Hear say your boats sail on sand.'

Our joshing stopped when we halted in front of the new, bronze studded doors to the Bishop's Palace. This was all new. Another addition was an arch, decorated with twining leaves and sculptures of a Goat God playing pipes and the Pagan Green Man. It was enhanced by holographic shifting colours. Very impressive!

With a blast of music, the portals were flung open. Natasha stood before us. She wore olive robes and was crowned with golden leaves. She was fantastic! Straightaway, I sent the picture of Natasha as a goddess travelling around the globe and across 400,000 miles to the entire Red Planet audience. Humbly, I acknowledged someone almost my equal in publicity inventiveness had arranged this image for the First Lady.

I was so distracted, I missed the opening words of her speech. Seeing I fumbled my cue to reply, Teena covered for me. When she curtsied, she forced down my arm, so I bowed as I was expected to do. Afterwards, she looked into Natasha's eyes with a friendly smile and chattered like a bimbo with a brain that rattled like a pea in a bucket to distract viewers' attention from me.

'Remember us having breakfast with you and Butch and that Sour Puss, what's her name? You look fucking brilliant. It's fabulous to see you.'

The male soldiers were staring at her thighs, saying, 'Ain't she cute!'

Teena was so natural and sweet. Natasha laughed with her and walked beside us into the palace. We found major improvements from the days of the slovenly wooden door that went into the dusty corridor of pissed up soldiers who confronted me on my first visit here! I approved of the security cameras and laser defences, so shockingly absent when I had strolled in to gate-crash the President's party.

At the bottom of the staircase, Natasha ordered her soldiers to let no one past this point, or any other routes to the upper stories. Beaming graciously, she turned to my red-haired young love.

'You are so very lovely,' she complimented her as she placed her fingers lightly on the girl's shoulders and drew her gently towards her to kiss her forehead. She added, 'I know how polite you are, Teena – and I have no wish to exclude you. At the same time, many friends of yours have joined our security and administration gang. I procured a list of room numbers for you of some old friends you might want to pop in and see. Please don't be offended.'

Teena again smiled towards her, aware of her meaning and appreciating the delicate manner of her request to leave us to a private discussion. Such consideration seemed odd from a lady talking to her husband's former girlfriend. Female psychology was always beyond me.

Alassam and I followed the Natasha up to the first floor. In every action she had a regal dignity, a contrast to her dishevelled, clumsy husband! I dug up an ancient maxim that warned, 'Comparisons are odious'. That was certainly true when Myrna came to mind! Both women were highly intelligent, even brilliant rulers. I was conscious many said they were the real brains behind their partners. I knew Myrna believed she was! Nevertheless, I identified Natasha possessed emotional intelligence. Conversely, Myrna was a device of cold intellect. At her core was a diamond, hard, sharp and

185

cutting. At best, her communication was usually of the mind. Natasha and Butch seemed to me to understand one another from their hearts.

We entered the Presidential private room. Six heavily armed guards were posted outside. When we were seated, we were offered refreshments. Alassam had been toking a spliff. Snacks did not interest him just now. Shaking those fabulous dreadlocks, he bellowed, 'Jon! He's my bo' wid the cheese and pickle hunger. I'm just wid grog!'

He was not stoned. This was a way he relaxed before diving into serious matters. I checked out the room in which we were ensconced. There were steel reinforcements for the door, even some walls, spy cameras all over, laser weapons set to kill assassins, plus emergency buttons on three sides. They were concealed by cosy decorations, cushions and sofas that provided a soft, cuddly ambience. Everything gave the illusion of being designed to relax visitors. More importantly, it also aspired to put visitors off guard.

'I'm happy to see you in person again,' Natasha said in her deep, husky voice. 'I miss the President being here, you know. How is he, Jon? Vid conversation is so antiseptic.'

I did not recall her addressing me so familiarly before. Perhaps favourable intelligence had come from her spies. The initial 15 minutes of our conference was taken up with chat about Maddigan. Only when Alassam shuffled in his overly-soft easy chair, did we get down to business. The First Lady apologized to us for her 'rambling'. The General's big white teeth shone as brightly as a Terran full moon on a dark night from his sympathetic, wide smile.

I was updated with little details about Stonehenge and the Isle of Wight. My own affrays were of minor interest to them both. I provided all I could, but felt there was nothing to say. What worried them most, all of us actually, were the American mercenaries. They had already received my encrypted copies of the interrogation of Barker and Kirk – and of their escape.

Alassam was in fuller flow than usual. 'Tell you what's rumblin' in my belly, man. Are them Yanky buttheads behind that

186

fucked up invasion? If they ain't, who hired them? And why was it all so easy to whack da mothers? I guess my bud, McNulty, had four times as many fighters and strato-craft as them, mind you.' He leaped off his settee and brandished his fists as if he was fighting. The gold braid on his red jacket glittered like lightning flashing through the dark room. 'They mighta bin layin' on the 'Henge altar and beggin' us to sacrifice them!'

Natasha turned her attention to me, asking, 'Where were you in the battle on Salisbury Plain, Jon? Were you close to routing the mob at Stonehenge? You've said nothing of what happened to you.'

'Well, I was observing and protecting Teena,' I fumbled. 'It's not that I was frightened…'

'I'm not challenging your masculinity.'

That grated on me. I answered coldly, 'Frankly, I don't know what you want to know.'

Taking my hand, she gazed into my eyes and gave a heartfelt, apology. She explained it came out wrongly. I was shocked when, unexpectedly, she kissed me on the lips. This, to say the least, was not a typical action for the First Lady of the British Empire. Her sincerity was beyond doubt. I asked her to reveal what it was that she knew about the action at Stonehenge. What was she fishing for that I had missed?

'Their giant. The ogre,' she burst out, attempting to discover if I had concealed something.

Alassam was skinning up a third joint. His thought processes were moving down different paths. To dramatize his horror at something he had witnessed from his own drones, he sprang up, towering over us and suddenly howled like a wolf. His ability with narrative had diminished so much, his cry actually achieved a greater shock than any cold military account. He was still semi-incoherent when he launched into the longest speech I ever heard from him!

'Was them Druids as summoned a devil from hell, man. Biological enhancement of da virus-man horror. Not science. Demon stuff, man. Ain't science we was watching. It was born outta test tubes and filled with the evil we never seen on them vids. Ain't no

187

godly man was ever born 15 foot tall havin' two pairs of arms, and strong enough to pull up one of them granite stones like it was a weed from yo' little front garden. Special laser-proof armour they done made it. Beams bounced offa him when he swung that old-style club fulla nails, just killin' poor boys of McNulty and Maddigan's. Druid "Super Soldier" is what that evil thing is. Lasers do fuck all and ain't no nukes in our boys' holsters. It was one of my hero warriors with African balls, ran at that fucker with a spear. Can you believe? A fuckin' spear! Stabbed it right into the back of that monster's knee through the space in its leg armour.'

Rastaman was the ultimate cool. He flipped his mobile viewer over his shoulder without his gaze shifting and caught it in his right paw. Directing its focus on the left wall he activated Natasha's ten-foot square screen for me to see what he talked about. He must have got it directly from McNulty, or one of his officers engaged in combat. Recordings made in the midst of battle are always wobbly. In this case, images of the giant troll in combat also kept going on and off and slipping into slow motion. If anything, that made it more sinister. It also confirmed this was genuine and undoctored footage.

The 'Troll' as we all thought of it, was an abuse of nature. There were aspects of a human body in the 12-foot miscegenation – provided you ignored its surplus limb. But it was diseased as well, having the warty skin that was green-hued with a slimy substance ebbing between its bodily scales and pus-filled boils. Under bushy, tangled eyebrows the eyes were slits, suggesting it was half blind. Its filthy hands were webbed and massive. Though the monstrosity was obese, it was inhumanly powerful at the same time. A flier descended too low. The Troll reached in the air, plucking it like a thief in an orchard. Then it was crushed. We discerned a trickle of the crews' blood substitute for fruit juice. Effortlessly, it smashed the mess of the machine on the ground. A screaming soldier, hysterical with anger and horror, tried to hack its hamstrings with his antique sword. The horror plucked him up, bit off his head and then it threw mangled scraps of his body far across the battlefield. Like a child in a tantrum the monster stamped a fat, fleshy foot on another victim. In seeming disgust, it shook its foot to discard the gore and the crushed flesh and bones of what had been a person from between its toes. The picture spun around. Then the ogre was shaking its head in a soundless scream. Here was the moment that another of Alassam's heroic Afro soldiers plunged his spear through its thigh.

There was shocked silence. Even from the general and Natasha who had already viewed it. I was conscious that my jaw hung open. So much for strutting idiots like me, proud to be lords of outer space, who created robots and went shooting across solar systems in awe-inspiring rockets!

'I live on a scientifically explicable world,' I finally said. 'General, Sir?'

'Yuh get bad mind,' Alassam mocked my imbecilic intellectualism. 'Yuh get a bun.'

That was polite patois for, 'Fuck off!'

More drinks were needed. My hand was shaking. Natasha produced a silver cigarette case neatly packed with spliffs. We still did not speak for a good three or four minutes. I was the one to resume. 'I need any information you can give me. A little bird told me that I am to be sent to Anglesey.'

'A little bird?' asked Natasha with a friendly smile.

I did not answer her.

The stoned General caught on. He said, 'I'se the best commander you ever see. Don' tell your man, McNulty that, Jon. If'n you do I will know. *Yuh a crassio.* Then I don't never believe you again. Unnerstand what I talkin' about?'

'Of course,' I lied. 'I'm a jumped-up admin wimp. I go where I'm told and do what I'm ordered. That's fine. And you can trust me.'

Natasha tossed back her hair. She said, 'a gossiping avian told me that you have a difficult path ahead, Commander Masque. Nevertheless, like Alassam, I realize I can place my trust in your integrity.'

Chapter 29

'Let's leave it there,' said Natasha. 'We will reconvene in the morning after a sound night's sleep.'

The First Lady left the sofa's nest of cushions and glided to a small table at the far side of her den. A tiny silver bell sat beside a wooden carving of a lunar goddess. Holding it delicately between forefinger and thumb, she rang it. There was a high-pitched purity in its tone. She had sensed her staff were awaiting her summons for light refreshments. My belly rumbled approval!

A concealed egress in the wall opened, and a dark girl and a boy with golden curls wheeled in two trolleys of steaming dishes. This was a flashback to the ancient Victorian period of the first Empire. This cosy politeness soothed me. Such mannered society made a refreshing contrast to our present world where behaviour was manipulated by technology.

We enjoyed a twenty-minute period wherein no one spoke; we could merely relax and appreciate the most succulent fare I ever encountered. In Helium, fresh meat and vegetables were a shameful luxury. Here was my 'bliss moment'!

Having jettisoned his patois game with me, Alassam enquired, 'How come you know the Doran boy so well? I can always tell. No offense for being nosey. We're friends and I'm direct, you know, hey?'

A slight flicker of his hazel eyes to Natasha's face, told me she had arranged his casual enquiry.

'You're a sharp blade in the armoury, mate. And spot on! Not so much Doran as his ma's business I knew well in the old days. I give ten to one you see a similar place on Rig 40. Maybe Luna?'

'Betcha!' he replied with another shiny white toothed grin. 'You ain't going to tell me you not done visiting houses here, have ya?'

'Ah, c'mon, bud! A guy of my years? My redhead angel is all I can manage. And I tell you something, pimps and madams are never friends. I got badly burned by Doran's ma. I figured she told that fuckin' Golden bitch lies about my private life. Really, I think she fancied me and got jealous, you know?'

The General thought that was a hilarious tale. He did not press any further. Nor did he make any sceptical remarks with Natasha present. He merely laughed and laughed. He said he couldn't say if Rig 40 had the recreational facilities of Rig 1. From all he knew it was as dead as the Moon. I was awkwardly conscious of Natasha watching me and weighing me up. She was too clever to believe my ignorance of Anais's accommodation. I was uncertain if I had sunk as low as possible in her estimation, or if she thought I only played some devious game.

Her single comment was, 'How modest you are for a sex god!'

'Don't embarrass me. Men grow up. I was a daft kid. I'm happy now. Teena. A one girl bloke!'

She casually followed through, 'Why did a brothel keeper's son show-up from nowhere as a Presidential pilot? You seemed very familiar when he collected you? I hacked your vid-system on your journey, naturally.'

'Doran – bless him – warned me that his mam told on me to Golden. Brothels are the best places in the world to find information. That was really why I had to run for my life from Mars.'

I decided my seeming openness laid Natasha's suspicion to rest. She liked my admission of love for Teena too. I chose the explanation she would approve of. I came to think she sensed truth in what I had said about my feelings for Teena. With renewed warmth towards me, she explained she'd arranged a suite for Teena and me. Perhaps she hoped I was a useful diversion for her husband's dearest teenaged girls?

As for Teena, she was eager for my return. Our accommodation was ideal for her youthful brashness and bling. Everything she selected for our room was gold and maroon. Pseudo-ancient Indian throws were flung across the *chaise longue*, the king-sized bed was all in colours that clashed with any conceivable colour scheme. She turned on a battery of flashing lights which nearly knocked me out as I entered! Swirling multi-coloured skeletons waltzed from side to side of the room in time to a singer, with a lyric that went, 'Ontology! Ontology! Oh, oh, oh! Ontology'.

She noticed my open mouth and hands reaching towards my ears, and kindly turned off the whole overkill. Impulsively, she threw herself at me and caught me off balance. We toppled backwards and landed on a divan with her on top of me. I loved her warm body and musk-scented skin. Her radiant visage was cheek to cheek with me. Joy and tenderness entered my heart. I kissed her. When I found a hairbrush under the cushions, I ran it tenderly through her gorgeous veil of red hair.

She touched her imitation emerald ring on the third finger of her left hand. It produced soothing music from the many concealed devices in our chamber. The melodies of an ancient harmonium and bass guitar multi-tracked and vibrated in parallel with our heart beats.

'I will never live on Mars again,' I said. 'It is a machine world made by mechanical intellectuals. There is more life and feeling on Earth than I have ever experienced.'

She was dumbfounded. All her life she was taught humanity's future lay with the Red Planet. Mars was the New World which would lead humanity to an ideal future.

'Settlers migrated, believing it would be like here,' I explained. 'Early expeditions like "Pathfinder" handed out "Mars Watches" to disoriented settlers, you know that? They were adjusted to Martian chronology time. Free trash to make the suckers feel normal. The days there are about the same length as here; they vary from 50 minutes faster to 40 minutes slower, with a year lasting for 690 days, but there are still similar seasons to Terra. A shame the air's too thin for birds to fly.'

My Jon Masque emotion overcame my Simon Edge coldness. I burst out, 'You don't realize how Earth's beauty inspires me every morning when I wake to hear birds singing. On Mars, no birds. They'd have nowhere to perch anyway. Martian winter's dry, cold and cursed with deadly sandstorms. The summer days are worse. A single occasion of sun-bathing at an unusual 70 degrees Fahrenheit beside Olympus Mons is my one pleasant memory. More likely I hid from 150-degree Fahrenheit heat punctuated by dust storms.'

This explosion of feelings shocked her. She said, 'Isn't it all being changed year by year, honey? Terraforming stuff makes more air for plants and woods. And what about those massive domes over cities? Helium looks magical on the Terra news.'

'Sure. But how many hundred years will it take? All we achieved to date are the biggest weapons, spaceships and the most complicated inventions to fight wars.'

'You know I love you,' I whispered, embracing her.

'I know, darling. You're not alone in that. I feel the same,' she sighed.

Chapter 30

I went out early next morning. It rejuvenated me. My confidence returned. One slip and I would die if I had made a misjudgement after my indecision as to who I really served. It was the first time I realized it.

I looked at Teena in the early light before I left. Waves of her ginger hair flowed all over the pillows. She was fast asleep, smiling, seeming so sweet, young and vulnerable! But my time was short. In many ways! I dry-showered, dressed and crept out without disturbing her.

I descended the old Victorian staircase, crossed the wide entrance hall. I said 'Hi!' to a bonny maid with a Scot's accent. Maddigan's security had been significantly beefed up these days. A score of Alassam's 'Rasta Elite', as I thought of them, guarded the front of the premises these days. They saluted me, and I returned it with cool wave. I felt grown-up!

Once I rounded the side of the building, I dropped my dignified pose and jogged over the lawn to the Abbott's pool so I could make a couple of furtive calls. Myrna topped the list.

I hadn't checked what time it was on Helium. When Myrna came on screen, she was sluggish, despite my opening jollity. Still, she seemed more relaxed and friendly this time. I had rehearsed to deliver a chat about the sandstorm season on Mars, and say it was a sunny morning on Earth.

'I'm, frightfully sorry, dahling. I'm obliged to be brief. The Caliphate have attacked our Hindu friends' province in the northern border territory. China, unexpectedly, I must say, contacted the British and Indian colonies proposing a three-way meeting. I intend to talk to your Chinese girlfriend before my Yea or Nay. A meeting in the flesh, you say.'

'Janine? Come on! I saw her with Alisha here. On Terra! You're lying! You invited Mossad Joe to your meeting, I expect?'

She switched me off then.

I remained beside the Abbot's Pond. Exhaling my stress in a great breath, I perched on the low stone wall, surrounding the pool.

My fingers paddled in cold, clear water, causing the fish to flip their tails here and there. Their circular mouths opened in anticipation of food descending from the surface. I drew in more fresh, sweet air. Bird songs from the trees and bushes continued to uplift me. What I had expressed to Teena last night were my true feelings about Earth. It was a surprise to myself that I acknowledged present day Mars offered only a soulless future of scientific marvels. I no longer accepted being a cog within a mechanism. Only Earth offered nature's heaven. Masque was replacing Edge even more.

I was disturbed from my meditation by a voice that funnelled through a mouth wider than those of the fishes.

'Not private, is it, mate?' Doran bawled, as he slouched across the lawn.

I forced a grin and waved him to join me. 'You're welcome any day, my son,' I lied, 'after you said about all them tarts drooling for me.'

I was still skilful with the common touch.

'I did a bug sweep here, boss. Whole garden's as clear as. People here ain't as savvy as we are on Mars with monitors, you know.'

'That's a relief! What can I do for you?'

'T'other way round,' Doran smirked. 'I know what's what. Plan is for me to take you around Anglesey base, all solo and secret. But that cool-as-fuck old lady, Natasha, plans to put half a dozen military on my flier. And even your General Rasta mate! Only wanted to alert you, Boss. Not sure whether your Rasta man knows, but the info I have says the Druids are doing tons of weird-as experiments there. She must 'ave sez to the Rastaman that you're the man what'll know what they're up to. All you got to do is tip us a wink if you have owt you want me to do about him.'

'I won't know till I've done these calls. I'll pass you a wrap with a note inside if I do. Last thing anyone thinks of in this world is writing messages! Excuse, will you? And cheers!'

He sauntered away. I touched my device to chat to Maddigan. I was diverted to Alisha because neither he nor McNulty was available. I was pleased. She was one person I wanted to speak to.

Her lovely light brown face, framed by her new spikey blue and silver glitter, came on screen.

'Been long enough,' she snapped.

I tried a clumsy charm offensive of, 'I respect you. True. No cheats. We both serve our people. No fingers crossed behind your pretty little bum!'

'Don't patronize me! I heard what a gossipy old woman you are, punter. Never deceived you behind your back with Joe.'

I was unable to stop the angry flush from rising to my cheeks. If she aimed to humiliate me, she had succeeded.

'I have to know how much you're in bed with Janine,' I snapped.

I learned the extent of how well she had honed her tongue through her relationship with a Mossad agent. As sharp as a razor was the answer because she slashed at me with, 'You can report to Mama Myrna I am not doing Tantric sex with your oriental fancy. Both my India and you Brits need an alliance with China. You were too slow. You failed your spy school exams! You obviously know zero about the Caliphate's incursions at the Anglo-Indian border. Scan a map and see where the Chinese Empire lives if you have a speck of brain.'

What I shared with the Chinese was a need to keep face. I switched Alisha off and searched again for the Welshman. Again, no luck. I touch-screened 'McNulty'. I was shown a wall of bodies, four or five deep who had defended the sea end of Ryde's High Street.

McNulty appeared. He asked how I was doing.

'I was hoping for a chat with the bloke who used to be my best mate. Not with Myrna's double agent.'

I was sure a shadow at the top corner of the screen was cast by a hostile woman. I realized that might be my paranoia. I did not wait for the General's response. I switched him off and entered the Abbot's Palace.

I jogged directly to the Presidential building, up the wooden staircase and to Natasha's little room where the previous night's discussions took place. Intuitively, I knew something was happening, so I tried to take her by surprise. Despite my lack of a security code, I was able to go straight in. Alassam and the First Lady were completely relaxed to see me. I was concerned about my clinical paranoia. Why the hell did I consent to my brain being tampered with?

Natasha casually included me in their conversation. 'I know you're aware of Christian mythology. Judas Iscariot took the most difficult assignment of all time. My heart warmed to him as it does to you.'

Adopting a boyish grin I asked, 'Do I understand correctly what you are implying, Ma'am.'

Natasha glanced at Alassam. His massive palm patted my back. He was not hostile. Somehow, they understood what was happening to my mind. The lady reassured me, 'You are my friend, Simon. I am a politician like you. I've chosen to trust you. Your good motivations are as clear as Earth's sky.'

'I apologize for the murk of my Martian sky,' I quipped.

She continued, 'You have a very significant part to play against serious dangers about to confront both worlds. We both believe in you, Simon. Or would you rather I called you Jon?'

How long had they known about my duplicity? When I asked her directly, she performed more elegant verbal pirouettes.

'Surely you didn't imagine that the boy, Doran, would appear from nowhere, with no explanation, to undertake top secret missions without our most basic check-up? Or, thinking of how Butch appointed McNulty, no one but a bumbling idiot would believe my husband's miraculous rescue was genuine after such a clumsily performed assassination attempt? To appear dozy and inept is Butch's favourite pretence. Though, there is an element of truth about that side to his personality as well, I admit.'

In desperation, I cried, 'Natasha, sweet lady! Why would you accept the recommendation of Manitoba Joe, who is General McNulty, to appoint a dodgy refugee from a shack on Dinas Emrys to reorganize the English nation? That's greater madness than I'm experiencing.'

Her hand covered her lips in laughter. 'Oh, Simon! It's not *what* you say, but the *way* that you say it! Your charm succeeded. I am disarmed. We know what was done to you. However, your intelligence has emerged undamaged. I believe you will be our best asset.'

'Told you, ma'am. I love this guy. I trust him,' Alassam smiled. 'Even if he's romancing his teenage babe who sends every guy in my marines sky diving.'

There are times to impress people by decisive demands. I said, 'You decided to trust two agents from Helium. Tell me who else knows where we came from and how we shifted allegiance.'

I counted them off on my fingers – Maddigan, obviously, Manitoba Joe, who knew everything and every side, served Mossad, Butch and Myrna, and I was certain Joe had told Alisha. That left our ambiguous ally, Janine. The one person who mattered above all was Teena. But I was aware love blinds you as well!

What was more crucial was who was unaware of my duplicitous loyalties. Myrna and young Doran were on the list there. I felt a burden was shed as I came clean with the First Lady. Most of all I was free to declare every truthful detail to lovely Teena. Alassam was spontaneously happy there were no more secrets between us. Ironically, as my empathy with McNulty cooled, Alassam was still pleased to share military action with him. He saw a certain integrity in Joe. The Rastaman was a partner, not a rival by nature.

In addition, he was insistent about covering my back when I set off to the spying mission around Anglesey. He confirmed that a dozen armed marines would accompany us while Doran navigated.

I asked, absolutely straight, if I seemed mentally competent to cope with my duty ahead. Natasha replied that Masque had emerged from the chrysalis. If she was wrong in her judgement, she and the President would perish and the Empire would be destroyed by Druidic or Allah maniacs.

I sensed a cyclone of violence enveloping me. At the same time, I felt more able to face what was required of me. Goodbye, Simon Edge.

Chapter 31

McNulty exploded onto my screen. He went straight into serious mode; news had come from Mossad. The Caliphate was crossing the borders of the British and Indian Provinces on Mars. Such military aggression was unanticipated by anybody. It appeared to be directed towards every province. Already there had been bombings of several larger Australian and Russian settlements. McNulty was already directing the international retaliation here on Terra. Secretly, he also assisted in co-ordinating Israeli armies, who were already sweeping into Arabia. He was assisting India as well because they faced a similar unprovoked attack. In the last few moments, the Indians nuked Islamabad as a pre-emptive precaution against potential Pakistani-Islamic fighters. That fuelled a planet-wide 'jihad' with India's inevitable invasion of Kashmir.

Up to this point, China had chosen to stay out of the action. As Joe put it, 'They are delighted to let other powers slaughter one another so they can mop up any survivors.' Even as we talked, I saw an incoming news flash for him. He forwarded it. Chinese complacency had been shaken by a fleet of triangular vessels – which he termed, for some reason, 'flying saucers' – that abruptly appeared from a secret Antarctic base. At this very moment, they were hovering over Beijing and several other Chinese cities, although there were no laser strikes as yet. China held fire. Joe's intelligence revealed that Janine had informed Alisha they indicated an old North American manufacturing methodology. Maddigan was left with entire personal responsibility for the defence of England. However, support for him was on its way from African allies, thanks to Alassam.

Though I murmured, 'What the fuck?' I was glad to receive this news when I did. It gave me a brief window to consider courses of action before Myrna came back to me. My luck did not last long. Within a dozen breaths, the screen lit up to reveal her suspicious features. Giving her no time to utter a syllable, I said, 'Some news is arriving this minute. There's a hostile fleet over China. Israel and India are kicking the shit out of Arabian Islamists. Their aims are unclear. What information are you hiding? Why didn't you inform me? I want to investigate a rumour of you checking out secret weapons the Druids are developing on Mona. Is that correct? Are they planning to exploit the Caliphate threat to the Empire? It's in our interests for Helium to work with the President. Whatever differences we have with him, we all are part of in the British Empire, aren't we?'

I made up that Druid plot in an instant to get her off balance. My intention was to see that Helium and Wells would be united against a common enemy. I intuited she possessed less information than I had. Myrna's aggression was averted, so I quickly said I loved her and wished her well in whatever happened on the Red Planet. She replied in kind.

Historians act as if all events have planned and calculated intentions behind them. It's bullshit. Since the surgical interference in my brain, I learned differently. Everything happens accidentally. Half an hour previously I held conceptions of the way things could unfold. Once upon a time I was a tool in a petty plot for Myrna to overthrow an 'incompetent' Head of the Empire and make herself President. Later on, she hoped for an alternative scenario where Maddigan would be defeated by the Druids or foreign invaders so that Joe and I were cleverly placed to manipulate her coup. Neither she, nor anybody else, anticipated this spontaneous outbreak of war on two worlds. Then the big question remained. Whose technology produced the armada of 'flying saucers' that threatened Beijing? Surely not the Druids?

I raced to my quarters to collect Teena. Whatever might happen, I needed her to be with me. It was irrational for me to take her on the Anglesey operation that the Maddigans had planned for me.

My friend, Alassam, was waiting for us to arrive at the entrance to the palace. He wore camouflage fatigues. His unruly Rasta-locks were tied into a ponytail emerging from the back of his military cap. His visor was up and looking like a halo when it reflected sunlight.

The nickname of 'Rastaman' had stuck to the poor bastard. The only thing he shared with that odd faith was his fondness for weed. He accepted it with good nature. Once we joined him, he and Teena competed for who could produce the best toothy flash and laughter. He gave her a friendly peck on the cheek. While he hugged me as well, then he whispered in my ear, 'we got to vanish. Right now! No one seein' us go, know what I'm sayin'? We got a mega-flier to fit 12 of my guys. Even space for a token whitey Anglos or two. The thick boys done making such a goddam racket. I said da gobsters we join them about five mile north. At Old Glendower's shanty was good.'

'Ooh! My cosmetics!' squealed Teena.

'Yeah! I told my boys to pick up your stuff and put it on the steps there. Da fellas will guard it. Okay. Us three gonna play sky games. Happy wid dat?'

He led us around the side of the palace to where three sky-boards were waiting for us, each with its sidelights flashing. We were given a brightly coloured capes and masks. I asked Alassam if he was taking the piss, or what. With a patronizing sigh, as if I was lobotomised, he explained they were to fool spectators or spies that we were only idiots, letting off steam by playing a fad called 'Sky Spin'. I remembered a similar game when I was a teenaged brat. It broke the boredom of muggings in the alleys of the Helium slums. In maturity I preferred the comfortable bar in a tourist balloon. *Anyway,* his deception was dumb enough to work. Scrutiny by Arabs, Druids and Chinese observers might well miss us while they studied some nearby army training exercises.

Alassam bounced with excitement. He was one of those nut jobs who have no fear of being slaughtered. Life or death – it was just a game to him. He chattered away, teasing and joking with us.

'Hurry up, Whitey Boy and Red Head. Put on ya audio-visors!'

I tried out mine. It had the same additions as the specs Teena and I used. That meant they were state of the art. They provided sharply defined visuals up to two miles away, and clear sound, despite the breeze and the buzz of our miniature flier pads. I adjusted easily, being accustomed to the sandstorms on Mars. Those distracting multi-coloured flashing lights were purely for fun. No way did we look war-like. Laughing all the time, the general rambled on with his autobiography, life and loves, as we flew. Maybe his chatter was to help me relax because I had a slight tremble on.

'When I was a suckling,' he told us, 'Ma carried me to Morocco in a backpack. I musta watched them older kids on t'ings called 'skateboards'. I wanted one when I grew up and was famous hero of the Brit Empire. And here I am!'

Showing interest, I shouted, 'Morocco? And why help spooks like us?'

'We run outa Christian missionaries to put on spits 500 years ago. We wanted brains to eat and they don't have none!' he said with distorted laughter.

I looked up at the dazzling sky. It was wonderful. Clouds were wrapping themselves into white woolly balls, drifting from east to west. They floated through vast skies of purest blue. Everything was so bright, in contrast to Helium. I had to squint, though my companions seemed unperturbed. I needed my visor to filter it.

Teena was a lass who loved a dare. She shouted something I couldn't make out and streaked away to more than a hundred feet up in the air. Surely, it wasn't the first time she'd done this. I was embarrassed because I was trembling. I was a skyboard virgin. I pretended I knew which button to press for increasing my height. I made a lucky guess. My ascent was far slower than that of my companions. At 70 feet I faced a fresh problem. How did I operate the controls to level out, and keep from climbing through the ionosphere? Alassam was hovering beside me, thank heavens! With brilliant dexterity he drew his flier beside mine and patiently adjusted a control at the side of my visor. He was even able to show me how to do it while we flew side by side. Mercifully, he didn't laugh at me or tell Teena what a wanker I was.

We reached our destination shortly afterwards. That familiar cottage lay below us. There was no indication of the concealed battle class flier. As I descended, I spotted Old Glendower. The black Welshman sidled out and stood amidst his flock of sheep, his hands shading his eyes to confirm our identities. I tried to wave to him. A mistake! My skyboard went out of control, causing me to wobble from side to side in the air. Glendower must have recognized me – perhaps for that reason – for he started waving back. Once again, Alassam edged up beside me so he could help me descend. I let him take charge. Slowly, gracefully, thanks to him, I achieved a smooth landing. Once I was free of the safety straps, I trotted toward Teena as she reached the ground. Alassam and Glendower slapped a high-five.

Alassam asked, 'Where you hidin' it, papa?'

'Round the side of the 'ill,' Glendower answered with his regional lilt.

We went round the hillock beneath which the cottage sat. The old man teetered to a great heap of branches, piled up garbage and who knew what. A rake was propped against a lonely ash tree. Munching a plug of tobacco, he grasped it and began to clear away his camouflage. There, hidden in it, under a protective lean-to, was our king-sized cruiser. A shout came from within, causing me to jump with surprise. All the general's marines were lurking there! Khaki painted panels slid back, and we were invited to come inside.

When we entered, we discovered Alassam's soldiers were waiting for us. Twelve pairs of marine eyes – male and female – focussed on Teena's long, shapely legs. Doran, conscious of not being a uniformed fighting man, flipped a coin up and down in his palm, to appear cool. Seeing an opportunity to help him feel more confident, I gripped his arm and called to the squad, 'Me and my bud here need good English beer, fellas! This fine young flier's my friend, Doran. I'm Commander Masque. Who are you, fella?'

I had picked out one I sensed was group's smart-ass and eye-balled him.

'Bellington, Sir. Corporal,' he snapped, saluting.

He played a role of being friendly, but subordinate as he indicated the chiller unit. Inside were refreshments. I noticed the tin marked, 'Dope' too. Doran, keen to assert himself, albeit as my pet monkey, opened it and rolled a spliff. I shook my head and warned him that no way did we want a stoned pilot. We needed to be quick and keep a low profile. Having demonstrated my status, I lobbed a bottle to Alassam. He caught it without a glance and returned to being a general. Tersely, he informed the team about the route we were to take over Snowdonia. From the shore of mainland Wales, we would fly west across the new islands in the Irish Sea to fool any hostile surveillance. His plan was to make an abrupt turn of direction, away from the north and south isles of Ireland. Descending to sea-level we were to land on Mona, then cross by sea unnoticed to Anglesey itself. Our flier carried three inflatables for that purpose. Things do not always happen as you want!

I heard the buzz of an incoming message for the General. I drew closer to read his screen. Red letters announced, 'Confidential Grade Only'. Surprisingly, he beckoned me, and he also invited Teena over to share it. Seeing my expression, he explained she was Confidential Grade too. *Funny*, I thought.

On his screen was the sultry Head of Chinese Secret Services. Janine Suee regarded all three of us impassively. Batting aside polite niceties, she plunged into business with, 'Mossad's shared with the People's Republic of China the key to the advanced technology of the British Empire. Your wife, Masque, has committed to assist the President some say she aspires to supplant, with the same quick transportation devices. I ensured Alisha's nation has access to it as well. Politically, China does not wish Britain to be India's sole ally. China believes it is in everybody's interest if we act in unison.'

She paused for us to digest her information. I decided I would be more impressive being silent. She responded in kind. Like poker players we stared at each other, neither speaking. Neither of us claimed to have four aces. Fingertips together, Janine resumed, 'You are aware of my informal association with the Indian lady. Your Mossad comrade is prepared to co-operate with our diplomatic alliance?'

She allowed sufficient time for my dumb European brain to work out the implications of her 'informal association' with Alisha. That would include Alisha's stories of my relations with her as a working girl at Anais's Palace. I was embarrassed. Somewhere humour was concealed behind Janine's immobile features.

Both Simon and Jon fancied the Head of the Chinese Secret Service. Some drives remain strong irrespective of common sense!

Chapter 32

We varied our altitude to confuse enemy monitoring. I was bursting for action at last! Hopefully, we would uncover, once and for all, what the Druids were really up to. Alassam shared my high spirits because he was relishing a chance to try out the flier's advanced cloaking. I suspected McNulty was responsible for such rapid access to this equipment. He was happy to concede Mars was light years ahead of Terra in its technological expertise.

It seemed the extravert Rastaman and taciturn McNulty shared a mutual admiration society. Just one thing niggled me, and I must be truthful. I was angry how overwhelmed I had become by shifting and ambiguous events. Initially, I decided the root of my feelings came from my own confused loyalties. I arrived from Helium as a semi-hostile spy, serving Myrna Golden, governor and wife. Manitoba Joe and I reached Earth by means of a top-secret teleportation device. Being primarily a top-ranking Mossad agent, he had freedom of choice. I was an errand boy. My task was to assess the supposedly inept President of the Empire so my wife could overthrow him and usurp his Empire. Although Myrna's own ambitions were involved, there was a greater national threat. I was commanded to seek a means to counter the Caliphate's *jihad* against the civilization of two planets. That part, of course, demanded Maddigan's assistance. What once was totally straight forward had become contradictory or indecipherable...

Even more burdens fell on me. There were mounting uncertainties about my 'best mate' Joe, and several others had hidden motives. My ex-bed mate, Alisha, was Indian Secret Service; Janine, inscrutable as she was, was shifting from foe to friend; both Maddigans had been a puzzle; then Teena appeared from nowhere to become centre stage. Last of all I shifted, between desire to hatred for my wife and her people, to become a champion of those I had been dispatched to undermine. External political activities – the Druids, the Islamists, the Viking invasions with the monster, those mysterious 'flying saucers' – caused further earthquakes for interplanetary civilisation.

Intuition spoke again to me. I was being swept towards a climax. The denouement was coming.

We flew silently and cloaked from detection. I found refuge in research for my mission on Anglesey. Glendower's inconspicuous cottage lay far behind us. At present, we were passing over the mile wide channel that had made Devon and Cornwall an island. The next destination required a flight towards the we went east which was a place of deep green nature, such a magical contrast to the dull, orange harshness of Martian deserts. I decided it would be a good time to chill so I swallowed the yellow pill I had hidden in my boot. Since everything had become unreal, internally and externally, I might as well dive into its depths. What I had taken was a Fifteen Min Trip Tab. Originally, it was meant for agents who had the misfortune to be interrogated. You could get a break in another dimension while your flesh was tortured. I would need its power within me in time ahead! Teena jabbed me in my ribs to make me reach into the other boot. The wild child never missed a trick! I nodded to the General, but he declined. Discipline! Doran wanted to be accepted, impress us and get free drugs. I shook my head, gesturing for him to get on with his job. I don't allow cadets to take liberties. And I certainly do not permit pilots! Before he had time for sulks, a strange sight below made me exclaim, distracting everyone.

We had swung back down the coast of Wales. I believed I saw the remains of an Edwardian seaside town, bustling with people in stove pipe hats. I turned to Teena to share my vision. Already it was shifting. 'Dragon,' I whispered. The word was sufficient for her to enter the same place. Once, I learned that this bay was topped and tailed by mountains called Great Orme and Little Orme. My brain library informed me the name meant Worm or Dragon. For me, the Great Orme seemed to have a shiny green scaled head; a fin ran from the creature's snout to upper spine. The Little Orme was a serpent coiled in many-hued reptilian scales.

Teena breathed, 'He's gorgeous! Oh, I'd love to ride on his back and feel him beating the air with those tremendous wings. I want us to drop from the sky with him breathing fire on Mona.'

I opened a bottle and studied the screen's breath-taking views of Snowdonia. Mists swirled around the snowy peaks, towering into pale blue sky. My old hideaway was too well hidden even for me to pick out. Although it was near noon, I saw a translucent full moon over Cymru. This was my first chance to study Earth's sole satellite. It felt mysterious, in a way that Phobos and Deimos were not. The latter were just pieces of rock. A final wave brought me back to the war and plotting reality.

'Back?'

'Guess so, love.'

When I stood up to check the viewer again, I observed we had dropped further southward. For a moment I thought I had got a flashback. I saw a giant Buddha, and strikingly odd architecture around a long, narrow pool. This was for real, though. Files supplied the name, Portmeirion. Alassam probably detoured as a misdirection before we approached Anglesey. No one would think of Druid's Island invaders sight-seeing a tourist folly! Wisely, the marines took this opportunity and were arming the flier's weaponry and reinforcing Rig 1's latest cloaking upgrades as a precaution.

'Are we going to blow away these fuckers?' asked Doran, manly gruffness in his voice. He appeared ignorant of the identity of 'these fuckers'. Like any youngster who had never been in combat he believed he was invulnerable. He could kill and not be killed. The soldiers around him inflated this confidence. He was happy to bomb anybody without personal danger.

'Shut the mouth up, batty boy!' the General hissed. 'Information! We here for information. We aim to see but not be seen. Got that?'

The reprimand stopped the blather. Alassam guided a descent until our craft almost lopped off the tops of the pine trees that ran to the shore. Turning to me and Teena, he informed us, 'I'm hoping the enemy anticipate cloaking being used high above the ground. I want us under their laser-webs.'

That shut up everyone. We accelerated, skimming the waves in a silver mist. In moments we were hovering over the sand dunes of Anglesey's wind-swept shore. No people, no defences! How peculiar! As we edged slowly inland for less than half a mile, I discovered there was an ancient archaeological site. A viewer app directed my attention to some faint circles, marking the foundations of dwellings of 5,000 years ago. My interest in this treasury of prehistory was interrupted. The left stabilizer blew up. An enemy overhead had scored a decisive hit on us.

Alassam instantly responded with, 'Hang tight. They can't locate us easy, guys. Shielding's still on. If we have to land, we run or fight. No other choices.'

Doran wept. He had wet himself. The boy who had been eager to bomb people did not live up to his imaginings. The young girl with the flowing ginger hair had to stroke his face and kiss his brow to reassure the lad. Of all of us, she was the least fearful. She smiled and spoke to me in a calm voice, 'See our screen, honey. Check at the sky.'

Overhead the heavens were darkened by swarms of black shiny disks. They could blow us to smithereens if they chose to. That appeared very likely. I hoped Doran would not wet himself again.

Chapter 33

A very different drama was taking place 400,000 miles away. In the murky mid-day sky above Helium a flotilla of zeppelins hovered. They displayed an array of national coats of arms belonging to Britain's allies on both Earth and Mars. Several were equipped with advanced weaponry, shared by Myrna, desperate to maintain their support. To ensure security the balloons enjoyed the support of a host of glittering strato-cruisers, buzzing like angry bees. An array of security devices protected every conceivable area. A variety of media were to broadcast approved recordings for their interplanetary audiences. Discretely, concealed recorders were located above the city and particularly in the Governor's Palace. Again, there was careful censorship of what the public would see.

Naturally enough, all of us missed the live event. I was engaged in preparing for being murdered by Grand Druid Haggard on distant Earth! Weeks later Joe described the attendees to me, and what went on in that meeting in Governor Golden's governmental palace..

Teleportation brought the Earth delegates through to Helium in a highly secretive manner. The only participants to travel by their own means were the Chinese Ambassador and entourage. The word 'teleportation' was not spoken. There was an unspoken recognition that the two dominant nations present were the British Empire and China. Both were suspected to possess the secret of teleportation. Mossad did too. But nobody knew that.

There was a common desire for united action. All parties at this summit saw the seriousness of their situation. Invasions, nuclear war and references to mysterious American weaponry appearing on Earth worked everybody to a state of immense concern. This was in addition to the threats and aggression of the Caliphate on Mars.

Seriousness and grim faces epitomized today. There were none of the intoxicating 'jollies' I had been used to at Myrna's cabinet sessions. A modest diet, minimal alcohol and drugs and an hour's privacy before discussions were the only permitted preliminaries. Once everyone arrived, security escorted representatives into the dome of the Governor's Palace. They were taken into the fortified main building, then through the high Golden Doors to the Great Hall. They sat in allotted places in a circle of simple desks. Jars of precious spring water were provided to each of them.

Not a minute was wasted. Myrna welcomed her 'friends' and made a short, if pompous, opening address. I imagine she expected polite applause and thanks. Later, Joe described for me with relish how he upstaged her before she was sat down. Without warning, he appeared out of nowhere in a truly dramatic entrance.

That wrecked Governor Golden's stage-managed performance. Even the diplomats dropped their masks of probity rehearsed for their audiences of interstellar constituents on planets and Rigs and gaped in astonishment. Unannounced, he strode into the chamber. Moreover, he was accompanied by Janine, Head of the Chinese Secret Service, and India's Earth liaison officer, Alisha. Interestingly, despite his surgical facial alteration, everyone instantly knew who McNulty was. The Indian Consul was visibly shocked to see her Senior Intelligence Officer colleague, Alisha, beside him. One thing I admired about Myrna was her aptitude for appearing to be unperturbed, no matter what challenge she faced. I have no doubt she was really tested when McNulty came through her supposedly inaccessible entrance to the conference room without shindrance. He was present without invitation too! She found the best course of avoiding even a ripple of consternation.

With admiration, he described to me later how she glared at him, then rapidly shifted it to the pretence he had arrived late for the meeting.

With customary hostility she snapped, 'You look as if you're still disorientated from your transportation. I hope you have an update on the situation of Earth, I was expecting it from you to prove you're as up-to-date as we expect.'

Determined to assert herself, she looked round the table and asked Israel's Ambassador whether Joe would be speaking for Israel, or for Mossad. That was a winner! He admitted, honestly, for once, she 'caught him off balance'. In fact, he became flustered. A scowl might have worked better. Instead, he attempted to deny knowledge of the rumours that Mossad had any part in what was going on in England.

'I am informed that Mossad sent some agent or other onto a Druid Island. I have some access to the organization, you see? Apparently, their agent ran into trouble, ma'am, and has disappeared. He was, it seems, with a party accompanying the English General, Alassam, and a small team of Special Forces. It seems to me their enemies are interested in Alassam rather than Mossad. I guarantee to keep everyone updated if they make it.'

Israel's Ambassador knew that to lie effectively, one must add a few seeds of truth. It was some English person with Alassam according to my sources, certainly not a Mossad agent. It was clever of him. Joe had already provided the Ambassador with a full update about what was taking place in England. Israel's government needed its strong relationship with Mossad. Joe came to the meeting to aid him, not Myrna, if information was required. They had pre-arranged signals indicating a Yes or No response.

The conference room was surgically bright. Psychologically, this said, *'No hiding and no secrets here'*. Myrna demanded, 'we want the punchline, Ambassador. No preambles. Then we can go into the presentations by other friends of India, China, the African Free Nation, Australia, Great Britain and, of course, Israel for shared updates regarding global situations on Mars and Earth. Fire away, Sir!'

Joe spoke, rescuing the entire assembly by dropping a bombshell.

'An alliance of the supposedly extinct United State of America established a base on the far side of Luna, half a century ago. Despite telling lies to our goodly friends in China, the Russkies have been working with the Yanks over this entire period.'

Janine, sitting beside the Ambassador, punched the palm of her right hand with her left fist. I think she felt obliged to present some pantomime anger to assure the gathered Western powers the Chinese Empire had never been privy to such information. Joe said he had prepared to detail their technology, but Myrna wanted to spit out the flesh and get at the bone. I am certain she was feeding ego and asserting her authority.

'Are they allied to the Caliphate on Mars? Are they a major military part in the wars on Earth? Is someone else involved?' she asked, looking round the hall.

There was a universal shaking of bewildered heads.

The Indian Ambassador sought to play down the situation. 'An armistice was agreed between Helium Province and the Caliphate. You even permitted mosques here. As far as reportage informs us there is a similar agreement between President Maddigan and his Druids. Druids are pretty damned few. Anglesey and Tintagel are microscopic, ma'am. Americans and Russians on the Moon are fantasy.'

McNulty let loose a hoarse laugh. 'The true danger is an alliance between the Yanks and Terran Druids. The USA return is true. I've seen it. However, the greatest threat is not them, not Muslim scum – it's the pagans with eugenic labs on Anglesey! They're creating biological monsters.'

This was the second time he stunned the assembly. He told me, with relish, there was a full minute's silence. Then a chattering between delegates.

Myrna became impatient and angry. She shouted, turned her speakers to full volume and exclaimed, 'Eugenics!'

For the benefit of any lacking inter-planetary English language, the Chinese Ambassador explained, 'Genetic manipulation! Germinal choice technology! Half human hybrids!'

With dry humour, Joe added, 'Zombies and monsters and giants!'

One area both Governor Golden and McNulty skirted around, were the exact whereabouts of the African marines. Neither had anyone an inkling of the details of our mission. Nor could they have guessed the danger we faced 400,000 miles away.

A degree of accord was reached by the attendees. On Maddigan's orders, Myrna had already negotiated with India and, to a lesser degree, Australia that in return for military support they could acquire extensive tracts of land currently under British control.

In return they would contribute unconditional military support to the Empire. There was no doubt about the inevitability of the Caliphate's incursions into all Martian settlements, or renewed terrorist activity. A similar agreement with the other allies was imperative. An added inducement was that the Islamic borders on Mars could be seized and occupied by the victors of conflict.

China expressed a concern. Their ambassador demanded assurances of allied support. Long ago, Chinese Terran policy had included alliances with Russia. It had included hostile action on Earth and Martian settlements. Then the plan went dead. Oddly, the Russians ceased to be of significance on Mars. If what the Mossad agent (Joe shook his head, apparently) were true – as she believed it to be – there could be a massive assault on Chinese territories on both planets.

Consequently, it had become blindingly obvious that an Anglo-Chinese alliance was the only means of achieving stability. After all, China now possessed the British Empire's secret of teleportation. Teleportation must have been the British bargaining chip to ensure their alliance. It was also the only means by which the Caliphate or Lunar Yanks could be checked. Everybody had to accept that.

Discussions took an abrupt lurch. Nobody was fully aware of the Druid agenda. It was common knowledge the Druids once tried to convert Maddigan. Some still speculated about his trustworthiness as President of the British Empire. They feared he might still have associations with mystic or Pagan insanity. McNulty watched Myrna puff herself up as if she might exploit these doubts. It must have looked to her like an opportunity overthrow the old fool. Everyone was utterly amazed when Janine stood up to declare the position held by the President of China.

'Many months have I observed and worked with President Maddigan,' she informed us. 'As a result, many issues were clarified for the Peoples' Republic of China. Those were games he plays. They were to deceive Druids. He courageously exposed much of their intention. Though he fails absorbing them into British Empire, he takes them by surprise; fights against them now time is right. Do you realize that with Mossad assistance it was he who defeated them and the thieves and evil ones in Salisbury? With his leadership we allied to stop attempted invasion of Wight Isle. So much USA fear him, two of their soldier men came to assassinate him. You, general, captured them. Maddigan proved to my nation he is the man without deceit. Honestly, he shares arms and strategy with China. And, most of all, teleportation is presented to my people. I believe he shares even this with all friends who fight beside him. My respect, China's respect, is with President Maddigan.'

Hands together, she bowed. She sat back down. The Ambassador nodded approval for her speech on her behalf. With such endorsement no one would be fool enough to abandon their leader in the alliance.

It would be spitefully cruel of me to repeat McNulty's description of Myrna at this moment. I couldn't help but recall her constant digs about Janine as 'my girlfriend'. I understood this cunning attempt to confirm any hunches and hints she might have had about China and Maddigan, using me as go-between. Accepting the reality of the situation, she applauded Janine's speech. Her self-control that allowed her to accept the success of the alliance came before her own ambition.

Had I realized that Haggard and the USA were as big a danger as the Caliphate, I would not have accompanied Alassam on the current mission to Anglesey. Neither would I have continued to view Maddigan as a lovable, benevolent old gentleman. After Janine's revelations, I discovered he was deviousness incarnate. Still lovable, mind you!

Chapter 34

Nobody was injured when we were lasered and smashed down on Anglesey. I silently offered a toast of thanks for the safety features of Helium technology that were integrated into the strato-cruiser.

Alassam sent nine of his 12 marines from the base hatch and running from our fallen ship in the direction of Druid research labs. We needed to check how imminent soldiers were in coming to capture us. The floor of the flier opened again for the rest of us to escape. Before we could do so, he told us to freeze. Intense laser beams burned 15 feet into the Earth beneath us. I thought we were being fired at. No, it was the General burning out a hideaway for us underneath our vessel. He jumped in the pit he had made. We leaped in after him. Concealment canvas dropped over the hole. It was cover in the dusk. The bottom of the ship closed up again. 'Come together, guys!' he hissed. We were crushed about him in the blackness. I thought of mass burials, especially from a perspective of unlucky victims who were accidentally left alive.

Tomb-time was mercifully brief. I heard Alassam breathing heavily and fumbling in his slimline backpack. A viewer screen lit up. This was top-of-the-range Rig 1 kit. Such tech was way outside the competences of Maddigan's technicians. The source was most likely from Mossad. Another compacted item the size of a man unrolled too. The General's purpose was to create and expand a secure underground den for us. An illuminated dial showed his huge, brown fingers dancing round a vid-screen. To everyone's infinite relief, a lining formed about the walls of our chamber and forced them apart to create a wider underground accommodation. The sound of hissing reassured us that air was already feeding through from above. The General was desperate to activate the external cameras. Like a good leader, he understood his troops needed one more thing before they could exhale their carbon dioxide of relief.

I was awed by the rapidity and efficiency of Alassam's actions. His training and instinct were completely merged .

'Let there be light!' he proclaimed with a guffaw.

The military viewer amplified the light for us a thousand-fold. We relaxed from our huddle once we realized we were safe in the adequate space of our warren. The acid coating created by electrical shocks to the artificial coatings pressurized on the sides so it could safely burn into more soil. The resulting expansion was hardly a skate boarder facility, but we were thankful it had evolved from a cremation chamber to a gym. The lining substance gave the entire hideout an olive- green sheen, which was comforting. The largest viewer I'd ever seen rolled out from a man-sized bundle. Alassam adhered it high up on one of the walls, to provide illumination, warmth and oxygen. Being incredibly efficient, he did it all all by himself.

I had a free moment to monitor what was happening up top. The soldiers who shot us down surrounded the ship. Sound was excellent so I immediately discovered why we were spotted so rapidly. I saw that accompanying Haggard was former Eco Minister, Sheila. Smugness was embossed on her face, as she was faced our concealed exterior cameras. She held the place of honour beside the High Druid, Haggard. In her talons she held the President's strato monitor, which would track any ship, any place.

It looked like Maddigan had been shamefully careless when he was having sex. I imagined her picking his pocket whilst her feet were in the air! She had struck me as looking impressively acrobatic for a mature woman. She must have concealed the national fleet monitor after she had stolen it from her panting old lecher. As a consequence, we were hearing her implicit boast how she had directed the High Druid to follow Doran's vessel with the device. I suspected Haggard would as inept as the President with technological applications. Such matters were, to him, jobs for underlings. Earlier Alassam had no time to initiate auto-destruct on the cruiser. That was most fortunate because now we were able to pick up careless gossip.

Sheila wanted to uncover all the technical information she could about our ship. It might be useful, she declared, as back up for her white-bearded priests. The longer she took to break in, however, the more time we had to snoop on their plans. The Druids believed we had all abandoned our vessel and fled, panicking into the night.

As a precaution, Alassam had programmed all the flier's screens with a red flashing announcement to offer intentional misinformation. 'Total Evacuation! Meet 23.30. Mound.'it repeated. The warning concealed our presence and assisted the nine marines who had been sent ahead check out for danger.

The enemy faced their own problems. I had studied them on the screen carefully. I noted Sheila's permanently combative tone of voice when she spoke to Haggard. Any view he expressed seemed to be perceived by her as a slight.

I had already fantasized how she must have offered a satisfactory sexual performance to lure lusty old Butch into her boudoir, despite the toll of age. Unfortunately, it was obvious why he tossed the Presidential lariat around my Teena as his reserve pony! I suspected the Chief Druid had less interest in getting his leg over. Like his rivals in evil, like the Catholic clergy, he more likely had an appetite for kids. That might be why the Priestess of Chalice Well showed him such scant reverence. Respect was entirely missing when she addressed the patriarch.

I had assumed Haggard had been consulted about where our incursions were likely. That was not what happened. Sheila only informed Haggard after she herself called together the fleet that brought us down. I wondered where they came from. What did amaze me was her idiotically transparent arrogance and ambition. Also, I was perplexed why he suppressed his anger. He gave no reply to any of her observations and mutely blanked her. I used close- up visuals of the party above our concealment. I freeze-framed the twitch of irritation on the right side of his mouth. He might find her useful for her insight and intelligence, but that would surely be superseded by his absolute, though silent, rage at her failure to respect his status. Perhaps the answer lay in her possession of Maddigan's tactical monitor by which she controlled a treasury of information.

Taciturnly, Haggard moved away from her to investigate our cruiser more closely. His flowing white robes accentuated his dignity. The former Eco-Minister lacked this poise. To me, she sounded shrill. Or, as Myrna used to say, 'common as a fish wife.'

'You've no idea who began spying on Mona? I'd say someone with more brain than that bitch, Natasha?' Sheila screeched. 'Fucking talk to me!'

Wearily, Haggard drew his fingers across his eyelids. He recovered his contemptuous dignity, observing, 'None of your thoughts are hidden from me, regardless of how ineffably intelligent you believe you are. I see you think it was the dualistic playboy, Simon Edge? He is hardly an indicator of wisdom.'

Not an indicator of wisdom, my arse! I thought as I switched off.

I asked Alassam if I could have a few minutes with Teena. He grinned and nodded. We high-fived. What a great guy! I retreated to a small alcove next to the luminescent screen and beckoned to Teena. She sensed my confusion and came to me. Such long legs! However, this was not my intention when I lay down on the mud floor. I placed my head in her lap.

A rarely opened compartment in my mind opened its door. I told her I was having identity problem. I wondered if, in some mystical way, Haggard had seen me watching and got into my brain. When he looked directly at the camera he might have telepathically pressed my psychological keyword 'dualistic'. I fled inside my mind and saw a door. It opened. I grew frightened of entering to see what it held. That led to my full story. I told Teena as best as I could about how a brain operation had made Simon Edge into Jon Masque. Her face showed shock, comprehension and, finally, pity.

'Each morning when I wake up, I don't know if I'm Simon or Jon. I might never wake at all. I'm frightened my brain could be wiped clean. I go off on one then. Sadness and terror eclipse some "me". Jon Masque dislikes Simon Edge. That is reciprocated. Trouble is, I was and am them both. The me watching them both sees them as alien as a pair of 15 feet tall, green, bug-eyed monsters. In the old days, even minor surgery had repercussions like infection. What complications have my brain operations created? Medical tampering has not merely affected the grey mush of my cerebrum, cerebellum, hypothalamus and so on. But what about the damage to my brain's product that they call the mind! My mind, not tissue like my brain. Without you, Teena, anchoring me, my mental sepsis would become insanity.'

I blanked out. Apparently, I was gone less than two minutes. Suddenly, I was back again, growling and muttering. I saw Teena's beautiful face, filled with concern. When I asked what I was saying, she said that the only words I uttered were rubbish about reaching Mars by astral projection. Then, I lay like a corpse beside the screen, repeating, 'monster factory'.

Before I could speak again, I was gone again. Some electrical current of memory was taking me back in time. I saw something I'd missed on the Stonehenge battlefield. My inner eye revisited the 15-foot-tall, brainless giant, lifting men up and biting off their heads and limbs. From there, I struggled to remember the word Myrna later used to describe processes used at Tintagel and Anglesey that would explain it. *Eugenics!* The word worked like magical invocation. Once that entered my brain there came a flash of vision that intensified and held. More buried memories. No. The future! I saw hordes of horrors storm from the Caliphate to cull the infidel. Right across the frozen red sands they came. Their mutated bodies were modified to shrug at cold, starvation or darkness. My final mental image was of two colossal Americans, Barker and Kirk, standing with their legs astride the miniature moon, sneering at their Terran victims.

I heard deafening screaming. My body was vibrating. Then, I was being roughly shaken and I heard Teena crying my names. This shouting was coming from me, and I was drenched in sweat. I saw Alassam was here as well. I asked him if he was okay.

He looked relieved I was returning to sanity.

'Am *I* okay? You jokin' me! You been out and away wid psilocybin, man? Have you done swallerin' mushrooms and licking tropical toads, baby?'

A last eddy of intuition rippled through my head. I genuinely knew what was about to happen. I also knew what remedial action was needed.

'We're detected,' I warned. 'You must use the laser burners to head 500 yards left so we surface and run. Do it, please. Now!'

It is quite astonishing in the face of such irrational lunacy, but calm, sensible Alassam acted on my request. I laughed at Simon Edge inside my head screaming in fury.

We had sufficient power left to burn through. Our tunnel's walls held energy we could divert. A corridor was cut through the subterranean hiding place. As the general yelled the order, everyone ran. Our escape shaft inclined upward. All of the others obeyed me without hesitation. We emerged into the darkness of Earth night with a sliver of crescent moon providing no light. I sprinted in front, leading Teena and Doran and the general and his three remaining guys towards those circular foundations that marked the homes of the villagers from 5,000 years ago.

'Down the holes!' I commanded everyone.

We all dived at the instant a wall of fire blew sky high. We were deafened by the aftershock. Why had Haggard demolished our strato-cruiser? It was filled with scientific and political information as well as Helium's latest weaponry? Had Sheila received a message from someone, friend or foe? Was it a mistake? Or was this sabotage Natasha had programmed to protect security secrets? What was strange to me was an alteration of Alassam's attitude. There was a kind of awe in the depths of his dark brown eyes. He had just experienced my intuition warn us and save our lives. I was becoming different from who he previously thought I was.

There was no time to waste. We must seize the opportunity to escape before our enemies could track us. Worse disaster might begin raining on England in the form of shiny, black American ships swarming from Luna. I sensed that would signal the start the Caliphate's insurrection on all the allied provinces of Mars. After that, I knew most likely they would teleport armies and weapons to assist Arabia to repel Israel. Even more terrifying, was my fear India's old enemy, Pakistan, launching nuclear retaliation on Mumbai.

Chapter 35

Whether inside your head, or in exterior reality, there's always something lurking in the darkness, ready to leap out when it is least expected. The surprise on this occasion was definitely advantageous for us. Without warning an air fleet attacked Anglesey. Lasers shot from the dark sky. They were not after our sad little gang. Their fire was targeting the Druid's research and development facilities.

Were these friends here to rescue us? I was slightly doubtful about that. Their insignia were impossible to make out in the gloomy sky. My first guess was that this had been sanctioned by Natasha. because Wells was geographically close to Anglesey. McNulty was on Helium, so he could not be leading it. Maddigan was organizing Southern England's defences against any further threats. That only left the First Lady with both authority and ability to make such a decision as an assault on Anglesey. If so, her reasoning was unclear to me. Natasha would be more inclined to accept us as collateral casualties than risk a fleet of craft just to rescue us.

There was no further time to speculate. Someone waved and yelled from the perimeter of the buildings. I identified three of the original nine marines Alassam sent to reconnoitre while he created our hideout. The general charged forward to greet them. Teena, Doran and I, with the remaining three marines, followed after.

My spirits were uplifted by the sight of Teena's flowing red hair as she overtook me. For a moment her loveliness seemed, to me, otherworldly. I was inspired about to do something brave – or maybe just reckless. She would remember me if I died in my attempt to save us all. I noticed Doran desperately gripping her hand. Although she must have been at least three years younger than him, he needed her as a mother-substitute, a lady who would lead him, rescue him and wipe away his tears. My goodbyes to them would be painful and pointless. I was going to do what I had to do. Without a word, I ran. All alone, I sped towards the Druid's hell palace. Chance directed me blindly, but accurately, toward a collapsed wall that led inside the facility.

Having activated my visor and oxygen, I jumped over debris, enshrouded by smoke and dust. I stepped over dozens of white-robed corpses. I entered through the hole in the wall and, like a man possessed, careered down debris-strewn corridors that took me toward the centre of the complex. With my legs racing automatically, I arrived in a large, high-ceilinged room. Its roof had received a direct laser hit. It must have been of great intensity because after piercing the ceiling when it had penetrated right through the floor to expose a huge circular hole, that had been designed for access to a lower level. If there was a gravity device fitted to the sides – and if it was still operational – I would be able to descend and discover what was hidden down below. Of course, should the gravity control be fucked, I would end up a mess of blood and bone waiting to be unearthed by historians of 1,000 years in the future.

Act. Don't think. Hesitation results in wrong decisions.

I plunged into the cavity and found myself floating downwards in total blackness. It was lucky the gravity device was undamaged. I drifted like a feather. Very lightly, I touched down in a place with dull, artificial illumination. How else would I be able check out hell? A noxious stink hung in the air, making me feel sick. Vats filled with noxious substances seemed to have been knocked over by quakes and explosions. Or it was possible someone had tried to destroy evidence.

I was confronted by more passages. Picking one, I followed it. This took me through a subterranean maze with archways leading to rooms that echoed with howls, barks and screams. I chose the darkest, noisiest one. When I entered, I pressed the night vision sight on the side of my spectacles. Lines of cages stretched down the sides of this frightful place, for as far as I could see. I quickly identified what was happening here with increasing horror.

Each cage imprisoned an animal, being casually used for cruel experiments in cross breeding and for far worse reasons. Some creatures I could name from a general knowledge of genetic manipulation. There were felines known as Tigons, Ligers, Leopons and Jaglions. Most had been implanted with steel claws. Further along the path of pain, I identified a Zonkey This a sad creature was given a comical name that was brutally inappropriate. I walked a short distance up the aisle of experiments to identify a Grolarbear, a Mangalig (a pig/sheep cross), even, in a tank of sea water far too small for it, a Wholphin. Tears of empathy ran from my eyes for these unfortunate beings.

I knew it was essential for me to shed my spiritual empathy if I were to survive here. I needed to access reserves of brutality, cruelty and ruthlessness I had once possessed. All I desired, while I struggled to stop my crying, were any numbing narcotics that could deaden my horror and fear. They would have assisted me to cope with the situation. That was the moment one of this hell's inhabitants attacked me. Claws began ripping my arm, and it kicked me so hard I nearly fell. Demons of callousness and savagery filled me. I had to slash and kill him, feeling no pain or remorse! If I failed, I would be dead.

In calling the attacker 'him', I am not attributing an iota of humanity to the thing that lacerated me. Three-inch fingernails swiftly slashed my cheek, narrowly missing my eyes. My attacker's visage can only be described as 'hideous.' One of its eyes was misplaced, far up its forehead and was double the size of the other one. There was a nose – more a trunk – where its ear belonged. The other eye had switched residence to where you would have expected its nose to be. The miscegenation's lips that hung loose and flabby were those of a congenital imbecile. They failed to hide the rotting fangs or prevent green slaver from dripping to the floor. I was obliged to reach for my weapon. My laser shooter was gone! I must have dropped it. The only defence I had I had was a primitive a dagger. But it was stashed out of easy reach. The nine inch blade was sheathed within the false lining of my crotch-padded leather pants. Imminent death empowered me. I grabbed with the speed of terror, by ripping through the material of my right-hand hip pocket. In a flowing motion, I blindly lacerated my assailant. Instead of scarlet blood, a vile-smelling yellow ichor pumped from its wound. Before that mutation hit the ground, another one had attacked me. This thing had a serpent head with a human visage. The horror lunged at my thigh with envenomed fangs. The only reason it missed was because I was still tottering away from the first assault.

The most awful feature of the snake man was when it uttered maniacal laughter, that resembled bestial howling. It had stinking slimy hair that slapped my face. My emergency torch slid down my sleeve and accidentally came on. I almost wished I hadn't seen what else stalked me! A pack of four or five deformed dog-things crouched preparing to encircle me. I think that, before the modifications to their bodies, they might have been beasts that were called 'hyenas'. There was madness in their eyes that made me shake in fear. Somehow, I could tell the 'hyenas' were highly intelligent. In some way their brains had been tampered with and warped. Something had gone wrong with these poor beasts. Perhaps they had the perception to be aware of their own monstrousness. They might have emotions like me. I dare not follow that thought into pity that would overwhelm and immobilize me. I grieved for them, even though I knew I must kill them or be killed. If this was my last moment, my ego insisted that I die a hero.

I feared I was about to lose control over my bodily functions. Already my whole body was shaking with an adrenaline rush. Frantically, I scanned the gloom for my laser weapon. Close to me, beside a rocky wall, my eyes alighted on an ancient altar. Miraculous! Two swords lay on top of the stone. I imagine this played a part in some Pagan magic ritual. Being a product of the late 23rd century space age, I never had the opportunity to assume a heroic stance holding a blade above my head. This was the moment to do it!

In bored periods on Dinas Emrys, I had watched dramas about Vikings. I recalled how those warriors faced impossible odds. I attacked the pack. Shocked, they hesitated just a moment. I did not falter, and continued running at them, swinging the sword I had grabbed from the altar. Although they still meant to take me down, they never expected me to suddenly leap to the left and launch into them from the far side of the altar. I grasped the hilt of that three-foot sword as if the weapon was a part of me. My very nature was transformed by a sublime charge of energy. The blade swung around my head, then circled down to hack into canine flesh. My cries of joy, my exhilaration at being a warrior, like ones of ancient legend, possessed me. It was ecstasy. I could slay the entire slavering pack!

The berserker fury was terminated by a dart piercing my chest. A second struck my shoulder. A third one completed the job. Then, darkness. My heroic last words were, 'Fuck you, CUNTS!' I was ready to join my Earthly ancestors in death, filled with the same defiance as the Vikings of old making their last stand.

Although I remained in silent blackness, it was not non-existence. I was unaware of any intermission of time passing. Perhaps this was the calming moment before complete oblivion.

As if someone was gradually bringing a faint sound then infinitesimally increasing the volume, a scratching noise came to my hearing. In my imagination there was a mediaeval scribe in a castle, recording his history. Abrupt light dazzled me. Then I could see again. Before me was an ancient man with the long white hair and beard using a goose feather quill writing on a yellow scroll of parchment. Some ancestral fear cried out that this was the Catholic entity called God. I had died in that eugenics laboratory and my name was being inscribed in The Book of the Damned!

Gradually, reason returned to me. It was no divinity in the afterlife. Utterly the opposite. This was the Arch Druid of Tintagel. I was ashamed of my terror! I tried to excuse my cowardice as being due to the reshaping of my brain by Rig 1's surgeons. I needed to be Simon Edge. That would restore my psychological swagger. Imitating me as Simon, I demanded, 'Why'd you pull me out of there, you old bastard?'

Haggard ignored me and continued recording whatever it was with his quill and ink. I rejected an infantile urge to chant, 'Druids are butt plugs' just to annoy him. A bit more subtly, I declared, 'If a cockroach has your forked tongue, I'll go and nap.'

More swiftly than I could see, he reacted. Something like a snake fang pierced my calf. I shrieked.

With calculated calm, he informed me, 'That was the electric whip with which I just saved your miserable life. My enhanced hyaenidae were getting out of hand – thanks to this American treachery.'

His assumption about the Yanks was curious. I laughed, knowingly, 'So they gave you a sucker punch you were too stupid to see coming.'

Of course, I actually knew nothing. The bluff had consequences. Mocking him was bound to infuriate his pride. I realized he could easily react by further punishment from the electric whip. Also, I realized I was naked. With a degree of self-control, he merely flicked my balls with the tip of his lash. Tears of terror poured down my cheeks, but I gritted my teeth to hold back screams. I prepared to imitate my fantasy heroes.

As though he had done nothing to punish me, he remarked, 'I wonder how secure Britain's relationship with China is, behind that pomp and circumstance. Come to that, I heard rumours of internal duplicity. It's closer to you than you are capable of noticing. What would happen if Maddigan was removed by your Myrna Golden? A ruthless atheist like her is somebody with whom I could do business. Of course, there seems to be a plot afoot, involving the English First Lady and her husband's black general. Not so secure is your happy alliance, is it?'

When I refused to take his bait, he went on, 'From what I know of your character, you worry less about political ideals than why you're not dead.'

'That's because I'm a charming intellectual and more than your equal.'

His laughter resembled a tiger's purr.

'Words such as "arrogant" or "deluded" persist in entering my mind when I study you. I shall provide an honest answer, Simon. I kept you alive because you are unique. You epitomize the philosophical factors at the core of our conflict. After the superb butchery in your cerebrum, you exist in both of them. Science and Spiritual. Do you possess sufficient intelligence to comprehend my meaning in my observation, stupid young schizophrenic?'

He was indeed shrewd. My dual identity as Jon Masque and Simon Edge, mirrored the increasing division within my psyche

227

between science and magic. Changes were not merely in physical appearance. The cynical materialist, Simon, had imperceptibly become Jon, who was buffeted chance and intuition. Many would think he was a magician. I suspected he had a degree of telepathy. Cunning too.

There were a multitude of explanations demanding answers. Why had the sacred Isle of Anglesey become a eugenics laboratory for madmen to create monsters? Then we had Haggard's association with the reborn USA. These were most materialistic of Protestant Christians. Why would they ally with pagans, closely akin to Black Magicians if USA history could be believed?

Furthermore, why – as seemed to be the case – U-turn and renege against their allies? Equally bizarre was that the only possible alternative ally for America would be the Caliphate. Yanks saw them too as agents of evil. Equally, there appeared no way the Muslims could curry favour with a Jewish derived culture the Prophet had demanded be eradicated. Lastly, what about Britain? Why had Tintagel abandoned President Maddigan, who they once prepared as their public front in the Tor rituals?

Trying to catch the old man by surprise, I enquired, 'How come you plotted to kill our team? As I see it, you lured us here entirely for that purpose, didn't you? Come on! You could have killed me any time. For what reason am I your prisoner?'

Haggard's reaction chilled me. He gnashed his teeth like a maniac. I grew afraid. He raised his voice for the first time: 'America shall face its second apocalypse. I shall punish the treacherous, big lipped, square faced, boy scientists with mouths filled with lies and big teeth. You shall serve me to access your invention that will assist me in their destruction.'

With that, he whirled around and rammed a gigantic hypodermic needle into my arm. There were better ways to administer knockout drugs, in this day and age! As a sadist, I guess, the High Druid preferred the archaic means. I've no doubt he relished my scream of pain as I passed out.

Chapter 36

I came round in a stench of vomit. There must have been something noxious in the knockout injection. Haggard had done it deliberately to prevent me starting trouble. More likely, he merely enjoyed suffering. I was lying on the cabin floor of a king-sized strato-cruiser. The moment my eyelids flickered, icy water sprayed over my naked body as a primitive cleaning solution. My head cleared with the shock! A towel landed over my face. Automatically, I rubbed myself with it, despite my aches and my shivers. Someone threw some items of clothing at me. I tugged on the pair of cream-coloured cotton baggy gym pants and loose jacket top. Cotton was a novelty for me. My kit was natural, not artificially made. I had been told by someone, probably Glendower, it was like wool they either grew or trimmed from Welsh sheep.

Through mildly blurred vision I discovered my comrades were prisoners as well. Teena (thank the stars!), Alassam, Doran and two marines, all shared this misery. I was incredulous to see they were in metal chains. Rather a medieval touch that was, I thought! My sight was clearing, though my eyes felt sore. While I collected my senses, I became aware we were aboard a highly advanced battle cruiser. I had no idea how we all ended up here. Thanks to the knock-out jab, I missed our escape from Haggard's torture chamber.

So far as I could guess, the Druids' cruiser had been hidden some distance beneath the interrogation room. They must have lugged me down there to make a getaway from that unexpected air-attack. It would have been hair raising when they all absconded from those eugenics test labs.

Simon Edge's patronizing voice sneered from the back of my head. War? Ancient history? Military tactics? He knew it all. Physical resistance, he observed, would have been out of the question. The aggressors clearly possessed the most sophisticated technology in existence outside Helium and Rig 1. The Holy Isle launch pad on Mona proved immeasurably more successful protecting Anglesey's Druids than in what occurred in legendary Roman days. Overall, their modern foemen's strategies were vastly more daunting than anything the Romans came up with. That said, the assault followed the traditional military method of Rome, which was a big, brutal action generating a firestorm over the land. Weapons change, but military tactics do not.

Jon Masque pushed Simon away and assessed our situation from a different perspective. Here and now is all of importance when one's death is so close.

I saw the High Druid perched in front of the central screen with the control pads. Going onto manual, he personally piloted. From all the mumbling and chanting he was doing, I figured he was trying to invoke assistance from Pagan gods. There would be little help coming from his stunned, demoralized Druid retinue! His devotees comprised six male Druids and High Priestess, Sheila. Once my vision improved, I realized there were another four Druids I had been unaware of on either side of us.

Young Doran was scared shitless. Stammering, he leaned towards me for reassurance. This was an error. Talking was forbidden. His attempted blather was terminated by a flick of Haggard's electric whip. I took heed. However, I did not draw attention to the fact that I was the only prisoner not in irons. For that reason, I did not ask Alassam and Teena how they had been captured and brought aboard. I still felt sick and in considerable pain from head to toe, but I was alert. Sometimes I can be observant. By studying the nearby water pressure and oxygen readings, I deduced the flier had escaped through a tunnel under the Menai Straits. Afterwards, it must have re-surfaced fairly near to shore and ascended to a high altitude. The central screen readings indicated we were travelling at top gallop across a night sky in a southerly direction. Tintagel was the most likely destination.

I felt the High Druid's gaze on me. He was trying to penetrate my thoughts while my mind was in a weakened condition. When that failed, he whimsically surfed the computer menu. Miraculously, he accessed Rig 1. I caught a glimpse of Anais, promoting her girls. Fate had thrown the dice of randomness into my life as it had so often before. Before the High Druid could pull back from his accidental intrusion, a 'spread transmission' penetrated to the cruiser's central communications. Visual intrusions were almost impossible to capture. Such trespassers could not be tracked to their location so long as no messages went out from them. Haggard realized he had been spotted. With impressive speed, he pulled out and hit 'random scan'. It was his breath-taking misfortune to enter through the enemy fleet's server. Admiral Barker's face sneered at him from the central frame. He was far quicker than Anais had been! Behind him hovered his toothy servant, Lieutenant Kirk.

'Hi, you mother-fuckin' savages of Brit-land! Uncle Sam's raised his flag again! Down but not out. Know what I'm sayin'? America is back!' Barker announced. He tugged his neat moustache to remove any loose bristles. His following words astonished me. They clarified the direction events were moving.

'Democracy, freedom and belief in God!' Barker announced in a deep, sonorous voice. 'We've returned with true American values that we shall restore to Earth and share with Mars. No more British imperialism! Your tiny island will be cleansed of blasphemers who defile the word of the Lord. Praise God! Mankind will be redeemed from Pagan superstition no less than from Islamic heresy! We come with science and rationality! Jesus has restored America. The nation is re-baptized, risen again from the oceans! We are born again of the water and the spirit!'

Here was the hellfire sermon enhanced with the most lethal arsenal ever assembled by mankind. Once, I had considered Haggard the epitome of religious hysteria. He could evoke an almost lethal charisma. Once, he had been on the path to dominate the Head of the British Empire's President, making him Tintagel's puppet. With the same complete conviction in himself he then took a new approach when his clever brain uncovered reborn Americans. He got closer to his goal then anyone ever guessed. His conquest of Lyonesse by defeating Alassam could only have been achieved by using the assistance of the USA and its advanced technology. I concluded he did it again when he masterminded the Stonehenge uprising. At the same time, he co-ordinated the invasion of the Isle of Wight, though likely with the Yanks participation in discussions. Finally, all of it made sense!

Treachery was his payback. Treachery! No wonder for his deranged fury. He was doubly betrayed; first by Maddigan, then by Barker. Right now, he attributed most of the blame to Maddigan, who had made a fool of him in the first case through his deception. Irrationally, he saw the other contributory cause as the teleportation secret Helium had concealed on Rig 1. There was no doubt in his mind about a deceitful deal occurring between Maddigan and Myrna. He could not comprehend such idiots as them possessing the intelligence to out-manoeuvre his own divine genius. Unbelievably, to him, they thought they could crush all their enemies like the Druids and Caliphate and two worlds would be ruled by the British Empire. That explained everything to me. Devious Haggard had been blinded by ego.

Ignoring all security precautions, he transferred his communication from Barker to Rig 1. The High Druid again became a madman. Once again, he began shrieking and gnashing his teeth, froth pouring from his mouth as if he was rabid. Confidential codes must have been accessed during his idle surfing, since Madame Anais appeared on the screen. This time it was she who was caught unawares by the drooling maniac, open mouthed and bellowing.

'Black bitch! Your miscegenation should have been ended. You have betrayed civilization and the Goddess and Cernunnos of antlers! You! You! You! You made deals to lay your filthy hands on the progeny of machines so Britain could eradicate humanity! Your whores seduced your soldiers to wipe out nature.' His eyes rolled back in his head while his sandalled feet stamped the floor. I felt the terror that comes from being entirely at a lunatic's mercy.

The violent fit continued. Spitting and choking, he tore a machete from the fingers of a priest beside him. In the same motion, he rammed the semi-blunt end of it into one of Alassam's two remaining of marines. His foot placed in the dying man's chest he pulled the weapon from his body, almost slipping in streams of his victim's blood. Coherent speech left him. Fixing mad eyes on Anais who stared, horrified, on screen, he grabbed young Doran's collar.

'See punishment coming to you!'

Still in his chains, Doran was hauled onto his unsteady feet. With a sweeping arc, Haggard decapitated the boy. Straight through the vertebrae, his blade cut. Blood fountained, spurting from the neck and torso as his corpse fell to the floor. Haggard stared, unblinking at the mother's tear-covered black face. He gripped the decapitated head by its hair and held it to the cameras. He swung it round his head, screaming and drooling down his beard. Doran's dead face was pressed up to the viewer.

'Here's my reward for your treachery, vile whore-trader! I will shit on his head, traitor of America! Science is powerless before Cernnunos's judgement!'

Hot tears ran down my face. I could not bear to look at Doran's mother.

What disturbed me above all else was that my own intelligence role never detected the secret survival of North America nor their alliance with Russia. Alassam nudged my foot with his toe. When our eyes met, he gave me a half nod and I felt the empathy in his brown eyes. I was grateful for that.

At this moment, Fate balanced my luck with misfortune. Haggard's strato-cruiser went spinning across the heavens after a laser hit. This occurred within moments of Haggard's maniacal contact with Rig 1. His malice had revealed our exact location to Barker and Kirk. He was oblivious. In his fit of insanity, he began kicking Doran's head like a football, that oozed blood and brains. Sheila stood by her psychopathic guru gagging. She started to vomit over the deck.

Alassam could be an inspired leader in any situation. He indicated he was free of his chains. Teena's criminal abilities were activated as well, for I realized it was she who freed him. Sheila, white with shock, stumbled onto the control panel. She began piloting manually to level out the gyrating craft. Before the other Druids were able to recover, my dreadlocked Rasta buddy made it to the emergency escape panel.

He resembled a black-maned lion when his massive paw smashed the plasteen cover of the emergency button. Shouting, 'On!', he threw Haggard's anti-gravity back packs to me, Teena and his marine. How I admired his cool, in grabbin' a trio of anti gravs without even a glance!

He was so efficient, he had secured his own device before anyone else even began. It was his role to take charge and lead us. There was no time to piss about. With another order, 'Go!' his broad two-inch-thick brow butted the escape hatch switch. The Chalice Well Priestess screamed when Alassam jumped out first. A gale tore through the doomed ship. The marine attempted to follow him. To my shame, I knocked the guy aside, grabbed Teena's hand and we both fell out of the exit. We fluttered in space for a moment, shocked by the chill and the night darkness. The sole sweet thought in my noddle was that if I ever saw Druids again in the land of the living, I'd blow the bastards' heads off.

These happy imaginings yielded to my urge for self-preservation. Nudging Teena to copy, I pressed the anti-grav trigger on my backpack. We activated them just in time. Another few seconds and we would have been revolving helplessly at high speed toward the ground. However, we wore the finest of Helium's technology. Silent jets blazed from our backpacks, delicately suspending us motionless for a few moments. I had leisure to look down at the forest of hair beneath us that identified Alassam. He must have sensed my gaze because he looked up, activating sufficient illumination for me to spot his big white teeth grinning away. Teena and I both waved. Before our gradual descent started, I checked that the soldier above us was safe too. Also, I wanted to check whether the Druids' damaged flier was likely to collide with us. I wondered if the Druidic fuckers had sufficient gravity-kits for all of them. Or maybe old Maddigan's Ecological ex-shag had control over the battered cruiser? There were self-preservation factors for me to weigh up. For example, how far across the Irish Sea had we travelled? Worse, I could hardly swim with my injuries once we hit the sea. My Jon Masque body lacked the ingrained skill it had when I lived in my former Simon Edge body. That was food for thought.

SPLASH!

Chapter 37

I was in the midst of drowning in the Irish Sea at this moment. Naturally enough personal survival occupied my full attention, so I was unaware of what old Butch was up to. The President's actions determined the future of the human race on two planets. Our own offshore floundering was significantly less important.

Later, I discovered the boss had vanished to a level I could never have imagined.

He took his elderly Welsh mate, Glendower, and mysteriously left the Isle of Wight. He was confident the victorious allied forces controlled entire region. This was guaranteed by the support of the whole local population. Alisha, surprisingly, had been selected to direct the entire coalition – though with his detailed instructions. Her appointment was an appreciative diplomatic gesture to India. This helped to show the equal status held by all members of the alliance. It would make betrayal almost impossible. A shrewd psychological assessment lay behind this decision. His philosophy was that same trust he gave would – within calculated parameters – be reciprocated by others.

That arrangement being made, the two elderly Welshmen next streaked northwards in their luxury two-seater flier through bright blue skies toward a prehistoric site named Avebury.

'Glendower! Look you, me friend,' said the President. 'Come you to be a privileged witness this day. You are to learn about the key that unlocks the Druid brain that manufactured abominations with genetic engineering.'

Years later an opportunist created the 3D blockbuster about the President. It was a biographical dramatization. Special effects fabricated more hair and less belly flab for him. Drama needs had him deliver a messianic speech to his companion. Apparently, there was considerable applause from audiences everywhere at the moment he drew a big breath and declaimed, 'My friend, you witness my spirit opening the gates of wisdom. The fate of two worlds must be decided. I must find guidance for the actions by which we must take to liberate the Red Planet. At the same time, Terra, birthplace of humanity, must be restored. America was corrupted by faith in false sciences. For the third time that country must be punished. It blew apart in the Yellowstone event. Before that the same wickedness pulled it under the oceans when it was named Atlantis.'

I doubt he ever said anything so laborious and pompous. I cannot bring to mind the fake drama attributed to Glendower in his response to the Welshman's inspirational gospel. If he lived long enough, his mucky nails must start scratching his woolly head in complete bemusement. Furthermore, Maddigan would, no doubt, have let loose the reins on his bardic spirit during their short flight because he liked a bit of fun and jokes.

When they descended on Avebury, their flier made a wobbly landing in flat meadows a quarter of a mile from the northern arcade of standing stones. He was a poor pilot! When they stepped down to Earth, they slowly went towards a fallen monolith where they could sit side by side. Maddigan resumed with an explanation of the alignments of the arcades of stones. Butch sometimes deserved the 'Welsh Windbag' nickname, often whispered behind his back. In my opinion, he picked Glendower to come with him because the old chap's ignorance made him an ideal sounding board for some mystical analysis.

The President led the way to the north entrance of the Earth works. More tourist guide than President of an interplanetary Empire, he halted before they entered the outer circle and pointed to a half-buried monolith.

'Knocked down by vandal farmers in the vaunted "Age of Reason,"' he shouted, clicking on his own visual record. Abruptly he crashed the spy drones above them. However, they had already recorded a secret record I was to see much later.

I am unsure whether it was by fraud or some atmospheric anomaly, but what I learned from this record was odd.

From his grunts and vague comments, it appeared Glendower was looking at something different from what I saw. The old man was in a half-demolished ring of old boulders. I started when I first looked at them closely. These monoliths had distinct faces! The President explained the left-facing were feminine, the right facing, male. Some female stones suggested snakes.

When I viewed this episode at a later time, I was fascinated to watch a tourist guide to Terran prehistory turn in a more peculiar direction. You would imagine interplanetary war ought to occupy the mind of the man at the head of an Empire. Instead, he began to instruct his school friend become shepherd, of the weirdest inner beliefs I ever heard. There were two inner circles within the larger complex, he explained. They represented the two inhabited worlds within the Solar System.

He brimmed with enthusiasm. He said they were sitting in the northeast area, or 'Cove'. Below was what he called the 'Obelisk' ring. The President spun around in the middle of the ring.

'Tara-tara!' he hailed. 'We are within the orbit of Mars, here in the "cove" of science and logic. Despite the phallic "Obelisk", its stones mark the feminine path of Planet Earth. Like Yin and Yang, each energy contains within it its opposite. The 21-foot phallic Obelisk lies in the space of Mother Nature; within Martian masculinity, behold the stone with five faces of the feminine!'

Without warning, he collapsed on the grass at the foot of the huge monolith. Whenever I see the recording there are, I believe, five faces. A vulva is also clearly created in the granite. Probably through a transmission blunder, Maddigan's features become blurred when he makes his last remark. 'On May Day dawn the Obelisk's shadow falls across the vulva. They unite – as I've faith humanity shall.'

For ages I lay in a trance. I often wondered if I worked for the Master of an Empire of two worlds, a shaman or another fraudulent Haggard. Nevertheless, something was happening that went through me every time I ran the recording back. Could it be that there was some knowledge deep within his unconscious mind to which he opened unique access at this moment? For me, it remains strange beyond words.

He turned to primitive pseudo-science. Elements of Fire and Air formed the essence of Mars, whilst Water and Earth lurked beneath Terra. His description of a power waiting, even now, under our ocean to awake, made the hairs on the nape of my neck stand on end. Poor Glendower mumbled the disrespectful assessment, 'blather'. Maddigan ignored him, literally a man possessed. The astronomical correspondences became psychological. Most I could not understand. He said that West Kennett Long Barrow, the waters around the Silbury Pyramid, along with the stone circles, represented different hemispheres within the brain. Maddigan interpreted the Earthly landscape and planetary symbolism as his roadmaps for action, as a political and spiritual map, guiding his actions. All of it was too arcane for me. If his subjects were aware of it, he would be locked in the next cell of a mental hospital as the High Druid.

Madness dispersed. The day trip ended with Butch lying in the late summer's clover, a gentle breeze carrying sweet scents of grass and wildflowers to him. Assisting his return to being sensible, he struggled to tug a pair of bottles from his coat pocket for him and his pal. In the next Terran 24 hours the continued existence of the entire human species on two worlds would be decided. No one knew how near the end was.

When he restored access to the drones outside the atmosphere, less joyful news came on his screen. Lines upon lines of the Caliphate war fleet fighters, of Marian manufacture, materialized over Earth to assist Saudi Arabia drive back Israel's invasion. The Jewish soldiers were taken by surprise. The first target should not have done so, given Saudi Arabia was Islam's sacred site. What was seriously unprepared for was the speed with which they arrived on Earth and the power and quantity of their weapons. *Jihad* became synonymous with genocide.

Jon Masque was facing a danger just as personally dire. It was doubtful whether there was anyone could rescue me, bobbing in the icy Irish Sea.

Chapter 38

I grew light-headed when I got into a rhythm of spitting salt water from my mouth while more sea trickled from my nostrils. Nothing had ever taken me closer to craven terror than this floating in the sea in pitch black night. I was utterly alone! When I shouted there was no answer, not even an echo. It is dreadful to die alone and unremembered. As was my wont, I pretended none of the bad stuff was for real. If I could feel my movement in the water, maybe it was happening. If not, it was definitely a vivid nightmare. Then my imagination betrayed me with a thought of sharks cruising around the Irish Sea.

Out of nowhere, came a wooden 'raft' with two people holding onto it. Were they rescuers? I was near to weeping with relief, but I did not dare yield to false hope.

No! I actually was saved. It was like a light coming on. People pulled me between them, one on either side, helping me to hold onto their driftwood, bouncing on the waves. A woman was on my left and a man on my right. Differences in their weight told me that much.

With something of a shock, I identified them as Teena and Alassam. The latter illuminated our faces with his emergency light. My tears mixed with salt water when I stared at his black face with drenched dreadlocks. The beautiful girl with long ginger rats' tails kissed me before I could speak. Alassam realized my emotional condition. He promised help would come any moment. I thought he must have signalled a friend on the mainland. With an impulse that would later embarrass me, I said I loved them both.

'I couldn't go on without you,' exclaimed Teena.

Alassam interrupted in a sad tone. 'We lost Marine Walantoia. Came from Libya. Joined me there. In them days, before the 12 thousand of us came rescuin' you British soft, white boys, he signed up. Know, what I'm saying?'

Once I'd have snapped back that he was getting Lyonesse back as payback. Along with his appointment as Commander of all England's armies, this was a pretty solid thank you. Tonight, I did not want my sharp tongue. I abruptly went all tearful, wobbly and afraid of an attack. Shock, I believe it's called.

The blackness of the sky was split briefly by a searchlight that flickered over the waves. Alassam announced, 'I believe there's a lady up above.'

A twelve-seater strato, bristling with more lasers than ancient Terran hedgehogs' 'spikes', went round and round less than 20 feet above us. Side portals slid back, and slides appeared so a pair of soldiers with anti-gravity back jets descended to assist us from the Irish Sea. I spotted the white robe of Natasha Maddigan behind them. We were delivered into the cabin within minutes. She waved joyfully. General Alassam returned it, laughing in relief.

I remained weak and disorientated. I had been through as much as my stamina could cope with on Anglesey. Teena helped Alassam to heave me onto a medical couch. Always alert, the First Lady saw I was wounded. My companions were embarrassed they had been unaware of my injuries. Even I had not realized it till I was pulled from the icy sea. Most of the damage was from my fight with Haggard's mutants. After temporary salves were applied, I grew aware of another half a dozen injuries from fangs and claws. A blade had pierced my side at some point. Worst of all was an injection site which was red, swollen and infected.

Imperiously, Natasha swept across the cabin and pointed out, 'Your young princess trained as a healer. Teena, please treat him immediately with your semi-science of magic.'

Feeling unstable in both my emotions and body, I desperately needed to recover my tough pose. At least my brain was coming back online, full power. Concealing the trembling of my hands, I faced Natasha.

'What is it you need from me, m'lady? My intuition's always sound, and I'm always a lucky dude. Something big time is happening. You're not telling me what it is. I'm getting the feeling you require my humble skills.'

'Humble?' she replied. Alassam laughed. After a pause, she did likewise. She began again, 'You seem oblivious about what you are needed for.'

I tried to anticipate her intentions. Someone could have implanted secret stuff within my brain without my knowledge. She meant something less devious.

'I met you as Jon Masque. Once, by reputation, I knew you as an entirely different person. Simon Edge would have been too arrogant to consider my espionage resources would even match Helium's. Hours after your appearance in Wells, I had secured an extensive databank to analyse your reputation prior to your teleportation. I initiated in-depth research into your history, plus a dossier of Simon Edge's psychological evaluation. Naturally, everybody knew you were Myra Golden's consort. Frequently, only a man who was ruthless, egocentric and cunning would be a useful instrument for Helium's Governor. After all, the sobriquet, "Ice Maiden" was generally applied to that woman. What was difficult for me to adjust to was the fact that you were not Edge *pretending* to be Masque. You *were* Jon Masque. You know, it was really difficult for me to accept that surgery and psychological indoctrination could, together, remake your entire character. It was bewildering when I met 'Jon Masque'. That person was utterly contrary to the character I previously studied so thoroughly and detested.'

She sighed deeply and looked into my eyes. She continued, 'Some things, bless you, don't change. Not always bad. I am relieved that you were not a recording that was wiped, then totally replaced by what someone deemed a more "appropriate" character for espionage. You won't be upset if I admit I find you are personable. It might make you feel better if I say you're an egocentric bastard who grew on me. In fact, I liked you – occasionally. Often, you are amusing. The achievements of modern science can be daunting. Ironically, you experienced little difficulty in adapting to your altered psyche. You woke one morning knowing you were Jon Masque. That was all there was to it, for you. I'd guess you also like Jon more than Simon. Truly astonishing! You were fully aware of everything that you had experienced in the past and of the mission for which you were assigned. I surmise you simplified it for yourself using a fantasy like, "*I'm in England, disguised as Jon Masque. Of course, I'm the same Simon as always. I've had a face-lift as a disguise. That's all."'*

She was right. I was different, if not the opposite from the who I used to be. There is no doubt I was still as charismatic as I'd always been. That goes without saying, of course. I couldn't have handled it were there no core ME. There are questions there I would not want to go into.

Natasha studied me, discovering that I was less secure than she'd previously thought.

'I must be brief,' she explained hurriedly. 'The crises of the last few days make bluntness unavoidable. I've only ever known you as Masque. Despite my aversion to most aspects of your former Simon Edge character, we're both aware of that personality's diplomat and planning skills. I disliked your Simon self for being a devious, lying swamp of self-aggrandisement. Originally, he was merely a distant stranger we monitored on Mars. I confess, my reaction to you is different now. I have grown to like and respect you, John Masque. I can think of no other man who could have survived all that you have been through!'

Her light kiss on my cheek was unsubtle. However, my emotional recovery was assisted further by Teena, who continued to stroke my back as if I was a cat to be calmed and loved. I'm not sure how far ahead the First Lady had considered the means to win me over. The bottle of 500-year-old Black Label Whisky, smuggled from her Butch's hidden store, was her most inspired tool in her plan. Whisky was an indulgence shared by me as Simon and Jon! I knocked back a shot, then savoured the aftertaste. Natasha was too parsimonious a host for my wishes. I was obliged to hold out my tumbler for more. She got the message. When my tumbler was brimming again, I became more comfortable and attentive.

She made her concluding remark, 'Butch found it easy to identify potential in you, even in your first encounter. That was why he gifted his beautiful girl to you. It was a personal sacrifice for him. Dear Butch loved Teena. Nonetheless, her contribution was essential for us to awaken your latent power that will serve to defend billions of human beings.'

'You what?' I cried, too pissed off to say anything else.

'I always knew you would be pivotal in the events coming to Terra and Mars. Unfortunately, it seems that at this time we need some Simon Edge skills that are housed in your subconscious if we are to survive. In short, I want you to invite unscrupulous Simon Edge to emerge from within you, Jon Masque. I am ashamed for being so calculating and demanding so much of you.'

This was the point at which she changed the subject from me to a more abstract theme. She attempted to describe her husband's transmission from Avebury. She hoped to demonstrate he also had an alter ego. Simon Edge would have dismissed everything as being the metaphysics of an imbecile. My modified mind was prepared to reserve judgement: even when she likened it to an internal representation of Mars and Earth. I promised to watch the recording, using the security code she gave me.

My head spinning, I made an excuse, 'I can't cope with this stuff, Ma'am. I'm too exhausted. Send me wherever you want.'

She was disconcerted by my tone of confused resignation. She wanted to demonstrate her concern for me. Turning to Alassam, she pleaded, 'Please help me! Here we are, in Earth orbit, practically waiting to be attacked. We have moral obligations to assist Jon. He's a friend. And a good man. I don't want him to revert to being that bastard Spymaster on Helium. There's a worse danger if he endured another operation for a personality restoration…'

I interrupted in the voice of Simon, 'You could donate me to the Anglesey eugenics labs.'

Much of the pain from my injuries and potential poisoning was easing, thanks to Teena's ministrations. However, I became uncharacteristically emotional, if not tearful. Partly, I wanted her to feel guilty about what she wanted me to do. Upon reflection, the real reason was different. Those casual words, 'he gifted his beautiful girl to you' kicked it off. I wondered why I was the sort of wimp to be upset by such a trivial remark. What was wrong with me? Despite the gravity of the situation, Jon was incapable of making a firm decision!

From the main vid-screen came a deafening racket. Alassam marched up to turn the volume to ear-bleeding maximum because he was so angry with my wavering. Seizing my shoulders, he shouted at me.

'Two mother-fucking worlds are gettin' blown up!'

He turned my head to face the screen. A major offensive was shown breaking through Britain's Martian territories. I detected fires in areas of Helium. It was deep into the long Martian night. The familiar blackness of the dark, frozen season was shockingly broken by fire and explosions. I glimpsed multitudes of men and women dying before us in flashes of laser light. Corpses were piled on the main thoroughfares. The ionospheric drones sent endless images through the chain of Rigs so that Earth too would witness lesser settlements south of the capital being eradicated. Alassam rapidly scanned a dozen regions of the Red Planet. Every sector between the border with the Caliphate and the British Provinces resembled what ancients called 'hell'. That included the Chinese and Indian provinces. A full scan of the 400 million miles between Mars and Earth presented a collage of rocket ships soundlessly erupting in the void. There was war in space! It was unheard of. The aggressors were using weapons of unbelievable sophistication. The name *America* was in my mind! Alassam's last pop-up flashed pictures of the destruction of one of the central Rigs, probably Rig 20 or 21. At that point, the transmission went fuzzy. It must be that the Caliphate had begun to destroy both drones and the rafts of communication hubs. Soon, we would lose all surveillance.

'Where is McNulty?' I cried in horror.

Natasha frowned. She wafted her slender fingers to summon her Rastaman General, indicating she wanted England on screen right away. The destruction of just one intermediary Rig had impaired transmissions. Another malfunction kicked in. Sabotage, no question. It caused visuals to move at high speed, fast forwarding across the continents of Earth instead of where she wanted. Despite the blurring it was clear that destruction was even worse on Terra than on the Red Planet. Wars were being fought by sea, on land and in the air. We could see that much. Two countries had made pre-emptive retaliation against Arabia. First, Chinese forces crossed the deserts. From the west a massive fleet of fighters from Israel flew to assist them. They were determined to eradicate the birthplace of the Caliphate. So far as I could tell, Australia was the sole nation to hold back. Maybe they had been wise to abstain from the Great Adventure of space! Worryingly, there was no trace of McNulty.

Matters worsened. Alassam's immense forefinger rapped on the screen, where he'd freeze-framed an air armada, coming to support Arabia. We went dumb with shock. The fliers displayed the insignia of the USA. Across much of the globe American strato-cruisers appeared from nowhere.

The general voice-directed his cursor north. Our hearts leaped and a loud moan of relief came from all of us. Above the English Channel, we identified McNulty's markings on a shoal of little silver fighters that suddenly burst from the skies above the Bishop's Palace.

'Butch!' Natasha uttered with reassurance.

What happened next again took away our breath. A small group of US cruisers, large vessels, were crossing the Channel to engage our little silver fliers. One minute the strait was vacant. The next a US war party was in full attack! A second party manifested so the Americans had doubled their strength.

Joe's response was even more dramatic. He brought them down in minutes! His actions had always been unexpected. This day he excelled himself with a miracle. Of course, there are no miracles. His team had directed what Alassam identified as Muon Magnetic Field beams towards the American aggressors. Although he knew what it was, the Rastaman General was equally stunned. Even he had not known this force had been successfully created. Turning to me, he declared, with shock, the firepower derived from muon g-2 was able to disrupt particles within the enemy vessels. They simply froze up in the sky. Then they fell to the ground and smashed. There was no blood, no screams – no people. All that was left was scrap metal, littering Somerset fields. No soldiers existed anymore.

'Jon? Did you know about McNulty's work, man?' the General breathed. 'Gimme truth.'

I answered, truthfully, I had no idea. Natasha touched my arm in a friendly way and nodded to her general. With her habitual dignity, she moved towards the screen to survey every part of the palace grounds. She was seeking her husband, an expression of concern on her face.

Teena held her body next to mine and I was restored.

'Advise me, Alassam, because I trust you. I'm frightened of returning to being cruel, arsehole, Simon Edge if I tune up my brain on Rig 1. I don't feel like I have a choice if Natasha needs Simon Edge's devious, ruthless skills to work for her. Know what I mean?'

He was puzzled and asked, 'Why pretend, man?'

'On Rig 1 they could reverse mental upgrades. That way you can get me back to being a ruthless liar and killer, the man who can scheme and achieve mass extinction of any threats to the Empire. What frightens me more is myself. If I fuck up in dabbling inside my brain, I'd be dead or a lunatic.'

His reply was as honest as ever, 'My job is to lead our soldiers. Teena? Hold his hand. The First Lady and me's going back to Earth. Our worlds be needin' us. He needs you. You gotta go to Rig 1 with my buddy and change his nappies!'

We all become slow on the uptake when we are stressed and tired. I did not question his manipulative skills until I found myself awaking to Teena and I lying on a surgical couch. Flexible metal strips slid around us where we lay side by side.

Teleportation can be terrifying when it is unexpected. One minute there. Then here. The conversation we were having seemed to have taken place a thousand years ago. A compact portable teleporter, likely bestowed by Mossad spies had directed its beams on us. My pulse rate doubled and blood shot to my head. Neither fight nor flight had been available as options as we were sent across 400 million miles to Rig 1 where my mind was to be invaded and transformed into Simon Edge. That's what happens when someone else makes your decisions.

Chapter 39

Only once before had I experienced my atoms, molecules, electrons – with a pinch of Quark, Strangeness and Charm – spinning through the void during teleportation. My first teleportation remains a shocking experience! Long ago, in the Rig 1 labs, my brain was sliced and diced to create a new person, who would serve as Myrna's snooper in the court of Maddigan. Initially, the experience was sold to me as being a simple affair. Lie down in the lab. Whack! I would wake up appearing to be a different person. It was but an illusion to deceive my English audience. Reality was crueller. There was no time to adjust or recuperate. I still find it disturbing to explain that trauma.

I had woken up on a couch in Snowdonia, a million miles away from icy Mars. I felt a different body. My traits were, somehow, different. Impossible, it sounds! It was. How can I express what it is like to realize I had been made into a person who wasn't me? I was an alien personality.

I spent a long time alone in my cottage. I had to adjust to being Jon Masque of Earth. Simon Edge was a fantasy man from a dream. In the cottage I had woken up. Wales was real and Helium was fiction. I was months in isolation before I was be fit to meet with Manitoba Joe and we would become moles burrowing beneath the heart of the British Empire.

This time, my second teleportation to Rig 1 was even more shocking for me. Where were Alassam, Natasha and Joe? I had been with them a moment ago but now I was alone. I was familiar with being drugged. The symptoms were present now. For some reason I had been separated from my friends and I found myself dumped on a surgical couch. The smells of this place were familiar, but I could not recall where I was or why I was there. Recently, I thought I saw that of the 40 Rigs between Mars and Earth being blown to smithereens. Maybe that accounted for why I was so agitated and confused.

This teleportation had been more extreme than I thought it was before. Instead of experiencing an 'Eyes closed on Rig 1, eyes open in Wales,' I felt I had been as nothingness. No taste, touch, no nothing. No me!

A bluesman sang, 'I woke up this morning.' I opened my peepers to hear my own magnificent voice rendering, 'I woke up on a surgical couch in the laboratory of Rig 1.'

The gruff voice of Madam Anais was calling me. I swivelled round and I saw her black mourning weeds. Poor woman! Her youngest son was lost forever. Her eldest, Darren, was standing here, beside me. He saw I needed assistance. He helped me get my feet to the floor. Standing was an effort for me. Leaning heavily upon his arm I managed to reach his mother and hug her.

A slim oriental girl with skin of a light green hue was also trying to comfort Anais. Her name? My memory still impaired. I was scared that the physical transference had malfunctioned, and my brain got damaged.

Madame Anais had aged shockingly. Once she had been a blazing comet of energy and merriment, that comical wheeler-dealer, brothel empress, surrogate mother of happy young prostitutes, quick-witted organizer of espionage. All of it had deserted her. Now her dark face was haggard; white streaks defeated the black dye of her hair. She ignored her appearance. She wore no make-up, or whatever she once did to conceal wrinkles. Instinctively, I held her closer to me. Despite my own fragility of mind, I wanted to filter some of my positive energy into her. I heard Teena breathe, 'Jon, baby, bless you.' Anais moaned pitifully. Her black mourning weeds smelled heavily of tobacco and dope. That did not matter. I kissed her forehead and cheek.

An altar had been set up in a corner of reception. Once the girls paraded here for customers making their selection. Today it served a different function. Bottles of brandy, a bowl of blood indicated some kind of Voodoo shrine. Alassam would have known what it all meant.

Anais finally returned my kisses and told me, 'You a saint, boy. Not your vain face and body. Matters none if'n you be Masque or Edge. Them names speak fo' themself. You more'n either of them fellas. I don't care what body you dressed in.'

Before she could release her tears, Rig 1 was attacked.

There was a display of token shooting and a few theatrical explosions. I use that word because this was an obvious publicity set up rather than a serious military strategy. And I was immediately aware of the identity of our attacker. Our central vid-screen showed banks of search lights that served a dazzling exhibition for subsequent live newscasts. Here was my own trademark production!

Anais enquired, mildly, 'Do you need to hide, Simon? I have a place…'

'I won't drop you in shit,' I assured her. 'But if this red-haired young lady falling asleep on your couch could be concealed safely? Romance. You know? An obvious someone is here in person to uncover imaginary plots against them. Being bitter and being vengeful they will lash out at youthful beauty to hurt me and punish my girl, Teena.'

'Brainy decision, boy,' replied Anais, 'if it's the woman we think it is.'

Turning to the discreet keyboard I knew to be hidden under the lid of an old wooden desk by the wall, I touched the second green button on the upper left of the layout. If I had pressed anything else, the hard drive would have been eradicated. I would have been killed by a shock as an added extra! Strange security for a brothel, if you know what I mean.

A muon ray eradicated the entire side wall of Madame Anais's secret refuge. It heralded the person who had given muon to McNulty. There was a deal that involved me being presented to my closest enemy. I did not blame Manitoba Joe. Without the ray, England would have been lost. Through the debris of the demolished wall space, there burst a score of armed, uniformed soldiers. I didn't anticipate the vicious punch to my chest that brought me to the floor. I lay moaning, attempting to recover my breath. My sole thought was one of relief that Teena was clear of this brutality. The girl would likely have attempted to protect me and been injured if I had not emphatically shaken my head. The leader of the invading thugs was tall and slim. Despite appearances there was a lot of force behind the boot that stamped on my body. Body armour generally enhances the wearer's strength. When the protective helmet came off their identity was as I had expected. It was as well I had no breath left in my lungs to express my pain and rage. Some relationships end with, 'Have a good life.' Not this one!

I looked into a face filled with fury. My darling wife was angry beyond all belief! Her close-cropped ginger curls were flattened and sweat ran down her face. Removing her boot from my carcass she made as if to leave me for a moment. Then she suddenly kicked me in my ribs again.

'Bastard!' she roared. 'The plot for you and your pal Maddigan and his bitch wife to take over Helium failed! What weaponry have you and your bitches designed to overthrow me? And how about your deal with the Yanks? I know you so well. You'll promise to be double-crossing Maddigan to save your weasel skin and play both sides. I remember how cunning you are doing that.'

I shook my head as I lay prone. I was sure that her kick had fractured a rib. It was impossible for me to cough to get rid of the phlegm on my chest. It hurt too much to cough! None of it hurt as much as my heart when I realized what Myrna had become. Despite her ambitions for the presidency, she had once behaved honourably. That Myrna had been a calm, intelligent woman who played politics like chess without visible emotion – and without malice. No personal spite was involved. She simply moved pieces over the board. Her primary intention had been to benefit her people. Such impartial, rational actions were the signature of a capable and incorruptible Governor of the Province. Moderate policies of *détente* had kept the Caliphate at bay. Whilst regarding President Maddigan with scepticism, she still implemented his designs to the best of her ability.

I no longer recognized her. I was at the mercy of a dictator in the making, who distrusted everyone and would murder on impulse.

Wisely, I did not speak while she had me bound up and thrown into a cell at the rear of the brothel's 'naughty room'. This was where violent clients were imprisoned before fitting punishment was administered! Anais protected her girls at all times, and no one would get away with harming them. The lock-up was 12 by 12 feet with a high ceiling. All four walls, and the floor too, were shiny, white reinforced plastic. I had been given a bedding sheet and cover, a cushion to sit on and a toilet and shower unit. Nothing else. Not even a mirror in which I could examine my lexicon of injuries. Knowing Myrna as I did, I did not waste my breath by telling her anything whatsoever or, in fact, making any reply at all. That was one trait that had not changed in her! Her rationality was based on the premise that she was always right and anybody who demurred was a traitor, trying to mislead her. Safer to be dumb! Just the same, Simon and Jon shared the characteristic of an inability to be clever.

As the panels slid tight on my cell, I risked the irony of, 'Naturally I'm guilty and that's why I arrived to see you, risking my life.'

She didn't kick me again.

I decided to use new Jon Masque abilities in my hour of need. Staring at the blank white walls in front of me, I unshackled my mind. Whether it was illusion or something else, I imagined I hovered above Glastonbury Tor's maze, where I once watched Maddigan on his route to the summit. This time it was me winding the terraces around the ancient site. I thought the journey might take place inside my mind.

Reality broke down the doors I had opened. Myrna's crap fighters were under attack. Fuck knows who it was this time! The metaphor became tangible. My cell's door was smashed and the debris flung aside. A green-tinged oriental featured babe, who I might have recognized earlier, was liberating me. Her name surfaced. She was skinny little Melanie. The front area of the Sex Palace shook as if there was an earthquake on Rig 1. This was a major attack.

Melanie yelled in her high-pitched voice, 'Caliphate, they here!'

'A mirror!' I replied with my mind completely elsewhere.

Chapter 40

Chance takes decisions if we fail to make them ourselves. As we headed towards the rear of Anais's Rig 1 Palace, I expressed my thanks to Melanie for saving me, running my hands around her small, firm body. Though I was aware of war cruisers lasering us, I simply had to embrace her. My smooth charm triumphs over my fear of death! So slender, so…happily, I recalled the last occasion she had sex with me. I felt a stirring in my sweaty crotch and joy stiffened my cock. She giggled and grabbed it. I was astonished at myself when I suddenly said, 'No. Not now. Honestly, though, thanks for my rescue.'

She looked surprised – disappointed too, I believe. Then she smiled and answered, 'I see you good guy. Nice fool guy. You save me. Bomb time? Now I save you.'

'How did you recognize me, though?'

Melissa looked puzzled. When she asked me why, I thought I must look totally different. I was not Simon now. She shook her long black hair.

'Mirror! Bollocks to space battles. I have to look in mirror!'

We had walked through the wrecked observation deck of the palace until we reached a cubicle which Melanie identified as a 'dressing room'. There was quite a lot of damage in there, but it had what I wanted so much, I even felt my eyes starting from their sockets! I had to see to the face of ME. Only one mirror had survived intact. It was antique with a gold frame decorated with intricate Chinese dragons, vines and blossoms. It was not the priceless art that interested me. Just my reflection. To my relief, the hansom features of Simon Edge smiled blissfully back at me. Since it was a full-length mirror, I was glad to see my former fit and healthy body was restored. No more spectacles and scholarly stooped shoulders! Not only had I been teleported from Natasha's ship, but also the operation on me had restored all the physical fitness I had lost. I hesitated. Something worried me. I was scared I might not only have lost only the Jon Masque weedy body. My psychology, my personality; was that regressed to Simon Edge's? Could I actually have achieved the body of an athlete with the soul of a saint?

There were star and sickle insignia on the sides of the destroyers, exchanging laser fire with the fleet, identifiable by the red, white and blue coat of arms of the British Empire. The latter fanned out, symmetrically, with three lines of battle cruisers at the front, followed by a trio of super destroyers that indicated China's support. A pair of giant Indian Battle Cruisers formed the apex of the triangle. I detected McNulty tactics. Here was another purpose behind his gate-crashing of Myrna's conference on Helium. Once the Chino-Indian commitment had been firmed up there, he had teleported back to Earth for the defence of England. To prevent disclosure, he was reported as having 'gone missing' or 'vanished'.

Here was my own opportunity to act, rather than be acted upon! No one was giving directions to the alliance of Martian provinces. Joe once taught me that what all soldiers look for was someone at the top telling them what to do and assume responsibility. The timing was fortuitous again. Teena emerged from the debris near the brothel's main passage. I was concerned to see she had been injured. A closer inspection reassured me that it was a small cut to her forehead. Teena's nature was to help others first. I saw Anais was looking frail and in need of the lovely redhead's assistance. Once she had assisted the old lady to a chaise longue I beckoned and indicated the control board below the viewer. Melanie discreetly withdrew from my side.

I asked Teena if she could assist with Anais's communication systems. She nodded immediately so I told her, 'If you can operate the screen function and encrypted channels for the old lady, I can get us out of this mess.'

A fresh vitality restored Teena despite her shock from the small wound. She welcomed the opportunity to join the action. I realized this must have been had been another role she had served for Maddigan. She had never been the bimbo I initially mistook her for. She had constantly watched and learned when I thought she was painting her fingernails.

With absolute self-assurance, she formatted my image to appear on all of Helium's military channels. With a small smirk, she created a golden aura about me, and my voice was enhanced to a level tone of confidence. Knowing I could rely on her technological ability, my task was to create the words.

'This is Commander Edge. I am summoned here by Governor Golden. I have been put in charge of Special Ops by my wife to quell the insurrection on Earth which has also endangered our President and Empire. I have experienced communication disruption with Governor Myrna. That is being resolved. She did, however, order me to assume command of the fleet. Please assure me you have adequate muon energy to decay the neutrons imminently for our strike?'

I was authoritative. Folded arms and a solid body posture are immeasurably more effective than explanations. I knew nothing of Myrna's real plans. Teena had broken through Helium's inner coded channel to confirm that McNulty had already transferred the muon appliances to Helium's fliers. Strategy was more Joe's area of expertise. If in doubt – guess. My guess was that our fleet outnumbered the Caliphate. Intuition informed me they anticipated support from an ally. Whoever they were, it appeared they had not turned up. Delays might give them time to do so. Even worse, hesitation would lead to questions from my own captains. I gave no one time to think. On my command all the Helium ships bore down on the enemy, dispersing muon rays to create terrible destruction in the void. I waved my arms and screamed, 'Show the camel fuckers Allah got lost in space. Save us all from these fanatics!' Memories of the decades of threats and terrorism made to their families and lives, the fighters of Helium flew silently screaming at the enemy fleet.

They used chemical shells to remove the protective coatings of the Caliphate ships. Muon beams were an unknown to me. Some people might have hesitated. Though Simon Edge would say, 'What the hell! They deserve it,' Jon Masque within me acted with some caution. I ordered the captains to begin by unnerving the enemy by zipping between and around their ships. Naturally enough, they focussed upon the destroyers with their huge laser cannons. That caution had led me to a serious misjudgement. The Command Cruiser exploded. Almost a thousand of our soldiers perished.

There was no longer an alternative. On my cue, our stratos pounded their fleet with the muon devices. Muon fire is almost impossible to detect, the beams being as slim as cartoonists' pencils. But their accuracy is mind-blowing. Within minutes the mobility systems of half the Caliphate's fliers were disabled. Then white beams of surrender illuminated space.

My dilemma was how to go about taking their crews as prisoners or enforce a Caliphate retreat from the vicinity of Mars and Rig 1. There was no time to search prisoners for weapons and no place to lock them up in prison. Simon would have waved them on their way. Then blown the lot of them to oblivion.

Another party silently accessed my insecure encryption. I started when the screen suddenly lit up, dazzling me with a display of crimson dragons on a turquoise background. Here was our major partner in the Alliance. Janine Suee's immobile face came on screen. The Chinese lady's game skills beat my own! I decided the presentation was Chinese humour. Janine was laughing underneath her serene surface. She watched me, saying nothing. This was generally a successful technique for an interrogator. I remembered our last meeting and my reactions to her made sense. She was obliged to speak at last, although I am certain I detected a latent smile.

'My, oh my, Commander Edge! The rapidity of your actions is remarkable. I comprehend the esteem your "buddy" has for you.'

Always, she managed to convince me of hidden meanings in every word she used. Which 'buddy' did she refer to? Was there a motive behind the vagueness? I knew I could never match her. Instead, I plunged in with naive bluntness, which was an evasive ploy.

'We are in the midst of a battle which I am directing without authority from anyone. My life is in danger. Myrna Golden has become a monster. With respect, be brief and tell me, without subterfuge, how we can progress to mutual advantage.'

There was a slightly stilted style in her explanation. 'The position of the Maddigans in England is successfully maintained by President McNulty and General Alassam. I possess details of their top-secret plan to defeat a USA invasion. Additionally, I have perception of the means by which they plan to eradicate the eugenic creations of your Druids. It is my firm belief you and I should jointly focus upon Mars and the Caliphate. If we are to achieve future harmony, the British Empire must agree to a revised territorial map of Mars. This would include not merely China, but also favourable arrangements for Joseph's Israel, Alassam's Africa and Alisha's India.'

Her democratic generosity to our other allies surprised me. Janine was way my superior in the league of intelligence. I was in awe of her. I accepted there must be sound political reasons for her direction. She realized these were affairs in which I was not in a position to make solid commitments. However, she judged me trustworthy when I answered, 'I give my word that I shall support the solutions you propose. I also agree to you alone, no other person, my transparency in these specific goals.'

Sometimes honesty is reciprocated. I trusted her and I believed her. Had I become Simon, I would not believe myself, let alone trust or be trusted by anyone else!

Madam Anais, still assisted by Teena, chuckled beside the viewer controls. 'All you need are Casinos for the Chinese, who are the greatest gamblers in the Solar System.'

Janine overheard her and laughed politely. Maybe that idea would appeal to her! Before I could contact respond or contact Joe again, Teena called me.

She stood, studying the main screen. Anais's fingers flew around links, accessing more communication routing than I knew existed. Teena passed on the information that Myrna's team were attempting to get back into their network to regain control of the fleet. Their war cruisers were becalmed in the void of space, where they had fled during the battle. That meant they were unable to make any physical intervention.

'Good work, Lady-Love of my life,' I told Anais. I kissed her curls.

The old Madam gave a throaty chuckle, adding, 'You's a smoothy, Simon. Know that don't you? No wonder my girls were happy to do sex while they picked your pockets, spied on your messages and dug out your secrets! If'n you moved your cock to where your brain oughta be'd, you be a genius!'

'I love this guy!' retorted Teena. 'I am not his candy, you know, ma'am?'

I responded with affectionate kisses for her this time. I assured her this love would be returned for as long as she lived. Simon Edge whispered to me of his distrust of all humanity. He reminded of the words Natasha had let slip; Teena was 'gifted' to me by the President. Even then, even if it had grown into a deep affection for me, our age difference was enough to warn me there would be no joyous outcome. Also – it is humiliating to admit – she was too beautiful to choose me. Every man she came near to wanted her. Wise men select ugly women assured they'll be loyal and subservient. Teena was just dazzling in her loveliness.

Simon's cynical speculation was disrupted. Rig 1 swayed and shook as if the palace was under attack. Anais told me not to worry. She was trying to block an attempt to tamper with the orbit of Rig 1 itself. I was disturbed to see the reason. It was Myrna breaking through our firewall. Either she wanted to redirect our laser fire down to the Martian cities in order to deceive the civilians we were hostiles who had to be brought down – or sabotage our programmes to malfunction and blow us up.

I hovered indecisively. An anonymous recording came through. The voice alternated from high, then low, from falsetto to bass growl:

'India, China edge. Now, Master. What a bore dere master. Unless there's meat I will go mad again.'

There is cryptic and there is incomprehensible. Who this was and what it meant was beyond me. Bemused, I looked to Teena and Anais. They were both laughing. Teena, I recalled, was an obsessive mistress of puzzles. She explained the message as if I were a kid with learning difficulties: 'Obviously, it's Butch! He's wanting you to meet him on the China and Indian border, Mars. You see why I say that now. Can't you?'

'Obviously,' I lied.

Three months later, I really did work it out. He had recorded Janine a message and bounced it to me. Janine had once explained to me that spoken Chinese derives its meanings through vocal pitch and inflection. It does not come from verbal ambiguities like most European languages. In fact, the high and low tones had been exaggerated to remind me of this. Once you knew that you could discover what it told you.

Teena tried to stop giggling at my slowness. She said, 'You never played code-crackers when you were a teenaged burglar, did you? Listen now, 'It's a *bore dere, Marks* me. Or I'll be *mad again*' gave the words *border, Mars* and *Maddigan*, for example. Even you, honey, can work out what *meat* means. Kids' stuff trick hidden in nonsense sentences. Idiotically obvious, isn't it? But who listens to a mad person's voice swooping from falsetto to bass?'

It took Alassam just as long as me to catch on. That was a relief to me.

Anais squeezed me close. She said, in a broken voice, 'If we don' meet again in life, remember an old woman, please.'

I had spokens my last words on Rig 1.

There was no time to hesitate or be tearful. That would have embarrassed me, anyhow. Before Simon's malicious chatter in my brain started up again, I realized Teena was already moving me into the Main Control Room. We were standing beneath the miniaturized teleporter. I squeezed her hand and turned to kiss her. And the teleporter beam hit us.

Now we found ourselves, still holding hands, at the border of the Indian and Chinese territories of Northern Mars.

Maddigan hailed us from a hundred yards away. Alisha and Janine were accompanying him. How on Earth did the Chinese Agent manage to be everywhere at once? Then I stopped and gaped.

To my horror, High Druid Haggard stood next to him too!

258

Chapter 41

Shared scientific advances between China and India had been more jealously hidden than our Rig 1 teleportation device. Upgraded surveillance and defences had promoted India to become a genuine super-power, almost the equal of that British or Chinese technology. In the days when my psychological character was that of Simon Edge, I was proud of my deviousness in concealing everything I knew. No one could penetrate my duplicitous concealments. That vanity took several knocks, once I realized many others had acted similarly. My self-admiration made me oblivious to it. The Druids hid eugenic horrors, the Yanks obscured their very survival after Yellowstone, not least the military complex on the Moon they shared with declining Russia. Topping the 'League of Deception' was the guy I once accounted my closest friend. Manitoba Joe was originally a dealer named Spike. He transformed into my confidant, then my minder. He was simultaneously the star agent of Mossad, but it gave me no hesitation. Such a chameleon was this fella, even Simon Edge had no idea what he was scheming or who he supported.

Materializing on the Martian Province boundaries, I was confronted by fresh intrigue and a totally unexpected shift of alliances. Being inured to such events, I did a Janine Suee concealment of expression. Putting it bluntly, my face showed fuck all! I created a minute for me to weigh it up by acting as if I was disorientated by my teleportation. I stared, blankly, up at the sky.

Above us were orbiting air balloons, generating artificial sunbeams. Amusingly, they created a visual illusion of a halo around Maddigan. It was better than the one I had created a while back! Smiling happily, he could read my thoughts.

'The omission of information isn't the same as telling a fib, my lad.' The Welshman's benevolent grin stretched even further. 'A new wealth of wisdom will be yours when you next gain time for introspection.'

Janine shoved me deeper in the swamp of obscurity by reciting, 'The Army requires perseverance and a strong man. Good fortune without blame.'

I was confused. Her flawless face revealed zilch. I could tell she quoted the I-Ching. I could not tell if she was taking the piss though.

The President teased, 'You could match our friend's reference to Confucius' *Book of Changes* with the Aryan *Mahabarata*, dear Alisha. Maybe I could dig into my Pagan *Book of Shadows, or Aradia* provides similar ancestral wisdom. You support me in this, don't you, High Druid?'

He knew full well how I loathed this gaunt fiend, but his gaze deliberately flickered between Chinese Agent and me. I must abide with his subtle hint. As Janine advised, I must be that strong man who acted with perseverance

Haggard shrieked his response in the off-key voice of somebody who's on the brink of insanity: 'I am not here to hear Chinese platitudes. I was summoned for my mission. Americans betrayed me. Rather as you betrayed your Goddess, Maddigan. In exchange for their support, I have shared our eugenic discoveries to assist the salvation of floundering Helium. That's why you now serve as my weapons against the even more evil Caliphate who rage across this bleak planet. Furthermore, my disease spores are primed for use on Earth. Be warned, all of you! I shall exterminate your China and India bitches within moments if deceit crosses your minds.' He glowered at Alisha and Janine.

Alisha retorted, angrily, 'You were fucking stupid to shift your germ facilities to the other side of the world to Pakistan, weren't you? We disinfected it with our nukes.'

Janine added, 'You figured China and India, adjoining Pakistan, made it simple to slaughter any country, give or take a few million deaths. Their distance from Tintagel meant you were safe too.'

She tried to calm down her tone. It failed to defuse the fanatic. The High Druid ranted again, 'Because the Americans broke their word to me, our Goddess of Nature, who inspires my every action, did command me that I must shift my allegiance to your assorted interests. So was I received by General McNulty. He directed my priests, laden with virus spores, to visit our treacherous former allies. Their moon base will be uninhabitable for a century now that the wrath of Hecate is purging the lying American dogs and their tame Russians. Death skulls grin in anticipation of the imminent arrival there of my Druid emissary, laden with spores. Thus, I say to you, fat President, should you or your lackies betray me, retribution will commence with a hideous death for your wife.'

Maddigan's restraint surprised me. He assumed a placid smile and his voice was soothing as he promised the ancient madman, 'McNulty will obey every detail of what I approved to assist you. In truth, High Father of Wisdom, we serve you being the essence of Albion's soul.'

Such blatant deception left me gob-smacked! What worried me was that I found difficulty in processing my own reactions to the shifting situation. I was Masque, then I was Edge. I was like a pack of cards shuffled at disorientating speed, and each card bore my new face. I switched from being emotional Masque to logical Edge. Never before had I experienced a situation in which I was incapable of distinguishing truth from lies.

Again, the President was gazing upward to the source of the artificial sunlight. The zeppelins provided warmth and light by means of the energy bursting to and fro between their generators and the ground reflectors. In addition, their dynamos created the power for light which was reflected and magnified to give the illusion of a dazzling blue sky that replaced the familiar gloom and darkness of Mars. Despite the extravagance of the technology required, his marvel was only operative for a maximum of half a mile.

He enveloped himself securely within his persona of the benevolent chubby old man we all loved. The image formed with the immense wastage of resources was well worth it when it enhanced his image for the billions of the two planets. The soliloquy he delivered was a conscious performance that would sway the emotions of the billions of awed viewers.

'A warm and fertile Mars awaits an awakening,' he sighed, blissfully. 'From this moment our technological skills and resources shall be shared. We are bringing sunlight to every region of this planet of hope. Forests, meadows and crops will grow. Greenness will cover this world, generating oxygen. Our climate will change. Animals and birds will be living across the globe. And the Druids will nourish nature's bounty in celebration of the Goddess. The name Haggard will be honoured by all men.'

With such glib flattery he demonstrated his political adroitness. Who would not preen as the High Druid was doing on receiving such compliments and adoration? I knew Simon Edge would! With Natasha beside him and China won over with the firm guarantee of territorial expansion through his gift of Caliphate lands to his allies, the scales were tipping decisively in the jovial Welshman's favour. Because he had never sought to be the head of the allied alliance, he was cast as the saviour of two worlds. It was also the reason he received the unconditional acquiescence of everyone who joined him

The beautiful Head of China's Secret Service was visibly relaxed about the situation. Janine understood she had joined a man genuinely without personal ambitions. Other races and nations gathered about President Maddigan. He was not the material of a tyrant or conqueror.

Maddigan and Alisha were having an intense discussion with Haggard. I walked a slight distance away with Teena and Janine. For the first time the latter responded to me in a friendly, almost human, fashion. We paused at an area of flat, orange sand. This was the unmarked border between the British and Chinese provinces.

Janine confided, 'my *chi* was fortunately aligned when first I visited Rig 1. It was long ago. I remember that it was before you assisted Governor Golden to attain the "throne" of Helium. Madame Anais pleased to serve more than one employer once your wife offered to reward her for intelligence. Naturally, communications passing across 40 Rigs between Mars and Earth were shared with The Chinese People's Republic. And vice versa, I'd guess. I never revealed who was responsible for the bomb that day you jumped from the balcony, Commander. That was a flawed outcome to another plan I had. I can be sentimental, which might amaze some. I ensured you escaped unscathed.'

Janine was the one who tried to murder me. What the hell! All I could do was smile admiringly at the slim, oriental genius of espionage. Sex with such a cool, calculating woman would be a fascinating challenge. Teena had gripped my arm. It took me by surprise. The sun sparkled on her spectacles. I lifted them up to enter the depth of her magical eyes. Filled with emotional warmth, I turned her around and kissed her.

When I glanced back several dozen yards away, I noticed that Haggard limped away with a milk curdling expression. I wondered if Sheila had died when his craft was hit. I kept this question to myself. Alisha was rolling out a portable screen. She perched it on a rock in the red sand, presumably to work out precisely where the borders of China, India and the Caliphate met.

Maddigan touched his own vid-screen and forwarded me what was coming through. He had no wish for Haggard to hear or see what the feed was telling him. Myrna had recorded the destruction on the attackers of Rig 1. This is what he had hacked into. That meant she had regained access to her encrypted systems. I watched Helium's fliers chase the remnants of the Caliphate strike force, fleeing back to their home province on Mars.

A fast-forward followed. This was more was worrying. Their retreat was a feint to lure Helium's fliers into danger. Their entire main fleet began a launch from their Red Planet bases, evidently with an order to obliterate Myrna's military whom they outnumbered ten to one.

The President wasted no more time suspense-building, much as he enjoyed displaying his flair as a techno. The Islamists' feint became a tool of its own defeat. From nowhere, the Chinese fleet appeared above the red sands. Since there had been no take off from the surface, the Chinese must have teleported from their Martian Province to take the enemy by surprise. In less than two years, teleportation processes had been refined to the degree whereby they could fit teleporters within most battle fliers.

From above Mars itself, another ally's armada joined the melee at the brink of the ionosphere. At first, I assumed they were Myrna's. However, all but a score were air balloons. I recognized the dancing elephant insignia of India. I was still confused as to the strategies operating from the array of motives involving so many players.

Adopting the expression of a simpleton, Maddigan waited for Haggard to approach once more. The old Druid was furtively reaching within his robe. He was attempting to hack into our viewing. As the manoeuvres went from his picture, the Welshman pretended he was oblivious to the Druid's action. He held up his viewer to simulate himself lauding Haggard as the hero of the planet, as if to an audience of billions of watchers. In decades ahead he announced, loudly, it was Haggard who would use Earth seeds, cuttings and biological eugenics to bring life to Mars in celebration of the Earth Goddess. Inflating the elderly psychopath's vanity further, Maddigan revealed his plans for the High Druid's statue to be raised in the centre of Helium. He added that a similar memorial was already in preparation to tower over Wells. I was surprised the old Druid had not drowned in his slimy sea of hyperbole.

Seeming already a foot taller, Haggard assumed a dramatic posture. He pointed to the heavens where Phobos and Deimos raced, and told us, 'When the creatures of the Earth accept the redemption that I bring, they will look up at their own moon and they will celebrate my vengeance upon America.'

Alisha, of the spikey, silver hair and smooth light brown skin, looked at me askance. But the President followed the old wanker's line of thought.

With a smile, the President elucidated, 'The Mossad ruthlessness imbued in General McNulty is shocking to me. Sometimes that is the sole solution. He devised an appropriate punishment for the threatening American killers. As my dearest comrade, the High Druid, is well aware, it was he who enabled a

Druid delegation to visit the Americans' lunar base. How indebted we are to you, Haggard, for directing him in the plan.'

'It wasn't all Mossad!' interrupted Alisha. 'I too assisted him.'

For the second time I have ever seen, Janine laughed. The sound was musical. Teena and I were bemused, ignorant of all these schemes. We had missed crucial events that occurred between my escape from Haggard's crashing strato-cruiser and more recent action on Rig 1. However, I had witnessed the Yanks destroy the eugenics centre. What was hard to swallow was how Haggard had accepted reparation to return to being Admiral Barker's ally.

The reason lay in the core of the American psyche. Men like Barker and Kirk epitomized the sense of cultural superiority, of a special destiny and, most of all, their martial pre-eminence. To them Druids were superstitious retards. They were akin to savages who were awed by mighty weapons. They would be grateful to these futuristic men once the USA bribed them with a bit of modern technology in the manner of ancient explorers giving trinkets to stupid savages. I believe Haggard was given an apology, face-saving explanations for the Anglesey bombing. The Yanks adopted reasons which were contemptible even in their country's heyday. The attack was a heart-breaking mistake. Massive reparation would be awarded. This would include gifting the Druids with Lyonesse, along with Devon and Cornwall. Then there were vast areas of Mars that America would assist them to cultivate and become all theirs! Improbably, the Christian USA would sponsor the Pagan revival that would sweep away the capital of the British Empire at the Palace of Wells. Haggard meekly accepted every inducement. There was to be a 'Special Relationship' between the pagans and Americans.

Haggard had the choice of accepting the excuses gracefully, or be completely eradicated by superior forces. Inside, hatred festered, and he planned his vengeance. The goddess must have heard his thoughts. Salvation arrived, miraculously, in the form of McNulty, of all people. Like the voice of temptation, he whispered in Haggard's ear. Now the opportunity for vengeance arrived. The fruition was to come the day of the Druid visit to the lunar base.

McNulty planned every detail for them. Through his Mossad influence he secured a number of teleporters (no questions asked) which he had reconditioned for a kamikaze mission. They left Tintagel by this means. With their seeming naivete, they bore gifts for their new allies. Statuettes of the Green Man, Aradia and so forth, showed their desire to bring good fortune to their 'friends'.

The Russians and Americans had nothing to fear from the band of Pagan priests. Moreover, the visitors came not simply with little idols. They also brought evidence of weapons of biological warfare which would decimate the British and Chinese Empires. Barker's crew were promised the plagues and armies of monsters created in the eugenics labs. These atrocities would ravage Mars and Earth. America would rule an Empire of two planets. No further decades of hiding on the Moon. Later, analysts discovered that Barker had major reservations about using such questionable weapons. He was sufficiently confident in the strength of the Russo-American strato-fleet. Nevertheless, the proposal in itself was sufficient to convince the majority of Americans and Russians on the Base. Also, the rift with Haggard would be healed. Thus, it was greeted with open arms.

There was a catch. The eugenic experiments and plagues were to be released on the Moon. It was McNulty's black humour that originated the way this would be presented to the Americans. How loudly would the Yanks whoop when they saw crates filled with thousands of Coca Cola bottles. The luxury looked and tasted exactly like the formula prescribed. There was one special additive. With timed release, designed in Anglesey labs, the gifts would reveal their horrifying symptoms. After 12 weeks physical mutations with unique genetic qualities would begin to slaughter every human being on the Moon.

During the President's account, Haggard could barely restrain his joy. I thought he would start prancing and singing any minute.

My eyes met those of Butch Maddigan. Our hearts contained similar emotions.

It was too late to stop it. We would live with it on our consciences.

Chapter 42

Teena and I made our final teleportation from Mars to England. We suffered none of the damage or trauma that I had previously experienced. Chinese technology had refined the rough edges. Janine was pleased to impress Maddigan – for whom she had once served as a humble secretary, whilst spying on him! Not only did she use a compact mobile teleporter, powered by solar power from the zeppelins above the desert border, but also, she directed the beam of our atoms into our chamber in the Bishop's Palace in Wells.

From our private room, we watched drone transmissions of the appalling scenes unfolding on Luna. Monsters, hatched and assembled in the eugenics labs, stalked through the dust on the dark side of Earth's satellite. We gazed in horror at a column of abominations staggering into the interior caverns of the Moon. This was where American and Russian technology was concealed. It was difficult to make out many details, despite Teena's juggling with light clarity. What we were able to make out was sickening. Rotting, diseased corpses were strewn all over the place. *Science!* I thought. *Give fire to a Stone Age man, and he'll use it to burn down his neighbour's hut!*

Admiral Barker had already taken a grandiose gamble in his mission to recover his nation's supremacy. His orders were to assist in restoring the USA's military domination of the worlds. Since the lunar station was beyond hope, being destroyed by treachery, his only alternative was an immediate attack on Earth! Future historians might describe that decision as madness. An assault on an entire planet was truly ambitious! As the Moon became uninhabitable, the one fallback strategy was to use the martial power America and her ally had developed there for almost a century.

Teena and I were open mouthed, seeing the incredible scenes unfolding before us. We couldn't believe it when uncountable numbers of American battle cruisers appeared over the South Atlantic. A pin-point camera shot into the lead vessel's cabin revealed the invasion was led by Admiral Barker's freshly promoted lackey, Lieutenant Kirk. He too was inspired by a grandiose vision of the USA's resurrection. I was more worried than I admitted to Teena, because Earth's inhabitants were unprepared for military forces of this magnitude.

Haggard's plans interested me. In many ways he was the motivation for much of what had taken place. He had shifted and changed alliances in an instant. Like an exotic spider he bounded from one strand to another.

After the idea of using Maddigan as a Pagan puppet failed, he abruptly swept into Lyonesse, with US military guidance, it seems.

There were no qualms about overthrowing his peaceful neighbours. Then, he set to work on eugenic creations which he was able to test out at Stonehenge. His colleague, Barker, personally organized an opportunistic invasion of the Isle of Wight. Once the USA betrayed him, he became Maddigan's friend again. Finally, by using McNulty's advice, he dispatched his plagues to Luna.

McNulty was always fully aware what the Druids and Yanks were up to. He palmed Barker's documents during that Ryde interrogation.

In my youth, before I grew fond of 'space opera', I noticed a revival in the popularity of a crime-unravelling fiction called 'Whodunnits'. They ended, predictably, with a detective explaining a series of clues, that explained a murder. This is precisely how I saw myself in this moment. Whilst sipping a refreshing cut glass goblet of rose, liberated from Maddigan's cellar, I analyzed the detail of the plots devised by participants from Terra and Mars. Partly, it was to impress my lovely, red-haired partner.

'Being with me,' I instructed her, 'you are blessed with two men, Simon and Jon. The superlative diplomat and the cultured historian together form a dual faculty genius. Thus, you will never be bored with me!'

Teena put an arm round my waist, let her hand slip, then squeezed my bum cheeks. When I jumped, she warned, 'Which end are you talking out of, Simon Edge, the old *poseur*?' I was shocked by such irreverent crudity. Her insightful response was, 'You don't need to worry about our difference in ages. I don't give a toss if you're made from two or a hundred blokes. Leave it there.'

Affection had scored over logic again. I took an apple from the nearby fruit bowl. Then I took a big bite so I could compose myself. Crunching enthusiastically, I cut the crap to surprise her with some fascinating information that might save us, and our planet.

My preamble was, 'Right! No academic swots were about to record events four and a half billion years ago!'

She mimed a big yawn.

Still attempting to look cool, I flung the core of the half-eaten apple over my shoulder and out of the Wells Palace window and said, 'This planet can destroy Barker.'

Teena said nothing and waited.

I described how a Mars-sized planet called Theia careened into Mother Earth, whilst she was still forming. Theia hit the Earth like a rock from a slingshot. In the explosion, tons of debris from Terra and Theia were flung into orbit. After mere millions of centuries, these rocks and minerals from the two worlds coalesced, until they were bound together in a satellite we call the Moon. This cosmic crash had a legacy which could protect us today. The planetary impact formed a 'dent' in Earth's magnetic field. This increased over time. A mere 400 years ago, before the Yellowstone event, scientists became aware that the collision point had affected our magnetic field. They realized it because it caused malfunctions in mankind's earliest satellites and space craft. The epicentre was the Atlantic Ocean between former Latin American and South African continents.

'Of all the targets for the Americans to select for commencing our conquest with their invincible lunar armada!' I exclaimed, 'the USA's ignorant, idiotic military chose the Theia impact site for them to teleport invasion forces! Look at the screen! Unbelievable! Bated breath time!'

Every other person on Mars, Earth and the 40 Rigs was hypnotized by the armada's materialization from out of nowhere. Being ignorant of the information I had accessed, they were probably preparing for death or enslavement by the USA. Teena and I continued gawping at our thirty-foot vid-screen on the far side of the Abbot's Chamber.

Knowing Mossad, they possessed some record of the Earth's ancient origins in a secret vault. The Vatican – that Christian version of Paganism – were once rumoured to hide such types of information. How could I have doubted Manitoba Joe? The guy who was the loutish mate and bodyguard of my genius was actually far more knowledgeable than I had ever been! That was casually demonstrated now. Though it was impossible to pick me out from a billion faces of the audiences on two worlds, he did. His stubbled face appeared on my private channel. He looked straight at me, gave a thumbs up and laughed.

His face revealed his exhaustion. He was running on amphetamines. The causes were obvious now that all the puzzles around his disappearance were explained. Even for the chief Mossad agent, his multiple deals were beyond mortal capacity to handle. Both the Americans and the Tintagel Druids had been convinced of his loyalty to them, when he provided his variant fictions of how he intended to betray Maddigan. Yet he convinced these suspicious, deadly people.

It was he who instigated Admiral Barker's attack on the Anglesey eugenics labs. Barker was convinced of the need to break his alliance with the Druids. His final resolution to wipe out the Druids on Anglesey was made when McNulty suggested they were re-forming a Pagan conspiracy into which Maddigan had been recruited again and converted. As his finale, Joe warned Haggard of the American scheme to attack him before he had time to act.

Ironically, Alassam, the most open, honest man I ever met, believed in Joe throughout all his brain-twisting manoeuvres. Mr Mossad was lucky in having another loyal friend – Alisha. He provided her with information about links between Pakistan and the Caliphate on Mars. It enabled Alisha to present it and influence the Indian Government's decision to launch the nuclear attack on them. Lastly, I think he had persuaded Janine, a fellow in the spy-fraternity, to agree to form a Chinese alliance with Maddigan in return for him sharing teleportation information. Everything was so simple, I reflected, once you tied those loose strands together!

Alassam appeared on the split screen. He was in command of all British fliers and fighters involved in the space war around the ionosphere. I watched him checking his fleet's preparations for engaging the American and Russian forces. Grinning, as he always did, he reproduced McNulty's chummy thumbs up. We replied in kind. He returned southwards towards the threat of the endless materialization of the enemy fliers. The Rastaman Fighter, as he had been obliged to name it, led from the apex of the Imperial fleet. Already, the Americans were experiencing difficulties while they attempted to complete their formation over the South Atlantic Ocean. I thought, *Bless you Theia for penetrating the womb of Earth all those millions of years ago!* The Yanks were too occupied with trying to operate their cruisers to fire at Alassam's rapidly approaching fleet.

At this point the defenders of Terra paused in their dazzling attack, just south of the Equator. They had had been instructed to stay clear of the Theian magnetic area, never to venture more than ten degrees below the Equator. From this point, they launched swarms of missiles and laser beams at the struggling invaders. Their intention was to create dismay, rather than engage in combat between the ionosphere and the ocean. Significant numbers of the Russian and US fighters were simply dropping from the sky. So far, they were unable to fly further north to do battle because disruption of the magnetically attractive field was resulting in wide-scale malfunctions of their weaponry and controls.

I could not contact Helium. I suspected a similar battle was in progress there against a Caliphate invasion. A rapid media scan gave me their sensationalistic clips yelling this was 'Crusaders and Saracens Revisited'. Their posting lacked legs because the ludicrous religion of Christianity had ceased to poison the Red Planet long ago. The outcome of the battle around Helium was as certain as the Terran defeat of the USA. There were no allies supporting *jihad*. The Caliphate were finally recognized at last as friendless fanatics, about to be confronted by an alliance of Britain, China and India, as well as newly arrived regiments from Australia and Africa. Like all religious fanatics, the Caliphate was assured their big, bad Allah would perform a miracle that would reward them with rape and murder of the Unbelievers! In reality, no politically aware nation backs a loser.

'Jon, my love!' exclaimed Teena. 'You've got to see this!'

Placing my arm lightly round her, I studied the progress of the USA's attempted invasion. Kirk's flagship was stubbornly forcing its way north towards the Equator, where lines of allied strato-cruisers were waiting. There was no doubt about his tenacity and courage. Without warning, his flier just froze. I imagined tentacles of seaweed appeared in the green gloom and, reaching up from the ocean, plucked him from the sky.

It was most likely psychological conditioning. That instant of mental aberration came from a recollection of a mystery called The Bermuda Triangle. Added to that, brain damage sustained through surgery and teleportation might have done in my perception! My resolve never again to leave Earth was reinforced. Geographical tracking informed me he had approached an island once called Puerto Rico. When he passed above Bermuda, he encountered the nexus of the magnetic void initiated by Theia. The proud flagship with stars and stripes wobbled, incapable of further progress.

What happened next remains a mystery. Endless theories fail me. Kirk started screaming about being 'in a place where there's no land, just grey nothing.' My location screen offered only the cryptic word, 'Sargasso!' The American was in a desperate rage and said he was arming all nuclear missiles to blast his way out. I had a touch of respect for this heroism from a man who would fight when he had no more to lose. At the same time, I was terrified that he was about to initiate a nuclear launch as his final vengeance before Americans were swallowed up again by the ocean. He would leave Terra as a chunk of dead ash in the bleakness of space.

I had missed Kirk's communications with his Supreme Commander, Admiral Barker. I was taken by surprise when a sparkling silver dust indicated atoms were transferring from the Moon to the Atlantic Ocean. More red, white and blue stars and stripes manifested. This time they ran along the sides of a second flagship. Fearlessly, Admiral Barker had teleported with his fleet of the last Americans, coming to aid his friend! His ships accelerated to maximum velocity to the last location of Kirk. As soon as they hit the Bermudan skies, full force, there was a tremendous atomic explosion.

Flames rushed over the South Atlantic sky. While the air itself was on fire, black clouds formed and swept in sheets of lightning across the hemisphere. Before we lost all vision, I witnessed the birth of the tsunami that would create the 199-foot tidal waves that would deluge South America. The planet itself was shaken. Even in Wells we felt it.

Perhaps we always experience pity and chivalrous emotions towards our enemies once we have destroyed them and are safe again. I 'tipped my hat' as an archaic saying went, to Barker. The arrogant Yank with his entire country and people were forever wiped from human history. Not just that. There would be no second reincarnation of the USA. The eugenic monsters and incurable plagues created by the religious order of Druids had dispatched the lunar base to hell on a handcart. All life there ended.

For the sake of memorable publicity, I put together a soldierly tribute to Admiral Barker. Teena recorded my rehearsed spontaneous requiem for posterity. I was refused to use such words as 'Victory' or 'Celebration'.

EPILOGUE

Seven years had passed since the assassination of Simon Masque.

He had chosen to be known by that name when he became Terran Governor of the British Empire. Maddigan and Natasha led the remembrance ceremony for him on this anniversary of his death. It was held on his birth planet, Mars. A complementary memorial event was taking place at Wells, conducted by Teena and his younger son. Mossad Joe McNulty and his companion, Myrna Golden, attended too. These days, transmission was instantaneous. It was possible for every moment to be synchronized on Mars and Earth.

On the Red Planet, the balloons were creating sunlike radiance, and successfully mimicked a hot summer's day in distant England. Artificial as it might be, this sunshine assisted vegetation to flourish in and around the geodomes. Already grass and bushes were proliferating across large areas of former desert. President Maddigan seemed ecstatic to behold the positive outcomes made possible by his genetic engineering of beneficent nature in the plant world. Ironically, the rapid advances in terraforming owed a considerable debt to the late High Druid's experiments in eugenics and genome manipulation. Unsurprisingly, no statues to Haggard appeared on either planet! One of the most attractive results of introducing vegetation was the profusion of giant butterflies fluttering around and within the domes. Maddigan smiled to himself when he reflected that Simon's ghost – if it was around – would most likely have made some quip about Haggard being as successful with lepidoptera as he was with murder plots.

Despite dramatic extensions in the human lifespan, the years had taken their toll on the President. He leaned heavily on a staff when he made his way to the dais from which he was to deliver his eulogy. As always, Natasha was there beside him. Time had been kinder to her. It was not solely surgery and eugenics that maintained her attractive physical form.

Over 30 people had gathered on Mars to remember Simon's incredible life. Janine Suee, retired Head of the Secret Service, represented China. But she came more for personal affection. Alisha was there too, for the Indian Government. Maddigan saw she was crying. Her affection for Simon had gone deeper than he had believed. Melissa, successor to Anais as keeper of the Rig 1 Sex Palace, was here. In the tradition of Anais, she offered more than her brothel-keeper facade. She was sponsored by McNulty to be facilitator of communication channels between the Red Planet and Earth.

The most popular and respected figure was General Alassam, New Africa's Head of State. He was Maddigan's closest friend and ally. Though his bushy plaited beard and dreadlocks were peppered with white, he still exuded the power of a born leader. There was no self- importance in his demeanour. He freely shed tears in his remembrance of Simon. He had been requested to perform an African song at the end of the remembrance. Alisha asked if she might accompany him. He grinned and gladly consented.

The President faced a massive screen that provided a 100-foot-wide backdrop to the dais. This linked him with Simon's people on Terra. His warm welcome was returned by Teena Masque. She was ageless, even though Simon's six-year-old son jumped about beside her.

The most controversial attendee, in the background of the ceremony on Earth, was 'Mossad Joe McNulty'. Despite his Israeli citizenship, he maintained the rank of Military Commander in the Empire's British province. He was famous as the general who restored order after the disastrous American invasion. He managed to be invisible most of the time. The other reason for his fame was that he was the man who publicly executed High Druid Haggard and Sheila, the woman who had stabbed his 'best buddy' to death in the reception chamber of the Bishop's Palace.

Maddigan knew details about the assassination that would be carried with him to his own grave. In his memory were images of Simon, sprawled in the corridor outside his bed chamber. Blood was pouring from a dozen stab wounds. A line of female sandal prints marked the floor of the corridor. A dagger was discarded outside the doors to his private area. Four laser-armed guards' corpses lay contorted from inhaling the noxious fumes from some genetically engineered substance, applied by the murderer.

Despite the evil perpetrated by the Druids of Tintagel and Anglesey, people still accepted Maddigan as a bit of a mystic and lovable eccentric. In fact, it was his consultation with a seer beside Chalice Well that guided his decision to move his seat as Head of the Empire from Wells to Helium.

With a symmetry dictated by this decision, he deployed Simon Masque, as *defacto* Regent for the Empire at Wells, England's capital. Being a shrewd politician, he saw he could implement any necessary checks and balances from a more distant relocation in the greater safety of Helium. From there it proved easier to maintain Britain's alliance with Janine's people of China and Alisha's Indian modernists when both of them too, removed to positions as governors of reorganized settlements of their Red Planet provinces. His intention was to avoid nationalistic fervour and thus potential wars. The African allies were the other crucial partners. He honoured his commitment of giving substantial areas of territory to the establishment of the Afro province of Mars. These comprised over 50 per cent of the former Caliphate possessions and over 20 per cent of the southern portion of the British province. This made a firm foundation for an even closer partnership with him and Alassam. The latter chose the title of 'Imperial Chief of the African Nation'. Like Maddigan, he chose to rule his Earthly territories from the Red Planet.

The anticipated moment approached. The President was assisted onto the stage by his wife. He looked into her eyes, glad that she would perpetuate his idealistic legacy when he was gone.

With a slight smile he said, 'We're wise to divert our minds slightly away from a religion of technology and enhance the intuitive sides of human evolution.'

Natasha discovered a crystal glass of apple wine in her hand. She was relaxed again and understood his achievement.

'Emotionally, you are a Pagan Head of State. I agree with you that Mars was a one-sided world of reason. You have helped achieve sane balance.'

'Ah, my lady, remember my epiphany in the two inner circles?' And he lost his thread. This was happening more and more frequently. He was embarrassed and glad his remaining time was brief. He tried to salvage the connection of his thoughts but was confused. He went on. 'Teena, that sweet young woman, widow of Simon, is responsible for assisting in presenting aspects of McNulty's reason to Earth.'

There was a long pause. However, his audience, still awaiting his speech, were patient and compassionate.

He ended his thought, 'my tired old brain. I think I was going to say Joe is important. You'll need him to contain Myrna Golden.'

Natasha kept the sparkle in her eye and joked, 'McNulty needs every iota of his adaptability now he's her paramour and probation officer.'

Maddigan seemed not to hear her. Normally a man of his age would choose to shed a burdensome body at 150 years. He had extended his span to almost 170 years because he felt a duty to complete the unification the planets. Absent mindedly, he recognized the site for Masque's memorial was on that same border between China, India and the former Caliphate where he had held the meeting with his allies before the Americans attacked Earth.

A young man with ginger hair assisted him to the lectern. He recognized the lad as Simon's older son. Patting the boy's shoulder, he turned to face the vast vid-screen behind him. For a second time, he raised his hand in greeting to Teena, whose flawless face had appeared in close up from distant Earth. She smiled, returning his wave. He took a final glance across the green grass, the flourishing laurel bushes and the recently planted saplings beneath the adjacent geodomes. That uplifted him. Now was time to address his people.

His requiem for Simon Edge of Mars, aka Jon Masque of Earth, would not be forgotten. Against all odds, Simon Edge transformed into Jon Masque and had demonstrated to him that a balance between heart and head could restore humanity on two worlds in the blackness of endless space.

THE END